Drowning a Ghost

Janson Mancheski

To my mother Dawn,
who taught me to read as a one-year-old.

Also by Janson Mancheski:
The Chemist
Trail of Evil
Mask of Bone
Shoot For the Stars
The Scrub
The Greatest Hits—Best of The Chemist Series

Drowning a Ghost
The Chemist Series – Book 4
Copyright © 2021 Janson Mancheski

ISBN: 978-1-950316-09-0
Printed in the United States of America
Fearless Publishing House

Table of Contents

PART ONE

THE FORMULA

"The world is a stage, life but a passage. You came, you saw, you departed."
— Democritus, 470-270 BC (Greek Philosopher)

CHAPTER 1

The drug dealer in the light blue Renegade swung into the far-right lane. Hidden four cars behind him, the detective matched his maneuver.

Five minutes earlier, Lt. Cale Van Waring had eased to a downtown stoplight where he'd spotted Amos Nick—who sported tight blond hair and scruffy facial growth. Nick was driving window down, elbow extended, and if he'd had the tinted glass rolled up, there was little chance Cale would have spotted him.

Whatever the case, he told himself what-the-hell, then swung a crisp U-turn and began tailing the vehicle.

The Monday morning traffic was congested. Half the stiffs were gunning for action, the other half dreaming they were on beaches somewhere. High buildings shaded the sunlight. The stoplight changed, and the vehicles grunted another block forward as if part of some holiday parade.

Trapped in traffic, Cale pondered the whims of fate. An eye blink. It's how fast your life can go sideways. He was headed to an appointment, minding his own business, when he had spotted Amos—a pot dealer he'd busted seven years ago, who back then supplied ganja to college kids and first-job millennials.

Cale could not have cared less about the man he tailed, except it appeared Amos had upgraded. The Renegade sure trumped the dented PT Cruiser he'd been driving years ago. Alarm bells to a former narcotics investigator.

He eased the Bronco forward, remaining in the conga line headed south. They were a block from the murky Fox River, which cut through the heart of downtown Green Bay. He stayed four cars behind the Renegade.

Cale's phone chirped a familiar number. Det. Sergeant James "Slink" Dooley was his longtime partner in both the Narco and Homicide Units. Slink was filling Cale's spot now during his current thirty-day suspension, and he could not be happier for the guy. If no dead bodies happened during the month, his best friend might be promoted to Lieutenant. Good for Slink. He deserved a pay boost with a wife and two young boys at home.

Cale kept one eye on the Renegade ahead and answered.

"Lomiller's a tourist aboard the boat, Slink whispered. "The bust's going down in ten."

"Where did you say, again?"

"It's a boat, dude. I told you—the river."

Slink had shared last week that GBPD was helping investigate a local meth ring. An upstart cruise operation had opened two months earlier. *We B Foxy Cruises.* A name-play on the waterway they traversed. Besides sightseeing, the fifty-foot vessel held a liquor license and was, in essence, a floating cocktail lounge. One of those "Sights of the City" numbers, it chugged the river by day, then after dark drifted romantically along, lit with blue lights like a luxury yacht. The cruises had started after the winter snowmelt, and the PD began receiving reports of watercraft zipping to-and-from the tour boat as it moved to various points along the river.

The scuttlebutt reached local politicians. Rumors began flying how the vessel might be double-dipping. Thus, Green Bay PD, the DEA, state cops, and the Brown County Sheriff's Department had formed a task force. Slink was invited, thanks to his background in narcotics.

DEA Agent Gwen Galman headed the task force. She was a petite black lady who enjoyed letting her stature deceive both cops and criminals alike. Cale had once seen Agent Gwen kick a cocaine dealer's scrotum into his throat, hard enough to match the hang-time of the current Packers' punter.

"Reason I ask," Cale said, "I ID'd a guy at a stoplight a minute ago. Amos Nick ring any bells?"

"You're kidding," Slink came back. "He's the perp County thinks is running the Foxy drug thing."

Rolling to the stoplights ahead, the Renegade performed a right turn down Cherry Street, headed toward the riverfront. Cale lost his visual, finding himself now three vehicles behind. With no opening around him, he flipped on the Bronco's flashers. Gesturing to drivers on each side, they responded with helpless shrugs.

Honking, signaling, cursing, he freed himself at last from the cluster and executed another U-turn, accelerating back in the opposite direction. If Amos Nick was headed for the riverfront, Cale was now a block away, moving parallel. He recalled another way down to the water through a parking garage.

Tall buildings blurred as he accelerated. He shouted into his phone at Slink, "Your mastermind just cruised toward the river condos! Blue Renegade."

"Son of a…we're on the opposite bank near the museum."

Cale braked through an intersection, eyes alert, scanning. "I'm on it. Don't tell Lomiller—it'll burn her cover."

He swung the Bronco toward a visitors' parking ramp. Emerging out the back a minute later, he cut the flashers and began a slow cruise along the waterfront. He hugged the shadows beneath the building's high façade, spotting the Renegade parked at a small landing pier about forty yards ahead. It was angled butt-end toward the fenced dock. Cale watched while listening to his phone, heard crashing noises, followed by Slink's excited voice.

"We're moving—we got a jet ski zipping away from the cruise boat!"

Cale tossed his mobile on the passenger seat. The tour boat was behind him upriver, sliding through the iron-gray water. Breaking away port-side, a watercraft was headed toward him. Cale advanced the Bronco cautiously up the pathway. Dozens of joggers and walkers moved around him, and he pictured them as scattered bowling pins if he accelerated toward the Renegade.

He reached beneath the seat for his tosser, a blunt-nose .38 revolver, then glanced across at the approaching jet ski now fifty yards away. A young man at the helm wore a satchel strapped over his left shoulder. He was bee-lining toward the dock with the parked Renegade.

Cale had to move fast. The task force remained at least five minutes away, likely lodged in bridge traffic. He increased his speed up the pathway, nudging through gaps in the scowling pedestrian traffic.

Inside the Renegade, Cale saw Amos Nick's head turned to view the approaching jet ski. He also spotted a concrete perma-bench in front of the deck, lodged just left of the blue SUV. At the river's edge, sloshy waves lapped at the pier. Wooden posts poked above the waterline like balding old men, and seagulls cruised on a wind current.

Cale eased the Bronco forward and stopped short of the Renegade's front bumper. It could neither back up into the deck nor ram forward into his heavy vehicle. The concrete bench further prevented an attempt at a Y-turn.

A grandmaster's chess move, he decided, the main piece wedged in solidly. Cale slid the revolver into the left pocket of his windbreaker, flipped on sunglasses, and exited, leaving the door ajar as he moved around the Bronco's rear bumper.

Amos swung his head back around at Cale's approach. "Hey! Jackass!" The windshield muted his shouts, and he watched the man fling his door open and jump free. "Move the truck. Now!"

Cale walked toward the Renegade.

Free of his SUV now, Amos barked, "I'm picking up my friend here! Right now!" A wave slapped the wet dock nearby.

"Is there a decent perch fry in one of the taverns back there?" Cale indicated the string of restaurants behind them, back up the walkway.

"What? What the hell are you—"

"All-you-can-eat buffet, maybe?"

The drug dealer glanced across at the approaching jet ski. He screamed back at Cale, "Are you stupid? Move your damn truck!"

Only three yards separated the men now. Cale's left hand remained inside his jacket pocket. Amos turned to his open door and leaned into the Renegade, and Cale pictured him emerging with a weapon. He charged up and grabbed Amos beneath his armpits, lifting the startled man, spinning him around, shoving him toward the river's edge.

Amos's hands were empty as he stumbled in front of the shore's low safety fence. He steadied himself and spun back around, ready to charge, but Cale front-kicked him in the sternum before this could happen.

An *ooof* sound escaped, and with his arms windmilling, Amos plunged backward over the two-foot barrier into the deep water with an ungraceful splash.

The jet skier cut his power fifteen yards from the landing deck, half-standing. He watched his partner's head bob back above the surface. Amos hacked up water, but when he spied the man in sunglasses holding a revolver, his face turned crimson.

"Good seeing you again, Amos. Long time."

"Van Waring. I remember you now, you prick."

His attention back on the jet skier, Cale saw the man reach for the throttle. "Hey! Unh-uh," he called, motioning with the weapon, and the man pulled back his hand. "Now, toss the satchel onto the deck over there."

The skier obeyed. The bag landed on the treated wooden surface like a shot crow.

By now, a dozen pedestrians had paused to watch. A cruiser swept up the Riverwalk with blue lights flickering, forcing the onlookers to each side. The DEA's ride was an unmarked burgundy Taurus with dancing dash strobes, and it sped down Cherry Street behind them. Both vehicles eased closer to the action, angled to avoid parking the Bronco in. Two uniformed officers exited and crouched behind their open doors, sidearms drawn. Slink was in the Taurus with AIC Galman. He slipped from the passenger door, staying low. They were joined by

6

another pair of cruisers behind them, parked now with their roof and dash lights flickering.

The officers popped from their vehicles, weapons drawn and ready.

Cale half-turned their way and raised his free hand in the air—a signal to them all was under control. Agent Galman rose, keeping her weapon pointed at the ground.

Swinging his eyes down to the dog-paddling Amos, Cale slipped the .38 back inside his jacket. He called to the men in the water, "Neither of you saw my water pistol, did you?"

Amos growled, "Screw you."

Cale turned back to Galman, saying, "You've got a pair of drug runners, Agent. Along with their bag of product." He stepped between the SUVs, reentered the Bronco, and then buzzed down the front passenger window as Slink joined Galman.

Cale called out: "It seems some tourist pointed a finger-gun at these skiers. Spooked the dumb one into jumping in the water."

Slink snickered. Galman glanced at him, and he gave her a *Why not?* shrug.

The Agent said something into her walkie. Then she called to Cale through his passenger window, "Thought you were on vacation, Lieutenant. Fishing or something?"

"I am!" he called back. "It's why I was never here."

She nodded, knowing his situation with the PD.

Cale gave her a thumbs-up and powered his window closed. Two officers kept the crowd pressed back along the walkway as another secured the deck with yellow tape. This was a crime scene now, and gawkers were advised to disperse. No fireworks here today.

Reversing the Bronco, Cale eased between the cruisers and headed up the river-access street. A minute later, he was back in the congested morning traffic again, navigating toward his appointment.

CHAPTER 2

Dr. Pamela Ranula's psychotherapy office sat in a five-story, brick-and-glass building, an easy nine-iron from the riverfront. Cale pulled the Bronco into the parking lot and parked in a front spot reserved for patients. He was about to exit when his phone buzzed.

Likely Slink thanking him for the drug bust assist, and he answered with, "You can repay me with a case of Pabst."

Silence. Then a hesitant voice asked, "Detective Van Waring? My name is Cho Lin. James." After a beat, the voice added: "You arrested me twelve years ago."

The name brought the memory back. He had arrested James Cho Lin over a decade ago when he and Slink had headed a meth bust twenty miles north of the city along the bay's eastern shore. A ventilated cabin surrounded by trees was an ideal place to bake product. It was secluded and private, and yet this had also aided the Narco unit. They'd encircled the site with bullhorns and convinced the drug cookers to surrender. Not a shot fired—no running down suspects through bushes or forest, and no hot car chases.

Best of all, no one was injured.

Three meth chefs had emerged from the cabin that day, kneeling on the grass with their fingers laced behind their heads. It was every cop's dream bust.

Twenty-two-year-old James Cho Lin proved to be the mastermind. To the young man's further detriment, a state congresswoman's niece had OD'd a mere month before his arrest, and evidence traced back to his product. As a result, Cho Lin was charged with negligent homicide on top of the manufacturing and distribution charges. To save the people a jury trial and reduce his sentence, he'd pled guilty. Though not a hardened criminal and not an actual murderer *per se,* nevertheless, the last Cale had heard was he was serving time at the state's max-security prison in Waupun.

"Hello, JJ," Cale said. It was the young man's preferred handle back then. "Been a long time."

Cale had always enjoyed Cho Lin. He'd been polite, articulate, and very bright.

Nevertheless, with newly released cons, you never knew what to expect. Who could guess what dark thoughts might have percolated in their minds over the years? Most let bygones be bygones. They accepted they'd screwed up and allowed society its pound of flesh.

With others, it was the opposite. Revenge seekers. Their lives had been ruined by "The Man." For all Cale knew, Cho Lin could be up in one of the building windows right now with a sniper scope centered on his forehead. He peeked through the Bronco's upper windshield while lowering his butt into the seat.

"Got out four months ago," Cho Lin reported. "We're cool. No worries, you and me."

"Good. Great." Cale exhaled. "So, what's with the call?" The ex-con was too smart to be calling for a loan. They both were aware of how the world worked.

"I need to speak with you, Lieutenant." After a pause. "In person."

Cale checked his watch. "I'm in an appointment for the next hour. I can meet you later. If that works?"

"Yeah. I'll text you the address." Cho Lin then added, "I wouldn't bother you, but it's kind of a matter of life and death."

"Mind my asking whose?"

"My own."

Seconds after hanging up, Cale's phone pinged. The address was a room number at the old Union Hotel in the nearby suburb of De Pere.

Cale rode the elevator to the third floor of the downtown Bellin Building. After a brief reception wait, he was ushered into the office of Pamela Ranula, Ph.D., the department's contracted therapist. He took the same spot he had occupied on his initial visit a week ago, the ox-blood leather couch's left side. He crossed his leg, feigning relaxation. The doctor was on her phone and not looking at him, though he sensed she was analyzing his every move. It's what shrinks did: figure out your attitude from your first sixty seconds of body language.

There was a broad window overlooking the river below. The same waterway he had deposited Amos Nick into minutes ago. They'd be processing him by now. He wouldn't put it past Slink to have allowed the guy to dog paddle for an extra ten minutes, just to underline the fact that crime didn't pay.

Although everyone acknowledged, it paid pretty darn well, at least until you got collared.

From behind her desk, the doctor swung to face the window. She was discussing a patient, and Cale imagined it was part of their ongoing game. They both understood his suspension had mandated his attendance, and he was not here in her office by choice.

She ended the call and glanced his way as if seeing him for the first time. Cale shifted his stare from his shoes to the window, looking out at the cloud formations in the hazy sky. Wasn't that Vince Lombardi's profile? Or it could be Batman hanging on a cross. He would tell her anything to hasten his departure from this purgatory.

"Call me Dr. Pam" was how she had greeted him at his first visit a week ago. He'd decided she was not how any lady shrink was supposed to look. Today she had on a crisp black pantsuit, the kind Maggie donned when headed for court. Dr. Pam wore trendy oversized eyeglasses. They made her appear as if she'd read every psych book from Jung to Glasser. He couldn't guess what shoes she wore but knew they'd match her outfit slicker than a magazine ad. Her dark hair was pinned up, shouting to the world, "I'm smart as hell, but I also work my butt off for a living."

He'd noted as much on his initial visit.

She set her muted phone atop her tidy desk. Rising, she walked over to a comfy chair with soft arms while offering him a cursory smile. She had her notebook and pen poised and ready.

"So. Detective Cale." She widened her eyes while sitting down. "Visit *dos*. Anything you'd care to share upfront?"

Twenty minutes ago, he'd been pointing his weapon at two criminals on the river. Now he was supposed to relax, blab about his wounded childhood. Not easy to pull off when you felt like a lab specimen. It all seemed "unnatural" if he had to put a word to it.

"Little drug bust on my way over." He shrugged it away. "Living the life, I guess."

"You know you're on thirty-day suspension, right?"

"Just helping out some friends."

Dr. Pam scribbled on her pad. "Your secret's safe." She winked at him, twirled her pen with slender fingers while studying his file. "The auditory migraines? Still getting them?"

"The pills my regular doc gave me help."

She reached for the digital recorder on her desk behind her, waved it. "Mind?"

He didn't. She pressed a button and set it down on the coffee table between them. "All right. When you hear the pounding in your head? You take an Imitrex?"

Cale nodded.

"Patients with migraines often feel dull pain to start. See flashes." She paused. "Auditory hallucinations can occur. Even voices that sound real." She stared at him probingly.

"I think...I hear the witch doctor sometimes." His mouth was dry. "It's nuts, I know. But he talks to me. Out loud in my head."

The doctor thought about it. "You don't answer him back, do you?" She faked a grin.

"It's all BS, right? So no, I don't talk back."

"Then what happens?"

"Same stuff. The pounding starts low—log drums, shakers, jungle sounds."

She chin-tapped her pen.

"You know this is from your PTSD, right? We discussed that last time."

Who was he to argue? He was just the schmuck on the couch.

"You went through a traumatic encounter with a lunatic, Cale. Not many people can say a voodoo priest attacked them in their home!" She paused. "I'd be surprised if you *didn't* have side effects."

She had the attack part right. The invasion of their home by Colonel Mabutu had been one of the most harrowing things he'd ever encountered. Or ever wished to.

"Repressing bad memories is how we cope," she said. "Yet things are going to surface from time to time. Often under stress."

"Guess I need a pill refill."

Dr. Pam scribbled on her pad, raised her eyes. "Is Maggie doing okay, by the way?"

"Pregnant. Seems happy." He wanted to believe it.

She studied him. "Maggie's dealing with similar trauma." Paused a beat. "Shooting a man dead in your living room—it can't have been easy."

Cale's neck warmed. What he hated most was how Dr. Pam kept bringing up the things he was trying to forget. He sat forward, elbows on knees, and told her, "Moving forward, you know? Both of us."

The doctor's tongue worked inside her cheek. "It isn't so simple." She frowned. "La-de-da. You have the baby, all ribbons, balloons. Paint rose petals on the nursery walls."

"How it's supposed to be, isn't it?"

"Most fairy tales are based on delusions."

Cale responded with silence.

Dr. Pam pursed her lips. It was her signal to shift topics. "Remember to pass along my offer. If she ever needs some gal to gal."

At $350 an hour. He kept the thought to himself.

Cale's phone was on the nearby coffee table. A glance told him fifteen minutes had passed. He wondered what James Cho Lin wanted. Life or death? It sounded a bit dramatic. Maybe he just needed a parking ticket fixed.

The therapist continued:

"I revisited your history file, Lieutenant. About your former girlfriend's death." She arched her eyebrows. "The shooting in Chicago years ago? The reason you became a cop?"

Her look at him was earnest and sympathetic. Still, the topic caught Cale off guard. He rarely conversed about the incident twenty years in his past, when a botched robbery attempt had claimed his girlfriend Mary's life.

"I'm over it," he said.

"Meaning you've buried it inside. Do you still think about her sometimes?"

"We all carry around our pasts, don't we?"

"Not human if we didn't."

He turned quiet again.

"Sorry. I didn't mean to probe." She drew in a breath. "It's just that some people remain haunted by their old wounds. The deep ones that linger."

After a pause:

"I think about her at times," he admitted. "Wonderful girl. I wish she'd had a chance to live her life."

Dr. Pam sighed. "Forgive me for sounding insensitive, but do you still blame yourself for what happened that day?"

Cale gave it thought, allowing the buried sadness to rise in his heart. Much the way one touches an old scar and the memory of the pain flashes back.

"I was nineteen." He glanced at the window, then back to her. "Emotion over logic, guess you'd say."

"Touché." The doctor wrote in her notepad, then stared at him again. "You ever regret becoming a cop?"

"Not a bit." He shook his head and as if to emphasize. "Bad luck happens to us all. I suppose it's the one decent thing that came out of the ordeal."

The doctor nodded, changed topics. "Just yesterday, I recalled the opening line of my doctoral thesis." She smiled coyly. "I'm not going to confess how long ago, but it was elegant in its simplicity."

"I'd enjoy hearing it." Cale reminded himself, why not? Anything to pass the time.

Dr. Pam's expression was open, and she recited: "'The demon named Pain waits for us all in the shadows.'"

Cale rolled the idea around in his head. He doubted she needed a response.

Shifting the way a punt returner cuts against the grain, the doctor announced: "We got your MBTI results back. The questionnaire you answered last time?" "

"Confirming I'm looney tunes?"

He recognized he might be validating whatever diagnosis his answers had revealed. Like the many crazies he'd busted over the years—the more they told you they weren't drunk, stoned, or clinically insane, the better the chance they were just that.

Dr. Pam nudged her glasses up her nose. "Your Myers-Briggs says you have an interesting personality. INTP, they call it. Just three percent of the population."

Cale was unimpressed. He imagined that Michael Myers, the infamous slasher, was likely an "INTP" as well.

"A 'Logician,'" she continued. "Ninety-percent logic over emotion. Analytical. Assertive. A cool head in a storm."

Cale pictured kicking Amos Nick in the chest. "I try to make smart, fast decisions."

She wasn't too far off, he admitted. He'd always prided himself on using common sense in a crisis, cutting out as much BS as possible. Still, his result wasn't one-hundred percent accurate. For one thing, he *did* show emotions. Namely anger— and often when it came to A-holes bullying weaker persons. Cale had always been an advocate for underdogs. Especially

14

anyone brave enough to challenge the massive bureaucratic machine.

The same machine which had now suspended him from duty for a month.

Dr. Pam continued reading her notes. "On the plus side, when your ten-percent emotional cues show up, they can register off the charts. Happy, angry, or just about any other emotion." She glanced at him.

"You're saying I'm, what? Bipolar?"

"Not at all."

She shifted in her chair, adding, "It's like when you shot that poor man in the leg some months back. Instead of just handcuffing him."

"You mean the poor man who raped and tried to murder my fiancé?" He would never forgive Tobias Crenshaw until the SOB had given up his final breath. Not even then.

Dr. Pam issued him a searching look. "Sherlock Holmes. Einstein. Isaac Newton. Even Abe Lincoln. They were all Logician personalities."

"How about Hannibal Lecter?"

"Him, too." She arched a perfect eyebrow. "You don't think you're a psychopath, do you?"

"Sorry, Doc." Cale shook his head, chiding himself. *Never joke with a shrink about other nut jobs.* "Just a little yuk."

She smiled without smiling. "The list I just gave you, they were all pretty good problem solvers, wouldn't you say?"

This time, he nodded and kept his mouth shut.

CHAPTER 3

Cale sat gazing out the Bronco's windows. He was parked across the street from the historic Union Hotel, a three-story, cream–brick building on a corner lot constructed a century ago. He'd been inside three or four times prior and knew the place had a ten-seater bar and beautiful, ornate chandeliered dining rooms. The guest rooms and suites were on the two upper floors.

Parking was on the street for the most part. The old gaslights positioned around the place rendered the hotel a quaint and stately appearance of a bygone era. The Union's reputation was for fine dining more than lodging, so there was little need for any doorman or glitz.

Studying the place, Cale decided things appeared kosher. No sleazy characters were lounging about, no visible crack pipes or needles strewn in the gutters—no glint of a sniper's scope from some third-floor window. The hotel was quiet and somber as if it hadn't quite woken up for the past few decades.

He couldn't fault himself for being cautious. He'd logged too many years on the force to stroll into a low-lit lobby to meet an ex-con he hadn't seen in over a decade. Not since the jury had pronounced James Cho Lin guilty, and the judge had gaveled the verdict.

The Monday morning traffic was sparse. There were three vehicles at meters along the side street, local shoppers. A dark-gray Buick Regal sat parked a quarter-block behind him, perched beneath the tree shade. A man with his tie askew was tapping, he guessed, on a laptop—a salesman figuring quotas. A large Dodge Ram pulled into the parking lot catty-corner from the Union. The driver exited and headed for the front doors of the bank across the street.

Still, there was always a lurking undercurrent of crime. The news blabbers theorized each night that criminals were becoming bolder. Civil society, once sustained by law and order, seemed to be pissing itself down the drain. Cale had seen his share of senseless violence as head of the Special Crimes Unit. He prayed his inquiry into Cho Lin's phone call wouldn't fall into any of the above categories.

Crossing the sidewalk, he entered the unceremonious front door. He'd decided to forgo the reception area or the elevators. Due to his suspension, the fewer eyes spotting him, the better. He slipped through the compact lobby and climbed the side stairs to the third floor. The hallway carpet consisted of dark swirls, and the wallpaper appeared upgraded. No music or TV noise sounded from any of the six compact apartments on the floor.

"Quiet as an empty house" was how he'd describe it.

Cale rapped the door of 308, and the occupant answered. Cho Lin was now thirty-two and seemed to have aged little from when he had received his sentence. Somewhat wiser about the eyes, more suspicious, but incarceration did that to you, didn't it? You learned to keep one eye over your shoulder.

The men greeted one another clumsily. While allowing him into the room, Cale noted how the man's eyes swept the hallway behind, satisfying himself the detective was alone. Cho Lin appeared edgy and nervous.

"Thanks for coming, Lieutenant. I wasn't sure you'd take me seriously."

"Had some free time today. You sounded stressed on the phone." *Life and death? My own!*

They stood in the sitting area of the one bed unit. The bathroom was to the left, with a double bed extending out from the same left wall. Cale supposed you could call it a suite the way a pickup truck was a flatbed. The windows were set against the back wall and peered over a side street—no tiny French balcony. Set off opposite from the bed were two sitting chairs with arms. They bracketed a small lamp table. The lamp's shade would have been comfy in his grandmother's old house.

Cale eased into one of the chairs and pulled his mobile from his windbreaker, setting it on the table. No ashtray. A sign of the times.

Cho Lin swept a stack of papers aside and positioned himself on the edge of his bed. He appeared frail, Cale noted, his five-ten frame straight as a cue stick. On one pillow were pages of notes beside a laptop. The man, if Cale had to guess, had been doing research. No surprise. The guy had a head for numbers. A science dude. Come to think of it, it's what landed him in prison.

"Somebody's been busy," Cale remarked, bobbing his chin at the mess atop the covers. He gave the ex-con the once over. "You're not using, are you, JJ?"

"Clean going in and coming out. I take a pill to sleep. Nothing else."

Cale believed him. Cho Lin was a whip-smart math whiz. The type who enjoyed walking around with a clear head.

"So, why am I here? Not just for old-time's sake, I'm sure."

"I was hoping you'd do me a solid." He rubbed his hands. "Fact is—I still owe money to some bad people."

The admission came as no surprise. When you dabbled in the narcotics business, you either had a stash hidden somewhere or, like the other ninety-eight percent, could barely float a ten-dollar lunch tab.

"Mob guys? Other dealers?" Cale arched an eyebrow. Every ex-con he'd known had debts. Legal fees, family, friends, the IRS. Or else old enemies. The latter was the worst. Enemies never forgave and forgot.

"Sharks," Cho Lin answered. "I tried legal services to shave my sentence but doing so cost a chunk in attorney's fees. But my old connections are even worse. They claim I never delivered on some product back when I got busted. Say I still owe them for it." He looked down at his feet.

Cale pictured the type of hombres he meant. When you swim with the sharks, he told himself.

"What's the tally? Ballpark?"

"It started at fifty-K." Cho Lin grimaced. "But they added another hundred to my number. *Compound interest*, they're calling it."

Cale wasn't a good whistler, so he didn't try. JJ confessed how the current sum would grow to a cool million in a couple of years. When he asked if there was any silver lining, the younger man let slip: "The DeSaul family. Uh, sorry. Hope you didn't hear that."

Cale's shrug prompted him to continue.

"They say if I pay full-up, they'll burn the paper. I get to 'stay living' is how they put it."

An age-old story. In this case, the good news was that the guy possessed marketable skills—even if most of them were illicit. "When's the note come due?"

"A month," Cho Lin said. "From last week." He glanced at his laptop on the mattress. "I've been holed-up here for two months. E-mailing, web searches. Calling anyone who knew me before."

Cale's phone lit up, and he glanced at it. "You're no ghost, JJ. Someone knows you're here."

Cho Lin rose and paced a few steps, flashing Cale a "zero" sign with his fingers. "It's how many people I can trust."

Cale wondered if he was only getting half the story. He was overly suspicious these days due to the insane home intruder's attack a month ago, followed by his disciplinary suspension. He had good reason to be.

Was Dr. Pam right? Perhaps he was too much "logic over emotion."

Cho Lin sat back on the bed's edge. He eyed Cale. "Okay. Here's the rest." He let out a breath. "They gave me a work detail in the prison library. Got me out of gen pop. Because I'm what they call a pacifist. Right? A soft fish."

Cale kept his eyes on the slender man. "Big brutes would make you grow your hair out, wear red lipstick. Turn you into their pet Fan Bingbing."

"Not much of a compliment, Lieutenant. But, yeah, that's the gist."

"So you hid in the library among the books?"

"There aren't enough incarcerated Asians to form a brotherhood." Cho Lin smirked. "I asked myself, JJ, what is it you do best?"

"Not sure I want—"

"I was a cooker." His eyes surveyed the room windows as if listening for street sounds. "I sent word up the chain. All I needed was baking soda, Visine, vinegar, hand sanitizer, and a couple of Zippos."

Cale let him tell his story.

"I promised a dust that would float 'em to the moon and back."

After considering this, Cale asked, "Why tell me all this?"

"The drug world has shifted," Cho Lin said knowingly. "Inside, it's a golden ticket for anyone who can turn canned prunes into a hundred proof. Or dried shave cream into powder." He chewed his lower lip. "Once I figured out the landscape, I worked out a plan."

Cale thought, A druggie with a strategy. How novel.

"I never use." The young man read his thoughts. "I make the product. That's it."

Cale rechecked his watch. "And this is where I come in, right?"

"It's nothing illegal," Cho Lin said. "I just need a Hail Mary pass to escape my debt."

A voice in Cale's head warned how the smart play was to exit the room right now. Still, he felt he should at least listen to the young man's story. Perhaps the guy was using him as a sounding board—a cry for help sort of thing.

"Look. My new idea will also help you. You meaning law enforcement, even more than it will help me."

Cale's phone lit up again. Maggie. "Hold the thought." He grabbed for his mobile, rising. "My fiancé." He advanced toward the door. "Anybody else staying on this floor?"

20

"Some dude in 302. He's never around during the day."

Cale eased out into the shadowed hallway. The forty-foot corridor revealed dust mites dancing at the far windows, and he pressed his phone's call-return. Maggie should be at home. But being pregnant, she had doctor appointments and other whatnot going on. She now had flex hours with her Public Defender's job and could work on her own schedule.

Maggie picked up on the second ring. "How'd things go with Dr. Pam?" she asked.

No emergency, thank God. "She reported my test score. Thinks I might be Hannibal Lecter's cousin."

"Great. That narrows down my Christmas list." Her words conveyed mock seriousness. "You want a butcher knife or a hockey mask?"

"That's not why you called, I hope."

"Slink says thanks for helping them." A question in her voice.

"Some small commotion by the river. I stopped to lend a hand."

"What about *suspended,* don't you get, Cale?"

"Some moron slipped on a river deck. Fell in." Before she could counter, he added, "Remind Slink he owes me a case of Pabst."

With a sigh, she shifted topics. "I'm on the way home. Want a Kroll's cheeseburger for lunch?"

"Had to play your trump card, didn't you?"

CHAPTER 4

Inside the hotel room a second time, Cale resumed his position in the familiar chair. Cho Lin remained on the bed, sitting cross-legged, typing on his laptop.

"Got things going on." Cale set his mobile on the lamp table. "Ten more minutes of sob story, then I got to run."

Cho Lin's eyes were wide and soulful. "Long story short, then. I perfected my cooking to stay alive."

"And the prison library was a perfect cover?"

"The shot-callers became my protectors. Got me all the supplies I requested. All copacetic."

"Copacetic." Cale peered at his phone.

"I met another fish in the library. Guy named Kilo Kemp."

Cale was close to drumming his fingers.

"Transferred in from Minnesota. His dad used to be a crime gang big wig. Rivals would snuff Kilo in a minute if they ID'd him." He massaged his neck. "They assigned him as my cell bro. The warden figured my protection would extend to my bunkmate as well."

"You watch too much cable, JJ."

"His dad was a Minneapolis underboss." He paused. "So, we had to keep Kilo's ID on the down-low."

Cale glanced at his phone again, patience thinning.

"Here's the deal," the young man said. "I've got a cousin, Benny. He lives in Shanghai, works R&D at a huge Chinese drug research lab." Cale remained unimpressed. "Where three-quarters of the world's fentanyl is produced."

He should have guessed anything Cho Lin touched would come back to narcotics. The warnings all cops had learned flashed into his mind: *Fentanyl. One-hundred times more powerful than morphine.*

"Benny's a neurological researcher—a pharm genius," Cho Lin continued. "I'm not kidding. A few months back, he created this new version."

"Version?"

"Fentanyl. Eff. China Girl or fifty other names."

Cale arched an eyebrow. "You mean the biggest killer opioid on the planet?"

"That's what you'd think." Cho Lin nodded. "But in this case, it's the opposite." He took a deep breath. "Benny has created a non-lethal form. One that doesn't shut down the heart or lungs."

Cale wasn't sure what to say.

The young man rose and stepped to the nearby dresser, leaned his back against it. "What if I told you we could end the opioid death crisis?"

"I'd say wacky weed has fried your circuits."

"I don't mean stopping sales." Cho Lin's voice hardened. "But the needless deaths." He waved one hand. "What if fentanyl became just another drug?"

Cale understood how the narcotics racket worked. The futile "War on Drugs" this country had lost decades ago. What he didn't comprehend was why him? The Why-am-I-here part?

Cho Lin pressed on about the massive waste of money fighting the never-ending cartel wars, the over-burdened healthcare services, wasted law enforcement hours, legal system strain. The devastation to families and communities.

"It's a black hole death pit," Cale agreed. "And everyone knows it."

Cho Lin moved back to the bed's edge, still standing. "As I said, I owe serious money to some nasty people."

"And this is your solution? A new drug? Buy your way out of debt?"

"I'm a cooker, Lieutenant." He shrugged. "Beggars and choosers?"

Cale glanced at his phone on the table. "We got a bottom line here?"

James Cho Lin had on a gray cargo shirt over dark jeans. He withdrew a folded piece of paper from his shirt pocket and extended it the way a teen shows ID. Cale studied the chemical formula on the note.

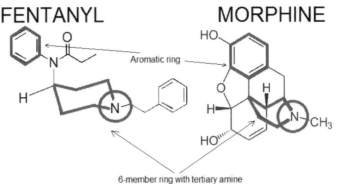

He asked, "This is your Hail Mary pass?"

"It's a designer compound. A new Acryl-synthesis."

Cale thought about it. "They tried it with NA beer, didn't they? Total flop." He handed the paper back to his host.

Cho Lin was undeterred. He explained how most cookers out there were cutting milligrams of fentanyl into other opioids and diet pills, pot, coke—even lollipops. It was cheap and enhanced the buzz. He shoved the folded paper into his shirt pocket before adding how a one-milligram flake too much caused a person's lungs to shut down or created heart arrhythmia.

"TV news screams it every night. At least they used to."

"My cousin," Cho Lin continued, "discovered that if you tweak a certain fentanyl molecule—he says the key is *bind,* not *bond*—it suppresses the respiratory depression. You get the bliss, the floating, the pain-free euphoria for two to three hours."

"We've already got NARCAN to save the OD-ers."

Cho Lin scoffed. "If you trust your stoned friends to spot if you're breathing or not." He pointed at his upper pocket. "*This* solves the problem. There's no need for NARCAN if there's no breathing depression."

"That's not the—"

"Look." Cho Lin's voice rose. "There will always be drug abuse deaths. But if you prevent the respiratory failure ones caused by fentanyl? More than ninety percent of them?"

He sat on the mattress's edge again.

Cale pondered the ramifications. A new opioid, cheaper than heroin and cocaine, one hundred times more potent than morphine. But it doesn't kill anybody. Who'd profit the most if such a drug reached the market? The inventors of the stuff, that's who.

He looked hard at Cho Lin. "Again, why tell me all this? I'm a cop."

Cho Lin reached across the bed and spun his laptop around. He spoke while he clacked some keys. "My cousin says it's too dangerous to make over there. The Chinese government controls everything, you know?"

Cale shrugged. Common knowledge.

"He sent me *half* of his formula. The note right here." He withdrew it back from his pocket. "I copied and stored it on a safe site. Dark web. Password protected."

"Half?"

Cho Lin rose now and crumpled the formula note. He walked into the bathroom, and the toilet flushed. Emerging noteless, he said, "I don't trust it written. Room cleaners and whatnot."

Cale stayed quiet, the clock ticking.

"There's another part." Cho Lin pursed his lips. "Knowing which molecule to tweak without affecting 5HT receptors. You also need the cooking recipe. It's accomplished with a precise polymer adhesion method."

"Where's the second part of the formula?"

"I'm meeting with a courier. Someone Benny trusts."

Cale at once understood the danger involved. He'd gone undercover at least a dozen times back when he had worked Narcotics. There was one primary rule in the business: *Trust No One*. "And you guys hatched up a plan for this?"

"My cousin is sending me the other half." Cho Lin looked over at him. "Along with his prep and cooking method. I get it from the courier, put it all together, then bake samples of the new product."

"Okay."

"Then I contact my old prison cellmate. Kilo. The guy I mentioned. He knows about my plan. We auction it to three or four different buyers."

Cale frowned, puzzled. "Why him again? This Kilo guy?"

"If the Big School teaches you one lesson," Cho Lin said, "it's how everything's a tradeoff." His look was knowing. "His dad's name still has cred in the drug biz. The connection makes us look legit to potential buyers across the world."

Cale supposed it made sense.

"It's my own neck on the block." The young man's voice hitched. "There's no crime in selling a math formula to the highest bidder, is there? To pay off debt?"

Cale was still processing the crazy idea.

Breaking the silence, Cho Lin said, "Or?" He pantomimed a knife slicing his throat.

The young man's options were indeed limited. Owing money to the mob was no joke. He'd concocted a plan to free himself, and whether it worked or not would prove iffy. Still, JJ's bizarre story left him with more questions than answers.

"This all goes down when?' Cale asked. "Getting the other half of the formula?"

"They're texting me the location." Cho Lin looked away then back. "But here's the crazy thing, Lieutenant. It's going down tonight."

Cale was aware that druggies needed to move fast these days. Too many tipsters and leakers out there, cutthroat competition. He said, "So you called me because you need backup? In case things turn dicey?"

"Not backup, Lieutenant." Cho Lin spoke in a low voice. "What I'm asking—admitting I'm out of my league on this stuff—is if you'll do the pickup for me?"

CHAPTER 5

Cale departed the old hotel with his head buzzing. He replayed the unusual conversation with James Cho Lin. The guy's out-of-the-blue request for assistance was stuck in a repeat loop in his brain.

Navigating the Bronco back to the city, his inner voice kept nagging: Why are you even thinking about this? It's insane! It was the voice of common sense, he guessed, and the voice had a point.

Despite his disciplinary leave, Cale remained an officer of the law. It was his obligation to consider the puzzle from every angle, wasn't it? On the one hand, he'd be helping an ex-con, a free citizen now, out of a significant jam. On the other, the situation involved illegal narcotics. He supposed the third part was how the entire thing was none of his business.

What don't you understand about suspension, Cale?

Nevertheless, suspended or not, he was still a cop.

Couldn't he lone wolf a case on his own? Especially if a new opioid were about to hit the market. And working with Cho Lin made sense. After the guy sold his formula—and he was correct, people bidding for a piece of paper was not a crime—Cale could pass the intel to the DEA. They'd have a ringside seat for the whole shebang. Bust the operators before any new "safe" fentanyl ever hit the streets.

Cale remembered his undercover times years ago, both users and dealers. He'd learned their habits, memorized their operations, got close enough, in the end, to slap on cuffs and read them their rights. Those had always been long-term affairs. This one, however, appeared to be spur-of-the-moment, whim-wham, exchange a few words, accept a piece of paper from a stranger. Walk away.

Easy cheesy.

His internal debate continued as he drove the Bronco home. Cale wrestled with the twisty parade of convoluted thoughts until he could take it no longer.

Cruising along the scenic river drive, he reached for his phone. Maggie would be wondering where he was. Still, ten minutes away—enough time to call Slink. Run the scenario past him.

His partner answered on the second chirp, saying, "Agent Galman's doing cartwheels. The satchel we recovered from the river contained a thousand Mexican oxys."

"Those blue-green ones?"

"Yeah—the ones slabbing users across the country."

It was because of the fentanyl additive, Cale knew. He now had fentanyl on the brain.

Slink said, "And get this. Cap's crediting me for the Amos Nick collar. Talking both promotion *and* commendation."

"You earned it. Johnny on the spot." It was about time his partner received more feathers in his cap. "I was never there, though, right?"

"Haven't seen you in weeks."

Cale swung the Bronco onto his block.

"Hey! I got to pass on having drinks with you tonight," Slink informed. "Janet's got me doing a soccer thing with the boys."

There was no time to discuss Cho Lin. Not when Cale wasn't sure, himself, what he might do. He told Slink they'd get together later.

"And amigo," Slink said, "your case of beer is on the way."

Turning into his driveway, Cale marveled at how the subconscious mind worked. Without any effort, he had just cleared his schedule for tonight.

Maggie served them a casual lunch at the dining room table. It was Cale's favorite local cheeseburger and a bowl of spicy brown chili. The food treat was a bribe of some sort. But it did

28

reveal one fact: If she was eating burgers and chili, it meant the worst of her morning sickness had subsided.

She continued probing his meeting with Dr. Pam. What did she think about the migraines? And the crazy sounds he sometimes heard in his head?

"PTSD. Says it'll fade."

She studied him. "Did you get more pills? The ones that help?"

Cale swallowed a spoonful of brown glop. "She called in a refill." After a pause, he added: "She also thinks I should use more emotion with things."

"Things like kicking people into the river, for instance?"

He swallowed more chili and changed the subject. "I got an interesting call from a citizen we busted years back. A meth cooker named Cho Lin."

They had been dating for two years now. Cale had shared so many bizarre crime stories and other cop tales that they all ran together. Maggie arched an eyebrow now, listening with a glazed look. He gave her the basic Cho Lin rundown, keeping the details sparse. It was about debts and cartels and if he might be able to help the guy out. She asked why the man had called him after a decade.

"He's got some problems going."

"An ex-con, right? This Cho Lin?"

"Released a few months back." He sipped his water. "Turning his life around."

Maggie's phone chirped, and she moved to the kitchen island. Her office was requesting she write a legal brief. She could do it from home.

Cale's thoughts remained on his meeting with the ex-con. It was what he missed most about his job—it kept his brain focused. One case after the next. Clues to locate and patch together. Every case was a convoluted puzzle in need of assembly. Still, sometimes the best approach was to shove all the clues in a box and let it percolate the way computers ran background scans while people slept.

It's what he did now with Cho Lin's request.

Nevertheless, while setting aside this newest problem, he couldn't prevent the "Big Kahuna" of quandaries from elbowing to the front of his thoughts. Maggie was now ten weeks pregnant. Neither of them ruled out the sperm donor might be Tobias Crenshaw—aka the Chemist. The pervert had incapacitated her with sedatives, then kidnapped and raped her while she'd been unconscious.

They hadn't yet run DNA tests. But the odds forced them to accept Cale might not be the biological father.

He, of course, had wrestled with the dilemma before arriving at his most logical solution. Since he loved Maggie so much, the best play was to support whatever decisions she chose. The thick and thin of it. They would get married and raise *their* child together.

For better, worse, so help me, God. All the rest.

The craziness they had shared over the past months had forced them closer. Cale felt as if they'd been married half their lives already. There would always be road bumps, of course, but if you took it all one day at a time, things had a way of working themselves out in the end.

Trite, perhaps, but old clichés were old for a reason.

Maggie remained on her phone, ironing out work details. Hank, the cat, eased up chairside. He blinked at Cale, making him wonder if cats had a taste for chili. Why not? He slipped his empty bowl to the floor while considered asking Hank's opinion on Cho Lin. The answer would no doubt contain the word *insanity*.

Maggie ended her call. Instead of rejoining him at the table, though, she stomped down the hallway to the den in her stocking feet and was back seconds later, waving a yellow legal pad. She had a pen tucked behind her pinned-up hair, and her glasses were now on.

Maggie yanked the chili bowl up from the floor, ignoring Hank's scowl. She plopped on her chair and set the pad between them the way a reporter readies for an interview.

"I've digested what you told me," she said. "Wrote three columns here. For the one titled *Sheer Idiocy*, I drew your face at the top."

"My good side?"

She spun the pad around, and he narrowed his eyes. He said, "Hardly Ryan Reynolds, is it?"

She was all business. "So, what does this Cho Lin want?"

"Wants me to meet a courier in a warehouse." It sounded creepier out loud. "To pick up…a chemistry formula."

"So, you're in a Le Carre spy novel?"

"Maybe more Dr. Seuss."

She leaned back. "What's the risk equivalent?" He angled his head, looking at her. "These are drug people, Cale."

"There's an upside—"

"And a danger level." She scowled. "Scale of one-to-five?"

"Low. I'll be armed."

"Ex-cons and drug people? Warehouses at midnight?" Her eyes pinned him. "What could possibly go wrong?"

Cale crumpled his napkin. "Either I go, or it's Cho Lin himself." When she didn't respond, he added, "The formula's worth a fortune." He paused. "What detective wouldn't dive into the deep end?"

"How about a *suspended* one? One who hears drums in his head?"

He gazed at her notebook. Not a single word was scribbled.

"It's a good cover, my suspension." He locked eyes with her. "Means I don't have to involve anyone else."

Maggie set her pen down. "All right. Let's say you get this *worth-a-fortune* formula." Her stare was tight. "Then what? You hand it to the guy? He says thanks, here's a hundred bucks for your troubles?"

Cale hadn't thought about the backend part. The whole thing had unfolded too fast. He shrugged away her concern. "Guess I'll cross that bridge when I come to it."

31

CHAPTER 6

Ten p.m. Monday night. Cale wore navy khakis and a dark polo shirt. After donning his burgundy windbreaker from the hallway closet, he realized it was the outfit he often wore when heading out to examine a murder scene.

He sloughed away the irony.

The small set of steps led up to the family room, where the TV volume was low. Maggie was stretched on the couch, half-covered by an afghan. The air smelled of popcorn from the plastic bowl on the coffee table. She wore leggings and a scarlet Wisconsin sweatshirt and offered a silent headshake of disapproval.

"Not sure when I'll be back," he said.

Cale was aware of how trite it sounded. He leaned over the couch behind her and pressed his face to her hair. Hank was on her lap, and she stroked his fur. Cale stood back upright, saying, "I know you don't approve."

She kept her eyes on the TV.

"It'll all be fine," he said predictably. "If it isn't, I'll call." Then he turned and departed from the room.

A minute later, he slipped inside the shadowed Bronco parked out on the driveway apron. The outside security lights illuminated the backyard as brightly as a softball field. Moths flitted up near the lights, drawn to both danger and heat. Cale wondered if he'd been a moth in a previous life.

He turned the Bronco's key.

By 10:45, he was back in Room 308 of the Union Hotel.

Cale wanted to verify Cho Lin's final directions. He also required assurance that the plan remained stable with no last-minute alterations. He'd been on prior tip-off raids where the event had turned into a cluster job. Eyeballing the guy one final

32

time would verify that the situation remained as planned. He'd gauge how nervous Cho Lin appeared. Perspiring? Jittery? White knuckling his phone?

These were all tells. Cale understood how being in the familiar room again, with no panicky vibe, would quiet any internal alarm bells. Plus, it was a final chance to call things off if need be.

Cho Lin stood at the foot of his bed. "All I know is he's a friend of Benny's," he said. "So, I'd trust him with my life."

"It's *my* life we're talking about."

The ex-con nodded. "I appreciate what you're—"

"You're sure he knows it's me coming?" Cale interrupted. "Not you?" He had his jacket unzipped. The third-floor room felt stuffy.

"I texted him ten minutes ago." Cho Lin said. "He's at his hotel. He'll Uber to the warehouse just before midnight."

They repeated the verbal code once more and exchanged emergency numbers. No need for a good luck handshake. If all went as planned, Cale would return here after the exchange. He stepped toward the door.

"Lieutenant!" Cho Lin called, and he turned back. The younger man's eyes were heavy with gratitude. "For doing this, well, just thanks."

With a nod, Cale slipped into the subdued hallway. He didn't recognize it now but would later recall that if Cho Lin had uttered some banal comment—*Break a leg!* or *Remember the Alamo!*—he would have ditched the plan and high-tailed it for the hills.

However, what he'd read in the guy's eyes was the fear given off by people who have reached their lowest rung of desperation.

Cale navigated the Bronco west across the Walnut Street Bridge, which ran through the city's downtown heart. His dashboard reported 11:12 p.m.

He swung left at the stoplights onto Broadway Street. He drove six blocks south past coal plants and storage buildings and the defunct old railroad switchyard. The neighborhood was bleak and low-lit. Only two other vehicles had come the opposite way.

Cale continued along the straight street. It was a strange configuration of old neighborhood homes on one side and industrial warehouses and plants opposite. The smaller houses were packed close, with slender driveways and side yards, tattered duplexes sprinkled in. The street was narrow, and bits of sparse light spilled from around the shaded house windows. A voice in his head reminded him he wasn't getting paid. Yet his rational mind argued that the goal was worth the effort. He could help Cho Lin out of a jam while at the same time uncovering a new drug that might help slow the opioid crisis.

Countless lives could be spared.

He stayed at a slow cruise. Anticipation tightened his chest. His head felt heavy, and he prayed a migraine wasn't forming the way thunder clouds did. He told himself he'd rather be home with Maggie on the couch, but that had all changed with Cho Lin's phone call. He accepted the risk. It's what cops did—even suspended ones.

It was a humid night with rain predicted later. The air felt swollen. The river flowed about forty yards away.

Cale slid past a string of warehouses not far from the riverbank, continuing below the speed limit. They stood in a shadowy row. The furthest building south, his target, was bordered along a chain-fence area and perched this side of the railroad tracks.

He eased the Bronco curbside, parking beneath two pitch-black elms. He was across the street from the meeting place. Almost 11:30 p.m. now. His plan allowed for fifteen minutes of recon, ensuring he wasn't walking into a situation he couldn't handle, a trap of some sort.

On the opposite side of the street, the empty parking lot appeared frail in the gloom. He was meeting the courier inside at midnight. But right now, other than insects buzzing around the light pole, the place appeared deserted. Cale hoped he had the correct address. He also prayed no river rats had chewed their way inside. He wasn't keen on rats—river or otherwise.

While driving, he'd pictured the courier arriving in his Uber lift. According to Cho Lin, the front door would be unlocked. The security alarms disabled. The driver would remain parked in front until after the exchange, then transport the courier back to his hotel.

It was the logical way to play it.

He surveyed the warehouse in the darkness, the calm before the storm. Once the courier showed up, Cale guessed the exchange wouldn't take more than five minutes. His orders were to drive around to the rear entrance, then slip inside the unlocked backdoor. Once they had traded passwords and exchanged the information, both men would walk away like spies on a foggy London bridge. Simple. Clean. Anonymous.

Cale's years in law enforcement had taught him many valuable lessons: Expect the unexpected was at the top of the list. To this end, he had tucked the .38 revolver inside his jacket pocket.

He was still thirty minutes early. Cop time. He wondered if his connection might already be inside. But no sign yet of the Uber. And with no other vehicles in the parking lot, he had no way of knowing what might be happening inside—hopefully, nothing but ghosts.

Arriving early allowed Cale a decent time to study the neighborhood. The homes were older, and many had small front porches. Every other house had toys cluttered in the driveway or sparse front yards, and lawncare appeared discretionary, but it was tricky to discern without the aid of a mid-block streetlight.

The clock kept ticking. No vehicles had cruised past while the Bronco sat in the shadows. A cluster of bushes lurked nearby, a weedy open lot behind them. The street, both ahead and behind, showed vehicles parked in front of the half-lit homes.

Further up ahead, the train tracks crossed an open area. Beyond the tracks stood a house converted into a neighborhood tavern. An unlit Schlitz sign in front was the only giveaway. "Daisy Chain Tap," the porch sign read. Three cars stood parked on the gravel side of the house. No music. Cale doubted the neighbors were thrilled, but who was he to judge?

Enough for the local flavor. He glanced at his mobile, no message from Cho Lin.

It was twelve minutes before midnight, time to check out the back lot of the warehouse. Cale reached for his ignition. Before he could turn the key, a lightless sedan came cruising up the street behind him. The tinted windows blocked any inside view as the vehicle accelerated past. It bounced over the train tracks ahead and continued two blocks further, still driving dark. It turned right at the far-off stoplights and disappeared.

No chance to read the license. It happened too fast, a car appearing out of nowhere on the lonely street. His cop brain thought, Love affair or slumming? No lights, so little chance any neighbors would recognize them. Or perhaps it was a housewife earning some easy late-night cash?

Not his concern.

He keyed his ignition, and the dashboard lit up. He was ready to flip on the Bronco's headlights when a second vehicle swept up behind him in the dark. He caught a side glimpse of the driver this time: a sharp-featured Asian female. Mid-20s, if he had to guess. Though her silhouette was backlit, he'd managed to make out her profile.

As the SUV accelerated away, his eyes fell to the rear license tag. The last digits...*469*. Cale also noted a middle letter appeared as a "J" or "L" before the numbers, so he had J or L *469*. Also, small lettering on the base: "ukes" or something similar it, tricky to decipher, out of state. He'd run a check later if need be.

The SUV—maybe a Toyota—accelerated beyond the tracks and passed the house-tavern. Only then did it flip on headlights. It swung a right at the same far-ahead stoplights as the previous vehicle before vanishing.

Internal alarms were sounding in Cale's head. This night was getting odder by the minute. One lightless vehicle was fate, but a pair, in short order, seemed beyond coincidence. Two passionate lovebirds escaping beneath the shroud of a moonless night. How poetic.

He returned his attention to the warehouse back across the street. It stood desolate under the low, soot-colored clouds. No vehicles, no visitors. Just the solitary pole light. And still no sign of any Uber.

His dash clock read 11:55.

A tight delivery drive ran up the warehouse's left side, and he navigated the Bronco along it. The path bordered a patch of lawn, which separated the neighboring warehouse property. Approaching the back, he noticed the rear parking lot ended in a weed bank that sloped far down to the river's edge. Another faint security light was attached to a single tall pole.

Cale parked ten yards from the unmarked back door. The original plan was for the courier to be inside already, awaiting Cho Lin's arrival. The code words were easy enough, and they ran through his head as he approached the door. The courier was to say, "*John Wayne.*" Cale, in turn, would provide his answer. It was the "KISS" method former athletes, military, and cops were all familiar with:

Keep-It-Simple-Stupid.

The red light was off on the keypad. It indicated that the courier was already inside. How he wasn't sure, but it didn't matter. He was on time, and the door handle turned without effort. Cale dipped into the inner darkness, easing the door closed behind him. The place smelled musty. He stood listening for a minute, allowing the graveyard stillness to fill in around him.

He flashed back to his undercover years, remembering he'd slipped into warehouses far creepier than this one. His left wrist brushed his jacket pocket, felt the weight of the .38. His muted phone was in easy reach. A cloak and dagger game now, and the stakes were high. He reminded himself that if the fentanyl formula weren't unique, they could have done all this at some nearby Denny's.

Cale advanced along an invisible path between a pair of shoulder-high wooden crates. Perspiration pooled along his lower back, and his gut reported a greasy unease. Cho Lin had confessed there might be "bad actors" involved. People willing to risk their lives to possess the formula. The narcotics game was ruthless, and lives were snuffed with little hesitation.

The crates became lower at the row's end, and he could discern open air ahead. The upper windows were grimy, allowing in a faint, translucent glow from the outside pole light. He stopped his advance and imagined the courier hovering frightened nearby.

Cale withdrew his phone and pressed the flashlight app. The beam was enough to illuminate a penumbra about ten yards out, and he remained frozen.

"Hello! *Mucho gusto!*" His voice echoed through the musty dampness. "James Cho Lin sent me here, in his place." Silence. "I say my part after you say 'John Wayne.'"

Only quiet shadows. Maybe the contact's English was shaky. Could they have mixed up the verbal sequence? Cale tried again:

"Rooster? Rooster Cogburn?*"*

He could sense another heartbeat. The quiet, however, revealed no sound or breathing. The warehouse floor was cold cement, filled with crates and boxes piled fifteen feet high—an open, triple high ceiling. Ahead of him, walking paths branched this way and that between the clutter.

Cale focused his beam outward as he moved, keeping the rear wall behind him. "Anybody in here?" The darkness swallowed his voice. "John Wayne?"

38

Nothing. Could their wires have gotten crossed, and he was supposed to be speaking Chinese? "Rooster!" Cale tried again, and more silence caused his gut to warn: *Get the hell out of here!*

"We work together, right?" He eased the revolver from his pocket. called out: "I just need the notebook—then I leave."

Walking across the pitch-black floor, his hand was clammy around the gun handle. An attack could come from anywhere at any moment. Cale's eyes scanned for whatever lurked outside the light beam. He detected a faint aroma in the musty air. Poison? Dead rats?

After a left turn, he entered a more expansive area. Felt eyes on his back as he cross-stepped forward. Jungle tigers attacked from behind, didn't they?

He stopped, his instinct telling him to sweep the light to the right. The beam located dark smears on the floor, and the coppery odor jived with the crumpled form laying in the half-lit shadows. Cale swept the narrow beam across the man's ashen, bloodless face. Murdered. Brutal fashion.

No doubt this was the courier. The snarky voice in his head taunted: "Somebody beat you to it, Ace."

39

CHAPTER 7

Cale had seen enough cold bodies during his career not to be affected much by death. Nevertheless, finding a deceased stranger on a warehouse floor, blood trickling from the crimson smile across his throat, still had a sobering effect.

He also calculated that if he'd entered the place fifteen minutes earlier, it might be his body lying there.

Images of the earlier pair of vehicles escaping down the dark street sprang into his mind. His senses were on high alert. He wondered if the perpetrator could still be lurking inside the building.

Cale listened for a minute, his trained ears bouncing their radar off the warehouse's inner walls. The hackles on his neck weren't rising. His gut wasn't tightening with each passing second. Instead, some deep inner voice informed him the killing was over, and he was safe.

He decided to trust his instincts.

He took a minute now to study the body with a sharper eye. The man's hands and shirt were drenched with blood, and he lay halfway over sacks of powdered cement. Cale knew how long it took a body to bleed out. By now, the killer had escaped, and the notebook containing the second half of Cho Lin's formula was with him.

Little evidence of a struggle. He imagined the assailant had sliced the victim's throat from behind; or else startled him, so when he had spun around, a butcher's slice through his windpipe had done the trick.

Cale noted one of the dead man's hands had fallen from his throat and the other flung aside. Handprints on his jacket revealed someone had searched him. Or else he'd fumbled for his phone in his final desperate moments.

Cho Lin had suggested the cartels would do whatever it took to get hold of his cousin's formula. They would then force him to manufacture the product, and afterward, he'd be deemed disposable baggage.

Same as the man on the floor right now.

Cale doubted Cho Lin himself was the murderer. He recalled how the prison authorities had described him as a pacifist. Instead, the bloody nature of the courier's death had "cartel" written all over it.

This was an execution. Brutal. Savage.

Another fact was also apparent. Cale was deep in the middle of a murder investigation.

He surveyed his surroundings again. The detective in him was grabbing the reins. Besides, the man on the floor was in no hurry to get where he was going.

Straddling the blood pool, he leaned over and probed the man's pockets, wishing he had gloves along. He searched for folded papers or envelopes, a wallet, or a phone, knowing everything was long gone by now.

Rising, Cale studied the surrounding area again. The darkness was layered, pale moonlight filtering through the dusty windows near the ceiling. The warehouse was a giant maze. His eyes wary, ears perked for the slightest sound or shuffle, he turned and retraced his steps back to the exit.

Outside the building, Cale scanned the empty parking lot. He could discern the flow of current from the nearby river. He withdrew his phone and climbed inside the Bronco. Slink Dooley answered, his voice groggy.

"Grab your call bag," Cale said. "Meet me at a warehouse off South Broadway. Last one before the P&G mill."

Scrambling sounds in the background. Cale pictured his partner dressing in the dark. Janet, Slink's wife, would turn into her pillow with resigned indifference. For investigators, night calls were routine. Real crimes happened after dark.

"Want to fill me in?" Slink asked.

Cale pictured him tying his shoes. "Some guy I was supposed to meet. More blood outside his body than in."

"You call the techs?"

"It's your job now." He added, "I'm a ghost, remember?"

Slink grunted and ended the call.

The protocol was to alert the station and get whichever detective was on night shift rotation. Yet Cale decided his partner was a better bet at covering for his involvement. With a corpse lying on the floor inside, he was already in this mess to his eyeballs.

The first patrol car arrived in less than four minutes and two more a minute later. Their flashing strobes reflected off the trees and low clouds. Cale stepped from the Bronco. He knew Sgt. Liz Juana from previous cases. She'd told him once how she enjoyed the graveyard shift. To her, it was like working some backstage production out of the spotlight.

"Strange time of night for a river stroll, Lieutenant," Sgt. Juana said. Her partner was a patrolman with a bulldog jaw.

"Strange times we live in, Sergeant."

He informed them of the body inside. The perp was in the wind—no witnesses to detain. Detective Dooley and the forensic team were on the way. Cale watched them walk to the rear warehouse door, flashlights drawn and sidearms ready.

He sat inside the Bronco with the door open. It was his best chance at replaying the details he had witnessed. With a dead body discovered, the pair of earlier mystery vehicles became more relevant. The first car? It could have been a Chrysler, Buick, or Lincoln. Decent-sized.

The SUV was easier. He'd gotten a look at the petite Asian woman's profile. Odds were, she had nothing to do with the situation, yet two vehicles driving lightless a minute apart. Midnight lovebirds, he had imagined. Did he need to hunt them down? Throw them into the midst of a messy murder investigation?

Of course, he did. The body on the warehouse floor was answer enough. Besides, what if one of them was the perpetrator? Or were they partners? A murderous duo?

Cale decided he'd feel things out before revealing all his cards to Slink. With no witnesses to detain, there was no need to overwhelm his partner at the onset. Keep both his presence and involvement sketchy. Meals were always best when served one dish at a time.

Cale's brain jolted. Sweet Jesus. He'd been processing all this with a cop's mind. Grabbing his phone, he dialed Cho Lin's number and got three busy signals in a row. He hesitated at leaving a traceable voicemail while searching for the Union Hotel's main number. He dialed the front desk, no answer—only an options menu recording. They were a mom-and-pop operation and probably shut down incoming calls before midnight.

He redialed Cho Lin, knowing he had to warn the guy. The voicemail option beeped, and Cale said firmly:

"Courier dead. Get out of there *now!*"

He stared at his phone then, wondering if he had just shot a hole in his life raft. The voicemail was traceable proof. It didn't matter. Cho Lin would be screening his calls and hear Cale's urgency. He'd be halfway down the stairs already, sprinting to whatever hidey-hole he chose.

Dark scenarios paraded through Cale's head. Too many. None ending well.

A pewter-colored Taurus wheeled around the building's back. Slink's cruise car pulled beside the Bronco. He would have called in the suspected homicide report to Watch Command, been assigned the case. Slink would also have a CSI team on the way.

Cale exited the Bronco, unable to avoid his partner's narrowed eyebrows. "I should've told you about Cho Lin," he said earnestly. "I only met with him earlier today."

Slink appeared puzzled. "You mean that cooker dude we busted years ago?"

Cale explained the phone call and hotel meeting and how he'd agreed to assist with a third-party intel exchange.

"At midnight? In a warehouse by the river?"

43

Cale understood how it appeared. "I walked in. Found the courier bled out on the floor."

Shaking his head, Slink deadpanned, "So, how's your new NSA job working out?"

They started toward the warehouse's back door, where the officers had propped it open, lights blazing now inside. Before they could enter, however, another vehicle came churning around the back of the building.

Dr. Heinz Mocarek was the long-standing Brown County Medical Examiner. He exited his Honda sedan, medical bag in hand. "Rain, snow, gloom of night," the doctor quipped, not smiling.

When Cale cocked his head, the ME added, "I live just three miles away."

Slink's phone chirped. It was the DA's electronic warrant, and he dutifully X'd it. It allowed them to enter without waiting for a CSI team. They slipped on gloves and booties, Slink loaning Cale extras from his call bag.

The inner warehouse appeared alien in the light. He led them back down the paths he'd taken earlier, between the high shelves and boxes and various clutter. A minute later, they stood looking at the body where he'd left it.

Dr. Mocarek stooped in close, peered at the starchy face, probed one cheek with his gloved fingers. He spoke without looking up.

"Dead an hour now, give or take." He studied the throat wound. "Serrated blade, from behind. Your perp is right-handed. Good chance he's a pro."

"And you think that because—"

"Not easy sneaking up on someone nervous in the dark. Getting it right the first time."

They continued observing the doctor in silence. Seconds later, Slink turned to Cale. "Anything else I should know?"

"This is how I found him."

"What about Cho Lin?"

"Never here. Left him back at his hotel."

Slink thought about it. "Let's hope he can prove he stayed there."

Cale side-eyed his partner. Slink wore a light jacket, eyes puffy from sleep. His recent coffee-ground stubble cast his face in shadow like a French actor Cale had seen in a noir film.

The front door of the warehouse swung open now as the forensic techs arrived. Half of them would shuffle around outside in their Tyvek suits. Another handful would shoo the detectives from the body to preserve trace evidence. Photographers and the usual others would join in. The ME would sign the death certificate and make it all official.

Both detectives continued staring down at the deceased victim. "How can a guy just stand there," Slink asked, "while his throat's getting slashed?"

"Drugged, maybe?" Cale threw it out there. "Before it happened?"

The doctor's knees creaked as he rose. "Can't say much until he's on the slab. Bloodwork will tell us about drugs."

"If he's got any blood left," Slink said, eyeing the scarlet puddle on the floor.

CHAPTER 8

City lights twinkled around them, reflected double by the flat surface of the wide river. Slink rode shotgun as the Bronco sped across the main De Pere bridge. The late-night traffic was sparse. Grill and visor lights blinking, they circled a roundabout, and seconds later, they squealed to a halt in front of the old hotel.

Cale had phoned three more times while driving. No answer. He pictured James Cho Lin squirreled in some basement storage cellar or similar dark place.

The detectives flung open the hotel's main doors and swept across the small front lobby. A white-haired lady staffed the front desk, her eyes widening. She lifted from her chair but sat down when Cale motioned his silent finger upward.

"No one else comes up," Slink warned her, trailing behind him. She nodded and watched them disappear.

Halfway up the stairs, Slink said, "Not the Kress Inn, is it?" He meant the 5-star hotel just across the river.

"Out of prison four months ago. Any port."

"Good place to gopher it. I'll give him that."

No lodgers poked their heads from any of the top-floor rooms. The ambiance was old-school spookiness, and Cale recalled a movie poster he'd once seen, where sales guys checked in late, and ghosts patrolled the dim hallways. The Union could be the prototype.

Their senses on alert, they crept along the hallway's dark carpet. Cale noted some odor, maybe citrus, which lingered in the stodgy air. No room service trays outside the doors, and the spectral aroma faded as they progressed. Outside Room 308, he held up his hand and withdrew his .38. Behind him, Slink stepped sideways and did the same.

Cale's ear to the door, listening for voices or sounds. Nothing. Quiet as the night lobby of a car dealership. It was an old-fashioned door employing keys instead of card-slots. He searched up and down the hallway for security cameras and spotted none, reminding himself that Cho Lin would not be peacefully sleeping inside.

Stepping back, Cale front-kicked the door below the brass handle. The old wood shuddered. Another two kicks splintered it, and they eased their way inside the room.

Heavy bleach odor. Cale covered his mouth and nose with his elbow. The room was dark and bleak, the window shades drawn—rendering the place an ominous silence. Behind him, Slink flicked on the room's dim lights.

Cale surveyed the scene. The chairs were at different angles than earlier. Most notable, however, was the lengthy lump on the bed beneath the blankets. Slink cleared the bathroom behind them before moving across to the far windows. They weren't meant for opening, so he crashed his gun butt through a lower pane to help air the place out.

Cale stood bedside and eased the blankets down to reveal the torso, then raised the pillow where it covered the victim's head. He had already pictured what he'd find, and his guess proved correct.

The lifeless face of James Cho Lin stared back with the open eyes rolled sideways. The pillow and upper mattress were a mess of bloody bone bits and oozing steaks of gray matter. A pair of close-range bullets had exited the skull, penetrated the lower headboard, and then lodged into the wall.

They heard a vehicle pass on the street below. Other than this, the room was as still as an empty jail cell.

Pulling the covers down farther, Cale observed the rest. Cho Lin had been forced to lie with his clothes on and cover himself for execution. Why he had put up no struggle was anyone's guess.

Cale said, "Two to the head. Close range."

Slink stood behind him, looking down. "Double-tap," he said. "Suppressor would be a good guess."

Glancing around the room, Cale realized the man's laptop was nowhere in sight. He scanned the place, then searched through drawers and inside the closet. He peered beneath the bed. Nothing. Cho Lin's phone was gone as well.

"The entire floor's a ghost town," Slink said. "No shots heard, or people would be milling around."

Despite the cracked window, the bleach odor persisted. A dark thought struck Cale, and he cast his eyes about. He stepped away from the bed.

"Don't breathe or speak." He motioned Slink to follow him. Together they slipped back into the hallway, where Cale removed his jacket and tossed it to the floor. Slink did the same, and they hastened down the stairs and exited onto the empty sidewalk.

Taking deep breaths, Slink asked, "That was about what again?"

"Fentanyl," Cale explained, also catching his breath. "It's what this thing's been about from the get-go."

Slink shook his head, breathing hard.

Cale was already heading back to the front entrance. He'd return in a second, he informed, but the entire hotel needed evacuation. "Fire and Rescue!" he shouted over his shoulder. "Call it in."

It was nearing two a.m., and the bizarre night was lasting forever.

The response team examined the hotel for toxic hazards while Cale and Slink sat inside the Bronco. They discussed what had transpired, what they knew, and how much they didn't. Cale admitted, in hindsight, that he and Cho Lin had been out of their league from the beginning.

He felt like an amateur. He was supposed to be a drug crime expert and should have recognized the high level of danger from the start.

"Don't beat yourself up, Kemosabe," Slink said, consoling him as a friend. "The Chinese government monitors all their scientists. It's a fact."

"I thought we'd sneak under the radar."

Cale was frustrated by his apparent lack of caution. As things stood, when word got out about his screw-up, the Department ought to suspend him for an entire year. Just for being a jackass." Hell, even Maggie had warned him of the danger.

He scolded himself: Stupid, stupid, *stupid!*

Slink put a capper on the fiasco. "The important thing is you came out the back end in one piece."

"Yeah. At least I'm good at that part."

Cale waited for a punch line that never came.

Fire and Rescue had cleared the hotel for poisonous hazards. The front desk lady and two upstairs occupants roused from their sleep had returned inside. A second CSI team had been summoned to examine Cho Lin's room, and Slink had signed another electronic warrant.

Dr. Heinz Mocarek had also made an encore appearance, one crime scene to the next. Cho Lin's body was driven off in the meat wagon, and the ME emerged from the hotel now, appearing frazzled. He informed the investigators he would perform both autopsies tomorrow morning and welcomed their presence.

They bid farewell to the doctor, acknowledging they'd all had a crazy night and needed sleep.

Slink exited the Bronco, and before closing the door, he leaned in, asking, "By the way, any killers come to mind who enjoy shooting people in the head?"

"Just a few dozen. I'll let you know."

Slink patted the Bronco's door frame. He then slipped inside a cruiser that would drive him back home to bed.

About to turn the key, a thought flashed through Cale's head. He exited his SUV and headed back toward the hotel's front door.

The front desk lady still had the same burgundy fleece tracksuit—the kind soccer moms once wore. She appeared seasoned, someone who'd seen enough of life not to be rattled. She watched Cale approach from behind the small front counter.

"I don't have to worry about passing out anymore, do I?" the lady asked. "Nerve gas or anything?"

He offered a weary smile. "I'm Cale Van Waring, one—"

"The detectives. I know," she interrupted. "I'm Millie. Night shift here for twenty years. And we don't take calls after midnight, in case you're wondering."

"Just a quick question," he said, "about James Cho Lin?"

"Always so polite." Millie blinked through her bifocals. "Can I ask?" She glanced around the place. "We're not what you'd call a hotbed of crime around here."

"Bad drugs," Cale confessed. He supposed it wasn't a lie. "You didn't notice any strangers hanging around recently? Or earlier tonight?"

She thought about it. "Not too many shady characters around here."

"How about security footage?"

"Never needed it." She frowned. "Hick, our bartender, he doubles as security when he isn't pouring Old Fashioneds." She winked at him.

Cale handed her his detective's card. "My partner from earlier, Detective Dooley, he'll want to ask you all this same stuff in a day or so."

After studying the card, her eyes widened. "Van Waring? I knew I'd seen that name before."

She turned around and withdrew an envelope from an open mail slot on the back wall. She glanced at the writing, then extended it to Cale. "James came down earlier tonight," she informed. "Told me to give you this if anything, well, you know?"

Cale studied the envelope before pocketing it. Was it a message from the grave?

He thanked Millie and turned to leave.

"Hope you find whoever did this, Detective!" she called, watching him stride toward the door. "James was one of the good ones."

CHAPTER 9

It was three a.m. by the time Cale pulled into the driveway of his home.

Inside the dark garage, he cut the Bronco's ignition. He sat in the faint inner light and withdrew the envelope from his pocket. Best to read it now. If not, he'd spend a sleepless night wondering what secrets the note might hold.

Cale employed his key to slit the envelope open. The note was hand-written on beige-colored Union Hotel stationary, folded in half. He read the three meager paragraphs. Then re-read it slower:

Lieutenant. If anything wrong happens, I just wanted to thank you for trying to help. As you know, I took some wrong turns in my life but never with any malice intended. I was hoping to make things right this time, get out of debt, start over. I was never a "criminal mind." I think you recognized that back when we first met. (lol)

If you're reading this, it means things didn't turn out like I'd planned. My cousin Benny's real name is Muri Chow, in case you need to contact him. My half of the formula is in an encrypted dark web file, buried in my laptop. You'll have to access the Tor browser. Peel the onion layers. Find the dark web's equivalent of Facebook. You may have to special search for it.
Login: Cyclops616<JackietheFU+Chan.
PW: =@/v)=(44^%$$)
PS: The bastards can hack all they want, but they won't find my part of the formula without the above logins. Guard them with your life. My final thought is: Thank you again. And don't trust a cute lady named Syan. Dangerous! DD!! – JJ zài jiàn

In the first-floor den room, Cale took a moment to hide the envelope. He climbed the stairs half-exhausted, moving into the dark bedroom in silence. Allowing his clothes to drop to the floor, he slid between the sheets beside Maggie without making a ripple.

As he settled onto his pillow in the extra-wide bed, her voice sounded husky. "Everything go okay?"

A loaded question. Cale was too exhausted to get into it. "A little sideways," he mumbled softly. "We'll straighten it out tomorrow."

The phone charger's glow provided faint illumination in the room. It was on the nightstand at Cale's side of the bed.

"You weren't in danger, were you?"

The night's events slid through his mind in Fellini fashion, a parade of characters marching in a surreal conga line. James Cho Lin, his cousin Benny in Shanghai (now ID'd as Muri Chow), the invisible man in the dark car, and the courier with his neck sliced open. The shadowy Asian lady driver, Slink and Millie and Doc, the CSIs in their white Tyveks. They were all trailed by some faceless assassin who had two-tapped Cho Lin in the head execution-style.

They marched along a hillside in an undulating line.

"Not real danger," he said, his voice heavy with fatigue. "You doing okay?"

Her body shifted. "Fine. I'm going in to work tomorrow. And I'm having a talk with Chloe."

Cale turned toward her shadow in the dark. "I'll tell you everything. Promise." He located the side of her forehead and kissed it, and they both fell asleep within a minute.

Or at least one of them did.

Though it was late, a mile across town from Cale and Maggie, her sister Chloe wrestled with her own insomnia. It was closer

53

to dawn than midnight, and here she sat, alone at the dining room table in the flickering candlelight. There was no point in waking her husband, Ed, or the kids. Chloe sipped from a cup of warm chamomile tea. A lavender-scented votive candle provided the room's faint light.

The dream had left her rattled.

The Liberian witch doctor's cackling laughter, even now, still haunted her dreams.

Chloe sipped her tea. Tomorrow she was meeting with her sister to tell her how bad things were getting. She was losing weight and unable to maintain concentration at work. These past few weeks, it had gotten worse instead of better.

Of course, Maggie had her own basket of issues. The baby was on the way, and the wedding date was scheduled. Chloe had agreed to be the matron of honor. And with all her sister had going on, she was hesitant to bother her with personal issues.

She hated being a burden.

Chloe had prayed the images of the "voodoo man" in her brain would dissipate over time. No luck. She decided she needed a more powerful weapon to deal with the situation. One that would scrub her mind clean of the taint.

Visiting Father Larchezzi was a good idea. Seek spiritual counsel. He had helped her before, and Chloe hoped he might do so again.

She finished her tea and extinguished the candle. Headed back to her dark bedroom, she decided the best remedy for purging her of the tormenting dreams was the most radical solution of all.

An exorcism.

The hour was late at the English manor house. The home was the principal dwelling of three large structures set deep amid twelve acres of Wisconsin woods, not far from Tar Creek, a Little Oconto River branch. The night sounds were the usual owls in the trees and the stream's gurgle as it swept over the weather-worn rocks.

Miguel DeSaul, the CEO of industrial dairy giant Fillmore Farms, had risen from his sleepless bed. He'd grown up a city boy, with sirens and car alarms, screeching tires, and gunshots. Thus, the quiet of the northern woods often felt like torture.

Accepting that his efforts at relaxing were futile, Miguel had padded his way downstairs.

There he sat now in the front room of his mansion. The windows were tall and quarter-paned, stretching to near the top of the room's two-story ceiling. A four-piece leather couch-and-chair-set matched the burgundy bookcases constructed from oak supplied by the surrounding forest. Paintings and other artsy decorations dripped from the walls in an opulent version of good taste, especially in this Podunk—Miguel smirked—part of the state, where viewers wouldn't know a Monet knockoff from a Manet original.

Though neither, he admitted, would he.

Through tired eyes, he stared at his brandy tumbler on the coffee table. His phone sat beside it. He was considering a move to the wet bar for another splash of brandy when the mobile buzzed.

Miguel fumbled to answer.

"Things went as planned," came the icy voice of Frank Kemp, the head of Fillmore Farms' security.

"You got the formula, Frank?"

"Courier had the second part on him," Kemp explained. "He was kind of bleeding a lot by the time he handed it over."

It was not the news Miguel had hoped to hear. But he also accepted that with Kemp, you got what you paid for.

Miguel had been pondering earlier in the evening about how he'd arrived at this crossroads in his life. His father was Sevastian "Sevvie" DeSaul, founder and king of the DeSaul crime syndicate, based in Minneapolis.

Started in the cocaine-snorting 1980s, the gang had made a fortune by employing a spiderweb of street hoods and taking over the city's urban drug market.

Years later, to shelter his ill-gotten gains. Sevvie DeSaul had branched into downtown real estate, making a killing when property values had exploded. The gang boss was an instantly legitimate businessman who had moved the family up to safer, saner Duluth, Minnesota. There he'd ventured into corporate farming as another tax dodge, just as the concept of industrial agriculture was beginning to sweep across the country.

Though Sevvie had come up hard as a ruthless gangster, no one argued that he didn't possess the golden thumb of good timing. Not when his millions continued to multiply faster than libidinous hedgehogs.

Sevvie had christened his new venture Fillmore Farms, Inc. and ridden the tsunami of success into the future. He hadn't known a lick about farming but was smart enough to turn things over to his corporate board of directors to run. Yet the father retained one wish: he requested that his only son, Miguel, work for a living instead of playing golf all day and living off the family teat. Thus, now at the tender age of thirty-five, Miguel DeSaul had been anointed as the Wisconsin Branch CEO for the past two years. It meant he functioned as the Farms' face across the entire state, part of Fillmore Farms, Inc.'s multi-state dairy conglomerate.

In truth, Miguel didn't give a chimp's butt about dairy farming. He couldn't discern a cow's snout from its backside and knew even less about how the beasts produced honest-to-God milk. Or even crazier, cheese curds!

In the end, it mattered little. Miguel did what his father told him. If being the somber face of the dairy franchise was what it took, then so be it. He lived an otherwise carefree lifestyle, even if it meant being stuck out here in the northern woods of Wisconsin.

But the current situation was about to change. Miguel had received—like the movies—an offer he couldn't refuse. He had avoided violence most of his coddled life, and listening to Frank Kemp's voice on the phone now caused his heartburn to kick in.

"Bleeding?" Miguel's forehead creased. "You mean the delivery guy? Or the Asian dude?"

"The courier. Cho Lin never showed at the warehouse."

"So you've got what? Half the recipe?"

"Somewhat," Kemp said. "But then it got interesting. I was parked in the shadows, waiting for Cho Lin to show, and you'll never guess whose SUV I spotted?"

"I'm not going to play—"

"Connie's bitch," Kemp snapped. "Syan. Spying around in the dark."

Miguel couldn't guess how his half-sister's companion—or whatever she was—could be involved in any of this. Was she after the fentanyl formula as well? And if so, how could Connie have found out about the warehouse exchange?

"Did you grill her? About why she was there?"

"No time. I moved straight to Plan B. She and I will have a little chat later."

It was the middle of the night already, and Miguel wanted to know the bottom line. "Frank. Have you got the formula or not?"

"Half from the courier. The rest is on Cho Lin's laptop. I'll bet my balls on it."

"Fine. Great." Miguel was relieved. "We'll talk tomorrow then."

Setting his phone back on the coffee table, Miguel knew he'd need another few slugs of brandy to fall asleep. Add a zolpidem chaser. Or else he'd be up whizzing St. Mark's half the night.

After ending the call, he realized he had been holding his breath. A deep inner voice kept asking, "Is this really what you want?" He looked around at the room's decorated walls. It was a beautiful mansion in the woods with all the fixings. Did he need more money? Or was going along with Kemp's crazy plan just a way to prove to his father that he could succeed on his own?

Miguel decided it didn't matter at this point. He had cast his lot with Frank Kemp. From here on out, it was in for a penny, in for a pound.

CHAPTER 10

It was well after two-thirty a.m. when Frank Kemp arrived back at Miguel's manor house. The glow of outside security lights illuminated the lawns and landscaping, the circular front drive, and the attached, multi-stall garage. The lights frightened away deer, raccoons, and black bears. All was dark inside. Miguel, Kemp imagined, had hit the hay right after their call.

After parking his shark-gray Buick Regal in a stall, Kemp used the back entrance and climbed the third-floor stairs.

The house was enormous—three stories high, seven bedrooms, and who knew how much other stuff? Kemp didn't care. He'd been nothing but a lodger here the past three months, occupying his apartments on the upper floor. Miguel had his rooms on the second level. Though never stated aloud, both men understood enough to stay out of one another's hair.

Entering his bedroom, Kemp dumped the contents of his gray leather satchel and other junk on his mattress. He'd stuck all the electronic devices in the Faraday sack. It blocked any attempts to trace them. He sat on the edge of the bed and kicked off his loafers. Right now, he was bushed. The euphoria of watching the blood spurt—first from the courier's jugular, then out the back of Cho Lin's shattered skull—had long worn off.

He was in the cooling-down phase.

He needed sleep now. But after a minute's battle, his curiosity won out. He reached for the wallet and notebook he'd taken from the courier. He flipped through four pages of chemical notes. These were followed by a depiction of carbon-hydrogen benzene rings (they reminded him of Tinker Toys) with double bonds. They comprised the second half of the formula for:

FENTANYL CONVERSION

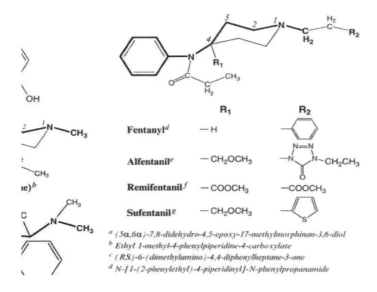

	R₁	R₂
Fentanyl[d]	—H	
Alfentanil[e]	—CH₂OCH₃	
Remifentanil[f]	—COOCH₃	—COOCH₃
Sufentanil[g]	—CH₂OCH₃	

[a] *(5α,6α)-7,8-didehydro-4,5-epoxy-17-methylmorphinan-3,6-diol*
[b] *Ethyl 1-methyl-4-phenylpiperidine-4-carboxylate*
[c] *(RS)-6-(dimethylamino)-4,4-diphenylheptane-3-one*
[d] *N-[1-(2-phenylethyl)-4-piperidinyl]-N-phenylpropanamide*

Kemp snickered. *Whatever.*

The following pages described the covalent bonding method for a unique new version of fentanyl, ready to be synthesized and manufactured. The subsequent pages contained a seven-step cooking recipe for the process.

The directions for "<u>binding constant</u>" versus "<u>bonding</u>" were both underlined with thick black lines. Insinuating this step was not to be missed or mixed up. The word "crucial**" was double starred.

Kemp smiled for the first time that day. With what he now had, in addition to what he'd soon locate on Cho Lin's laptop, he pictured a new and wealthier version of himself. His mission was to put the final formula together, then set up the private auction designed to make them rich.

Kemp slipped the notebook inside the bottom of his underwear drawer. Tomorrow he'd burn his clothes and the courier's wallet in the basement incinerator. He'd bleach-scour the Regal, leave no traces of what had occurred. It had been a clean operation. Even the part with the Syan bitch, which he'd address when the time was right. While his brain was still buzzing, he decided to take a stab at Cho Lin's laptop. See where he had stored his half of the formula.

Two hours later, Kemp sat back in his chair.

Three tumblers of Scotch had kept him going until five a.m. His encryption software had cracked into Cho Lin's private files. Then he'd dived into the dark web. His skills were far from Black Hat level. He had logged into the Tor browser then peeled through the various onion layers of nonsense.

But after locating a few dark Facebook equivalent sites, he had fumbled around like an alley drunk. Pulling numbers out of the air wasn't cutting it. Ten minutes later, he told himself, "Screw it!" and called it quits. He needed the correct password ID codes, or the fentanyl recipe might as well be sitting in a cave on Mars.

Kemp shut down the laptop and stuck everything back in the large Faraday sack. He took a minute to replay the day's events. That morning he'd been scoping out the Asian ex-con's hotel room from across the street, studying the entry and exit points, when he had witnessed some jackass in a windbreaker enter the place. The guy drove a silver Bronco SUV that stood out.

Even crazier, when Kemp had departed from the warehouse tonight after the courier's demise, he had parked along the gloomy street and waited for Cho Lin to show up for the formula exchange. Instead, the same Bronco had cruised past and parked at the curb opposite the meeting place.

There it had sat. With each passing minute, it reminded him more and more of a cockroach perched at the edge of a punchbowl.

Kemp didn't believe in coincidences. When Cho Lin never showed, he'd cut bait and headed straight over to the hotel in De Pere. He guessed right, finding the cooker holed up in his room.

Looking back now, he decided the driver in the Bronco had been a substitute. Maybe a PI hired by Cho Lin for the warehouse pick-up? He couldn't say why he had roared past the SUV in the dark with his headlights off. He'd been pissed off, sure. But whatever the case, it mattered little now. Cho Lin was in Buddha heaven. Or however their thing worked.

Kemp had scored the ex-con's phone and laptop and escaped unnoticed. He now had both halves of the formula in his possession. Nothing else mattered. Even though he was close to passing out now, there remained one thing he still needed to check. He withdrew Cho Lin's mobile from the Faraday sack and scrolled the messages. There. A trio of private calls out and back. He guessed the caller was the Bronco SOB and listened to the guy's desperate voice shouting for the Asian to vacate the hotel room. *Get out now!* Kemp smirked and secured the device. No chance the cops could ping-trace it tucked inside the Faraday.

He stuck all the items in his gray leather satchel and hid them in the top corner of his closet shelf. Away from the prying eyes of Mrs. Flench when she came to clean and dust his room.

The Bronco driver was the unknown player on the chessboard, Kemp decided. He'd ID the joker tomorrow. Whoever he was, it didn't matter—same result: double-tap.

As he undressed, Kemp knew he had other cracks in the plaster to spackle. There was Connie's bitch, Syan. And even Miguel was proving himself more of a lard-ass with each passing day. But he'd known as much going in, hadn't he? What mattered now was they were a hundred times closer to the payola than they'd been this morning.

Kemp understood he would figure out all the grimy little details eventually. It's what he'd done best for the past thirty years. Fix problems. Tomorrow was just another day at the mill.

His head hit the pillow, and he was out before the sheets even tickled his stubbled chin.

PART TWO

WARNINGS FROM THE GRAVE

"Soon, you will forget everything. And soon, everybody will forget you."
— Marcus Aurelius (AD 121-180), Roman Emperor, *Meditations* VII, 21

"Each passing birthday brings us each one step closer to our graves."
J. Mancheski

CHAPTER 11

Tuesday broke cool and crisp, typical of June days. The tree birds around the Van Waring house warbled and sounded content. Due to last night's late events, Cale had cut his morning rowing routine in half. He sat now at the kitchen counter with a water bottle. Hank was curled on a nearby chair, waiting for Maggie to set down his breakfast bowl.

All routine stuff. Just six weeks ago, the house had been filled with cops and forensic techs and the coroner carting away the lunatic's dead body. The bullet through his left eye socket was courtesy of Maggie defending their castle in the middle of the night. Good enough reason to limit much investigation.

She climbed the basement stairs, now in leggings and a sweatshirt. She carried a pantsuit on a hanger.

"All right, shoot," she said, arching an eyebrow.

Cale sipped his water. "Someone got there first. Killed the courier," he reported. "By the time Slink and I got back to the hotel, Cho Lin was already dead."

She fixed Hank's food bowl and set it along the hallway baseboard. She turned back to Cale. "Drug and gang stuff. We talked about it before."

He felt like a teenager in the vice principal's office. Yet, there was little point in denying the obvious. "If you want to say I told you so, you're right."

She stayed silent—a clever lawyer's tactic.

"It's Slink's case now," Cale said. "He'll figure it out."

Thirty minutes later, backing the Bronco out from the garage, he replayed last night's events in his head. It had all happened so fast, and there were still layers that needed working out. Somebody had executed two men over a drug formula. This much was fact. Yet weren't there already hundreds of synthetic narcotics floating around the country? Every city, town, and village? On thousands of street corners and seedy alleyways?

What made this one special?

Cale felt guilty about how terrible things had gone down. Responsible, even. He had underestimated the danger and shouldn't have just sloughed to Maggie how Slink had things under control. She deserved to know the facts. Except that between her pregnancy and job stress and their upcoming wedding plans—not to mention her sister Chloe's recent bout with depression—didn't she have enough on her plate as it was?

Besides, it was over now. He was confident Slink would figure out the puzzle. Cale was a material witness, sure, so he would do his part. He'd accompany his partner to the autopsy since Slink had already requested his presence, even if it was just to satisfy his curiosity. As for the rest, the clever play was to allow the detectives assigned to the case to figure it out.

The County Medical Examiner's autopsy room had a familiar aroma. Sterile, well-ventilated, with a persistent lingering scent of alcohol. Simple fact: fresh corpses didn't emit the "smell of death" many people imagined. Any odors detected had more to do with the forensics than flesh decay.

Slink stood leaning against one chrome countertop. The place was scrubbed and sterilized. They were the first warm bodies on the premises other than regular staff at eight a.m. Cale wore navy Dockers and a button-down shirt. He didn't have to worry about department dress codes for three more weeks.

James Cho Lin was naked on the slab. The non-breathing version of him.

"This gentleman first," Doc Mocarek informed them. He had on blue scrubs and extra-wide trifocals.

The detectives had noted the sheet-covered courier on a nearby gurney, waiting in the on-deck circle. His prints were being run through the IAFIS database for an ID. They were also searching local hotels for reports of any missing guests.

"Cause of death appears cut-and-dried," Cale said calmly. "For them both."

Slink smirked at his word choice.

Dr. Mocarek didn't speak as he removed the auburn-colored liver and set it upon his digital scale. He talked to the mic at his collar, then back to them. "Your man was not a junkie or an alkie. He's got the liver of a marathon runner."

"Sure he'd be pleased to hear it," Slink offered.

Cale accepted that his partner's levity was a cop thing. Many people around dead bodies did it. It was a reaction to the fear and anxiety death summoned.

A male lab tech entered with a manila folder. He was about to hand it to Mocarek but noticed his hands were buried inside the chest cavity.

"Tox prelim," announced the tech, waving the folder. "Rushed it through. Propofol injected above the right clavicle." To the ME, he said, "In case you haven't seen the site." The doctor stayed silent, and the tech added, "Lights out before any bullets were fired."

This explained for Cale that Cho Lin had been Michael Jackson-ed, then dumped onto the hotel bed before the two gunshots had ended his life. Talk about premeditated.

"Any other drugs?" asked Slink.

"Nothing street. Trace of Lorazepam for sleep or anxiety. That's all the prelim shows."

The tech handed the report to Slink and exited with no fanfare. The office functioned as all-business under Doc Mocarek's reign.

Reading it over, Slink stated, "No hair or fibers. No prints on the tables or TV or doorknobs. Clean bathroom."

They now knew the bleach odor was Clorox, not fentanyl.

They watched the doctor peer through his handheld magnifier ala Sherlock Holmes.

"Must've come up behind him," Slink said. "Jumped him with the needle."

Cale frowned. "Narrow hallway. Quiet. A tricky move."

Dr. Mocarek glanced over at them. "But leaving no trace behind? Your guy has done this number a few times before."

Cale thought about it. Cho Lin had been on high alert. He'd been expecting Cale's return to his room with the formula. The hotel wasn't large or noisy—there was no way someone should have caught him off guard.

"A room next door?" Slink suggested, his eyes wide. "I'll have a tech check it."

Cale observed the doctor placing Cho Lin's spleen on his scale. He gazed up at the second hand as it swept around the clock above the door. Mocarek moved to a lung, handling it the way a kid fondles a beanbag. He asked them, "Why not just triple the sedative dose? His heart would stop in less than two minutes." He placed the lung on the scale. "The gunshots seem like overkill."

"Send a message?" Slink arched an eyebrow. "Massacres. Mayhem. Both cartel signatures."

"Except they don't bother with cleaning up." Cale glanced at the awaiting corpse. "Citizen Two, there. Sliced throat. Not much cleanup attempt in his case."

"Maybe two killers?" Slink offered. "A single perp would have a short window—a fifteen-minute drive across the river to the hotel. Wouldn't risk speeding. Plus, sneaking into the place without being seen."

"Could be done."

"Why not just pop the first victim in the warehouse then? If you're carrying around a nine-mil?"

They watched the ME stitch up his efforts. Cho Lin had been taken apart piece by piece. But if it helped them figure out who had ended his life, Cale doubted the ex-con would mind.

Dr. Mocarek stepped back, snapping his gloves off. He removed his glasses and huffed the lenses. "You mentioned fentanyl last night and cartels today." He eyed them. "Care to clue me in on what we're dealing with here?"

Cale informed him about the supposed "safe version" of the opioid, which might soon be hitting the market.

"One not supposed to snuff people's lives." Slink added.

"Splendid," said the doctor, turning to scrub his hands at the small sink. "Maybe I'll get a vacation this year after all."

The northern sky was filled with puffy clouds high above the waters of the magnificent bay. Some poet might see them as battleships. Or a team of charging horses. But truth be told, neither detective was much of a Longfellow.

They stood together in the near-empty morgue parking lot. Slink said he'd search through listed kill teams around the Midwest. See if anything popped. Based on the evidence, they had to look at every angle. Cale agreed. It was what he'd do if he were in charge.

"It sounded a little goofy," Slink admitted, "mentioning 'safe' fentanyl. Did Cho Lin believe it?"

"Got him killed, didn't it?"

Slink mulled it over. He suggested it would be akin to a safe form of booze, perhaps, where you'd drink enough to get buzzed, then sober up before driving home.

It was a decent comparison, Cale supposed. Nobody in society cared much about the drunk or stoned part. It was the death and maiming accidents they could do without. Not to mention how the inventors of such a product—be it pills or booze—would become wealthy overnight.

How much would alcohol producers pay to get their hands on such a product? The short answer was they could name their price.

"So why kill him?" Slink asked. "Why not just rough him up? Or torture? Force him to reveal his login data?"

"They grabbed his phone and computer. Must've figured it's all they needed."

"What if they still can't access the site?"

Cale shrugged. "Good thing they don't know I've got the only copy. Username and login passwords."

Slink gave him a narrow look.

"After you left last night," Cale confessed, "the front desk lady passed along a note Cho Lin had left for me.

"I think it's called evidence?"

"Let me hold onto it for a day or two."

"Why?" Slink scowled. "You're no computer genius."

"Maybe I'll get lucky and crack it."

Slink fobbed his car door open. The pewter Taurus's doors were scarred like a shark who'd tried mating above his rank. The black tires and no rims screamed cop ride. Cale eyeballed his Bronco, and the front grill snarled back at them.

Slink was headed back to the station to begin working the homicides. Cale said he'd sniff around the drug side of things, see if their street CIs had heard any scuttlebutt.

With his door ajar, Slink said, "I don't care what Cap or IA say." He meant their boss, Captain Leo McBride, and the Internal Affairs investigators. "I'm a call away, you know."

Cale nodded. He was aware his partner was withholding the last phrase of advice his father had always added: *So don't do anything stupid.* He guessed Slink had wanted to add the final part.

He watched his partner drive off. Cale accepted that the murders had sucked him into the case. Viewing Cho Lin's autopsy furthered his guilt: how the tragedy could have been averted if he had played his cards a little smarter.

It seemed as if the decision had been made for him. Cale knew he would hunt down whoever had murdered the ex-con. If it involved psychotic cartel hitmen, Mafiosi gunners, or even Chinese assassins, then so be it.

He also understood he'd need more firepower than the little .38 tucked beneath his seat.

Inside the Bronco, he fished a small notebook from the glove box and located a phone number he hadn't called in three years.

He hoped she was still in business.

CHAPTER 12

Driving through the congested city traffic, Cale dialed the department's number for Records. He doubted a thirty-day timeout meant you couldn't research on your own. Some bureaucrats might argue it was *verboten*, but he decided his old friend Rosario would look the other way. Besides, she'd had a crush on him for years, and their exchange of playful banter always made him feel livelier.

"Hey, gorgeous," he said when Rosie answered her line.

"Heard about all the BS, Lieutenant," she offered. "My right foot would be a perfect fit up the butts of those fools."

"Can't fight City Hall."

"What they tell us." She held her tongue. "So, you're bored now? Decide to hit up my curvy booty for a date?"

Cale laughed. "I told you before, you're too much woman for me to handle, Rosie. We both know it."

"I'll take it easy on you. Promise."

"Let me ponder the ramifications." He allowed seconds to pass. "Meantime, how about a license tag?"

Rosario sighed, accepting the customary inevitable. "I know they requisitioned your weapon, badge, and ID, so I'll say it figuratively, shoot."

He passed along his information on the Asian lady's Toyota SUV, maroon, he guessed, later model, which could be out-of-state. He waited. Three minutes became four. At last, Rosario came back on the line, crowing how she gave him a "gold star" on the Minnesota guess. His guess at "ukes" for *Lakes* had narrowed it further.

He waited.

"Two names sound Asian to me." She read them out loud. "Parkay Luen. But the partial letter on your tag doesn't jive. The other one, Syan Hng. Female, age twenty-seven. St. Paul residence since twenty-sixteen. Tag: TDL 469."

"Bingo!" He now had a name.

"And you hit the daily double," Rosario teased. "DMV lists her mobile as a work contact. Folks seldom change their cell numbers." She relayed it to him. "You might be able to GPS her whereabouts—if she's still in the area."

"You're a living doll, Rosie. I'm going to dream about you tonight."

"Best dream since you were sixteen."

The arrangement to meet happened almost too easily. But why not? Cale asked himself. Sooner was better than later.

He was navigating the Bronco beyond the city's eastern borders. It almost felt as if the weapons dealer had been anticipating his call. Cale convinced himself to relax. After everything he'd been through last night, a pleasant drive in the country might even prove enjoyable.

The weapons dealer had selected a place both remote and wide-open. Not some seedy midnight warehouse. The timeframe for their meet proved even easier. "How about in ninety minutes?" her voice had suggested. It was no secret that private arms sellers were wary creatures. Always on the alert for phone taps or government rope-a-dopes.

Cale agreed to the hasty conditions.

An hour later, he found himself cruising the highway north. He drove past the County Sheriff's facilities and a stern-looking mental hospital, where a pauper's graveyard lurked in the nearby woods. He wondered what an ancient bone garden did for the adjacent subdivision's property values.

Passing the local university, he exited onto a county highway. He slid past miles of flat wheat and alfalfa fields, along with a dozen set-back refurbished farmhouses. The air smelled of hay and manure, a pungent blend baking in the morning sunshine.

He halted the Bronco at a four-way stop, staring out at the abundance of farm acreage. Thank God for GPS.

71

Cale navigated another two miles east before spotting a red F-150 pickup parked off the road's dirt shoulder. The driver stood fifteen yards further into the field. Behind her was a huge red combine, which appeared to have run out of fuel.

Cale swung the Bronco in behind the pickup and exited. He strode across the uneven terrain and shook hands with a lady in denim coveralls, sunglasses, and an International Harvester cap. The cap concealed her wheat-colored hair.

"Been a while, Detective," Jackie Glassen said, sliding her hands back into her jeans.

From a distance, Ms. Jackie could pass as a farmhand. She possessed long legs and narrow hips. Her eyebrows were dusky above Cherokee cheekbones, straight nose, dimpled chin. But close-up gave away the ruse—her skin was flawless. Not the sunburned jowls of someone who worked the land for a living.

"I suppose it's better that way, Jackie No Name." Adding: "All things considered."

The "No Name" part was a chuckle they shared. It was how her calls showed up on his phone display.

Jackie had survived a dozen years in the private weapons business by being one thing: discreet. She sold her wares to off-grid survivalists, to hunters who enjoyed an extra kick in their weaponry, and former military personnel—for whom staying well-armed was second nature. Jackie also supplied law enforcement members via private requests. A seasoned entrepreneur, she covered all sides of the playing field.

"Let's step into my office," she said. "Getting warmer out here by the minute."

Cale watched as she climbed up into the combine's cabin. She skootched into a seat behind the steering apparatus. He followed her lead and took the passenger, which was no broader than a 1930's rumble seat,

After they'd settled in, Jackie said bluntly, "Nobody's ever bugged a thresher."

No doubt she was correct.

"Your stuff's in my truck," she nodded, looking at him. "The Mossberg Shorty and Sig XL were easy. The Nighthawk 1911 a bit trickier. You've got expensive tastes, Lieutenant."

"The times we live in."

Jackie referred to the short riot shotgun with the raptor-head grip, the smaller concealed carry pistol, and the special 9mm Cale had ordered. He handed her a stuffed envelope, which she slid inside her coverall top. They'd known one another for at least a decade, back since the days when Cale had worked Narcotics.

"Hunting trip?" she asked.

"Just circumstances."

He didn't need to elaborate but figured he could use her counsel. In her business, Jackie Glassen heard rumors about many things, not just about weapons.

He said, "This opioid thing's got everybody lathered up."

"Sick world of ours." Jackie gazed out the cab at the fertile fields. "It seems they're all in a demented contest. See who can hook people on the craziest narcotics."

He said amen to that.

"Speaking of crazy, I've got to ask." Jackie widened her eyes. "That witch doctor business? The nut who attacked your home?"

Cale was hesitant to get into the gritty details, yet it had made national news. Several blog sites. "Some nut-case with a vendetta—what can I say?" He waited, and she was polite enough to drop it. He asked, "So the drug thing I mentioned. Any clowns out there you'd enjoy seeing out of business?"

Her right cheek dimpled when she grinned, and with her lengthy eyelashes, Cale imagined Jackie cleaned up smartly when she chose. "One group comes to mind, now that you mention it."

"Not the Sonoma cartel, I hope."

"Ever hear of an industrial dairy op? Called Fillmore Farms? Located up past Gillett?"

Cale knew as much about farming as he did knitting baby booties. "Sorry. Outside my purview."

"They'll be on law enforcement's radar any day now."

"An industrial farm?" He issued her a tight look. "You're serious?"

She explained how Fillmore was owned by a former big-shot gangster from the Twin Cities, how he'd moved into farming to launder drug money. They now owned a half-dozen corporate industrial farm ops around the Midwest. They'd expanded into Wisconsin four years ago.

Cale had read several mainstream news articles about massive corporate dairy operations placing smaller family farmers in a squeeze. The photos had unveiled oversized spreads with clusters of outbuildings, multiple silos, and seven or eight-thousand-head cow herds.

"Rumor has it," Jackie said, "this group is into more than just sowing and reaping."

They sat in the confined space. Cale pondered her words. He had brought up the drug angle, foremost on his mind, and she'd offered up a shady operation with, perhaps, a dark underbelly. Illegal narcotics walked arm-in-arm with unlawful weaponry. He'd thrown the word "cartel" out loosely, but the type of criminals Jackie was referring to were no less sophisticated.

Furthermore, she now claimed these supposed farmers had gotten their start in the next-door state of Minnesota. The same place Cho Lin had claimed his prison roommate was from, and the same locale the Asian mystery lady's license plates traced back to. Were these the people to whom Cho Lin owed his debts? "Dangerous people" was the term he had used.

Now both Cho Lin and his cousin's courier were dead. Each slain brutally and current patients of the county's medical examiner.

Coincidence? Cale thought not.

"So, this Fillmore group?" He looked into Jackie's bottle-green eyes. "You're implying they're involved in more than just milking cows?"

When she hesitated, he imagined he knew why. Tight lips were standard in Jackie No Name's business. Breaking the silence, she told him the locals claimed both the pot and pill business. But who knew what else they were up to beyond the mundane? What she did know is they roughed up a customer of hers a month ago. Badly. He'd spent four nights in a hospital.

Cale asked why, and she informed him how Fillmore was buying up farmland, and her friend had refused to sell. Her eyes then shifted out to the open fields again, adding, "Same strong-arm tactics bullies have used since Adam and Eve."

Cale processed her accusations. It was a familiar formula used in western film plots: Big landowners waging war against small-time homesteaders. While he pictured this, Jackie reached inside her overalls and withdrew his envelope. He gave her a questioning look.

"The worst part is, they're doing the same thing to others out there who are trying to feed their families." Her tight lips held back her anger. "Keep the cash, Lieutenant. Consider it payment for looking in on a few innocents for me. Let them know they're not entirely on their own."

He wanted to protest, but the distress in her eyes told him she was serious.

Cale accepted the envelope and followed her as they stepped down from the combine.

With his new weapons stashed in the back of the Bronco, Cale navigated his return along the rural backroads. He replayed his conversation with Jackie. He didn't know much about industrial farming, but he did understand how the national drug crisis had ransacked Midwestern urban cities for the past nine decades.

Over the last dozen years, even more players had entered the game—leeches who targeted smaller rural markets to pedal their poison. Even worse, they often disguised themselves as legitimate businesspeople, the exact way these Fillmore Farms phonies were doing. Jackie had described them as bloodsuckers, up to far more than just producing dairy products. As she saw it, they needed to be investigated.

Action on that level, however, fell into the DEA's lap. Cale decided he'd talk with Agent Gwen Galman. See if her intel matched what Jackie had revealed.

After working Narcotics for seven years, before his promotion to Robbery/Homicide, Cale understood the drug war's ongoing frustrations. Narcotics abuse and addiction had altered the country's social fabric. The nation was locked in a seemingly never-ending struggle, and regardless of whichever side was winning or losing, the bad guys were always three steps ahead in the battle.

Navigating back via the same route he'd driven, the sprawling city unfolded before him. The waters of the vast bay stretched to the northern horizon, painting a slate blue canvas as far as the eye could see.

Cale's phone buzzed. He peered at the screen's readout, "No Name." He answered, keeping it on speaker.

Jackie said haltingly, "I didn't give you the full story."

"I figured there was more," he admitted. "Close to the vest. I get it."

She exhaled. "There's a gal I've been palling around with. Her name's Rita Ross. Her daughter Feather is ten years old."

Cale didn't speak, and she continued:

"They live with Rita's brother, Ben. Co-own a small dairy farm they inherited five years ago."

"Let me guess. They don't want to sell."

"The group I mentioned. Fillmore. They've been turning the screws on them."

Making a lane change, Cale considered what she was telling him. Big industrial farmers threatening rural family farmers—more proof the world was losing its mind.

"Ben's been roughed up a few times. They've threatened him with worse if he doesn't reconsider."

Cale pictured the old Wild West days again. Cattle ranchers versus homesteaders. He wondered what character he might play in this movie. Not the washed-up gunslinger, he hoped.

"He's not the only one," Jackie continued. "The threats are always in the shadows. Anonymous phone calls. Stuff you can't prove."

"I'll take a run out there. Feel Ben and Rita out." Then he asked, "How about the little girl's dad? Is he in the picture?"

"Died when Feather was three. How sad is that for a kid? Lymphoma or something."

Cale exhaled, and she added:

"Watch yourself, Lieutenant. This whole thing might be one giant powder keg."

He swung the Bronco off an exit ramp.

Before hanging up, Jackie confessed there was one more thing she hadn't mentioned. Young Feather Ross, it seemed, had reported how some creep had begun hanging around in the woods at the edge of their property, scoping her out.

"You mean a pedophile?"

"Or maybe it's Fillmore? Ramping up the scare tactics?"

After ending the call, Cale eased the Bronco to a stoplight. The events of the past day circled in his head, and he couldn't erase the images of farmers battling Scarface wannabes.

When the light turned green, he accelerated through the intersection, wondering what brand of craziness he might be getting himself into this time.

CHAPTER 13

Maggie's Mazda was parked on the concrete apron that led to their house's side entrance. Cale eased the Bronco into the garage and exited as the double doors closed behind him. He began unpacking his purchases, not wanting neighborhood kids spotting him squirreling away firearms.

A sizeable, unplugged ice freezer sat alongside his corner workbench. He and Slink had heave-hoed the freezer up from the basement a year ago. It would make an excellent place to secure firearms.

Cale considered his new items from Jackie. The Mossberg could hold seven 12-gauge rounds. He held it this way and that, pumped it a few times. It was a short version riot gun with the bird-head grip. He set it aside and grabbed the combat-ready Nighthawk T4, which fit his hand like a second skin. It cost more than the Sig and shotgun combined.

Cale slipped the shotgun and Nighthawk inside a military-style duffel bag, wrapped it with a bedsheet, then tucked it deep inside the unplugged freezer. Along with the dozen boxes of ammo, she'd comped him. Insurance in case there was a need for real firepower. Cale prayed it never came to that and slid the twelve-round Sig under the Bronco's seat, trading it for the .38. He'd tuck the revolver in his bedroom nightstand in case more witch doctors attacked their house.

It was a little after noon now, and he discovered Maggie in their den redlining a legal brief, transferring notes to her computer. She gazed at him over her reading glasses.

"Sorry." Cale hovered in the doorway. "Didn't want to spook you." They'd both been jumpy since the home break-in. It would take months before they felt at ease again.

"Your autopsies go okay?"

"Crazy life, isn't it? When that's a normal question?"

He had informed her of his meeting at the morgue but not his rendezvous with the arms dealer. Some things went best unsaid. Cale moved into the room, casting his gaze at the tall bookshelves covering two of the walls.

"How'd the office go?" he asked. "Good being back?"

"I concentrate better here." She chewed the end of her pen, shifting topics. "Choe's coming over. Wants to talk. Didn't say about what."

Cale accepted that Maggie's sister was going through her own recovery phase. "She back to her cranky self yet?"

"That voodoo attack shook her up, Cale. Blew her world apart, guess you'd say."

Hank was on the room's couch and frowned as Cale sat beside him, his space invaded. Same as them all, the cat's world had also been upended that night. He'd lost one or two of his nine lives, though he seemed to have recovered faster. Cale supposed it was cats for you.

Maggie had on leggings, white trainers, and a lightweight summer sweater. Her hair was clipped shorter than usual. To Cale, she appeared the farthest thing from a sharp legal mind, but he knew better. She declined his offer to join her discussion with Chloe, informing him it was a "sister's thing."

"If she believes medieval torture might help," he said lightly, "I recommend Dr. Pam."

Before Maggie could retort, they heard knocks, followed by Chloe's voice at the backdoor. "Beware of Greeks bearing gifts! Anybody home?"

"In here," Maggie winked at Hank. "All three of us."

Hank jumped from the couch and trotted off to meet their guest. Chloe was his favorite, forever bribing him with treats. Psychics and cats, Cale told himself, talk about medieval.

Chloe appeared in the doorway. She said, "Hey, Rock Hudson! Thought you were out dangling worms with your time off."

"Animal cruelty jokes aren't allowed around here." He lifted from the couch. "Reminds me, I got to see a man about a horse."

79

"Thanks for sharing." Chloe plopped into his open spot on the sofa, hoisting Hank onto her lap. When Cale pecked Maggie's cheek, Chloe placed her hand in front of the cat's eyes, shielding him from his parents' hanky-panky.

"Nothing he hasn't seen before," Maggie joked.

Moving to exit, Cale studied his future sister-in-law. "You doing okay? You're not zipped on meds or anything?"

"Peachy." She stroked Hank's fluffy head. "I saw Father Larchezzi this morning." She shrugged, "I might even take his advice for once."

"This I've got to hear," Maggie said.

Cale departed with a headshake.

Chloe stared at the doorway as if Cale might reappear before swinging her eyes back to her sister. "Is he all right?" she asked in a low voice.

Maggie was chewing the end of her pen. "A little lost. The suspension thing…and everything else we've been through."

"Like a bad toothache," Chloe offered. "Takes time to heal."

"Is that what you and Father L discussed? Healing?"

Her sister narrowed her eyes. "I'm using tooth decay as a metaphor. What we talked about was my *soul*."

Cale polished off a sandwich in the dining room while the sisters chatted. The words "cleansing, spiritual warrior, and even *exorcism*" drifted from the den, beyond earshot for him to make any sense of it.

They'd figure out their issues together, the way sisters did. In the meantime, he had more important matters to deal with.

Cale grabbed his phone and strode beneath the archway, which led into the house's living room. Sunlight splashed in through the half-closed blinds. Perched on the edge of a loveseat, he auto-dialed Newman's number. She was a freelance hacker he used when he needed a phone or wireless trace outside the department's system.

His phone trilled seconds later. The readout read: "JC Penny." It meant Newman was on a secure burner phone, preferring voice to text.

"Long time, Lieutenant," came the tinny voice.

She had a modulator working. He pictured her in white leather and studs, some angel-demon out of *Dragon Tattoo*. "I need a location triangulation, Iris. Trying to hunt down a mystery lady."

"Aren't we all?" They smirked together in silence.

He informed her he had a name and number and needed to know where the lady's phone was and run a pattern trace. In-and-outgoing calls over the past twenty-four hours.

"Simple enough." Newman's voice was neutral. "I'll call back when I've got it. Crypto-cash, same as before."

Cale gave her Syan Hng's information that Rosario had provided, then ended the call. It's what he appreciated about Newman, few questions or other BS. He guessed it wouldn't take long.

He was in the garage when his phone buzzed ten minutes later. Newman reported: "She made four calls from a B&B. Some village called River's Bend, in Oconto County. She got one incoming from a Green Bay motel called SpringHill Suites."

"Near the Packers stadium."

"Yup. It doesn't look like she's planning a Brink's job."

Cale's laugh was polite. "Got a name on the B&B?"

"Called Burmeister House. All the calls were under four minutes, three to unlisted numbers. One pizza delivery."

He thanked her and ended the call.

It was one-thirty in the afternoon when the Bronco stopped at the curb opposite the downtown police station. Slink hopped into the passenger side. As the vehicle merged with traffic, Cale

81

asked, "You sure this is a smart idea? Cap might've seen us out his window."

"Last I checked, you're not Jeffrey Dahmer."

"Just saying."

Slink pulled his phone from his pocket, studying it as they accelerated away. "Besides," he said, "I'm following a lead in the Cho Lin murder case."

Cale had given his partner updates about what he knew. The entire mess was about drugs and gangs and murder. He still felt as horrible as he had upon rising. Pangs of guilt made his stomach churn.

They navigated through downtown. Slink informed him that Agent Galman had been in contact with the Waupun State Penitentiary's Records Department. They confirmed the identity of Cho Lin's cellmate: one Cary Kemp. Formerly a Minnesota resident."

"Kilo," Cale said quietly.

"Sentenced a nickel for armed robbery," Slink informed. "Released about a month after Cho Lin."

"And?"

"Cho Lin wasn't BS-ing about Kilo's connected papa. A lieutenant named Franklin Kemp. The dad's listed as a—get this—'security advisor' to a Minneapolis gang boss named Sevastian DeSaul." He paused. "For the record, Kemp's in his late-fifties now."

Cale thought about it. "How's it all connect to last night's double hit job?"

"Maybe it doesn't?"

Slink cast his eyes out at the river as they navigated the downtown bridge to the city's west side. "Galman says the DeSaul gang fell off DEA's radar about eight years ago. They exited the narcotics biz. Went legit."

"Into what? Real estate?"

"Try corporate farming." Slink let it sink in. "Wisconsin's their sixth Midwest state. The CEO is DeSaul's eldest kid, named Miguel. They buy up land and cattle. In four years here, they now own over four thousand dairy cows."

Cale adjusted his sunglasses. "Making it our job to speak with the guy, right?"

Slink replied while studying his phone. "Two gang-style hits last night, along with the drug angle." He glanced at Cale. "I told Galman I'd chat with DeSaul, both for the task force and working the homicides. Size him up, see if he knows anything."

Cale felt a bolus forming in his gut. "She didn't give you a name, did she? Of their farm operation?"

"It's called Fillmore Farms."

Cale GPS'd the address Jackie had provided. After navigating past the city's final subdivision, they witnessed countless acres of furrowed farm fields that stretched for miles on all sides. The rolling landscape was quilted around hills and dales and forests. Cale eyed the farmsteads as they drove, each containing various sheds, outbuildings, tall silos, and spreads of open grazing land. The predominant colors were in Norman Rockwell earth tones.

Early afternoon. Herds of cattle fed at their leisure in the sunshine. Cale couldn't guess at how many times he'd driven past identical farm acreage over the years and taken its simplistic beauty for granted.

Slink was in a text exchange with one of the sergeants. They had a new tip from an informant they hoped would pan out, but first, they had to get the lady out of detox.

Cale's thoughts shifted to Maggie. He wished she were riding here with him, sharing the pleasant scenery. He imagined they wouldn't have time for casual drives in the country once the baby was born. Not that they ever took one, anyway. He supposed they ought to talk more about it one of these days— the baby, not sightseeing.

An orange semi roared past on the left. Cale spotted their upcoming exit. They'd be heading north for thirty miles along County Highway 32. He couldn't recall ever being on the road before. Perhaps back in their twenties when he and Slink had ventured this far out to attend a summertime polka festival. He doubted either of them could recall the drive back home.

"So, what's the deal on Jackie's farm thing?" Slink asked, holding his phone in his lap.

"Can't you just smell the clean country air?"

"You mean the manure pit we just passed?"

Cale shook his head. "The couple are friends of hers. Corporate bullies are trying to run them off their farm."

"You're serious?"

"It's what she called them." He paused. "You're going to love who the bullies ID from."

"Fillmore Farms? If I had to take a wild guess."

Cale nodded. "You're going to make a splendid detective someday, Mr. Holmes."

Slink flipped him the bird.

They peered out the window at a John Deere fertilizing a field. Slink said, "This all sounds more *Shane* than Sherlock."

"Maybe a bit of both."

"We're not walking into some O.K. Corral, I hope."

Cale had thought the same during the autopsy, and Slink was right. At heart, weren't they still just boys playing adult-sized cowboys and Indians? Cops and robbers felt more apropos, he decided, at least in their case. Big corporations were pushing around smaller guys—an age-old problem for humankind.

Cale said, "I told Jackie I'd check it out as a favor."

Slink's phone buzzed, and he answered.

Cale's thirty-day leave was a burden on the investigation unit, but at least he wasn't wasting his partner's time by dragging him along on a random pheasant hunt. Last night's shootings remained at the heart of the matter—gang violence, drug formulas, and professional killers.

They were both working on the Cho Lin murder case. Just from different angles now.

Twenty minutes elapsed before they spotted the sign for the small city of Oconto Falls. He could already picture it: a Main

Street and two dozen secondary offshoots. Four or five downtown taverns, a restaurant specializing in pancakes for breakfast, meatloaf for dinner. A Kwik Trip on one end of town, a bank, hardware store, three beauty shops, some antique place, and the remaining cookie-cutter storefronts.

The high school would sit on the edge of town, and the surrounding homes would appear as studio props. A church or two, at least one of them painted white—a tavern on the last-ditch outskirts. Then nothing but barns and farm fields and woods in every direction, dotting the landscape as if they'd been there for a hundred years.

Many had.

Cale accepted that his canned description was a rinse-wash-repeat of over twelve hundred similar towns and villages across the state. Rural America, where ninety percent of folks were armed for battle if anyone threatened their homes, land, families, or freedom.

It took under twelve minutes to cruise through the village's three stoplights. Then they sailed out the reverse end the way you'd escape an abandoned Hollywood backlot.

Slink broke into Cale's thoughts. "I remember you once told me all crimes are about either cash, power, or sex."

"Never fails," Cale said. "They were after Cho Lin's drug formula. Maybe worth mucho bucks."

"And Jackie's gripe is what?"

"Bullies. Land grabbing." Cale pondered it. "Cash and power both, I'd say."

The flat road ahead was a solid gray ribbon, power lines proving they hadn't left civilization.

"So big guys pushing around smaller ones?"

"Implied violence," Cale said. "Threats and stuff. And how these Fillmore owners might have their fingers in more than one money pie, perhaps."

The Bronco continued down the two-lane stretch of road.

Twenty minutes later, they pulled into a farm property's paved driveway. It was a two-story home with siding, a barn, a silo, and three other large structures in the back. They saw a chicken coop, a small makeshift windmill beside real clothesline poles, and an old well with a wooden crank. Not quite Green Acres, but close.

A broad swath of forest loomed along the left side of the property, where it widened and bordered the next road over—if the map Cale had checked was up to speed. The woods ran north for a decent mile, separating two farmsteads from one another.

Five other large vehicles were already present at the Ross farm, parked at different angles along the driveway and front yard. Four of them were pickup trucks. The lone odd duck was a Tundra SUV. Cale moved past them all and pulled the Bronco to a halt on the soft dirt shoulder of the back driveway.

"Hope we're not interrupting the county board," Slink quipped.

"I'd keep it light," Cale said as they exited and made their way toward the back of the house. "These guys are battling for their livelihoods."

Ben and Rita Ross, a brother and sister duo, had inherited the farmstead five years ago from their deceased uncle. They lived there together now, along with Feather, Rita's ten-year-old daughter. The farm was ninety acres of barley and alfalfa fields and grazing land. There were some thirty spotted Holstein milk cows. The "ladies" needed milking twice a day. A bull named "Arnie," two dogs, four barn cats, and a dozen clucky chickens were added to the mix. Feather was home-schooled, with Ben and Rita trading off in a rotation between their daily chores.

As they moved across the backyard, they were greeted by a large brown dog of some mix. It trotted up and licked Cale's hand. "Good watchdog," he said, patting the animal's head. "Good boy."

An attractive brown-haired lady in jeans and an untucked checked shirt came around the side of the house to greet them.

86

"His name is Satchmo!" she called pleasantly. Cale figured this was Rita. He patted the dog's head again. "Good, Satchmo."

He glanced at Slink, who had his tongue in his cheek, no doubt wondering what they were getting themselves into. They both cast their eyes around, scanning the area the way detectives did.

Rita shook their hands. She waved away their showing IDs.

"No need, guys. Jackie said you'd be stopping." Her blue eyes glinted. "She also said you'd have cop dripping off you like wet paint."

CHAPTER 14

Rita escorted the visitors through the house's back door, blocking Satchmo from following. Inside the kitchen, they heard voices emanating from the front room. Catching a glimpse through the arch leading to the dining room, Cale counted six men and a lady perched on various couches and chairs. Heated discussion. He couldn't miss the gist of it—the financial plight and survival of Wisconsin's dairy farmers.

A speaker he couldn't glimpse was saying, "Country had thirty-six thousand milk farms back in two-thousand." He paused. "Half that now."

A bearded man in a Milwaukee Brewers cap agreed. "Wisconsin *alone* lost three-hundred farms in 2017. Gone like Hogan's goat."

"Same with poultry," added a tall man in a flannel shirt. "Used to be chicken farms spread across the country. Guess how many today?"

"Three or four giant ones."

"Hens in tiny boxes, too fat to move an inch. Crappin' out eggs."

"It's what they want with milk cows," Ben Ross said. Jackie had described him for Cale: six-foot-two, narrow-shouldered and jut-jawed. His head was a shaved cue-ball. "Want the whole state down to four or five mega-farms—cows all machine-milked by robots."

"Along with producing a quarter-million gallons of piss and manure," complained another bearded man. "And guess who's watching where they dump it?"

A lady named Lucy, mid-forties, had her hair cut short and wore a denim shirt. She said, "Yup. Nobody."

The group exchanged disgusted looks and headshakes.

While Slink and Rita listened from the doorway, Cale focused his attention across the kitchen at the young girl sitting at the table. She had a book at her elbow, writing in a notebook the old-fashioned way. He observed her in silence. She had tawny bangs over her forehead, and her mouth showed a bowed upper lip; she had on shorts and a red tank-top, revealing tanned legs and shoulders. As if sensing his gaze, she turned her head and pierced him with the bluest cornflower eyes he'd ever seen.

"You guys are cops, aren't you?" the girl asked.

"Guess so." Cale had his arms crossed and leaned against the sink counter.

Their exchange caused Rita to turn. "That's Feather," she informed. "My amazing know-it-all daughter."

The girl stuck out her tongue playfully. Her skin tone was a shade duskier than her mother's, rendering her an exotic look. She said, "Same as on TV, right? Cops always ride in pairs?"

Cale indicated Slink. "This is Detective Dooley. He's a real detective. Not TV."

Slink saluted her before turning back to the discussion.

"Can I see your badges?" Feather asked, swinging around in her chair. Cale noticed her eyes were large and almond-shaped, which further enchanted her appearance.

Slink dipped his hand toward his front pocket, but Rita stopped him. She frowned at her daughter. "Finish your homework. They're here on business."

Feather sighed dramatically and then returned to what Cale guessed were trigonometry problems. The girl dropped into deep concentration as if a switch had flipped, and the rest of them were invisible.

Rita and Slink remained fixed on the front room, where the arguing voices were heating up. Cale used the time to study the young girl. He was impressed by her ability to block the chatter out and stick to her task. She was all elbows and knees at her age, but he imagined when she filled out, she might reach levels beyond your average small-town cheerleader.

He edged closer behind Rita and Slink, watching the emotional fireworks in the front room. The bearded Burnski brothers, Kevin and Hans, were lamenting their situation.

"None of it worth a load of manure," Kevin was saying. "The way I told my brother, here"—he glanced at Hans in the Brewers cap—"they can offer me a pickup full of gold bars. I'll still tell 'em where to shove it."

Hans added, "An armored truck full. Then we'll talk."

Nobody laughed.

"Let's keep the BS real," Ben Ross suggested. "Nobody's offering any of us gold bars. Fact is that half of our friends and neighbors who've sold walked away with barely their shirt and shoes."

Heads bobbed. Cuss words. Grumbling. They stayed civil for the most part, though, aware of the young girl sitting not far away in the kitchen.

A slender black man lifted from his chair, knees creaking. "We know the party to blame." His eyes searched their faces.

"Now, Jacob, let's not get—"

"Those Fillmore bastards, that's who." After a pause, he added, "If it ain't one big outfit, it's the guv'ment." He spat the last word. "If one don't have their filthy hand in your pocket, it's the other."

"And getting worse!" the lady called out.

"Right you are, Lucy."

Murmurs of agreement. Jacob gimped his way across the room and out the front door with those words hanging in the air. The others followed, including Ben, exiting from the house and onto the sun-bleached front lawn.

Slink glanced at Cale and followed them all behind Rita. She moved through the dining and front rooms, trailing the last of the troops outside. A minute later, Slink was in an animated discussion with the Burnski brothers and Lucy. Rita talked among Ben and the other men. Their absence left Cale standing alone in the kitchen with Feather. After recording some tally in her notebook, she turned and looked at him with her forehead knotted.

"You're more than a regular cop, aren't you?" the young girl asked. "An army general or something?"

"I'm a lieutenant," he said. "I work with a special police unit."

"I knew it. I bet it's important."

Cale considered her comment. Not so essential, the upper brass couldn't demand him surrendering his shield and sidearm for a month. "Kind of," he said. "They're all important."

"Aunt Jackie told us you'd be stopping by."

"You get along okay with Aunt Jackie?"

"She's rad. Mom likes her. They laugh a lot."

Feather seemed to consider how much to reveal. "Mom gets lonesome out here." She looked back at her books. "Just what I think, anyway." Before Cale could respond, the girl swung around and stuck her legs out straight, knees locked, showing him her purple cross-trainers. "Jackie got me these. For washing her truck when she visits."

"Very...rad," he told her, and she grinned.

Feather closed her textbook.

Cale eyed the girl and her new shoes. She was beaming with pride. That was the thing with farm kids; they appreciated small favors and took few things for granted. Living off the land gave them a perspective on life. Animals and beloved pets lived and died, feasts and famines, the cycles of nature. Rising at five a.m. for chores, they learned important lessons that city youths were seldom taught.

A whine came from the back porch. They shifted their attention to the closed screen door. The moist brown eyes of a yellow lab were staring in at them—a different dog from Satchmo.

The girl hurried across the kitchen past Cale. "Trey!" she called, opening the door and hugging the dog's neck. Cale followed her onto the back porch. From her knees, Feather said, "This is Trey. He's my dog, and I just *love* him." Trey smooched her cheek, and she giggled.

The animal was smiling up at Cale as well. It licked his hand when he extended it, and Cale patted Trey's head and scratched his solid neck. He appeared a healthy seventy pounds if he had to guess.

"He's a good watchdog," Feather told him.

"He looks very brave."

She nodded. "He stays with me when I'm outside. Mom doesn't want him in the house because he sheds and tracks in prints." She ruffled her dog's head again. "He chases squirrels while I'm inside and guards the chickens. Else he plays with Satch." Her forehead wrinkled. "But Satch is getting old. He wants to run around, but Mom says he's no spring chicken."

Cale peered out at the back acres. The sun was steady above, and the plowed fields appeared like the corrugated surface of some planet. In a distant pasture, the cows grazed. The barn doors remained flung open, airing the place out. The same went for the main equipment storage structure—half the barn's height, its doors were also open. Within the shadowy confines, Cale could discern the front third of a green-gold combine.

It was time, he decided, to get down to the reason for the visit.

In the shade of the porch overhang, he asked, "Anything else your Aunt Jackie say to tell me?"

The girl anticipated his question. "You mean the men, right? Them both?"

When he looked at her, she added, "One's the *stalker*. 'Least it's what Aunt Jackie calls him." Her frown made her appear older.

"What makes you think so?"

"Because he's a creep."

She indicated the woods just beyond the chicken coop. Cale could see a few hens scratching in the dirt. But the afternoon was growing warmer, and he guessed they'd soon move back inside for the shade.

"How so?"

Feather explained how the man had studied her from behind the birch trees, remaining hidden. How he hadn't motioned or spoken a word, just stared out from the shadows. She confessed that she used to enjoy exploring in the woods and the running stream, collecting rocks and shiny stones, how she loved playing fetch there with Trey, and how her dog was keen to explore the forest.

"But now?"

"Mom says I shouldn't go in there anymore. Since the creep guy…" Her voice trailed off.

Cale focused where she'd pointed again. No one was present now, of course, as he sized up the shadowed woods with a detective's eyes. He imagined how the sight angles would look. A watcher would know when she was in the barn alone or inside with the cows. He could also observe unseen when she was feeding the chickens, hanging clothes on the outside lines, or performing her other chores. It was fortunate the dogs were around.

"You said two of them. Are they the same men all the time?"

Feather searched her memory. "I saw the other one just once. Older, with a mustache. But the main one hides in the trees and stares at me."

"How do you know it's him? The main guy?"

"His hair's shaggy. Like loose straw."

"You guess his age?"

She thought about it. "Older than high school. Younger than Mom and Ben. Skinny, too. Twenty? Thirty is too old."

Cale decided it narrowed things somewhat. Most rural boys in their twenties these days wore their hair cropped close. Sometimes tried their luck with facial hair. He imagined he could pick a skinny, straw-haired guy out of a group easy enough.

The girl was fidgeting now, tired of his questions. Cale still had one more.

"Do you have a cell phone, Feather? Or does your mom let you use hers when you play in the woods?"

She told him no, only for emergencies, or to text her friends about rides and things. Or to call Aunt Jackie if she had to.

93

It made sense. He doubted her parents wanted her carrying a phone around everywhere she went. He'd seen a laptop computer on the dining room table, so he knew they had Internet service out here.

"Besides," Feather added without prompting, "Uncle Ben says phones will rot kids' brains."

Cale smiled. He admired Ben and Rita more by the minute.

Car doors slammed. Engines cranked. The visiting farmers' group had driven off in their dusty pickups and SUV. All that remained was Ben's blue Dodge Ram at the driveway's edge parked about twenty feet ahead of where the Bronco sat.

Feather was back inside the house. Cale and Slink stood in the front yard with Ben and Rita, about thirty feet from the home, halfway to the road. Trey smiled as Ben petted his head.

"You heard how heated things get," Ben stated, watching the dust settle along the culvert. He turned to the detectives. "It's this Fillmore group. They've been pressing most of them to sell." He looked toward his sister. "Us as well."

"But you're holding out?"

Rita jumped in. "This is our life. What we've always wanted. It's hard work, but—"

"But they don't take *No* too kindly?" Slink offered.

"They even offered us jobs." Her frown was tight. "Me in accounting, Ben as a supervisor. A private tutor for Feth if we want." She squinted beyond the road at the open fields, then turned back. "Even said we can keep our house."

Silence held until a crow cawed from the trees.

"The problem is we're adjacent," Ben explained. "They bought all the land on the other side of the forest strip there. Then all the properties north, clear to the county line."

"Our land stands in their way," Rita said. "Blocking them like a chess piece, I suppose you'd say."

94

Cale considered what they were telling them. He shifted the topic. "I still don't get why they'd start messing with your daughter."

Rita crossed her arms. "Do either of you have daughters, Detectives?"

Cale shook his head.

"Two young boys," Slink offered.

The sound of the front door opening caused them to glance back at the house, where Feather now stepped outside. The old dog Satchmo rose from the tree shade and trotted over to her. She grinned and petted the animal, who at once appeared five years younger for being around the girl. Trey trotted up to join them.

It was then that Cale got a better look at Feather Ross. This time from a distance. Her dusk-bronze skin, tawny hair, coltish legs, and cobalt eyes made her appear unlike any ordinary ten-year-old he could recall. Closer to seventeen at first glance, if he had to bet.

Perhaps it was the fresh country air or the splash of sauterne sunlight caressing the young girl's cheeks. This time, Cale recognized that he was gazing at prepubescent innocence. Some teenage fashion model, he imagined, who'd just stepped from a magazine shoot.

Beside him, Rita worked her tongue inside her cheek. "You see it now, don't you?"

Cale turned at her voice. "I'm not sure I—"

"It's been whispered to us. Couched in several anonymous threats."

He shifted his eyes again to Feather, who was striding their way with her youthfulness on full display. He asked Rita, "What sort of—"

"Sex trafficking, Detective." She spat the words in disgust. "It's what their threats implied."

95

CHAPTER 15

With Slink checking his phone for updates, Cale accelerated the Bronco along the empty country road. More flat fields and rolling hills and forest glades, farmhouses half-hidden beneath leafy overhangs. Red barns stood with their silos stabbed in the earth. Cale handed his partner the hastily drawn map Rita had provided.

The road signs pointed north. They were headed toward a small rural town called River's Bend, eight miles away. Both men processed what they'd learned at the Ross' farm.

After glancing at the drawing, Slink turned to Cale. "Care to tell me what we're getting into?"

"Hard to say." Cale's jaw tightened. "The land-grabbing is BS, though. These people—their parents and grandparents—worked the land their entire lives."

"How weird a coincidence is it they're griping about Fillmore Farms? Miguel DeSaul? The same guy I'm out here to talk with?"

Cale checked the dashboard clock. After three p.m. now. "We'll get to DeSaul in an hour. One quick stop first, just to clear some stuff from last night."

"Meanwhile," Slink said, "we've got two bodies in Doc's cooler, along with a dozen men canvassing the warehouse neighborhood. Another bunch around the Union Hotel."

"I get it. But with everything going on last night, I want to verify this first."

"Meaning?"

"The warehouse last night," Cale said. "Before I entered, two vehicles cruised past me without headlights. I figured them for lovebirds."

"Lovebirds?"

He knew how vague it sounded. Cale explained his calls to Rosario, confirming the license tags as Minnesota plates and how Newman had traced the driver's mobile to the River's Bend area.

"That phone hacker?" Slink frowned. "Our people could have—"

"Off record. I'm suspended, remember?"

"And that's where we're headed now, right? Checking out your lovebirds' theory?"

"Quick chat. Then we'll meet DeSaul in the flesh."

Cale spent the next minutes sharing what Jackie No Name had revealed about the Fillmore Farms rumors. Of their not just milking dairy cows but also working side-hustles in the drug business; how their illegal narcotics involvement had grown locally and might stretch to the state's furthest borders.

Slink rolled his head as he listened, as if not wanting to hear it.

"It's something Cho Lin also hinted at," Cale added. "My brain keeps flipping back to it."

"The plot thickens."

Cale drove in silence for a minute. "It's also about the prison bunkmate he mentioned—Kilo Kemp." He paused. "Cho Lin felt he was the only one he could trust concerning the drug formula."

Slink arched an eyebrow. "The same Kilo Kemp whose daddy works for the DeSaul crime mob?"

"Uh-huh." Cale doubted there were two of them.

During her planned four-month stay in Wisconsin, the Burmeister House was a two-story bed and breakfast, which Constanza "Connie" DeSaul had rented for herself and her secretary, Syan Hng. Three months were up already. The sole daughter of wealthy mobster/businessman Sevvie DeSaul, Connie paid double the going rate to rent the entire B&B. Enough for the homeowners, a retired couple in their 70s, to take the summer vacation they had always dreamed about. They wouldn't return until after Labor Day, allowing Connie and her secretary to reside in comfortable isolation.

The afternoon skies remained pleasant, puffy clouds, and the temperature balmy for June. Being a Midwesterner, however, Connie understood the weather could shift from summer to fall in a matter of minutes.

She sat leisurely now in the front living room wearing a teal-colored workout jacket, leggings, and pristine cross-trainers. She tapped at her phone.

Syan was also in workout clothes. She'd just returned from a midday run and held a water bottle. She entered the room and sat on the front edge of a Queen Anne's chair.

"Run go okay?" Connie didn't glance up. She had her dark hair pulled back in a ponytail, and a few wayward strands tickled her eyes.

"Honked at by three pickups," Syan reported. "Teens in one of them. Also, by a farmer in bibs driving one of those giant-wheel tractors. He was kind enough to wave after I flipped him off."

"Remember my theory?" Connie tried not sounding preachy. "No matter where you are, this planet is filled with morons who can't keep their zippers up."

"The world, according to Connie DeSaul." Syan grinned, sipped from her water bottle.

"Am I wrong?"

"Not in the least."

Connie added, "Local yokels. But you can't blame them for honking at the second cutest butt in the county."

Syan rose and stepped over to Connie. She bent and kissed her forehead. When she pulled away and turned, Connie gave her a smack on her behind, which caused the younger woman to glance saucily back as she walked away.

"Why just the second?" Syan asked.

"Because I'm sitting on *numero uno*."

The younger woman laughed and traipsed toward the stairs. "I'm in the shower."

"Snap to it. We've got visitors—fifteen minutes out." When Syan arched an eyebrow, Connie added, "Couple of detectives from Green Bay. I told them I'd answer some questions about Fillmore."

Syan paused on the sixth step up. "Why don't they ask Miguel? Or his psycho-ass buddy, Kemp?"

"Because they're both idiots.

"The detectives? Or your brother and Kemp?"

"We'll find out soon enough."

Syan zipped up the stairs the same way she climbed a Stairmaster. Connie watched her rise to the top, thinking that if she were sitting on the actual numero uno, her best friend wasn't too far behind.

The sparse road signs informed Cale they were nearing their destination.

The village of River's Bend was incorporated. It possessed a low-division high school, renowned statewide for its football, wrestling, and track teams, sports where farm kids excelled. Everything appeared identical to how he had predicted, yet River's Bend did him one better. The stunted water tower displayed on one side an official proclamation:

HOME OF THE FIGHTING TROUT!

Cale navigated the Bronco through three stoplights until they reached the backend of town. There was a single-level, L-shaped motel located on the eastern outskirts. The more regal, white-shuttered Burmeister House stood perched across the street. A final stop for gas/convenience store sat thirty yards further beyond these, and on the opposite side of the road, further along, beckoned a cozy home tavern with an old-school Blatz beer sign attached high on a metal pole. Beyond these quaint establishments were expansive farmlands and rolling pastures that went on unabated for miles.

The Burmeister House was one of a handful of registered B&Bs in the county. River's Bend was not known as a tourist trap, although the local fishing was excellent. Cale swung the Bronco into the driveway at the side of the older red-brick home. He parked some yards behind a burgundy Toyota SUV with Minnesota plates, taking a long look as he analyzed the vehicle's rear bumper.

"It's your case," Cale said to his partner as he exited. "So, you run point."

Slink agreed.

A minute later, they were ushered inside the front door by an attractive brunette who introduced herself as Connie DeSaul. She possessed the self-confident demeanor of a successful businesswoman, one dressed down while on vacation. She had on a dove-gray tracksuit, which somehow appeared chic. She wore the kind of makeup that looked absent.

Shyly entering the room was a second female of Asian descent, who Connie introduced as her traveling secretary, Syan Hng. She was dressed in black jeans and a summer sweater. Cale noted that the dynamic between the female pair suggested something closer than the typical boss-secretary business arrangement. He sensed a certain comfort level between them.

After shaking hands, they were ushered into the well-lit front room. Cale eyed the pleasant interior as they advanced into the place. It possessed old wood finishing throughout, oaken floors and polished baseboards, and a pair of ornate chandeliers in both main rooms. It felt as if from a long-ago century and summoned images of his grandmother's old house. Minus the chandeliers, of course.

Cale felt out of place as Connie motioned the detectives to a wide floral couch. He imagined sixty years ago they'd be removing their fedoras ala *Dragnet*. He wondered why the secretary chose to hover alone at the room's back, leaning against a tall curio cabinet. Deference or decorum? Maybe both.

"Thanks for seeing us, Ms. DeSaul," Slink said once they were settled. "Nice place you found here."

"Connie. Please." She smiled from her spot on a loveseat. "Thirty-four more days on our lease. After that..." She lifted perfect shoulders.

Cale had sensed it as he'd pulled into the driveway. But now, his second glance at the Asian lady across the room carried the pulse of recognition. The Minnesota plates were a tipoff but hearing the name "Syan" confirmed it. He'd caught just a glimpse in last night's faint light, but there was little doubt this was the female driver who'd sped past on the street outside the warehouse a short time after a murder had taken place.

Was he sitting in the room with a killer?

Syan remained leaning against the cabinet near the stairway railing. Her eyes locked on Cale as he studied her, and he swung his focus back to their host. Connie's face reminded him of someone who played poker for a living. "I hope I can answer some of your questions," she allowed, issuing a half-smile at the visitors.

Slink was angled away from Cale on the couch. He pulled an old-school notepad from his pocket. He asked, "Why this place, Ms. DeSaul? If you don't mind our asking?"

"It's close by. I work for my father," she said in a firm voice. "Sevastian DeSaul."

"Owns Fillmore Farms, right?" Slink narrowed his eyes. "And your brother, Miguel? He's the local CEO?"

"Half-brother. Different moms."

Slink jotted in his notebook.

Cale imagined Connie DeSaul had grown up privileged. Her calm self-confidence enhanced her classic good looks. With her hair up, she could pass for a 70's movie actress. Natalie Wood, perhaps. He imagined her age around thirty.

"I function as our corporate troubleshooter," she said.

"Meaning?"

101

"When one of our six cattle farms has *issues*—personnel, management, or other things—I come in and assess. Find and solve the problems." She crossed her legs at the ankle.

Cale was still attempting to figure out the dynamic between this female pair. One of them was a dragon lady, he decided. He wasn't sure which one yet.

"You've been here for three months now?" Slink asked agreeably. "Does it mean your Wisconsin farm is screwed up, somehow?"

"We have several staff concerns," Connie confessed. She began adding a thought but caught herself. "Of course, I can't go into details."

Cale widened his eyes. "A couple of cows go wonky?"

His joke fell flat.

She blinked at him. "We've had over a dozen mergers and acquisitions this past year alone. So, our business plans are in constant flux."

"Buying distressed family dairy farms?" This from Slink. "That sort of thing?"

"We don't twist any arms, Detective. If it's what you're implying."

"Just reading the news."

Connie considered his comment. After a sigh, she explained how expansion brought with it different levels of complexity. She brushed a piece of lint off her thigh. Cale recognized the room temperature had dropped. He could smell the lemony scent of furniture polish. Was it one of Syan's secretarial duties as well? Housekeeping?

"How well do you get along with your half-brother, Ms. DeSaul?" Slink asked directly, and she cast her eyes his way. "An online article says you and Miguel fight like cats and dogs."

"Online?" Connie snickered. "The corny cliché tells you enough, doesn't it?"

Syan adjusted her posture behind them, hands behind her back, leaning against the cabinet.

"Miguel is what you'd call an alpha male," Connie further explained. "Daddy's blessed son. Wine, women, cars, the whole enchilada."

"A typical CEO pattern?" Cale interjected.

She frowned, not taking the bait. "My job is making sure he stays true to our father's vision," Connie smirked without humor. "My brother's personal life is his own business."

Slink scribbled in his notebook. Cale rose and walked a few steps toward the front window. Turning back, he said, "I read an interview with your security advisor—a Frank Kemp. He also claimed mega-farms rarely pressure smaller ones into selling their land. But when they do, the little guys come out winners."

Connie measured her response. "It's rough on them to stay afloat. Farm families don't have six or eight kids like they used to." She hitched her shoulders. "But my father trusts Frank."

"Even more than his own son?" Cale arched an eyebrow. "Or daughter, for that matter."

Connie didn't bite. "Frank's a long-time family friend. He visits all our farms, the same as I do. Often for months. He makes sure the security staff is up to speed." She parsed her words. "Then he moves on to where he's needed next."

The room was quiet for a bit. Slink said, "Seems as if you and Kemp do the same job." When they turned his way, he added, "You come in and fix problems, right? His job is preventing them in the first place?"

"We each have our talents."

"I'm sure you do," Cale said. He looked across the room. "How about you, Ms. Hng?" His question forced their eyes to shift to the silent secretary.

"She's my girl Friday," Connie interjected. "Does a bit of everything for me."

"Great. Then I'm sure she won't mind answering a couple of questions for us."

Syan looked at Connie for assurance. Connie asked, "Concerning?

"Where Ms. Hng was last night a little before midnight?"

CHAPTER 16

The two ladies were huddled together in the room's far corner speaking in low, strategic tones. They reminded Cale of doubles tennis partners discussing strategy during a timeout.

Connie stepped forward and at last announced, "We've agreed. If you insist it's necessary, Detective. But only a few brief questions."

"Just a few," Cale allowed, motioning the secretary toward the house's kitchen. "Outside back, then, in private."

Connie offered a resigned look. Cale followed the lithe secretary through the kitchen and out the back door. They stood in the middle of a wooden deck, where a three-foot-tall fence surrounded them. Four outdoor chairs sat around a matching table. Sunlight sprinkled through the branches of the adjacent tall elms and stately willow tree.

Syan faced Cale with her arms crossed. She appeared more impatient than concerned. His eyes focused over the lawn at the driveway, where the front of her burgundy SUV could be seen.

"I ID'd your license tags." He looked at her straight. "Your vehicle was spotted on the street along the warehouse district. Just before midnight."

"Do you write mystery novels, Detective?" The younger lady feigned a smile.

"Driving with your headlights off."

The challenge disappeared from Syan's eyes. She opened her mouth, closed it.

"Before you blurt out something you may regret," Cale warned, "ten minutes after you left, we found a man dead inside the warehouse."

"What man?"

"One with his throat slashed."

Frank Kemp pulled his gray Buick Regal into the parking lot of the Fillmore Farms main office facilities. He studied the flat building through his front windshield. In four short years, they had risen to become one of the top dairy operations in Wisconsin—America's Dairy State, no less. Nothing to sneeze at. The new $10 million bio-generator would be up and running by years' end. It would quadruple production and enable them to bring in another two-thousand-head of cattle.

Kemp had only learned about dairy farms over the past few years, not growing up a farm lad himself. Still, regardless of what business you were in, there remained one golden rule that mattered:

Keep the place making money.

Kemp opened the Regal's door and stepped into the afternoon sunshine. He was careful not to soil his wine-colored, tasseled loafers. Thus, rule Number Two was: Keep your eyes peeled to the ground when walking around a dairy farm.

The Tex-Mex named Ferlando emerged from the front office door to greet him. The guy had a bandito mustache and a bald head that glistened when he removed his straw hat. He could pass for a character actor.

"Swell day, Mr. Kemp." The man issued a carny worker's grin. "Cooler weather and all."

The fact was, even seventy degrees was too warm for Kemp. He had grown up in the shaded urban streets of industrial Minneapolis, where sixty-five degrees was cause enough for gals to dig through dresser drawers for their favorite bikinis.

Kemp nodded, all business.

"Cool breeze makes our ladies happy," Ferlando prattled on. He meant the cows, of course. "Grinners are the best milkers. So they say."

Kemp couldn't care less about bovines. He forced a smile, staying congenial. Part of his job was keeping the help enthused—especially Ferlando, who managed the farm's fifty employees and was also a central cog in their lucrative side-business.

Kemp gritted his teeth through the back and forth. The fact was, he already had his departure date planned. Once he had his hands on the fentanyl formula, he and Miguel would be on a direct flight down to Belize in less than a week. After that, they'd each possess enough cash to live on the sun-bleached beaches for however long their mortal lives lasted.

Or be free to relocate to wherever else on the planet they chose, for that matter, in case they happened to become sick of one another. The way Kemp pictured it, they could live the way actor Marlon Brando had in Tahiti years ago, with never-ending booze and surrounded by naked hula girls.

At least it was their long-term plan. For now, there remained hurdles that needed clearing. No such thing as a free ride, was there? But when you got your chance at the golden goose, Kemp's theory was you grabbed the sucker by the neck and held on with both hands.

It was how he viewed their current situation.

The two men stood in the warm parking lot now, mid-afternoon, between work shifts. At least a dozen vehicles were parked around them, but they otherwise had the lot to themselves.

"Step inside?" Ferlando offered. "Got the AC on full blast."

Kemp shook his head while scrutinizing the operations manager's moist brown eyes—the eyes of a Guernsey, he decided. Then he said, "Just touching base about what we discussed yesterday." Kemp pushed his sunglasses up his hawkish nose. The aroma of cow pies sweetened the air around them.

"Under control. I fired LeRoy right after we talked."

Kemp considered the news. "I told you about Iowa, didn't I? The stink storm there?"

Ferlando scratched his chin stubble. "I warned him two weeks ago: No selling to our workers!"

The manager had been the one who had alerted Kemp about an employee named LeRoy Roal. How he'd been a pot-dealer before being hired at the Farm. His desire to "turn his life around" had turned out to be a load of BS.

"I'm not messing around here, Ferlando," Kemp said, his tone straightforward. "Hope I'm clear?"

Kemp accepted that the manager had a soft spot for the workers. Might Ferlando have placed LeRoy on probation? Or reassigned him to graveyard shift? Hiding his presence until things cooled down?

"I warned him twice when I booted his ass out." Ferlando scratched his cheek stubble. "Said I'd call the county cops if I see his mug around here again."

Kemp allowed a long beat of silence. It felt right. He was convinced the ordeal was over.

Turning to depart, he strode a few steps toward his Buick, then called over his shoulder: "Call me if there's any trouble." He waved his phone in the air. "You're the cock-of-the-walk now, Ferlando. Keep your beak to the grindstone."

Kemp slid back inside his Regal. The tan leather seats hadn't had time to warm, and he cranked the AC on high and swept from the parking lot.

The lean country roads bordered the adjacent cornfields. Navigating the long rectangle, Kemp continued east for another mile before turning back southward again. After that, one more soft turn deposited him at Miguel's English manor home, where he'd lodged for the past three months. The monotony of the drive allowed him time to think, and his thoughts returned to last night. He harbored no regret eliminating either the ex-con, Cho Lin, or the courier in the warehouse. They were loose ends that required erasing.

Getting his hands on the drug formula was the primary objective.

Still, the thought of "loose ends" brought the image of Connie's secretary to mind. He'd have to decide soon on her status. But first things first.

Kemp's thoughts drifted back to the master plan. Once they—meaning he and Miguel—possessed the new fentanyl formula, they no longer had to worry about manufacturing their own product, transporting it, or selling it to some multitude of faceless dirtbags. Each of those steps placed them at greater risk of exposure, and each step increased their chance of scrutiny by the DEA.

The beauty of Kemp's strategy was its simplicity.

Once he put together the whole formula, he'd have Clive Bawdy, their resident cooker, produce a small batch of non-lethal opioid pills. He'd then offer samples to a select group of customers. Gratis, of course. When zero overdose deaths turned up and word spread that someone had invented a non-lethal version of fentanyl, they'd contact a handful of high-level bosses at the top of the illegal narcotics world: the Chinese triads, the Columbian and Mexican cartels, and Italian Mafiosi. Maybe one or two others.

Once these elite entrepreneurs were satisfied with their product's credibility, Kemp would solicit a trustworthy auctioneer to conduct a bidding sale on an ultra-secure dark website. They'd play it straight down the middle. Sell only one version of the formula to the highest bidder—payment in the untraceable cryptocurrency of their choice.

Then they'd walk away, as slick as art thieves from a no-alarm museum.

Kemp had convinced Miguel it was the smartest play. Manufacturing and distributing it themselves required too much effort, too high an exposure level. If they eliminated the headaches of the entire manufacturing and supply chain— production, distribution, sales, and then having to launder the money afterward—they'd reap faster rewards with far less risk.

They'd pocket a windfall of cash while staying above the fray.

Besides, Kemp had added, there'd be no looking over their shoulders for the rest of their lives. Miguel, of course, had agreed to the plan. Now all Kemp needed was to locate Cho

Lin's part of the formula, still hidden somewhere on his laptop. Thanks to last night's success, at least he now had possession of the guy's computer.

He needed to crack the Asian kid's password encryption. Then, once he put it all together, they'd be on their way to a lifetime of comfortable bliss.

Kemp's head was clear now, far more than late last night, so he figured the search shouldn't take too long. Some tech-savvy seventh grader would've had it figured out already.

As the Regal cruised the road's final stretch, Kemp's mind returned to the one variable that continued to torment him. They hadn't settled on what to call the new drug. These days it was all about branding, wasn't it? They couldn't call it "Safe Fentanyl." Or "No Death Fentanyl." Not much zing in either of those. Besides, Kemp understood how a distinctive name would also give their new product instant street cred.

Blue Crest; Wonder Lust; Floating Fog?

He needed it catchy yet descriptive. A buzzy name that honey-rolled off a dealer's tongue when trying to entice a would-be buyer. What had Walter White called his crystal meth product in *Breaking Bad*? Blue something or other, wasn't it?

Blue Marble; Blue Whale; Turquoise Tango?

Then it popped into his head like a starburst. *Blue Sky*. That's what they'd called it.

But even that famous moniker didn't sound too earth-shattering when you thought about it. Times had changed, so something even catchier was required. Kemp set the problem aside for the moment. Right now, the stuff's name was the least of his concerns.

He swung the Regal into the drive, which curled between the high trees with shafts of late afternoon sunlight seeping down through the leaf canopy. Driving the winding road, he marveled at the beauty of the English manor house. The strips of forest on each side hid the adjacent farm fields, creating a natural hidden sanctuary. The feel of comfortable privacy.

Despite the frozen Wisconsin winters, it was as if they were already living in their own secluded slice of paradise. Even though they hadn't quite become millionaires yet and northern Wisconsin sure as hell wasn't Tahiti.

CHAPTER 17

The Bronco cruised along the open countryside. Slink thumbed through phone messages in the passenger seat. He set the mobile in his lap and asked, "You get any vibe from Connie DeSaul?"

"Her story's plausible." Cale's eyes scanned the empty road ahead. "Family business. Siblings often keep watch over one another."

"As a troubleshooter, her job is to spy on her half-brother and the other guy, Kemp, right?"

Cale side-eyed him. "Notice how the temp cooled fast at the mention of her brother?" He paused. "As for Kemp, she'd have to run their personnel issues through him first, I'd imagine."

Slink thought about it. "This Kemp sounds bulletproof. Security guys work in the shadows, run tight ships—until some employee goes postal."

"Postal? You're thinking of Ken Bruen novels." Cale snickered. "Duh. These guys milk cows for a living."

"And postal workers sell postage stamps." A pause, then: "Anybody can snap. We've seen it ourselves."

They drove for minutes in silence. Cale reflected on how the voodoo priest had bewitched his partner's mind during their recent home invasion. Could it be what Slink meant now by saying, *Anybody can snap?*

"I wonder how Miguel views his sister's presence?" Slink asked. "Renting a place just miles from his backyard? For more than three months now?"

"You think a family coup's in the works?"

"Why not? Company founders have turned things over to their daughters before." Cale glanced at his partner, and Slink added, "Hugh Hefner, ring any bells?"

"The Playboy genius?" Cale shook his head. "You married guys! You're in a room with pretty ladies for ten minutes, and your thoughts turn to centerfolds."

"I'm talking about the business end."

"So am I."

They drove back over the same eight-mile road they'd navigated an hour before. The home of Miguel DeSaul stood a mile up from the Ross farmhouse, due north as the crow flew. It was across a small creek that ran inside the stretch of woods that little Feather now found so threatening.

The near-barren country roads were hypnotic, and with Slink busy with phone messages, Cale peeked at the GPS every thirty seconds. He recalled how neither Connie nor her pal Syan appeared shocked when learning about last night's murders. It was somewhat odd. People outside of law enforcement weren't usually so blasé when informed about bleeding bodies. Then again, Connie had grown up in a gangster household. Perhaps she'd heard too many sordid tales to be fazed anymore.

Slink answered his phone's buzz, one of the sergeants telling him their witness canvasses had produced zilch. He turned toward Cale now and asked him what Syan had revealed during their conversation out on the back porch.

"She copped to being there," Cale reported. "And she's afraid to her bones of this Kemp guy. I confirmed with her that he was there. Different vehicles."

"She sound reliable?"

"For the most part. Still…" He let the word hang.

Slink said, "I'll need her statement. After we talk with DeSaul, we should have a better feel for how this mysterious Kemp character operates."

Cale thought about it, and Slink's phone buzzed again— someone with a forensics update.

He listened with one ear as he drove. The afternoon sun was losing its luster. The sky turned quilted, clouds forming high in the north. Weathered old utility poles and electrical lines were their guideposts. The narrow road was otherwise empty.

Cale's thoughts turned dystopian. Could this be how the last two people on earth might see things? When he glanced across at Slink, he decided it wasn't one of his most nuanced thoughts.

113

His partner remained locked in his phone discussion, and the monotony allowed Cale to recall his deck conversation with Syan. She admitted driving past the warehouse late last night. She'd been tailing Kemp under Connie's orders, following up on rumors of his "shady dealings," is how she described it.

Cale ran their discussion through his head now, recalling it word for word.

"Shady involving what?" he'd asked.

The Asian secretary had sounded like a witness conveying testimony. "Everywhere Kemp goes, he's always got some hustle going on. Nothing to do with the Farm. Not officially, anyway." She'd looked him in the eye. "We're trying to nab him red-handed."

"We being?"

"Connie's my boss. She's loyal to her father's business."

"Including tailing people in the middle of the night?"

"I do what she tells me."

He'd decided it made sense. If Cho Lin had told him the truth, the entire mess was about illegal narcotics, the courier, the fentanyl formula, and the warehouse meeting.

"You think Kemp's involved with opioids?" he'd asked.

"And everything in between."

Cale's silence prompted her to add, "I was parked on the dark street, hidden. Kemp didn't know I was there." She'd shivered. "He drove up to the warehouse and went inside."

"He use a key? Or jimmy the lock?"

"No clue. It opened fast, though." She had paused as if picturing the scenario. "No way was I following him...not through an empty parking lot at night."

Cale recalled the foreboding warehouse, the breeze, the metallic scent of the nearby river. He'd asked her if Kemp was on his phone? Perhaps planning to meet someone?

A breeze had chilled the outside deck, and Syan shoved her hands in the pockets of her jeans. She'd told him Kemp had emerged five minutes later. Walked casually to his car, not as if anything unusual had happened.

"Not angry? Not looking as if he'd just sliced someone's throat?"

She'd frowned. "He drove from the parking lot, not in any hurry. But then things got stranger."

"Stranger how?"

"Kemp parked back at the street curb," Syan had continued. "Four cars ahead of me—and I swear he knew I was there. The way a cat teases a mole."

"For how long?"

"Ten minutes maybe." Her lips had been tight. "Then, you showed up. I recognized your Bronco now."

Facing her beneath the shaded back of the house, Cale had considered the tale. Syan's story jived with the time of his arrival and with the courier's death—long before he'd entered the warehouse. The man had already been bleeding out on the floor.

"I ducked down in my car." Syan's voice had quavered. "Kemp stayed at the curb waiting for you. Wanting you to either drive to the warehouse or leave."

"Except, I didn't do either."

She'd shaken her head and explained how Kemp had then started his car and driven past the parked Bronco without headlights. He'd sped across the train tracks and disappeared around a corner further up at the lights."

"And you tailed him? Why?"

Syan confessed to following Kemp a few blocks further until he'd turned for the bridge ramp. She then gave up and drove back to their home, where she had taken a sleeping pill and gone straight to bed.

She hadn't been aware of any murder until hearing the news that morning.

Cale now continued studying the farm acres and forest stands, his eyes unblinking as he gripped the steering wheel. Beside him, Slink remained conversing on his phone. Cale replayed how his talk with the petite secretary had concluded.

The young woman's eyes had turned fearful. "I'm afraid now, detective."

"You should be."

"Do you know someone I can call? In case I might need—"

"Need what?"

Syan had hesitated before saying, "Connie doesn't permit handguns. Even for protection." She'd shivered. "But from what you say happened...."

Cale had motioned for her phone and typed Jackie No Name's private number into her contacts. He handed it back, and after a glance, she'd asked him, "It's for real?"

"You can trust her. Use my name if you call."

The secretary then slipped back inside the house. Cale had remained on the backyard deck as the breeze caressed the leaves above him. The inevitable questions ran through his head: Was Syan credible? Or might she, instead, be feeding him an alternate version of the truth? Was there an outside chance she had executed the courier herself? That she might be an actual dragon lady executioner who was now pointing the finger at Frank Kemp?

Cale recalled the post-mortem note Cho Lin had provided him: *Don't trust a cute lady named Syan. Dangerous! DD!!*

He now halted the Bronco at a four-way stop. When he'd read Cho Lin's note in his garage late last night, he'd envisioned it might be a "message from the grave." Now, with more updated information, the voice in his head told him Cho Lin's words hadn't been so much a message as a warning.

From the Bronco's passenger seat, Slink turned toward Cale.

"You were saying?" he asked straight up. "Did our little secretary confess to being a double murderess?"

"She's hiding something. But also terrified."

Slink thought about it, glancing again at his phone. "While you were talking with her, Connie shared an interesting tidbit with me."

116

Cale's glance prompted him to continue.

"Turns out Syan was quite a fledgling MMA fighter, years back as a teenager." Slink continued, "But even stranger is, your buddy Cho Lin used to send her dozens of nutty fanboy letters."

"You're BS-ing me, right?" Cale said, assessing if Slink were joking. "He was in prison back then."

"Why would Connie lie?" Slink added, "Syan never wrote back, of course. She was what fifteen, sixteen? An older dude writing to her on prison stationery?"

Cale rolled the bizarre information around in his head and what it might mean. Some guys, he understood, never got over rejection. As far back as fourth grade, they carried it to their graves. Could it explain what Cho Lin had meant by writing Syan was *DD Dangerous*? His being rejected years ago by some puppy love crush? While serving out his narcotics sentence?

Why not? Stranger things have happened.

The GPS informed them they were less than a mile now from the DeSaul property.

As things stood, Cale had more questions than answers. Had Syan Hng been truthful? Was there a chance—remote as it seemed—that she and Connie had together slain the courier? Were they the "kill team" the autopsies had suggested? One with a deadly blade, the other preferring a suppressed 9mm?

And if so, where did Frank Kemp fit into the equation?

Cale was reminded of the evening's news shows and how increasingly insane the world was becoming. Nothing seemed impossible anymore.

He reminded himself of his need to stay focused. Okay, he thought, assuming Syan *hadn't* been lying. Just because Kemp had entered the warehouse and departed minutes later, it didn't mean he'd murdered the man inside. What if he had driven to the place merely to meet someone? Then discovered a dead man on the floor with his throat slashed. He'd have fled the scene like a lot of people, fearing the killer might still be inside.

Safely back in his car minutes later, parked on the street, might he have pondered reporting the crime? Remained hidden with his headlights off? Deciding what to do next?

Cale understood it was all supposition. There'd been no 911 call recorded by emergency dispatch, either from any Frank Kemp or any other "Anonymous" caller.

Syan reported the guy had sat in his vehicle for twenty more minutes after parking on the street. Why? Making calls to his partners? Or his lawyer? Or maybe he'd sat there in a frozen state of panic?

Folks often reacted oddly around bodies spurting blood.

If any of these were true, and Kemp wasn't the man who had executed the courier, then where did it leave them? And how did Cho Lin's bloody execution right afterward fit into the mysterious murders?

These were just a few of the puzzle pieces that needed sorting out. Cale hoped their discussion with Miguel DeSaul would shed clearer light on the matter. Once more facts were established, depending on how the chips fell, Slink would invite the enigmatic Mr. Kemp—it was Slink's case, after all—to the downtown station for an exploratory interview. They'd get a better picture of the guy's involvement and his statements on record.

Cale paused the Bronco now at a four-way stop. A two-tone pickup slid past, the only vehicle they'd seen for the past twenty minutes. He turned left, following it, asking Slink, "How's GPS looking?"

"Take the entry road a quarter-mile up on the left," Slink said. "House is on a dozen acres. Just two years old."

"Swimming pools, movie stars."

"More like cow pies and John Deeres."

CHAPTER 18

Situated a mile east of the Filmore Farms main entrance, the English manor house was tucked inside the pristine northern woods. You entered off the county road onto a curving drive that cut through thirty yards of forest until it revealed the circular driveway in front of the mansion.

There were no fountains or sculpted statuary. No line of Bentleys, Jaguars, or Range Rovers out front. No tailored butler ready to greet anyone.

Still, the manor house fit the needs of Miguel DeSaul, the Fillmore CEO. What he loved most was the isolation. This and the fact the tall trees and lavender bushes effectively masked the manure perfume, which emanated from the thousands of acres of surrounding farm fields.

Miguel lived in bachelor splendor inside the main house on the first two floors of the twenty-two-room home. The top floor had been assigned to his father's right-hand man, Frank Kemp, who also happened to be Miguel's godfather. Miguel didn't mind Kemp's presence. He'd grown up with "Uncle Frank" throughout his childhood. Kemp's four-month visit was acceptable because the house was spacious enough to each have private floors and interact at their discretion. And to even be companionable on certain days when both men were in convivial moods.

Besides, Kemp had already been here three months now. Long enough to get the Farms' side-business in order. It was this ancillary hustle, both men understood, which was their true source of cash flow. The dark secret of Fillmore Farms was how their dairy operations functioned as a cover for the more lucrative business of providing recreational narcotics to small cities, towns, and villages in the surrounding five counties.

Where the actual profits existed, as it were.

Nevertheless, things had taken an interesting twist for Miguel five weeks ago, when Kemp had gotten wind of an extraordinary business opportunity. He'd informed Miguel his son Cary—called "Kilo" since age twelve—had a former cellmate named James Cho Lin. And this Cho Lin's cousin, Kemp had revealed, presented him with a new narcotic, which the cousin had perfected in his Chinese lab. It was a non-lethal version of the synthetic opioid fentanyl.

Being in the street drug business for most of his adult life, Kemp had recognized the cash potential at once. Thus, he devised a scheme for procuring the formula for himself. His plan, however, depended on two significant points. *A*) He had to secure the drug's design free and clear. And *B*) Kemp needed a partner he could trust. As a confidant of Cho Lin, his son Kilo became the means of providing the first part. And Miguel DeSaul, heir to the family fortune and tired of living in his crime boss Daddy's shadow, had been offered the second.

Kemp shared his get-rich-quick scheme with Miguel one evening. He presented it as an escape from both their lives of servitude. With the drug formula in hand, they could make enough money to live like kings, even if they chose to go their separate ways afterward. It hadn't taken Miguel long to decide. The choice was simple: continue residing in the Podunk northern backwoods, a two-bit milk supplier to the masses. Or Door Number 2, live royally in some exotic locale—Belize, for instance—sipping umbrella drinks while surrounded by attractive senoritas in barely-there bikinis.

Being in the drug business anyway, the men had jumped in with both feet. They had spit on their hands old-school and shook on the deal. They both agreed it could be the opportunity of a lifetime, that is, if they managed to pull it off with their hides intact.

These were Miguel's thoughts now as he labored at his wet bar in the mansion's high-windowed front drawing-room. The walls were decorated with fine artwork. Miguel imagined the paintings might pass for originals, at least in diffused lighting.

But what did he care? He knew as much about art as he did working an abacus. He prided himself more as a "man of action," preferring golf or swimming at the club pool to staring at framed fox hunts on his walls.

As long as those worthy activities didn't interfere with his mandatory 4:30 afternoon happy hour.

Miguel now supplied a dollop of fresh-squeezed OJ to his four fingers of Kettle One. He'd heard Kemp's Regal cruise up the drive five minutes ago, knowing his partner would be joining him in a minute.

He couldn't wait to receive an update on their project.

Miguel had been growing antsy of late. He doubted he could endure another three months here in the Midwest. Snow-bound for most of the past winter, he was ready for a change of scenery. He imagined how twenty million dollars each in their pockets (to start) would allow them to blow this pop stand once and for all.

His father would be disappointed, of course. But this is where his sister Connie, love her or hate her, came in. Miguel told himself many times that if she wanted to run the Wisconsin farm operation so bad, she could have it.

One thing was certain: his father would soon get over it. Business was king, as far as Sevvie DeSaul was concerned. Furthermore, Miguel predicted his dad couldn't stay PO'd for too long. Not when his lifelong best friend Frank Kemp was also involved.

Miguel heard the connecting door from the garages open. The door led into the mudroom, which in turn led to the long central hallway. Moments later, he could hear the clacking footsteps echo off the high ceilings. Standing in the drawing-room, drink in hand, the sound caused Miguel to grit his teeth. He pictured Frank Kemp's cringe-worthy footwear. He wondered—for the millionth time—why the bloodless hitman Kemp would persist in wearing those maroon tasseled loafers.

But that was Uncle Frank for you, one unique gent. Miguel accepted that Kemp could dress however he chose, and any

121

punk stupid enough to snicker would be lucky if his heart were still pumping one minute later.

"Got a status update?" Miguel asked glibly, timing his question to Kemp's entry through the room's open archway.

Kemp replaced him at the wet bar, and Miguel stepped across the room.

"How's this Swedish vodka work in a Bloody Mary?" the thick-chested Kemp asked, working the chrome ice tongs. "You know I'm partial to the cheap stuff."

Miguel reached one of the room's high windows, stared across the manicured west lawn. He didn't want to get sidetracked. Did Kemp have the formula or not? He decided to try honey over vinegar. He said, "Tomato juice gives you acid, Frank. Remember?"

Kemp's nostrils flared. "If I get acid, it's from cracking that dickwad Cho Lin's password." Not bothering with a celery stalk or pickle, he chugged down half his drink and freshened it back up before the first glug hit his stomach.

"I'll get the passwords. No sweat," Kemp said. "Just a matter of time."

Miguel crossed his hairy arms. He had on a black polo shirt and linen slacks. He'd seen Kemp in testy moods before. The savvy play was to refrain from pressing him too hard.

"How about Ferlando?" he asked. "He straighten out the thing with the pot dealer?"

Kemp bottomed his drink and set the glass on a serving tray. He considered another refill. "Something about the guy gives me the creeps."

"Ferlando? You're the one who hired him."

"Because he's an earner, that's why." Kemp reached for the vodka bottle and poured again. "He fired that fool, LeRoy." Kemp thought about it. "I still might send the moron a message, so he keeps his trap glued."

Miguel sipped his drink, pondering things, knowing it was pointless to rush his partner. "Your business, Frank. Meantime, I think I'll hit the range and murder a couple of buckets."

"Don't pull your groin," Kemp said grumpily. He turned and departed from the room, gripping the Kettle One bottle by its neck.

Miguel heard the tap-dance steps as his partner neared the hallway stairs and gritted his teeth once more. At the wet bar, he unscrewed a fresh bottle of vodka he'd pulled from the lower cabinet. However, before he could pour a decent slug, he heard an unfamiliar vehicle pull up in front of the house.

CHAPTER 19

The Bronco eased halfway around the circular driveway and stopped before the tall double doors of the manor house. Three stories of gray, multi-windowed granite. Ivy vine creepers up the brick. Gabled roofs, the works. Half the outside shrubs and hedges wore 1950s flattops, courtesy of some groundskeeper wearing Wellington boots.

"The only thing missing is the gravel drive-up," Cale said as the detectives stepped from the Bronco.

Slink snorted at the absurdity. "Try running a snowplow over gravel twenty times a winter."

The doorbell chimed from deep within. It was answered a minute later by a middle-aged woman. She wore dark slacks and trainers, with an unmatching headband around her tight auburn hair.

"Hello there," she announced in a friendly tone. "I'm Mrs. Flench, Mr. DeSaul's housekeeper."

They should have called ahead, Cale understood. But Slink hadn't wanted the occupants—especially the man named Kemp—a chance to rehearse their stories. Or phone some Fillmore PR flunky who would rush over and serve as a corporate mouthpiece.

Slink flashed his ID and gold shield, and Cale, standing two steps behind, nodded. "We're Green Bay detectives," Slink announced. "Looking for Miguel DeSaul. Just a couple of quick questions for him if he's in?"

"Concerning?"

"About intruders on your property," Cale added smoothly. "Young girl on the neighboring farm downstream. Having problems with a stalker."

Mrs. Flench knitted her brows and turned, admitting the detectives into the spacious front foyer. She hurried off to

124

announce their presence to Mr. DeSaul before he left for the golf course.

An umbrella stand in one corner, and a couple of ancient castle paintings on the walls, embellishing the stately manor's theme. Cale was staring at one when an inner door opened from the hallway ten yards away. A man emerged and strode their way, smiling curiously. He was pleasant-looking, with tight salt-and-pepper hair, and his smile didn't fade as he neared.

"Detectives. C'mon in," said the greeter.

Closer now, Cale noted how the man's curved nose and narrow eyes rendered him a predatory appearance. This was furthered by his tight, open-collar shirt and casual gray slacks. The whole image fell apart, though, when he spotted the maroon-colored loafers complete with matching tassels. So much for predatory, his mind chided.

"I'm Frank Kemp," the solid man offered. "Miguel's house guest." They all shook hands, and Kemp ushered them into the high-ceilinged drawing-room where the quarter-paned windows looked out over the estate's manicured front and side lawns.

"Been visiting here long, Mr. Kemp?" Cale asked as they surveyed the room. His eyes slid to Slink, and as long-time partners, they knew enough to let things play out.

"Business lodger. A couple of months." Kemp kept the smile in his eyes. "Call me Frank, why don't you?"

Moving deeper into the place, the detectives noted how the room appeared bathed in the late afternoon sunlight and spoke to a pleasant life beyond most everyday annoyances.

"Nice digs," said Slink.

"Farm life for you, eh?" Kemp chuckled as he ushered them toward a set of leather couches with matching coffee tables.

Entering beneath a hallway arch behind them, a second man now spoke. He held a cocktail tumbler in one hand.

"Caught me on the way to the nineteenth hole," Miguel said, jocular. "Mind if I enjoy a bracer?" He stopped at the wet bar along the sidewall, arched his bushy eyebrows. "Join me, gentlemen?"

"On duty. Thanks, anyway."

"Ditto," Cale added, not precisely accurate.

Miguel moved from the bar with a fresh cocktail and extended his free hand toward the visitors. He flashed bleached teeth when he smiled.

The detectives seated themselves on a wide, burgundy leather couch. Cale felt pleased they'd advanced from the flowery version Connie DeSaul had earlier offered. As he settled in, he noted how the burly Kemp remained standing a polite distance away. His arms were crossed, short of flexing. If the room had held a pillar, Cale pictured the man leaning against it, though perhaps not wanting to crease his fancy loafers.

Miguel chose a matching armchair opposite them and crossed his legs. "Now, gentlemen, what can we do you for?" Before either could speak, he added, "Midwest jargon, by the by. Minnesota, born and bred."

Slink played along. "Not Vikings fans, I hope?"

"Long before we stole Brett Favre from you."

They shared hearty laughs, and Cale used the moment to scrutinize the pair further. They appeared more like Vegas pit bosses than anything to do with farming. Yet times were changing, he allowed, and with hi-tech, multi-international corporations running dairy farms these days, he supposed anything was possible.

Miguel sipped his cocktail. "We're in farm management. Both of us." His eyes roped in Kemp. "In case you think we don't fit the sodbuster image."

"I doubt either of you own a pair of bibs," Slink said. "But your business—it's not why we're here."

"Some mention of a trespasser?" Kemp piped in. "Mrs. Flench was saying?"

Slink explained how the young girl on the neighboring farm had spotted a man eyeing her from the woods. Maybe half-a-dozen times in recent weeks."

"The Ross farm," Cale said. "I'm sure you know them."

"Fine people," admitted Miguel.

Kemp added, "Real farmers. Salt of the earth."

"In fact," Miguel said, "we talked about an offer on their property a few times. Nice profit if they're ever interested."

Kemp stepped toward one tall window. He leaned with his back against the sill, continued studying the visiting detectives.

"Crazy times we're in," Miguel said, frustrated. "Perverts. Drugged-up college kids marching around and whatnot." He arched his eyebrows. "When's it going to end, eh?"

Cale agreed. He'd even heard of paid protesters receiving handouts to picket industrial dairy farms. Staying focused, he asked, "But you guys haven't spotted anyone odd, have you? Hanging around your property?"

Miguel sipped his cocktail. "We keep a close watch on this place. And on our workers." He looked across the room. "Frank, here, makes certain our ship stays buttoned-down."

"Had to let a moron go just yesterday." Kemp frowned. "Pot dealer." He flipped his thumb ala an umpire. "He's outta here!"

The detectives took it all in. Cale pictured Mrs. Flench hovering behind some corner, listening the way maids did in *Downton Abbey*. Miguel explained how the woods at their property's edge extended alongside Tar Creek for a mile, down past the Ross' place. But they hadn't heard of anything out of the ordinary happening in the forest.

"There's an old beat-up barn," Kemp offered, "halfway down the woods." When they looked his way, he added, "College kids used to party there on weekends. Pot smokers, pill poppers. You name it."

Slink said they'd look into it. Miguel rolled the ice cubes in his empty glass.

Cale decided to accelerate things. They weren't here on a social call. He relayed the latest Green Bay news from last night, how a pair of murders had occurred. A gang or drug hit.

Miguel frowned and confessed that, geez, they were isolated out here. He barely had time to keep up with the local headlines. His nod at Frank Kemp showed him in agreement.

Slink said they were out this way on a different matter. He added, "We're just crossing a few T's off our list. But FYI, one of the murder victims was an ex-con."

Kemp narrowed his eyes and suggested prison gangs.

Or perhaps migrants, Miguel theorized. Foreign gangs kept trying to recruit migrant farmworkers. He looked at them, measuring their response. The Farm's employment records were at the detectives' disposal if they wanted to check. But the system, he added, was riddled with false IDs, and searching for true identities was tricky business.

"It's the reason they never pay taxes," Kemp added, offering a frustrated shrug.

Cale reported how heroin, fentanyl, and opioids couldn't be ruled out, how narcotics were always in the picture. Slink added that he was sure they understood the score better than most.

The room turned somber, with their hosts' expressions indicating a sadness they couldn't be of more help.

Slink peeked at his phone, then back at Miguel. "Quick question. Unrelated," he said, arching one eyebrow. "Your sister Connie?"

"Half-sister."

"She claims she's in the area as a consultant. A kind of business overseer?"

Miguel placed his glass on a coaster. He glanced at Kemp, then back at the visitors. "Sadly, Connie is always meddling in things she shouldn't be."

"In what way?"

"Along with that, uh, gal pal of hers." Miguel reached for his glass again, arched an eyebrow. "Truth is, they're the same as dog crap stuck to my shoe."

A pin drop would have thundered on the polished floor.

Kemp stepped across the room and gripped the back of a vacant armchair. His knuckles were gnarled.

"Let me explain it," he told the detectives. "Connie and Miguel"—speaking as if he'd refereed their spats for decades—"there's always been tension." Kemp conveyed further how

128

Connie felt her father should've anointed her CEO of the farm here in Wisconsin and how she might be a shade delusional on the topic.

Miguel suggested his sister hoped he screwed things up, and Cale noted how voicing it made the man fume as if he'd just blown a hundred-dollar putt. Miguel added that Connie pictured herself as some Joan of Arc, swooping in to save the day wearing wings and a halo.

He glanced at the visitors, saying, "Her and her little carpet munch—"

Kemp's phone buzzed. He waved it in the air, saying he had to grab the call. He moved toward the hallway, with his voice muffled as he spoke.

Miguel rose and strode to one of the tall windows. He stared outside as if interested in the landscaping.

"I hear you, Mr. DeSaul. Er, Miguel," Cale said, somewhat out of the blue. He was sitting forward on the couch, elbows on knees. He added how he also had an unstable younger brother named Robin, who had plagued their family over the years.

When he glanced at Slink, his partner's eyes asked, Crazy brother Robin? Cale didn't wink but could have. He hadn't seen his wayward brother in years now, he confessed. Last he'd heard, the guy was backpacking through Malaysia.

Miguel turned back toward the room, his silhouette dark against the sun-warmed glass. He wondered, rhetorically, why his sister just didn't leave the area? Frustration colored his tone. Why didn't she go back to their dad and torment his life instead of Miguel's?

"Siblings." Cale spread his palms wide. "They've always got something to prove, don't they?"

Miguel returned to where they sat as Kemp glided back into the ornate room. His expression displayed concern. "Another headache," he announced with a grimace. "Damn milk carousel slipped a gear—I got to shoot over there."

Slink rose as well. "Before you fly off, uh, Frank. Can I ask one more thing?"

Kemp arched his eyebrows.

"Just wondering what kind of vehicle you drive?"

A pause. "Buick. Regal. Why?"

Slink was nonchalant, saying, "A witness claims there was a dark 4-door sedan spotted in the warehouse district last night. Where one of our victims was murdered."

Kemp looked at them all. "Ten-million sedans on the road every day, aren't there?" He turned and made for the open archway, barking into his phone as he escaped.

Minutes later, the detectives were escorted outside by Miguel. They thanked him for his cooperation. Standing near the boxy Bronco, they turned as Kemp's gray Regal accelerated down the tree-lined lane.

"Frank's one solid guy," Miguel admitted. "Loyal as a marine. I've known him since I was little." He chuckled. "I'm not BS-ing you. He's my godfather."

"You're a lucky guy," Cale admitted. "Close family and all."

Inside the steamy Bronco, Cale cranked the engine as Slink checked his messages. "Get anything out of that?" he asked evenly.

"Beyond how they both lie through their teeth?"

Slink glanced his way as they cruised beneath the high leaf canopy. Ahead of them, the curving lane was pierced by lances of afternoon sunlight.

"Sister Connie's not high on the Christmas list," Cale said.

"Add a lump of coal for her secretary."

Cale spun the Bronco out onto the barren country road. "I'd tell you the game's afoot," he said, "but you'll give me that stupid face you make."

His partner glanced his way, and Cale added, "Yeah. That one."

CHAPTER 20

Maggie was in the den at her computer when she heard the Bronco drive up and park on the garage apron. With last night's excitement behind them, she and Cale could relax at home this evening. Maybe even turn in early.

Chloe had departed hours ago, and her work on the legal brief had taken most of the afternoon.

The conversation she'd had with her sister lingered in her mind. It all boiled down to Chloe's plan to seek help from Father Larchezzi. He was their favorite priest, the man who had helped them recover from their recent assault by the lunatic. Just as they'd employed teamwork to survive the encounter, they also needed one another's ongoing support in the aftermath.

In Chloe's case, the post-traumatic effects still lingered. After revealing her plans with Father Larchezzi, Maggie offered her sister whatever assistance she could provide.

"Thanks, Mags," Chloe had said, hugging her at the door. "But I've got to do this on my own."

"You sound like you're joining AA."

"Except it's my soul, not my liver."

Maggie smiled. "You've got me on speed dial."

With a sheepish wave, Chloe had departed.

From her computer chair, Maggie heard the Bronco's door slam. She rose and ruffled Hank's head where he lay curled on the half-couch. She proceeded down the hallway and greeted Cale as he entered.

He looked frazzled. "Things go okay with the farmers?" she asked, filling her water glass at the sink. The sun was lowering in the western sky.

He pecked her cheek without fanfare and opened the refrigerator. "Too much clean country air. I feel like I just plowed the back forty."

She leaned against the counter. "So, you're not mowing the lawn after dinner?"

He fished a bottle of water from the fridge. "Think I'll hire a kid once I'm back at work." He strode to the dining table and pulled a chair free, spun it around, and sat with his legs extended. He complained his butt was still numb from driving.

"The farmers' gripe session was crazy." He sighed. "I know more about cows now than I ever cared to."

She didn't know how to respond.

"Do you know we've lost more than half our family farms over the last decade?" he asked. Over five hundred in this state last year alone?" His sigh was heavy. "Mostly to those industrial farms and nonsense bureaucrat restrictions. Running the small guys out of business."

"I thought you were working a drug case. Or that hotel murder?"

"They might all be connected." He sipped his water. "Something's rotten in Denmark."

"And you don't mean Denmark, Wisconsin." Maggie grinned. One of the cornpone jokes they shared.

Looking at his eyes, however, she recognized the sharp-edged glaze he sometimes got. It reminded her of how a bulldog with a bone won't let it go, even if you hoist him dangling four feet in the air.

"I'm sure Slink can handle it," she said, matter of fact. "He's got the task force behind him. City, county, state. All working together."

Cale polished off his water and rolled the empty bottle on the table surface, making the plastic cry annoyingly. He told her he was going to wash up. Then he'd start the grill and get going with the steaks he had spotted on a plate inside the fridge.

"I don't mind eating late," she offered saucily.

Maggie bumped herself away from the counter and stepped into the dining room. She draped her arms around his neck, straddling onto his lap cowgirl-style. Cale slid his chair further from the table as she kissed his stubbled cheek and then his lips.

He studied her with smoky eyes. "What's all this about?"

"Cooped up here all day. Now my badass detective is home to protect and serve."

"*Suspended* badass detective."

They kissed. Maggie swung to her feet and tugged at his arm. "C'mon," she coaxed. "You can't be too tired to join me upstairs for an hour?"

"Hmmm. Choices." His face revealed mock seriousness. "Upstairs with my wife-to-be, or mow the lawn? Hmmm."

She slugged his bicep and stepped away, her hips rolling as she moved down the hallway. She climbed the stairs. "I'll be up here!" she called back. "If I hear the stupid mower start, I'll be disappointed."

Cale rose and trailed her with that bulldog glint in his eyes.

Maggie had prepped a pair of rib eyes, and Cale seared them on the Weber grill he kept on the outside deck during the warm months. He held a bottle of Pabst in one hand. As he flipped the steaks, his thoughts returned to their meeting with Miguel DeSaul.

During the drive back to the city, Cale's guts had been churning. Things weren't kosher with this pair of corporate farm heads. Connie was jealous of her half-brother, and it was just as evident Syan was terrified of Frank Kemp. Both had suggested narcotics were being dealt on the side. Still, investigating those claims would take time. Especially if the transgressors were professionals who had been at it for a while.

Neither Miguel nor Kemp carried the look of unpolished hayseeds.

Cale's thoughts shifted to Jackie's original request that he also investigate the problems Fillmore was causing for her friends, the Ross family.

By nature, he chose to side with the little guys. And thus, when it came to an underdog group of farmers versus wealthy corporate invaders, well, the odds were going to fall with the local bunch every time.

How could they not? There was gracious and pretty Rita, solid Ben, and Rita's feisty young daughter, Feather. Along with the other farmers, all were fearful of losing the land they'd worked for decades. This motley group was in a battle for their lives against a conglomerate known for hitching cows to giant mechanical milk pumps, sucking out more in a day than a dozen family farmers combined could manage.

Cale supposed it was progress, yet that didn't make it any less disheartening.

His mind flashed to the scenario he and Slink had joked about, where land-grabbing cattle barons were bullying small homesteaders. The movie *Shane* again. He recalled how the film's hero had ridden off into the sunset with a fatal bullet in his belly.

So much for heroic Old West fantasies.

Cale stared out at the lawn and high trees and bushes, which shielded their corner property from the suburban street. On the opposite side of the house stood the bushes where the voodoo psycho had concealed himself—his stakeout position—where he'd planted the female college professor's severed head atop the three-foot-high pole.

Cale was thankful he was on this side of the house now. Looking at those same bushes again would no doubt ruin his appetite. Still, he was having trouble shaking the memory. The low throb of drums, bells, and shakers had filled their home that night. The sound remained imprinted on his brain. He couldn't fight it. It was part of him the way babies never forgot their mother's first smile.

He forced the memory away by concentrating on his time upstairs with Maggie. A more pleasant scenario.

Cale listened to the birds singing in the dusky gloaming. He detected the slow roll of traffic from blocks away. Some kids' far-off laughter reached him, splashes coming from their family pool.

He flipped the steaks again and swigged from his beer bottle. He'd call Slink later, get his partner's update on the investigation. Slink had reported how they were shipping the courier's remains back to Seattle. James Cho Lin was still in the morgue's cooler. His remains would be cremated, deposited in some nameless grave with a crooked white cross. Cale chided himself for being unable to shake off the Wild West motif.

He tonged the steaks onto a platter, grabbed his Pabst, and disappeared back inside.

They dined casually up in the family room of the split-level home. They watched a documentary about *The Top 10 Medieval Warriors of All Time*. Maggie had rolled her eyes, but Cale found it fascinating. He learned it had sometimes taken a year for an invading army to conquer a castle. Talk about persistence. Midway through the list, his phone buzzed, and he answered a number marked "Private."

Cale stepped across the room away from the couch while Maggie grabbed the remote and muted the TV.

"Detective Van Waring," came a bit too cheerful voice. "Hate like heck to bother you at home. But I wanted to touch base—after our little chitchat today."

The voice still rang fresh in his mind. "Mr. De…Miguel, right?"

"Hope I'm not interrupting."

"Just relaxing after dinner. Me and the little Missus." He winked at Maggie, who rolled her eyes a second time.

"Listen," the man said in earnest. "I was impressed with your demeanor today. You don't leap to rash judgments. Wait until your facts are straight. Am I right?"

Cale's mental alarm bells were ringing. The guy couldn't be calling just to fluff him. "The facts usually play themselves out, uh, Miguel."

"How true." The voice paused a beat. "You're wondering why I'm calling, I'm sure."

"Crossed my mind."

135

"I was touched by what you mentioned about your wayward brother Robin. His problems."

"Yeah, well, family. Right?"

"I hear you. My issues with Connie…" Miguel let it dangle before adding, "You might've caught wind during our talk. But Frank Kemp, from earlier, is leaving us in a month. Headed back to Minnesota. My father needs him for some other projects."

Cale pictured the hawk-nosed Kemp. Without them revealing as much, he remained a person of interest in last night's double homicide. With a pair of detectives paying a surprise visit, it came as no stretch that Kemp's departure plans may have suddenly accelerated.

"He seems capable. A Jack-of-all-trades-type."

"He'll be missed." Miguel didn't sound too broken up. "But here's the thing. Frank's leaving creates a gap in our management team. We've interviewed a few applicants already, but we're still searching for a new security head."

The conversation was edging toward the surreal, Cale decided. Was he hearing what he thought? Could Miguel DeSaul, CEO of a dairy farm, be offering him an actual job?

"I'm sure you'll find a great replacement." He peeked over at Maggie, who now sat with her head cocked, her expression somewhere between intrigue and amusement.

"Since you left, I've been doing some research," Miguel admitted. "Truth be told, the review board ruling against you was political BS. Your bogus suspension?"

Cale agreed without saying so.

"PC nonsense," Miguel added, "if you ask me."

Cale's suspension was public knowledge and had been revealed a half-dozen times in the local press. Nevertheless, he agreed with Miguel. The final decision had been a deal struck between the State Department and the State's AG. The Green Bay PD higher-ups had been leaned on, forced to discipline him in some fashion. They couldn't let a blatant case of self-defense

136

slide, could they? Not with a foreign diplomat being fatally shot inside his home and no one facing repercussions.

Even if said diplomat was a psychopath dressed up as a witch doctor and responsible for his own demise.

"Water under the bridge," Cale said evenly. "I'm getting some fishing in." It was a running joke among his friends. Cale had never landed a fish in his life.

"Still," Miguel said, "let me cut to it?"

Cut to what?

"We'd be offering you a splendid salary and benefits. A gold mine from what they're paying you now, Cale." He paused. "And did I mention this part? No stress?"

Cale wasn't sure how to respond and stayed quiet.

"Not much crime on dairy farms." Miguel chuckled. "And with your background, we'd match Kemp's current salary." He let his words dangle. "How's two-eighty-K a year sound?"

Cale was speechless. Seriously? Almost three-hundred-thousand dollars? To babysit forty or fifty employees? Half of whom started their shifts at four a.m. and spoke little English?

"Look. You don't have to decide anything right now." Miguel sounded like a time-share salesman. "But I've got some time tomorrow for us to talk if you'd like." He paused. "Lay it all out. Prove I'm not BS-ing you."

A giant roulette wheel was spinning in Cale's brain. The little ball stopped bouncing, resting in the slot marked *What would be the harm?* Right alongside *What have you got better to do?*

"I'm on paid leave another three weeks. In case—"

"Why I'm calling on short notice," Miguel said, his tone smooth. "Can't hurt to have a friendly chat, can it?"

A silent pause, then: "Yeah. I guess so—why not?" Cale mumbled. "How about I call you in the morning? After I've slept on it?"

Upon ending the call, Cale stood frozen near the couch, still surprised by the conversation. Maggie was staring at him with her eyebrows arched.

"Crazy. I know." She was an attorney. He didn't have to explain the call. "That farm CEO I was telling you about? Miguel DeSaul?"

She laughed. The words "farming" and "job interview" floated in the quiet between them, and Cale joined in her amusement. She'd be picturing him in a pair of bibs, denim shirt, pitchfork in one hand. Add a milk can or any of the other clichés you could toss in.

He rubbed his chin thoughtfully. "You're laughing at nearly three-hundred-K a year, by the way." His expression conveyed false seriousness. "With no POSs shooting at me." Cop speak for armed criminals.

Maggie pulled Hank onto her lap and scratched his neck. She relaxed her smirk. "You're not honestly considering this, are you?"

Cale resumed his spot beside her. He reached for his beer bottle on the coffee table and took a healthy swig.

CHAPTER 21

Typical June morning. Hazy sunlight and birds making a racket they called songs.

"You can't be serious!" Slink said, uncertain if his leg was being pulled.

"About taking a job with them?" Cale had his phone set on speaker as he drove. "I didn't say I was."

"Then why meet again?" Slink added, "I'm talking with the DA today. Both DeSaul and Kemp might be part of a murder investigation."

Cale stared out the Bronco's window. A tepid sun was disappearing behind smoke-bottom clouds. "Remember back in Narco? The times we went undercover?"

Slink caught the drift. "That's your plan? Infiltrate the bad guys on their home turf?"

"I've got the free time. How can it hurt to play along?"

Slink said resignedly, "Just watch yourself. And call me afterward. I'll fill you in on where we're at with the murders."

The Bronco headed west over the arching Tower Drive Bridge. It spanned the mouth of the Fox River, where it opened into the massive waters of the bay. The Wednesday morning traffic was sparse. Cale gazed out at the expansive body of water, a teal-blue canvas that stretched to the tip of the northern horizon. In the near distance, a trio of sailboats cut across the shipping lanes.

He had phoned Miguel earlier, hoping the man wasn't already on the first tee. It turned out Miguel, despite his affection for alcohol, was an early riser. Cale agreed to rendezvous with him for lunch and continue last night's discussion. The timing was perfect. He'd had time to mow the lawn while imagining how the job interview might unfold.

The idea still felt ludicrous, but he recalled how he had faked his identity in the past. Compared to many of those dangerous endeavors, this one appeared to be a walk in the park.

Cale planned to learn as much as he could about the Fillmore operation, especially concerning Frank Kemp. Determine if the guy had mentioned anything to Miguel about Cho Lin or the fentanyl formula. The man's responses would help him decide if Syan had been lying or if she was in deeper than she was letting on.

While he drove, he tried picturing what DeSaul did inside his mansion during the day. He didn't keep regular office hours, so what then? Made calls? Stamp collected? Internet porn? Regardless of how the CEO passed his time, it appeared to have little to do with farming.

Cale hadn't noticed signs of any wife or children. No bikes parked near the garages; no other vehicles perched outside the home. No signs of visitors or maintenance or landscaping people, and no signs of inside workers. Some small staff, at least, had to assist Mrs. Flench with general cleaning and housekeeping duties.

Kemp, as they'd learned, occupied the third floor. It allowed Miguel to wander ghost-like through the rest of the house.

A new thought occurred now to Cale.

Was it possible they were a same-sex couple? Miguel and Kemp? Neither had given off the usual indicators. But two guys living together in a secluded luxury house? Art dripping from the walls? The middle of nowhere?

He supposed he'd get a clearer picture during his second round with Miguel.

Cale's larger plan was to feign interest, perhaps accept the security job offer on a trial basis. Once on the inside, he'd uncover whatever shadowy secrets he could find on both Miguel and Kemp.

While he drove now, his brain kept pushing the idea further. The strategy would be to string it out for a week or two. After learning what he needed, he'd inform them his heart remained in law enforcement. A corporate job, though intriguing, just wasn't his cup of tea.

They'd shake hands and part ways.

Sometime after that, he pictured Slink and the boys returning to slap handcuffs around Kemp's wrists. Charge him with double homicide. As for Miguel? Perhaps indicted as a co-conspirator? Which he damn sure was.

Connie DeSaul, no doubt, would end up the overall winner in the deal. And maybe Syan, as well, being able to sleep better knowing Frank Kemp was behind bars.

For the moment, Cale didn't want to get too far ahead of things. First, he had to convince Miguel he was serious about the job offer. This was key. He replayed the scenario in his head, deciding his strategy wasn't too shabby for being cobbled together on short notice. But he would find out soon enough.

He now drove the identical route he had taken yesterday, heading west from the city. He wondered if Frank Kemp might also be on hand. Cale hoped so. Kemp would desire to have a say in his replacement, wouldn't he? So, the more, the merrier, he told himself. Perhaps Kemp would slip up, not suspecting Cale was working Cho Lin's murder case from the inside.

His phone's buzz interrupted his thoughts. The readout said, "Miguel DeSaul." Running late, he guessed.

"Mild change of plans, Detective," came the man's voice. "Listen. If my suggestion here doesn't work for you, we can reschedule."

"I'm just on the highway. What's up?"

"Are you familiar with the yacht club in Oconto?"

Cale pictured it. "It's north, right? Up the shoreline?"

"I'm purchasing a new boat," Miguel announced. "Would you mind if we switched our lunch to there?"

Cale thought about it. Changing the course wouldn't add much to his drive time. He wasn't in any hurry, regardless. And besides, talking to Miguel on neutral turf instead of his living room might prove advantageous.

"Fine. I'm fifty minutes away," he said.

141

Cale ended the call. He took the next exit a mile up, pausing at a four-way stop before swinging a lazy righthand turn. He headed back northeast, the same as taking the long hypotenuse of a right triangle. Still, it would be a scenic drive up the western bay shore. Clouds in the north were beginning to shield the sun. Even better. The traffic would be light.

He considered phoning Maggie but decided against it. He was not some tenderfoot who needed to report in every time the wind shifted. Besides, he was still having a business lunch with Miguel DeSaul. It mattered little that the location had changed. He'd get ahold of Slink afterward as well. Find out the progress on the Cho Lin case.

Brown and green farm fields and copses of thick forest were spread out all around him. Cale glanced in his rearview mirror. He imagined his reflection asking, Hey! Are you doing okay? Is the case going well for you?

"You mean for real?" he answered back, mocking himself out loud. "Let's see… I got two guys killed Monday night; my new shrink thinks I'm a nimrod; I'm suspended thirty days because a witch doctor was shot in my living room." He paused, awaiting a rebuttal. None came. "Oh, and my fiancé's pregnant. Odds are by the sick SOB who raped her."

"Your plate sounds full, laddie," his reflection said.

"On the bright side," Cale snickered, "I've been offered a job as a farmhand. Headed to the interview right now."

The reflection looked back sagely and said, "All we can do is move forward, right?"

With a sad shake of his head, Cale dissolved the fantasy conversation. He wondered, briefly, if conversing with his image in the mirror wasn't that much different than what he accomplished during his sessions with Dr. Pam. Less her dismissive pout and framed degrees on the walls, of course.

He set his GPS for the Oconto Yacht Club. It was on an inlet along the shoreline where it connected out to the bay's deeper waters. Cale set the cruise control and decided to relax and enjoy the drive. His private pity party was officially over. No more beating himself up.

The rest would take care of itself.

CHAPTER 22

"If we could just get a smidge of evidence that they're cooking meth." Connie paced through the front room of the B&B house. "Or importing oxys in from Minneapolis. Or Chicago."

"We know they are," Syan replied. She was sitting on the parlor couch in a burgundy tracksuit, legs extended, arms behind her head. "Kemp always has his side-gig going. You said so yourself."

Connie wore similar workout gear, though hers sported designer labels. They had just run two miles together, preferring the country air to the local gym, where the young yokels ogled their every move.

What none of these rural bumpkins realized, Connie marveled, was how her hundred-pound whip of a friend could kick any one of them to their knees in an actual altercation. Syan Hng had once held a record of 15–2 on the Taipei MMA junior circuit. She'd slip behind whichever dolt deserved it, apply a chokehold so tight he would pass out while his knees were buckling and robot-arms flailing.

But all that nonsense was beside the point. Right now, their dilemma was they were running low on time.

"I told you about Iowa," Connie said. "Remember? Where our managers got caught selling drugs to the workers?"

"Miguel was booted out, right?" Syan said. "Forced to either resign or face prosecution?"

"It's why I never thought they'd give him another CEO post. Not ahead of me." Connie's cheeks flushed. "Goes to show what a sexist pig my dad is."

"Kemp's got his ear," Syan said. And besides, he'll do anything to torment you."

Connie understood her friend would say no more. Syan knew better than to revisit the dark secrets Connie had once shared with her. She was the single living soul to whom Connie had revealed how Frank Kemp had raped her mother years ago. Repeatedly. Back when Connie had been ten years old. And if she hadn't warded the bastard off in their kitchen one night with a butcher knife, he would have done the same to her. Over and over. She'd slept much of her adolescent years with the same knife tucked beneath her pillow.

Connie felt the dark phantom of her memories slide behind her eyes. Yet, she knew if she remained very still and waited for the darkness to subside, she could avoid the depression and headache, which would force her to stay locked in her room for the next three days.

Both ladies sat in meditative silence and waited for the clouds to pass.

At last, Connie brightened. "I talked to Ferlando again." She pushed her headband up her forehead.

"And?"

"And nothing. Typical numb and dumber." She exhaled, frustrated. "He freezes up whenever I mention either Kemp or my brother."

Syan crossed her arms as if a chilly breeze had found an open window. "Speaking of which, I can't keep tailing Kemp anymore, Connie. Not after what the detective told me."

"You told Van Waring the truth, didn't you?"

Syan nodded. "But voicing it, I realized how much danger I'd been in."

Connie thought about it. With dead bodies accumulating now, whatever Kemp was up to, catching him at it was no longer a simple "gotcha" game. "Okay. I get it," she allowed. "Selling painkillers to farm kids is one thing—but killing people?"

"You know Kemp's nickname. His calling card?"

"Two-tap." Connie frowned. "For years growing up, I thought it was because of his stupid shoes."

"It's no joke now." Syan held her breath. She put one fingernail to her teeth, fought off the impulse to bite. "I know you don't want to hear this, but I'd feel safer if I had a gun."

"A bit over-reactive?"

"Not if what the detective said is true. Kemp might be a sadistic murderer." Syan rose from her spot and paced a few steps before turning back. "If he's killing people," she added, "why aren't we asking ourselves the real question?"

"Which is?"

"Who's paying him to do it?"

It was a question Connie was reluctant to dwell on. Rising from her chair, she swept off toward the stairs and headed for a quick shower before her scheduled doctor's appointment in an hour. "Let's talk about it when I get back," she called behind her.

After Connie had disappeared upstairs, Syan pulled her phone from her jacket pocket. Glancing at her contact list, she eyed the number the detective had given her.

The same as a thousand other yacht, cruiser, and sailing clubs dotting the shorelines of the nation's waterways, the Oconto Yacht Club members take pride in being thought of as an "exuberant" bunch. In group spirit with the few dozen highbrow, private club cousins on the coasts and ritzy inlets, these congenial local recreational clubs grant memberships to water lovers of every race, creed, and disposition. There stands group solidarity, displayed via each club's unifying motto:

HAVE FUN. RESPECT OTHER WATERCRAFT.
STAY SAFE!

Being based in Northern Wisconsin, a state renowned for its noble German heritage and lusty beer consumption, a fourth addendum might well be added:

PLEASE CONSUME
ALCOHOL IN *SEMI*-MODERATION

Nonetheless, Oconto pleasure crafters took their time on the water seriously. The long Green Bay arm was not as treacherous as Lake Michigan's colder, deeper depths, yet it remained a substantial water body. As part of the Great Lakes system, massive tankers and freighters made daily excursions up-and-down her fluid spine. A prominent U.S. Naval ship manufacturer was based just up the coastline in nearby Marinette. Deep waters equaled large boats and ships.

The Oconto chapter held her own. Many high-end luxury yachts and pricey cruisers were slipped at the club during the warmer months. And due to the club's emphasis on maintaining a relaxed atmosphere, a challenge arose toward distinguishing weekend warriors from the well-heeled wealthy class. At least while enjoying the airy, glass-enclosed luncheon room.

As Cale secured the Bronco and strode toward the doors, he noted how the wind had kicked up. The temp remained a warm 70-degrees, but the skies in the north formed a stretch of angry clouds. He wished he'd worn his windbreaker. Decorum be damned.

Uncertain if he was appropriately attired for a yacht club visit, he entered the front doors and strode to the hostess station. He had on charcoal Dockers and a button-down dress shirt. Surveying the thirty or so diners already seated, he was satisfied his clothing blended in. No jackets or ties were evident.

The pleasant blonde hostess wore a smile with dimples to match. She announced his name before he could speak. "Mr. Van Waring?" Cale agreed, and she added, "Mr. DeSaul is at his usual table. I'm LuAnn, by the way." Her brassy chest tag confirmed it.

Cale followed her Scandinavian form to a corner table.

Miguel looked up from his Diet Coke—Cale wondered if it might be rum-laced—and half-rose, extending a warm hand. "Detective," he said, smiling, "have a seat. Sorry about the sudden change of venue."

Cale accepted the leather-bound menu from LuAnn and sat as commanded. When she asked for his drink order, he pointed to Miguel's glass. "Same poison."

LuAnn drifted away without comment.

"Hope the drive was tolerable."

"GPS. Easy cruise. Set it and forget it." Cale was relaxed, off-handedly asking, "So what's the deal? You're buying a new yacht?"

"Friend of a friend's dumping a thirty-foot Sea Fox." He sipped his drink. "A fishing cruiser, less than a year old. Guy only took her out a half dozen times."

"I wouldn't have pegged you for the fishing type."

"I'm not. But I enjoy the water." He gave a conspiratorial wink. "Played Big Ten water polo for Minnesota."

Cale tried to look impressed. "It's a party yacht then?"

A headshake. "Smaller vessel. But I enjoy the open deck for when I take, uh, special friends out." He grew thoughtful. "For whatever the reason, ladies seem to be addicted to the water."

Cale recalled an obscure factoid. Threw it out there. "Did you know Wisconsin has more actual lakes than Minnesota? The famous Land of Ten Thousand Lakes?"

"Bull."

"Google it if you want."

A brunette waitress named Michelle arrived. She set down Cale's soda. "What can I get you sailors today?" she asked in a playful tone.

Miguel retook command. "Two Cod Florentines," he said as if Cale were one of his bikini boat pals. He glanced across the table. "Fish all right?"

Cale shrugged, no debate. He handed Michelle his menu, and she waltzed away. This was Miguel's show. The point was to keep the guy happy and talking. He sipped his soda, disappointed to find there was no rum additive.

"About my job offer," Miguel said, not wasting time. "I was serious. It could be a great opportunity for you."

Cale had rehearsed his game plan during the drive. Same as he'd told Slink, it wouldn't hurt to listen to whatever the pitch was. It'd be like playing a walleye on a twenty-pound test. Survey the landscape, find out as much as he could about Miguel and Kemp and their corporate farm operation.

He said, "Not sure I'm a good fit for security detail."

Miguel leaned back in his chair. "Not many homicide guys are, I suppose." He swirled the cubes in his glass. "But it's more a long-game play."

"I'm getting married in a couple of months. Baby on the way." Cale decided not to elaborate.

Miguel lifted an eyebrow. It was half-past noon, and his stubble was already coming in. He informed Cale he was no fan of sales pitches. But it was hard to knock the corporate life. Full benefits, low-stress nine-to-five hours, dental-medical, cushy retirement package. He allowed his words to float, then asked if his fiancée had provided any input?

"We talked. She's not a big fan of the idea."

"Yet with the family? Little Cale Junior on the way?"

Cale chewed a piece of ice.

Miguel accepted a soda refill, and Michelle deposited two plates of the steaming fish in front of them. Pasta and salads were on the side. He issued Cale a thoughtful look while asking, "Remember Scoop Skowing?"

"Of course." Cale blinked at the familiar name dropped out of the blue. Skowing was his former mentor back when he had first made homicide detective. He'd even helped Cale out by ID-ing potential kidnappers in his human trafficking case.

"He's the current Packers' security head these days," Miguel allowed.

Cale was aware of Skowing's crafty career maneuvering and gave a knowing nod. "It won't be easy stealing him away if that's what you're thinking."

Miguel swallowed a forkful of cod. "Just an example. He's a former detective who switched to corporate." He waved his empty fork. "Fat paycheck. Good security. And not out on the streets getting shot at every night."

Both men understood things weren't quite so dramatic. However, Cale had to admit that for a guy who didn't enjoy sales pitches, Miguel had thrown a couple of high sliders in for strikes.

CHAPTER 23

Jackie No Name's red pickup sat parked at the front curb of the Burmeister House. On the back outside deck, she and the girl named Syan were seated at the round table, sipping iced tea. The sky was turning darker in the north, with the wind swaying the branches above them.

Adding oddity to the scene was the silver .38 revolver sitting between them on the table.

"Lt. Van Waring? He's a straight-shooter," Jackie said. She had her hair clipped up and wore jeans and a white blouse. No makeup. But she felt the cool breeze adding color to her cheeks. "He's always played fair by me."

"I wasn't sure I should call you," Syan said. She glanced at the dangerous weapon with uncertainty.

"I was in the area. There's a farm couple I'm friends with nearby." Jackie studied the statuesque willow tree. "Cale must be convinced you need help."

"Says he'll delay telling the cops. Like I said, I was near the warehouse the other night, where that poor man—"

"You didn't do anything wrong, Syan. From what you told me. Just wrong place, wrong time."

Syan's smooth forehead creased. "That evil prick Kemp. I never thought he would hurt…." Her voice trailed off.

They were quiet as they considered her situation. "You didn't know him, did you?" Jackie asked pointedly. "The man who got killed?" She noted that Syan wore dark jeans and a bulky sweatshirt and clutched her collar from nerves or the breeze.

"I searched online," Syan confessed. "There's a news blackout or something."

"Next of kin delay. It happens."

Syan peeked at the handgun again.

"How about the second guy? Shot in that old hotel?" Jackie asked. She watched Syan, gauging her response. "Think they were connected somehow?"

"His name was Cho Lin James. Or Chin Loo," Syan said, hesitating. "Something. The news said he got out of prison a few months back."

"That's what Van Waring told me. He mentioned high-level drugs being involved."

The patio door opened, and Connie stepped out from the backdoor. She held a bottle of water. "Ladies." She greeted them evenly, but her demeanor cooled when she spotted the revolver on the table. She covered her response, shifting her eyes toward the high trees. "Breezy out here. Storm in the air."

"Connie." Syan's voice was tight. "I told you, it's for self-defense."

"I thought that's what martial arts taught you," Connie sniped. She released her breath, then turned and strode back into the house. The door slapped behind her.

Syan cringed at Jackie. "Sorry. I thought she'd be gone longer."

"She isn't PO'd for real, is she?"

"Just, you know, the surprise of it."

"Here," Jackie said, grabbing the empty revolver. "I'll hide it with a box of shells beneath the bathroom sink. We'll talk payment some other time."

Syan mumbled her thanks.

Above them, the clouds were sliding over a steamy sky. Both ladies followed Connie's trail, parading back into the house.

Syan's burgundy SUV was still in sight when Connie turned from the broad front window. She focused her eyes darkly on Jackie, who was sitting on the couch with her legs crossed man-style at the knee. Connie took the seat opposite her, tense, perched on the chair's edge. She said:

"Look. I don't give a crap what you do for a living."

152

"Syan called me. Asking for help. I happened to be in the area."

"I know what you are." Connie sat back, crossed the legs of her navy pantsuit. "Syan's a sharp-looking gal." Her eyes matched Jackie's tight gaze. "But when she's here—at my house—she's on my payroll, and we keep our relationship professional."

"She's not your pet, Connie. And with those killings the other night, I don't blame Syan for feeling spooked."

Connie inhaled, her temper rising. "We're both on a job. We're attempting to find out what my brother and his...his *scheming* cohorts are up to."

"By up to? You mean illegal drugs?"

"Among other things."

An awkward silence built between them. Connie studied the blonde, sizing her up. Jackie's skin showed a certain gloss ladies possess who've grown up with many niceties in their lives. Certainly not gals who dealt lethal firearms to make a living. She decided there was a darkness inside this visitor, some long-standing loss or even painful regret, a bleakness she sometimes recognized when staring in her own mirror at night.

Connie surveyed the blonde lady in silence, feeling the tension between them build.

"I see the score now. You're in love with her, aren't you?" Jackie asked bluntly.

The question caught Connie by surprise. Her cheeks flushed, and she jabbed back, "We keep things professional between us." Then added, "Unlike *some* people."

Jackie didn't take the bait.

Connie looked off at one corner of the room. She guessed she was conversing with a frustrated lady, one who hid her insecurities behind a need for control. It explained the business this gal was in.

"Look. I get you're an anti-gunner." Jackie brushed away a wayward hair strand. "I respect that. But I think Syan...she believes she's in real danger."

"Syan can take care of herself."

"I hope you're right. For everyone's sake."

A cold silence held the room.

"This is a small community." Connie's eyes darkened. "Tongues wag. You're the lady dating Rita Ross, aren't you? The pretty farmer's daughter?"

"My dating life is my own business."

Connie pressed her lips. "My point is," she said, "I need Syan's head clear around here."

"If you're talking about—"

"Two murdered bodies Monday night. Now we've got the cops sniffing around."

Jackie shook her head. "You don't think it merits her trying to protect herself?"

Connie watched Jackie's eyes scan the room. She spotted her guest's handbag on the hallway table outside the front entrance.

"Look. I'm sorry if I didn't clear things with you first," Jackie said, her tone subdued. She lifted from the couch, making to leave. "Tell Syan the weapon is optional. Her choice. Or yours. Whatever."

Jackie then strode from the room. She grabbed her handbag from the hallway table and opened the front door. She turned back, facing the trailing Connie. "Pass along my message, please. And I hope you both stay safe."

Connie observed the lady's long legs as she strode across the lawn to her truck. Jackie swung a U-turn after entering the vehicle, moving past the last-ditch tavern with the Blatz sign hanging, accelerating out of town. Connie watched the F-150 grow smaller as it swept along the distant farm fields.

Only then did she turn and walk back inside the house.

CHAPTER 24

Lunch was finished. Her mom preferred to handwash the dishes. Feather always helped with drying and afterward got to play thirty minutes outside. It aided digestion, her mom claimed. Exercise and fresh air cleared the girl's head for another three hours of afternoon studies.

Today, her mom sent her outside with the sky clouding up before the raindrops began to fall. The family lived by Mother Nature's clock. The cows and her dad had their daily appointments in the barn. Chickens did what chickens do all day. The dogs timed to the second when their food bowls would appear on the back porch. Even Rufus, the rooster, hollered at the first scarlet hint of daybreak.

Clockwork.

The wind was blowing stronger, Feather noted. The sheets ghost-flapped on the lines, and the three-foot-tall calf door on the old barn was clapping, at least when the breeze kicked up her dancing heels.

She was already outside with Trey, so her mom had no concerns. The dog's job was to look after her. With his ready muzzle and muscular shoulders and haunches, the yellow lab was well-suited to the task.

Feather lazed her way past the hen house and beyond the edge of the conifer bushes. She fired a yellow rubber ball off into the woods. Trey rushed for it and returned it a minute later. He smiled his lopsided grin and dropped it near her purple tennis shoes.

"Good boy," she said, smiling. She grabbed the ball, and he pierced her with brown eyes that would melt the heart of a princess.

Rufus cackled from the edge of the blood-colored shed. He strutted three steps one way, then the other, a dedicated private patrolling his turf.

"Thirty minutes!" Rita called from the porch. "And stay out of those woods."

Feather waved back. It was getting windier, and she was glad she'd grabbed her light green jacket. The screen door banged as her mom disappeared back inside.

Staring at her pet, she said, "At least we got out of drying dishes."

Trey whined, ready for another ball pitch. This time she crossed him up and fired it behind the barn, opposite the woods. The dog bounded after the rolling sphere.

She could hear Ben's tractor a quarter-mile off, bouncing over the soybean field. He wore headphones, she knew, listening to Z-Z Top or Lynyrd Skynyrd or another of his oldie's bands. Feather preferred modern songs flavored with a salsa beat, ones with more melody than lyrics, but she also had a soft spot for songs that told a story. Often about boys who left you then realized they screwed up. Or about confused passions like in *Twilight*.

Sometimes a rhythm got stuck in her head and kept repeating itself. But this only happened at times when Feather felt lonely, which was often, it seemed, because there was too much quiet amid the trees and hills and farm fields. Except when the frogs and crickets played their serenade at night. But that got boring about a minute in, without much story going on in their two-note racket.

She watched now as Trey got distracted behind the barn by a gopher. He dropped the ball, sniffed around a few steps.

"Bring it back, Trey!" she called. "Don't be a putz!"

It was a word her friend Iris used in bible study. But not when Pastor Roy's wife was around. Feather had tried it out a few times on her own and laughed at how the word rolled off her tongue. But she only used it on Trey.

Her command hit home. The dog forgot about the gopher and trotted back toward her with the ball in his teeth.

"C'mon, boy. Bring it back."

One of Ben's oldie songs popped into her head. Feather sang out loud, "Rolling, rolling, rolling, keep them doggies rolling...*Rawhide!*" She made a loud whip-crack sound and snapped her wrist, then laughed when Trey cocked his head as if to say, You're weird!

He dropped the ball at her foot. Feather picked it up, ignoring the drool.

She decided it was an excellent time to visit the stream—her favorite place on Earth and just a minute into the woods. The tree glade went about forty yards sideways before it ended, thinning into tall patches of weeds leading to the next road over. The waterway ran lengthwise down through the center of the woods. It cruised over smooth rocks and stuck logs and branches Ma Nature had placed there when she felt the urge. It was about two feet deep at most and was a low flowing creek. It gurgled in the spring and ran faster after the winter snowmelt.

Feather knew it was a fifteen-minute tromp up the opposite bank and through the denser woods beyond. They led to a clearing where the spooky old hay barn stood. It was an overgrown forest there, and she visited it sometimes. But don't tell Mom because she didn't want her wandering further than where the chicken coop stood. It would be peaceful now up in the run-down barn. Free from the wind shaping the clouds into bruise-colored battleships, which threatened to block out the sun.

Looking up, Feather saw the high branches doing their hula dance. The same dance she'd performed in her second-grade play. She was little back then, and not being home-schooled, and just a few years after her daddy had died. She missed him so much, or at least what she remembered of him. But it was how life worked, she'd learned. Everything lived and perished. So best not to dwell on dying too much. They would all meet later for a "Big Old Barbecue" party up in heaven, just as Pastor Roy told them.

Feather turned her eyes from the high swaying branches. She was ten now and no longer just a kid. She was ready for modern dances—even with boys and stuff. Leave the hula dancing to the younger kids.

She tossed the yellow rubber ball with the green "G" stamp deep into the trees once more. Trey's hindquarters disappeared after it. She followed in a slow walk, knowing he'd get distracted by smells and such. She stepped around a moldy old stump and some elderberry bushes. The air smelled loamy from damp leaves and moss and underbrush.

It was a netherworld of creeping shadows and gray light. Feather slipped further beneath the tree cover. Peaceful. Serene. A jaybird's trill called from above, and she knew a dozen fat crows were looking down at her.

Though in the woods, she could still discern the groan of Ben's tractor off in the far-away acres. Feather realized she couldn't see Trey, not anywhere. Nor could she hear him clumping through the heavy bushes. He'd probably found something more interesting to sniff at over by the brook, which was just through the trees.

She spotted the yellow ball in a cluster of ferns. She was about to pick it up when she stopped. A slender man stood about fifteen yards away, leaning casually against a white birch. She recognized his straw-colored hair, and she froze. She'd seen him in the woods a dozen times before staring out at her but never speaking, then disappearing, the way a magician does.

His crooked smile was disconcerting. Even worse, he held the matching green ball—with the yellow "G" stamp. It was the same ball she'd lost in here three weeks ago.

"Hello, Feather," the man said. "I found your other ball." He flipped and caught it.

A hundred thoughts rushed through Feather's head at once. She managed to stutter, "Where's my dog?" She looked past him at the opposite side of the stream, eyes swinging this way and that. "Where's Trey?"

The stranger glanced around with a concerned look, cast his eyes past her then looked back. "Maybe he went home?"

"Trey!" Feather shouted. The thick vegetation swallowed her voice. "C'mere, boy!" She whistled twice.

Only the wind's steady *swish* sounded through the high branches and the far-off chitter of tree birds and the thirsty gurgle of the nearby flowing creek.

"Trey!" she shouted more urgently.

The sun remained hidden behind the darkening clouds. The serene woods closed in around them, and still, the dog did not answer her desperate calls.

CHAPTER 25

"A beaut, isn't she?" Miguel asked. His eyes twinkled like a teenage boy who'd just purchased his first used car.

They had walked along the grass to the river inlet's edge, then onto the treated wooden pier of slip Number 14. In his street clothes and cop shoes, Cale felt about as landlubber as it got. Yet, he couldn't help but appreciate the shimmering crème-colored vessel perched in the water. It was a thirty-foot fiberglass Sea Fox with powerful triple outboards. The open hardtop covered the helm, and behind it extended two long lounge chairs. He imagined a pair of willowy swimsuit models lying atop the cushioned loungers.

It's how the sales brochure would picture it.

"Very nice," Cale said, studying the gently bobbing craft. The sun had disappeared behind the clouds by now.

Miguel ran his hand along a side rail the way a trainer strokes a thoroughbred. "The current owner took her across the lake to Grand Haven, Michigan and back, maybe five-or-six times tops. Says he wants something with more *oomph*."

Cale stood behind Miguel with his arms crossed. He was cautious of his footsteps, although the wide slats of the pier appeared dry. Up the inlet, other boaters were moving back to shore. The slips were beginning to refill with potentially nasty weather headed their way. A few larger engines slammed into reverse, churning the water as they backed into their slots, creating a brackish odor.

The breeze picked up again, ruffling Cale's hair. A bank of steam-colored cumulus formed in the north, though the temp remained sixty-five degrees. It would drop with the winds.

Miguel spoke over his shoulder. "I just want it for quick jaunts—business rewards and perks, that kind of stuff." He withdrew his mobile phone, frowned, pocketed it. "Reward our managers meeting quotas. Let them take her out for a few walleye runs."

"A business write-off?"

"What isn't?" Miguel's grin was cagey.

Cale studied the sleek power craft from where he stood. It appeared just off the sales floor. "What'd he say's wrong, again? The owner?"

"The nav system's a little wonky. But you get used to it."

"That's the GPS, right?"

"Seems our entire world's turning into nothing but one massive computer these days," Miguel groused. "Next we know, they'll computerize our flies to yank our dicks out to piss."

Cale laughed, unable to disagree.

Miguel grabbed the rail and swung himself onto the deck. "Beauty of this model is, you turn the key, and she flies." He removed his sunglasses, staring at Cale. "Sure you won't keep me company? Ten minutes out and back?"

Cale continued sizing up the Sea Fox. It made him wish he were twenty-three and living off his wealthy daddy's allowance. His father, however, had never gotten rich on a teacher's salary. And Cale's only allowance growing up had been a kick in the ass for not mowing the lawn or snow blowing the driveway on time.

Reality pulled him back to the present. He remembered the point of his plan with Miguel, why he was even standing here: *String him along, keep him blabbering.*

"Back right here in twenty minutes," Miguel repeated, cajoling. "Run out to deeper drink, spin her around, zip back in." His flash of teeth matched the sparkle of the Sea Fox's hull. "We even got ballcaps if you're afraid of mussing your hairdo."

Cale gazed out past the shallows where the watercolor pallet had shifted to a metallic iron gray. The flat horizon east extended as far as he could see. The waves were next to nothing. *The calm before the storm*, his brain cautioned. Perhaps the voice paratroopers heard before leaping from the backs of planes.

"You swear you know how to drive this thing?"

"Like Buzz Aldrin to the moon." Miguel chuckled.

Shedding his hesitation, Cale swung himself up and over the railing, landing on deck. His brain reminded him he had nothing better to do today, especially since he'd already mowed the lawn.

"In for a penny." He steadied his balance acrobatically. He wished he'd had on proper deck shoes, but at least his soles were cop-grade synthetic and wouldn't slip.

"Promise you'll get us back here before I puke?"

"Cross my heart."

Cale's brain snarked. *At least he didn't add the last part.*

Frank Kemp sat in his Regal with his phone at his ear. There were nine other vehicles parked in the Fillmore corporate lot. The voice on the line belonged to Clive Bawdy, the young chemist in charge of their drug manufacturing, who also doctored the products for distribution.

"The meth shipment arrived on time yesterday," Bawdy reported. "I counted it. Perfect card deck."

The guy's voice was tinny in Kemp's ear. Even though the lab—if you could call an abandoned feed warehouse lined with asbestos sheets a "lab"—was located just three miles from where Kemp was parked.

"Meaning fifty-two kilos," Clive Bawdy said, clarifying it for Kemp's benefit. "A-grade. Tested it myself."

"Excellent. When can you get it up to the barn house?"

"I spent all morning seasoning in the *eff* flakes." Bawdy meant adding fentanyl. "Ready in a couple of hours. I'll pick up Ferlando, and we'll store it there this afternoon."

"Good. Our guys are expecting delivery tomorrow night."

Kemp was satisfied with Bawdy's job performance thus far. Though twenty-five now, the guy possessed the rail-bone body of an adolescent. He had unkempt straw-blond hair and a hint of chin fuzz. Kemp knew thirteen-year-olds who appeared more developed than Clive Bawdy.

But as things stood, he didn't care how the younger dude looked. Bawdy got things done, didn't mess up, and he was making them money. Bottom line: it was all that mattered by Kemp's book.

Bawdy had worked for Kemp for over a year now, though he'd physically met the man only once during his latest three-month stay with Miguel. Bawdy had replaced their previous cooker, Browne, who'd been caught flapping his jaws in one of the local taverns. A negative by Kemp's rules. Mouthy Browne's carcass had since been deposited a few counties over, planted beneath a pressed dirt pile in a state-owned pine forest, the remains too deep for scavengers. In case of questions, a crumpled airline receipt hidden in his freezer suggested the man had relocated to Saskatchewan.

Bawdy's job was to cut the product to increase profit margins, then add fentanyl flakes to create extra zing.

At transport time, Bawdy and Ferlando delivered the goods to their various dealers and collected payments. The dealers were in seventeen different rural towns and villages, working over five counties. Kemp knew it was a six-hour circle trip there and back, but what did he care? He doubted either man would swap positions with any of the working stiffs who spent eight-hour shifts milking Holsteins and inhaling cow farts.

Kemp exited the Regal to stretch his legs. He focused on their discussion as Bawdy said, "After it's delivered, Frank, I was thinking about putting together a little gathering. Say next Friday night? Let our hair down, slosh a few brewskies to celebrate?"

Kemp felt his face freeze. He wondered, What the hell is he saying...? He can't be this dumb, can he?

"Nada!" Kemp barked, irritated and stunned at the same time. "And you don't touch so much as a doobie until after deliveries are finished. *Capiche?*"

163

"Loud and clear," Bawdy said, backtracking from Kemp's verbal firing squad. "Sorry. Getting a little ahead of things."

Kemp wasn't through with his tirade, adding, "And that warehouse better be scrubbed cleaner than a nun's butt."

Ending the call, Kemp thought he heard a dog's bark in the background. *Click.* He stared suspiciously at his phone. Faded connection? Tower interference? He let it pass, deciding he must be hearing things. No imbecile would be stupid enough to allow an animal into a drug lab.

About to reenter his vehicle, Kemp's eyes surveyed the distant grazing pasture. A lone burgundy SUV was cruising along the upper county road. He recognized the make and model. A single driver headed to town on some errand. Too far away, thankfully, for her to spot him among the lot's other parked vehicles.

He had been planning to sign a few papers inside. Screw it. There was now a new fish to fry. Behind the wheel, Kemp started up the Regal and swung it free of the Fillmore lot. A bloodhound on a fresh scent, he accelerated off in the direction the Toyota had been moving.

Ending his call, Clive Bawdy looked out the door into the adjacent room across the hallway. The girl in the jacket remained taped to the wooden chair. He had panicked at hearing the dog's yap and searched around for his .38. Fire it if he had to and call it self-defense. Instead, he realized the animal had only been coming around from the sedative, attempting to rouse the tied-up girl's attention.

The dog turned his way now, whimpered. The girl lolled her head, almost waking, moaning beneath the duct tape over her mouth. While he'd been conversing with Kemp, she had never glanced his way. Still, he wanted to avoid her becoming a screaming nutjob. Pointing his gun at the animal had thus far compelled her to obey. The barrel worked like a magic wand— aim at the pooch, she does what you say.

Bawdy grabbed his weapon, stepped out into the hallway. He eased the other room's door closed, separating himself from the pair. Problem solved.

Back in his processing room, he opened the refrigerator. He lifted a plastic container out and laid a paper towel on the counter, withdrew a fat clump of raw hamburger from the container, and plopped it on the paper.

He grabbed the baggie from the broad table behind him. It contained white fentanyl powder.

CHAPTER 26

The cracking sound surprised Cale. Loud as a gunshot.

Standing with one hand holding the boat's open hardtop brace, the noise caused him to turn toward Miguel with a surprised look.

They were a mile out on the bay now with the Sea Fox cruising east toward deeper depths. The width of the water body stretched twenty miles horizontally across. Behind them, the shoreline had receded, shrinking in size.

Miguel was at the helm. He focused on the computerized instrument panel and had pressed a couple of buttons, which set the craft on autopilot. He'd then bent down and opened a beer can—the *cracking* sound—after withdrawing it from the hard plastic Yeti cooler at his feet.

With the wind in their faces, Cale shouted, "What the hell, Miguel?"

The man glugged from the can and grinned. "This is the life, eh, Detective?"

Cale felt the hackles on his neck rise. He watched Miguel, still holding his beer can, turn and lift the container by its handles and carry it out to the aft deck, where he set it down alongside one of the loungers. Miguel's words echoed in his head. *Back here in twenty minutes.* They were already ten minutes out.

Cale wasn't bothered that no one was driving the boat. Everything was computerized. What concerned him more were the brutish clouds gathering along the northern skyline. These and the cooler of beer on ice. At the same time, he recalled a rule he'd learned from his years working undercover: Stay in character. Never blow your cover.

Thus, he didn't flinch when his new friend reached inside the blue-hued cooler and withdrew a second can.

"Here you go, amigo." Miguel held the dripping can out toward Cale.

"We're swinging back in a few minutes, aren't we?"

"Relax. Neither of us is punching a time clock."

Cale accepted the can. He popped it open and took a swig, reminding himself to stay calm, drink the beer. He remained standing just outside the helm, holding the hardtop's side brace.

Miguel hadn't put on a life jacket as they had cruised away from the yacht club dock. Cale wondered if it was some machismo test. Besides, they'd be back at the slip before he'd even manage to get the thing buckled. He searched around now, surveying the bins where they might be stored.

"You could get used to this, Detective!" Miguel called back over the engines, sipping his beer again. Despite the growing darkness in the northern sky, the man still wore his sunglasses. The wind ruffled his hair, and he became a two-bit version of Tony Montana for a moment.

"I doubt security heads cruise around in boats all day." Cale stepped closer to be heard over the stiff breeze. He kept one hand on the back of the lounger.

"They can if there're no problems to solve."

Cale took another sip of beer, noting the miles of empty water around them.

"It's called being proactive!" Miguel waved his beer can, shouting as he turned his head back. "You never allow crap to develop, so there's no crap to fix. *Capiche?*"

The water felt choppier. Cale again steadied his feet on the deck. They heard a beep from the navigation system. Miguel set his beer in the holder and stepped back to the helm. He analyzed the computer screen.

"Midpoint!" he shouted to Cale. "Seventy feet deep here." He turned, and his eyes scanned over the craft. "What do you think? My little souped-up jet ski?"

"Every guy's wet dream."

Cale squinted up at the sky to their left. Purple clouds glared back, and steel-gray water undulated all around them now. He watched as Miguel pressed a few buttons on the counsel, put one hand on the steering wheel.

"I'm idling," the man announced. "We'll swing around manually so we don't catch a roller." The Sea Fox reduced speed, the outboards churning the water to foam. The bow pointed north, and the boat rocked in the waves like a giant bobber.

Once they headed back to shore, Cale imagined that even the harshest wind would be no match for the trio of powerful outboards.

Miguel stepped out from beneath the hardtop and back to the foot of one lounger. He removed his sunglasses and perched them atop his head. Staring down at the cooler, he called, "I better get this back inside!" He grabbed it by the handles and lifted it waist-high yet didn't move from the lounger's base.

"Hey!" he called to Cale. "Mind checking your phone? I want to know if there's any reception this far out."

Cale withdrew his mobile and stepped farther onto the aft deck. The rocking boat caused him to stagger. He was standing just beyond the loungers and auto-dialed Slink's number. Around them, the wind snapped at the water. Whitecaps now crowned the undulating waves, and the Sea Fox circled in a slow rhythm.

Miguel remained a yard away, still holding the cooler's handles. It was heavy, with still twenty full beer cans and melting ice inside.

"Got anything?"

"Too far out." Cale squinted at his screen. He raised the device to the sky, angling it this way and that—still nothing. The boat pitched again, and he reached down and grabbed the guard rail, steadying himself.

"Here." Miguel stepped toward him. "Hold this for a sec. I'll try mine."

Cale pocketed his phone and accepted the cooler from Miguel. He held it by both plastic handles with the chrome side rail behind him.

Miguel worked his phone as a geyser of water showered them both. The wind gust swept the sunglasses from his head, and they bounced against the railing, dropping over the waterside faster than he could reach.

"Son of a...."

Miguel bit his lip and backed a yard from where Cale stood. The nearby engines roared, churning the iron water, moving the boat around the way a large shark circles a life raft.

Cale stood with his legs spread, his back to the rail. The fullness of the cooler aided his balance. The wind *whooshed* around them again, and another wave lifted the boat. Miguel's shoes slid on the pitching deck as if some high school bully had shoved the back of his shoulder. He was propelled forward and slammed hard into Cale.

Releasing one handle, Cale grabbed for the safety rail while being knocked backward. He missed it and found himself airborne, falling with his arms and legs flailing. He glimpsed the overcast sky and the side of the boat as the cold water swallowed him from behind.

The splash was lost inside the blustery wind and noise from the throbbing engines. Cale bobbed his head back above the water's surface, spitting, gasping. His legs and arms worked to remain afloat. The weight of his clothes became an anaconda's grip. More surprised than anything, he rubbed the water from his eyes and stared up at the steep hull of the bobbing vessel.

Seventy feet of water below flashed into his mind. It might as well be a thousand. Miguel was gripping the side-rail now, peering into the water with his eyes wide.

"Throw me a life vest!" Cale shouted. "Or drop the ladder down."

Miguel remained frozen, his eyes unblinking headlights.

Cale side-stroked closer but was careful to avoid the churning engines nearby. The hull was elevated five or six feet above the surface. The waves continued pushing him around. The deck was too elevated for Miguel to reach down and pull him aboard.

What in the hell's wrong with him? Cale's brain shouted. The man appeared half-comatose. "Miguel! Get moving—dammit!"

The rolling water scooped the boat up and down. Cale recognized a blue flash about thirty feet away. The cooler was on its side but still afloat. A blink later, it was swamped by a wave and disappeared.

The sky was a deeper purple. The wind slapped at the Sea Fox, and it seemed to free Miguel from his trance. Cale was drifting further away. "Get the long pole!" he shouted while dog paddling. "Something I can grab!"

Miguel stepped back beneath the open hardtop. Cale remembered spotting a life ring attached to one low door. Was it where the lifejackets were stashed? Miguel appeared back at the rail, holding a long aluminum pole. It had a hooped fishing net attached to one end. Better than a lifejacket, Cale decided. He tried paddling closer as he watched Miguel brace one leg over the railing. The man leaned forward and extended the telescoping pole out above the water. Cale lurched for it like a madman, but his furious flailing gained him no more than five feet. Another wave crested, rocking the boat. Miguel gathered himself and inched the pole out farther, stretching his arms.

With a lunge, Cale's fingertips caught hold of the netting.

Both men extended to their max. Between them, the pole quivered and dipped below the pulsating waves. Cale swung his left hand and caught hold of the metal hoop. "Pull me in," he gasped, spitting water.

Miguel adjusted himself until he had both knees braced against the inner railing. He leaned back the way an angler fights a marlin. "I'm trying!" he shouted into the wind.

"Hurry up."

"But first," Miguel called down, "give me the passwords!"

It didn't register. Water had invaded Cale's ears by now. Add in the engine noise and whipping wind. He shouted back, "What? I didn't—"

"The passwords!" Miguel demanded again. "From Cho Lin! The fentanyl formula!"

Cale squinted up at Miguel's ruddy face. He barked out, "Quit dicking around!"

"The passwords. *Now!*" A wave rolled, undulated, ebbing as the next one came. "You don't have much time."

The word "time" gonged in Cale's head like a funeral knell. Prior survival training reminded him—exposure, water rescue, body temps. He guessed the water at fifty-eight degrees, give or take. When hypothermia sets in, a person's blood rushes to protect their internal organs. Once this happens, motor control of the fingers, then hands and limbs, begins to fade. Soon afterward, mental clarity clouds. This is when statistics turn grim. Victims often drown because they forget they can't breathe underwater.

Cale didn't have many options. It was doubtful any rescue teams were being assembled. No one even knew they were out here. He considered his response. Miguel had set a trap, he realized now, and he'd been chump enough to walk straight into it.

"All right!" he shouted back, spitting water. He fixed his eyes on the man.

"The passwords. Now!"

"Okay. Just pull me in first."

Miguel's laugh was high-pitched. "Not a great time to be negotiating, Detective."

Cale bobbed beneath another wave. He spit out more briny water. His fingers were numbing, but he couldn't let go of the pole—his lifeline.

Holding a losing hand, he shouted, "All right! I'll give them to you."

Miguel now lodged his end of the extended aluminum pole high between his legs, his thighs holding it in place. He withdrew his mobile phone from one pocket and shouted down, "Ready. Let's have it."

Cale informed him he needed to locate a Facebook site on the dark web. With the mobile at his lips, Miguel repeated this into his voice app. Then Cale shouted to him the login ID and passwords, as best he could remember them from Cho Lin's final note. He watched as Miguel repeated it all letter for letter into his phone. When accomplished, Miguel ordered him to repeat it all back to him once more.

While Cale did this, Miguel verified that his mobile had recorded the letters and symbols all correctly.

The process took four minutes to accomplish.

"Now, your turn—pull me in." Cale's throat rasped against the wind, and the air held a briny seaweed smell.

Staring down from the rail, Miguel's smirk became a grimace. He pocketed the phone and freed his end of the aluminum pole from between his legs. But instead of pulling it toward him, he released the pole unceremoniously over the boat's railing. They watched together as the long handle smacked the water's undulating surface. It began at once to sink into the murky depths.

Cale scrambled to hold his end of the pole as it descended below the choppy waves. After a minute of frantic struggle, he accepted that it was pointless and relinquished his tight grip, paddling in place, scowling venom up at Miguel.

"You bastard!" Cale cursed, ignoring his inner voice's cautioning, Don't piss off the only man who can save your life!

"What can I say?" Miguel shouted down at him. "Business is business."

A rolling wave swallowed Cale's furious shout at him.

Miguel stepped back to the helm. Cale began swimming toward the boat with fury, his final chance at survival. As he neared ten feet from the hull, the engines revved, spinning the craft, pushing him below the water's surface. He quickly emerged, kicking and working his arms, hacking up water as he struggled.

Miguel popped his head around the hardtop support brace. Looking down, he shouted over the turbulent engine roar,

"About that job, Detective! I've decided to go in a different direction."

Cale held one middle finger high.

He watched as the Sea Fox blasted away, a rooster tail spewing in its wake. The craft bounced over the choppy surface and slapped away an insignificant wave. Then it curled around in the distance and sped back in the direction from which they'd come.

CHAPTER 27

Rita removed her garden kickers at the backdoor at the Ross farmhouse and slipped into sneakers, thankful the rain had held off. Her canvas bag held four handfuls of beets and radishes, and she ran them in the sink beneath cold water.

A glance at the stove clock showed 1:59 p.m. Feather was not in her spot at the dining room table. She was supposed to be doing math or physics problems today. Rita couldn't recall. The grandfather clock ticked, and she called out, "Feth? You in the bathroom?"

Silent house. Now the clock chimed twice from the dining room.

Rita dried her hands and drifted from one room to the next. She peeked in the den, the bathroom. She climbed the stairs to the second floor. Her daughter's bed was made, the room somewhat orderly—Khaki shorts on the bedspread, stuffed dolls, boy-band posters on each side of a crucifix. They all stared back at her with blank faces.

Downstairs again, Rita stepped out onto the back porch and surveyed the empty yard. Her eyes scanned the barn and storage sheds. On the move, she searched both sides of the house. She peered out past the henhouse and woods, concern growing, looking at the entry spot the girl and Trey took when exploring.

She whistled three times. A signal. Seconds later, old Satchmo drifted from the barn where he'd been dozing with the cows. Rita turned a half-circle and called out:

"Feather! Back in the house right now."

A blackbird answered from somewhere. She heard Ben's tractor grinding out in the field, but she couldn't see him around the barn. The sky showed storm clouds in the north. The first plops of rain splashed her forearm, and she knew Ben would cut things short and come in.

They had a system between them where his phone screen lit up for messages. Rita texted with her thumbs: *Seen Feth? Not in house.*

Her phone buzzed back: *Neg. Coming in. Rain.*

She walked through the yard and flung open the barn and shed doors, calling inside. Nothing. Then she moved opposite past the henhouse, shushing the cluckers and Rufus as he strutted about trying to impress her. Rita entered the woods between birch trees, stepping over the tangled brush beneath her feet.

She gave a crisp whistle.

"Feather? Trey?" Her voice echoed off the moss and ferns and was swallowed by the high branches. No answer. Not far away, she could discern the running creek's babble. A squirrel scampered somewhere. A woodpecker knocked a hollow sound.

Everything was calm and peaceful, the rain yet too soft to penetrate the leafy overhang.

Frank Kemp had always considered himself a clever SOB. He often reminded himself of how he could have been a master chess player, could see three, four, or even six moves ahead of whatever game was being played.

These were Kemp's thoughts now as he cruised down the street of the ten-block town of River's Bend. He'd spotted the burgundy Toyota parked at the fuel pump of a Fill-'er-Up station, its driver likely inside. He cruised on past. The Asian gal was clever, along with being self-aware. Not to mention she'd been trailing him around for the past two months. She would spot his Regal easier than a bird watcher spies an oriole.

Kemp pulled up two blocks ahead and swung into an alley behind an old corner tavern. He kept his car's grill pointed out toward the main drag, just enough to view the street traffic.

The wind around them was picking up, and the blotchy sky had turned overcast. Kemp observed a trio of boys as they strolled along the quiet side street, one dribbling a basketball.

He imagined they planned on getting in a few shots at a nearby park before the rain came harder and scurried them back indoors.

From his spot in the alley, he calculated where the Asian might head after her fuel stop. People bunched their errands together. The gal kept her hair cropped short, so the beauty shop was low on the list. This left the pharmacy or local supermarket. Kemp knew both locations were situated along the main drag.

He checked his phone for updates from Miguel—whom he knew was up to his own mischief. Kemp was anxious to hear any news. If all went well, the tricky part of their plan ought to be over with by now. But thus far, no messages.

Not that Miguel, whom he had always considered more flash than substance as a criminal, wouldn't have his hands full with the Green Bay detective. Van Waring seemed to have an edge about him, a cop who carried a chip on his shoulder. He'd been pleasant enough when the detectives had visited the house yesterday, but Kemp knew better. He had seen the type many times before. Van Waring was not a man to be taken lightly.

They had planned to catch the detective by surprise, out of his element. As for Miguel, Kemp gave the guy credit for coming up with the idea and being willing to take a considerable risk. It took *cajones* to attempt drowning a lawman. Kemp would report to Sevvie how his son had finally grown a pair if they pulled it off.

He glanced at the phone again. Nothing. But maybe "No news..." as the old saying went. Unless the twit Miguel had somehow dropped his phone to the weedy bay bottom. Stranger things had happened. Kemp knew this truth better than most.

He was frowning at the grim thought when he spotted the Toyota slide through an intersection. He waited a few seconds before shifting the Regal back in gear.

The Sea Fox had vanished. The wind had increased, and rain slashed down with force. Another wave swept over Cale, and it pushed him beneath the rust-gray water. He bobbed back above the surface and inhaled. How long can this go on? he asked himself, already knowing the answer.

How long before his legs stopped kicking, and he didn't come back up?

He was shivering so much now his anger with Miguel had subsided. He was locked in self-preservation mode. Another wave lifted him with its swell. He could not discern land in any direction but remembered there were sparse islands scattered around the bay. Where they were was anyone's guess. And swimming off in any one direction was suicide.

Cale was at the mercy of the chilly water and stiff winds. The storm would blow him wherever it chose.

Past rescue courses he'd attended came to mind. A fit human could stay clear-headed for about two hours in fifty-five-degree water. This, however, was *with* a floatation device. Shortly after that, your brain began hallucinating, seeing things not truly there. The same way lost desert wanderers imagine seeing water and palm trees from miles away.

Cale thought about drowning again. The final big gulp. Floating down, down, down like in the movies. He recalled that when pitched from the boat, he'd released hold of the beer cooler. Soon afterward, he had glimpsed it floating. But the plastic Yeti was long gone by now, having vanished in some random direction.

And as if things couldn't get worse, he heard the pounding of jungle drums deep in his head. You've got to be kidding! his mind screamed. Cale pictured some jokester demons looking down at him, laughing like drunks playing bar dice.

Did he have any tools at his disposal? The wet phone in his soaked pants pocket was useless—he'd tried it—unless it was somehow giving off a GPS signal. He considered the Navy SEAL trick, where the wind could turn your empty pant legs into a life jacket. Still, he understood it was the hypothermia that would get him before anything else.

There was nothing he could do to prevent it.

Another wave crested, pitching him up, dumping him back. The rain slashed fiercely, cutting across his face and neck.

Forty yards from where he bobbed, Cale spotted a small glimmer of teal atop the rolling surface. A log? A flash of pale blue? By some insane impossibility, could it be the floating Yeti chest? He began swimming with frantic strokes, battling the obstinate water.

The throb of hollow jungle drums grew louder inside his head. Ignoring the sound of bells and shakers, Cale thrashed his arms and legs forward. Whether real or imagined, he had to take the chance his guardian angel was somehow offering him a lifeline.

There are countless different ways to snuff out a human life. Some are quick and creative, others bloody, screaming, and messy. In Frank Kemp's four decades as the right-hand man to gangster Sevvie DeSaul, he had perfected most variations. Tire irons, garrotes, stilettos, machetes. Or, of course, the film industry standard, a 9mm with an attached suppressor.

The point is, they were all just options in the tool kit. You picked your instrument depending on the situation—the same as how a carpenter or plumber or brick mason would. But if you wanted to send a bloody message, you double-tap two bullets straight into a douchebag's cranium. The spatter of blood, bone, gristle, and gray matter sends an unmistakable message to anyone listening.

On the other hand, say you want things done fast, with little noise and a touch of finesse. In such cases, it's better to go with a fast-acting injectable substance. Take it from the Russians. You pump a chemical—potassium cyanide, for instance—into some jerkoff's bloodstream, their eyes roll back, and they lose consciousness in under a minute.

Quick, clean, simple. And not a single bloody smudge to soil your loafers.

Kemp had read the Asian lady's bio. Syan Hng had a history of being no slouch herself in the self-defense arena. She'd garnished a couple of black belts and won some MMA fights. The point was, either she could take a punch, or she couldn't. Kemp planned on not having to find out.

The drizzle was falling harder now as the Regal swept along the main drag of the small-sized town. He tailed the burgundy SUV from five cars back. It was easy to stay hidden with bright headlights around them. Two minutes later, Kemp noticed the SUV turning into a corner strip mall.

He navigated the Regal down the street alongside the parking lot. Then he turned the corner and eased to the curb on the adjacent side street. Better tree cover. The Asian gal, he saw through his blurry windshield, had exited and was fobbing her vehicle. He doubted she'd spot him in the rain.

Kemp reached into his glove box for his Rolljam radio device. It was smaller than a cell phone. A month ago, he had primed the Toyota and hacked the vehicle's rolling wireless code. Today was the day he would use it.

The SUV had pulled into a slot facing a string of five small storefronts. A dry cleaner, a card and candle shop, a health food store. Seven or eight other vehicles were parked in the front row. Kemp exited and strode over the muddy grass strip, then behind the stationary cars and SUVs. His head down, jacket collar up, he employed the drizzle as his ally. He was PO'd that his shoes were already damp.

Kemp stepped between two vehicles and swiped the Rolljam near the Toyota's front door lock. All five locks popped in unison, and he was pleased the headlights hadn't flashed on or horn sounded. He circled the front and passed back down the passenger side.

Small villages like River's Bend possessed scant security cameras. Kemp looked around anyway. With the coast clear, he raised the burgundy SUV's rear hatch and crawled nimbly inside. The roomy back provided ample space for his bulk. He pulled the hatch closed behind him, listening to the rain patter on the roof.

Kemp relocked the inner locks and slipped acrobatically into the wide backseat. No easy task. He angled his legs along the rear foot space, his shoulders hunched behind the driver's seat. Peeking through the gap between the front seats, he noticed a leather handbag sitting half-open on the passenger side. The gal must have grabbed her pocketbook from it before exiting.

He peered out at the food store to spot what she'd be carrying, knowing his presence would be shielded by rain steaks coating the SUV's windows. He hoped she didn't open the rear latch or back door. If so, he'd use the silent double-tap before she could react.

There he waited, figuring on around ten minutes.

It didn't take quite that long.

Kemp watched his target exit the store with two small carry bags. As she approached, he ducked himself down further. The driver's door clicked open, and the lady slipped inside, stretching her bags across the console to the passenger seat. She closed the door and buckled herself in, then fumbled momentarily with her ignition key.

From behind, Kemp extended his meaty left hand around the headrest and clamped it over the lower half of the petite woman's face. She went rigid, arched her back, too startled to scream. At the same time, his right hand slipped between the seatbacks, and he plunged the needle into the exposed skin of her neck.

His firm left hand muffled her cries. She herky-jerked her legs and shoulders, twisting, spasming, grabbing first for his hand, and then the seatbelt clasp. Then she stabbed at his hand with her car key, bucking around wildly. This lasting for a near half-minute. When her chin dropped at last, and she fell limp, he pulled the needle back and allowed her to slump sideways over the console. Still locked by the seatbelt, she reminded him of a crashed fighter pilot.

Kemp now caught sight of her purse again. The new bags she'd set there had nudged the flap open further. The silver glint of a revolver handle showed from inside.

He muttered, "Huh."

The narcotic was an extreme dose for her body weight. Her heart had twitched and spasmed three-four-five times before slamming to a stop. Kemp pictured her ghost floating above them now, giving him the finger as it drifted off somewhere.

He smirked. Neither she nor her ghost were any longer his concern.

CHAPTER 28

The rain-soaked Sea Fox now drifted a quarter-mile off the western shore. The waves crested and dropped. Rain lashed in sheets, stippling the water, a trillion shotgun pellets.

Miguel stood at the helm beneath the vessel's open hardtop, staring at the nav screen. He assessed the depth, the temp, the shifting wind direction. Thirty feet to bottom. No watercraft in any direction. Every sane boater had found safe harbor by now and was gathered at a card table or cocktail bar.

The roiling waters crashed over the vessel's starboard side. Miguel cut the engines and allowed the Sea Fox to rock and drift. He pushed the button for the thirty-pound anchor, and it sunk faster than a bowling ball tossed overboard. The craft rode low and bobbed.

Although their intricate plan had been hastily assembled, the storm played the lead actor in this play, cast as the perfect villain.

Miguel opened a front storage cabinet—time for his third act. The churning waters rocked the vessel as he removed and bundled his clothes and deck shoes, then slipped into the wetsuit. The water would steal his breath, but he'd be ashore before his adrenaline rush wore off.

Under twenty minutes, according to plan.

Stepping back to the stern, Miguel raised the floor panel that exposed the bilge pump and hoses. Water was seeping in from a hole drilled through the outer drain plug. He'd paid five-grand in cash last night to a harbor mechanic who had worked less than a minute. A fifty-dollar job, with the extra cash for the guy to imagine he'd dreamt the whole business.

On his stomach now, Miguel felt the inflow of water. It wouldn't take too long. A ten-foot squall might scuttle her, despite the fiberglass hull. He didn't give it much thought either way. Let the insurance investigators haggle it out.

Back at the helm now, he grabbed his mask, a pair of breathing canisters, and the Scuba-Jet. It was just inches longer than his forearm, capable of propelling him at five MPH underwater.

Miguel surveyed the choppy surface. A bolt of lightning flashed far off in the northern sky. Another wave slapped the hull, and he turned his attention back to the nav screen. They had decided against any "Mayday" call or firing a flare. So the story would go, a giant squall had swamped the vessel, pitching both Miguel and the landlubber detective overboard. The winds and waves had hit so fast that the explanation would hold up even under expert scrutiny.

The radar screen remained a colorless gray hue with no other vessels on display. Miguel withdrew his phone, hoping he had service this close to land. His fingers wet and numb, he texted Kemp: *Boat sinking.* The rest had been arranged.

Miguel powered off the phone and stuffed it into his waterproof clothes bag. He wanted to fling the bag into the deep waters, but his mobile contained the needed information. He slipped on the diver's fins, then velcroid the Scuba-Jet to his left forearm. The full canisters would each render him fifteen minutes of oxygen, more than required. He donned his snorkel mask and stepped to the outer rail.

Miguel had a fleeting image of Van Waring floating face down in the water somewhere, motionless. *Se la vie.*

Then he jumped from the listing boat with a splash and disappeared beneath the gunmetal surface.

Ben eased the John Deere tractor through the double-wide doors of the equipment shed. He left it sitting angled, not bothering with the usual parking job. He'd get to it later. The rain pelted the metal roof the way it did during hailstorms.

He secured the doors outside, then jogged across the soggy grass and mud of the backyard. The chickens were already inside their coop. The back door of the house opened as he climbed the porch steps, Rita holding it wide. She had on jeans and a sweatshirt, and her forehead was creased with worry.

"Anything?" he asked.

Her headshake. "No signs of Trey, either. Must be with her."

"Any note? Nobody pick her up for a church thing?"

"She'd have told us."

Ben considered this, wiping his feet on the soiled, all-weather rug before stepping inside.

"Should we maybe call that Green Bay detective?" Rita asked hopefully. "He gave me his number."

"Police?" Ben turned to her in the kitchen. "She's gone off before." His frowned. "You know how her imagination gets wrapped up in things."

"Think she went into the deep woods?" she asked. "Or maybe the spooky old barn? Up past the stream?"

"Better us looking than talking about it."

Ben grabbed his flashlight from the drawer and turned toward the door. Rita pulled her denim jacket off a hallway rack and put on a baseball cap. Back outside, they trotted once again over the sodden backyard, heading to where the high trees stood as if guarding their fortress.

His teeth were too frozen to chatter. Ripples appeared in the water as the heat seeped out of him. Cale imagined he saw a fish jump and was thankful he wasn't afloat in the ocean. Big fins would be circling.

Hallucinating, his mind warned. *Hypothermia...setting in.*

He continued dog paddling, nothing visible for miles. He had swum toward the blue flash earlier, but the spot was empty when he finally got there. He paddled in a circle until another wave crashed, pressing him below the surface, this time holding him there.

Cale emerged seconds later, spitting water like it was poison.

The waves had formed a new pattern, with every fifth one cresting. The wind gusts forced him low in the drink, and the slashing rain held him there.

The jungle drums began in his head again. Cale winced at their throbbing, surprised he could feel or hear anything at all. His flesh had turned blue, his body temp dropping. He recalled that anything under ninety was close to fatal, where you'd either pass out or start drinking the water.

The blue flash bobbed again. It disappeared just as fast, then there it was once more.

The mirage was twenty yards away. The teal-colored square bobbed, twisting with each crest and trough, spun by erratic winds. Cale summoned the last of his strength, and with arms thrashing, he kicked his legs like a cartoon swimmer.

He stretched one arm out just as a wave slammed in, nailing him with a liver punch. His fingers had almost touched the floating object—and then they did. He slipped two fingers into one handle, grasping it, numb. Cale lifted his left hand to where the second handle should be just as a new wave scooped and flung him back down again with spite.

This time he held on.

He gripped the cooler's handles with both hands, riding the wave in surfer fashion, not submerging. When the Yeti's tight lid had blown closed earlier, he imagined air becoming trapped inside. Now here he was, luckier than a miracle baby, floating. Cale worked to drape his torso over the flat, closed top, half sinking the object. He thanked God that he could rest his legs for a bit.

A small victory for mankind.

The skin drums continued in his head. Jungle drums. The ones which led to the stabbing-knife pain deep in his skull. The skies had darkened further, and the rain pelted around him. But the wind was behind him now, and he drifted with some invisible current, teeth chattering.

"Ah, Detective," oozed the oily, rasping voice in his head. "Always the survivor. Very impressive."

Cale's past flashed before him the way old wives' stories claimed. What you supposedly see before huffing your final breath. He was at the end now, wasn't he? Adrift, alone, half-frozen, and delirious. He tightened his numb fingers around the cooler's handles, his final hope. He imagined it was the same way pallbearers felt at funerals—the fear of dropping the goods.

The throbbing jungle drums reduced to a less frantic beat, still accompanied by shakers and low chanting. The cajoling voice in his head asked:

"Do you think you're dreaming all this?"

Cale forced himself to calm, not easy when shivering to death. "Dreaming..." he mumbled.

"I've missed our little chats." The voice needled. "I want to torment you like an insect. Or melt your brain to mush." It paused. "And yet, I strangely enjoy keeping you around. Your fight for survival amuses me."

Cale clamped his eyes shut as another wave heaved him. He vomited a throatful of water. Hacking, coughing.

"So, why don't I prove that I'm real?"

The log drums increased, and Cale's images of dancers cavorting around a jungle fire became more vivid. The same visions he had revealed to Dr. Pam, where she'd diagnosed him with "auditory hallucinations brought about by PTSD." What else could it be? Perhaps the hypothermia was tricking his mind?

Cale's teeth chattered. Yet his brain felt warmer somehow, the way a campfire behind you heats your back. After a minute, still picturing the bonfire, his shivering let up. Warmth swept through his bones akin to the first sip of morning coffee.

The voice cajoled. "See? You can trust me."

It was all some bizarre hallucination, and Cale doubted he'd recall it a day from now. He chided himself. A day from now? How about staying alive for the next hour?

He calmed himself, however, relishing the warmth while he could. Whether real or imagined.

"It's a spell, Detective," the voice in his head hissed. "I trip a brain signal that switches on your body's fever thermostat. Then turn it back off when I choose."

"Not...possible," Cale muttered this despite his mental fog clearing. He attempted ID-ing the voice, knowing he recognized it from somewhere. At last, with his brain fog dissipating, the answer slapped him hard.

Laughter cackled. "You understand now, don't you?" The tone hissed in his head.

Cale imagined the dream would dissolve faster if he chose to ignore it.

"Say my name out loud," the voice commanded. "Soft, if you choose—but *say it!*"

The drumming in his skull pounded louder again. His inner warmth evaporated, and his body temp descended. Within seconds, he was shivering in the wind and slashing rain like before.

"Have it your way," the voice said resignedly, and Cale imagined an invisible shrug. "A final chance offer to save your miserable hide."

Water whipped at his face, the icy prickles slapping him awake. His brain had slipped into survival mode. Cale debated with himself how if this were his price to continue breathing, for survival, then why not play along? It was all some form of hallucination anyway, wasn't it?

"What do you...want?" he asked. His thick words were barely audible. The campfire heat in his head flared again. It warmed his blood and cerebral fluid. "How did..." His lips were too blubbery to speak.

"A spell I learned as a child."

Cale wasn't up to responding.

The voice tsk-ed. "I've been inside your mind before, Detective." A pause. "The first time, if I recall, didn't you almost drown in that pool of hungry eels?"

187

The near-death incident remained branded upon Cale's brain. He'd been dropped through a trapdoor into a pool filled with moray eels yet managed to escape miraculously."

He asked in a low voice: "Are you, my guardian angel?"

Derisive laughter filled his mind.

"It's voodoo, you idiot," the voice angrily spat. "Of my own design."

A sudden tempest catapulted the cooler sideways, and an undertow threatened to submerge Cale's makeshift raft. His adrenaline surge helped maintain his grasp on the handles.

"You're dead," he managed after the violence abated. "Headshot. My living room."

"Say my name," the voice demanded. "Out loud."

Cale decided playing the imaginary sadistic game would cost little at this point. He recalled Dr. Pam's confirmation of how he made his decisions "by logic." She was correct; he was a problem solver. And his challenge right now was staying alive. If his hallucinations were from hypothermia, then why not play along with the voice in his head?

He muttered out loud, "Mabutu."

"My whole name."

"Tazeki Mabutu." A blusterous gale caused the metal-gray waters to churn. Cale added, "The Colonel."

A massive wave crashed over him. It drove his body beneath the murky surface as Cale pictured Satan himself grabbing hold of his ankles and refusing to let go.

CHAPTER 29

The water shallowed near the coastline. Miguel popped his head above the surface at last. His oxygen supply was low, and he stood up and sloshed his way to the beach of the public campground. The rain continued pelting the water around him. He removed his fins, opened his clothes bag, and swirled in bay water to drench the inner contents. He shoved the fins inside and proceeded further up the mucky sand, walking hobbled, his body drenched and shivering.

The bruised sky highlighted the gray undulating waters behind him. No campers around to witness his emergence. Miguel spied the Buick Regal at the edge of the nearby lot, where Kemp exited and walked to meet him, employing a protective umbrella. He paused at the concrete's edge and waited for his partner.

"Your clothes and stuff are soaked?" Kemp asked when Miguel reached him.

Miguel held up the bag of drenched clothing.

"Get out of that scuba crap and back into them." When Miguel hesitated, Kemp said, "Stick with the plan—it's got to look real."

Miguel wormed his way out of the wet suit. He was shivering for real now, his teeth chattering as he put on his soggy clothes. "Can I warm up in the car for five minutes?" he asked. Kemp gave him a smirk. "C'mon, Frank. I'm freezing my ass off here."

"No time. The swim go all right?"

"I'm here, aren't I?"

Kemp narrowed his eyes. "You got the formula? Where is it?"

"Clothes bag. On my phone, it's waterproof."

Kemp reached in and withdrew the mobile, sliding it into his front pocket. "Did the boat sink?"

Miguel's hair was plastered down, and his cheeks flushed lavender. "I was under the freaking water. How the hell do I know?"

Kemp gathered up the gear along with the Scuba-Jet and canisters. He stuffed them all in an oversized duffel bag he'd brought along, then tossed it into the back seat of the Regal, along with the useless umbrella. He stared up the deserted beach and out at the undulating waters. A bolt of jagged lightning flashed in the north.

By this time, Miguel was dressed back in his drenched street clothes.

"Now get back over there." Kemp pointed at the beach again, the rain continuing to pelt the muddy sand. The sky and water behind them were metallic shades with visibility reduced. Kemp ordered: "Same as we said. You passed out crawling ashore. I'll cover your footprints and kneel beside you when they get here."

"Can't I just warm up? Two minutes in the car?" Miguel's teeth chattered.

"I called 911 when you first came out." Kemp glimpsed his watch. "Should be here in a minute."

Cursing, Miguel turned and tromped back across the strip of grass and onto the beach once more. His soggy shoes squished. Twelve yards from the roiling water, he dropped to his knees on the sandy muck. He positioned himself as a beached survivor—his forehead propped down across one bent arm.

"Good enough for you?"

"You're a regular Brando."

Kemp knelt beside him like a man performing CPR. "Start shivering," he ordered. "You got hypothermia. Only mumble nonsense because you can't remember anything. Got it?"

"For how long?"

"Long as it takes."

Kemp gazed at his phone. In the distance, they could hear the whine and hoot of sirens growing closer.

190

"Showtime." Kemp peered over his shoulder through the trees and toward the approaching sound. "By the way, I'm destroying a good pair of shoes out here in this mess."

"Sacrifices. Right, Frank?"

The old "haunted" barn appeared as if some movie prop had been dropped into a forest clearing. The wood was gray and warped and worm-eaten. The high second-floor hay-drop no longer had outside doors and appeared as a giant cycloptic eye staring out at the surrounding landscape.

The ground-level barn doors were stuck halfway open on one side. They allowed a person or animal to enter at their own risk. A murder of crows had taken up residence in the upper loft. They came and went freely through numerous openings, most of which were gaps in the sideboards.

The creepy barn had become a haven for teenage pot smokers over the years. They had pulled in lawn chairs, tables, and even a few moldy mattresses. Yet the place proved spookier than it was comforting, especially if your buzz harshened and you turned paranoid. Thus, the teens had abandoned the site, spreading rumors that the barn was infected by ghouls and best left alone on nights when the moon was either out or wasn't.

Scattered on the outer grounds were a rusted Dodge Charger on cinder blocks and, not far away, the exposed ribs of a broken thresher. An ancient well had run dry decades ago. High weeds laid claim to everything in sight. Hoot owls patrolled in the moonlight with their sharp eyes peeled for juicy rodents.

All in all, it was a decrepit place to visit.

Ben Ross, of course, did not believe spirits possessed the old barn. He was a down-to-earth farmer who hadn't time for spooky tales or ghost stories. At least not when his farm was hemorrhaging money, and the wolves were at his door. Not to mention the latest bully on their block—Fillmore Farms—which owned over three thousand acres on the other side of the strip of woods perched between their properties.

The corporate giant's lawyers, of course, had looked into purchasing the mile-long section of forest. They would level the rotted barn and full woods in a single day, then sell chips to a clean energy plant thirty miles away. Hypocrisy at its finest: destroying forests while claiming to love the environment.

Fillmore hadn't stripped the trees away by now, so Ben imagined there were legal claims at play. He knew they'd get around to it sooner or later. They were corporatists, after all, loving the environment just as long as they received free government handouts.

Ben had been out to the old, haunted barn a few times in the past. His last appearance was two years ago. Feather had been eight then and had stumbled upon the weed-strewn place while walking her dog. Dotty was up in Doggy Heaven now, hit by a pickup truck. Consequently, they'd gotten the puppy Trey to help her get over her grief.

Feather was older now. She loved exploring the woods with Trey. She was allowed to venture over the stream but had orders to stay away from the decaying barn property. And she was forbidden to explore further beyond where the creek widened and meandered through even thicker woods. The northernmost sector of woods was owned by Fillmore, where their CEO's English manor house stood along with two other large structures.

Ben and Rita approached the weedy clearing now, where the skeletal "haunted" barn lurked in the off-and-on drizzle.

"What are you thinking?" asked Rita, eyeballing the derelict place from where they stood. The roof was caving in, and the worm-eaten slats were splintered. "Would she have come this far?"

"Doubt it. Besides, she'd have heard us calling out here by now."

Rita frowned, staring at the dilapidated relic. She turned to Ben, and he could read the worry in his sister's eyes.

Since leaving their farmhouse, they had separated after moving inside the tree line. They'd stepped through weeds and ferns and gnarled bushes, each calling Feather's name too many times to count. They'd moved around moldy tree stumps and lightning-stricken branches, slipping along the babbling creek on opposite sides.

"No worries," Ben announced gamely. "I'll check inside the place."

He stomped forward through the cluster of high weeds and overgrowth, a stiff walking stick in one hand, flashlight in the other, moving up a makeshift path leading to the front barn doors.

Anxiety gripped Rita. She stood near a clump of lilac bushes, where an invasion of jimson weeds also fought for territory. The plants gave off sweet, cloying odors in the dampness, reminiscent of the aroma in funeral parlors.

Five minutes dragged on before, at last, Ben stomped back outside. He brushed cobwebs from his jeans and ball cap. "Nothing," he reported. "Butts and ashtrays. Yellowed smoking bongs."

"Teenagers?"

"Must still gather here on weekends. Bongs, tin foil. Busted bottles."

Rita studied the rusted boneyard display of dead farm implements. Her eyes searched the landscape across the thicker tree branches, then back behind them, to where the stream ran. The rain had let up a bit, but droplets still fell from the wet leaves above.

"I'll call on Mr. DeSaul," Ben said. "If she went up through the woods, she'd have come out on his property."

"You know she wouldn't."

Ben was already backtracking the way they had come. "If she's not at home when we return, it makes the most sense."

Rita trailed dutifully behind him, her eyes scanning as she moved. "It's the drug stuff that frightens me. Teens can turn crazy. Or maybe—"

"Even farmworkers." He glanced at her. "We've both heard the rumors."

193

They were halfway back to where they'd entered the tree glade. Glancing at the stream on her right, flowing with fresh rain runoff, Rita froze. She moved down the leafy bank and paused at the water's edge.

"Wait!" she called to her brother.

Higher along the bank, Ben turned back to her. "Find something?"

Rita's focus was on the stream, staring at a jut of rocks sticking from the mud. She widened her feet, bracing near a tree with gnarled roots. She called up, "Hand me your stick!"

Ben extended the knobby branch down to her, and Rita dipped it into the water, poked it around the way a witch stirs a cauldron. After a while, she tossed the branch aside and removed one shoe and sock. Rolling her jeans up, she stepped one-legged out into the wet flow.

He watched her reach into the water. Seconds later, she rose back up, stepping her way free of the shallow current. She turned to him with her find. They couldn't take their eyes off the dripping, yellow rubber ball with the green "G" stamped on one side.

CHAPTER 30

Oconto Memorial Hospital, room 135. Miguel's head lay propped up on stiff pillows. He had been examined in the ER for hypothermia, exhaustion, and low blood pressure, along with other respiratory dysfunctions.

He was now in a private room, hooked to an IV saline drip and being pumped full of antibiotics. His significant organs seemed in working order, according to Dr. Latricia Seesi. She'd reported this to Frank Kemp, who'd been listed as Miguel's housemate, business partner, friend, and guardian. Besides experiencing dehydration and significant exposure to the elements, she expected this patient to make a full recovery in less than a week.

"We'll keep him here three days. For observation," she informed.

"Should he wait a day before talking to the police?" Kemp asked. "He's in shock—right, Doc? Besides the medications?"

"I'll let them know he's groggy," the doctor allowed. They stared down together at the unconscious patient. "But I'm sure they'd appreciate some explanatory statement of what might have happened."

Kemp nodded, said it made sense as both she and the nurse departed from the room.

While Miguel was being admitted to the hospital thirty minutes earlier, Sgt. Gary Lang of the Oconto County Sheriff's Department learned from dispatch that a boater had washed ashore at the County Park Beach.

The Oconto Yacht Club was in his jurisdiction. His call to the club confirmed two boaters had shared lunch and then left shore about fifteen minutes before the storm hit. Their slip

195

remained vacant, and the high-powered fishing boat had not yet returned.

The sergeant had checked with the Coast Guard logs. No "Maydays" from distressed boaters were reported, and it's likely the vessel would have sought safe harbor somewhere to ride out the storm. What puzzled Sgt. Lang most was that only one boater, a thirty-five-year-old male, had now been reported washing up on the beach.

Alone. And in a severe health crisis.

Ten minutes ago, Lang had pulled his cruiser in front of the hospital's main doors. His questions needed immediate answers. Questions such as: What was the status of the missing vessel? Why had they been out in dangerous waters during a storm? Why no *Mayday*? Where was the second man? What was his status? In short:

What the hell had happened out on the water?

Interviewing the survivor was urgent. Whether the man was half-groggy or on pain meds didn't matter. If he could blink his eyes and breathe, he could provide them with facts relevant to the situation.

Sgt. Lang sat now in a chair in the hallway outside of Room 135. He'd been informed that Miguel DeSaul, CEO of one of the state's largest industrial farming corporations, remained unconscious, recovering from a life-threatening ordeal on the bay. The Fillmore Farms' head of corporate security, one Frank Kemp, was acting as the spokesperson. He joined the sergeant now in the hallway chairs.

Lang spent the first minute sizing up the guy. Kemp didn't remind him of any farmer he'd ever met. His shirt and slacks were fitted, and those snappy loafers he had on? Though wet and dirt soiled, they still appeared sharp. Even after learning the guy was one of the company's higher-ups, suspicion formed a knot in Lang's gut.

"Why the Oconto Yacht Club?" the sergeant now asked, turning toward the man.

"Miguel was testing a new power boat," Kemp explained. "A mile run out, then straight back in." He sat with elbows on his knees. "Fifteen minutes tops. Must've thought he could outrace the storm."

Lang scribbled in a small notebook. "The club restaurant said he had a lunch guest. Never got a name."

"Van Waring. The guy used to work with Green Bay PD, from what I understand."

Lang jotted the name down. He asked, "Why would a law enforcement officer be lunching with Mr. DeSaul? You guys are in corporate farming, right?"

"A job interview is what I heard."

"Doing what?"

"Replacing me."

Before the sergeant could jot this down, a dark-haired nurse in pale blue scrubs stepped from Miguel's room and into the hallway. "He's conscious now," she informed the two men. "Groggy but responsive. A few very brief questions, please."

They trailed her back into the room.

Miguel's dark hair was plastered to his forehead. A half-day's growth shadowed his angular face. Lang had to admit he appeared like dung warmed over. Exactly how a near-drowned man should look.

Kemp stepped to the bedside. He grasped Miguel's hand. "Hey, buddy." His concern was heavy. "You know you're in a hospital, right?" Miguel glanced at their uniformed visitor, and Kemp said, "This here's a police sergeant, Miggy. He needs to ask some questions. Think it'll be okay?"

The patient muttered, his eyes half closing.

Kemp released his boss' hand, and it dropped limply to the bed. Then he stepped away, making room for Sgt. Lang to inch in closer. Lang asked about the boat—if they had called in a *Mayday*? Where was Officer Van Waring? How long had they been adrift? How had Miguel ended up in the water?

197

The bedridden patient blinked through these questions as if the sergeant were speaking Cantonese. He swallowed, then rasped. "Storm. Huge swale...swamp us."

Sgt. Lang frowned. "Any idea where the boat is?"

"Bilge pump snapped...water...couldn't keep...." Miguel's weary head pressed back into the pillow, with the questions taking a toll on him.

On the opposite side of the bed, the nurse gave them a look of concern.

"The boat was going down?" Lang asked, leaning further forward. "Did Officer Van Waring fall off? Or jump in panic?"

Miguel turned his head away. A tear slid down his ruddy cheek. "Waves...deep over rail...too deep..."

The room was quiet.

"So he's in the water, then?" The sergeant eyed the nurse, whose forehead was knotted with concern. Lang leaned even closer. "How far out were you when the swale—"

Miguel moaned and clamped his eyes closed.

The nurse said, "I don't think he knows. I'm afraid we'll have to end this."

"Near the shore?" Lang persisted. "Or way further out?"

Another faint gasp from Miguel. The nurse waved her hand over the blankets and motioned for the sergeant to step back. "Sorry. This poor fellow's had enough."

"Meds must be kicking in," offered Kemp with a frown. He turned and led the conga line out the room's door. Sgt. Lang was second, followed by the nurse, all moving back into the hallway.

She closed the door behind them, her voice whispering, "He's lucky to be alive."

The sergeant pocketed his notebook and thanked the nurse before turning to Kemp. "One final. I'm curious how you knew right where to look for him? The bay's shoreline's pretty long and twisted with inlets."

Kemp's eyes conveyed sincerity to both the officer and nurse. "Longshot hunch," he admitted sheepishly. "It's the same campground where we had our corporate picnic last fall. I just figured he might remember—"

"Any port in a storm, I suppose."

"So they say." Kemp swiped a moist eye.

"I'll notify the Coast Guard at once," Lang informed while moving away. "Get a rescue chopper in the air immediately."

Kemp turned back to the nurse. "I need to give an official company press statement. Would your front lobby be a possible option?"

Sgt. Lang was already down the hallway, out of earshot as she replied:

"Of course. I'll clear it with Admin."

CHAPTER 31

Two Oconto Country Sheriff's cruisers. A Wisconsin State Patrol SUV. A solitary unmarked vehicle with federal plates. All displayed blinking flashers while parked on the road's dirt shoulder and driveway of the Ross family farmhouse.

Inside the two-story home, Agent Gwen Galman—street clothes, blue DEA jacket, ball cap—sat with Rita and Detective Slink Dooley at the dining room table. Four photographs were laid out between them.

"She's ten?" the agent asked. "And these are recent?"

"Feather's a sensible girl," Rita said this, fighting the tears welling in her eyes. It was surreal. She couldn't believe they were talking about her daughter. "That's why I don't think she could have...." Her voice tailed away as if running out of air.

She glanced at Slink, who sat beside her. Initially, Rita had called for Lt. Cale Van Waring and informed the detective was "unavailable." They connected her instead to Detective Dooley, his partner. Rita had trusted both men from their visit to her house yesterday.

Slink had already been assigned to the Cho Lin murder case, which involved illegal narcotics and a possible connection to Fillmore Farms. Due to the potential child abduction, he'd requested Agent Galman's assistance. He had phoned Cale's number to leave an update but only received a "No Service" message. Cale's lunch with DeSaul would have ended hours ago. A bit odd, he'd thought, but understood how sometimes rural phone reception was a crapshoot.

Slink had ridden with Agent Galman to the Ross farm in her vehicle. Initiating an Amber Alert on the missing young girl was prioritized above all else. As a Federal agent, Galman would issue the Alert and inform local law enforcement the case was now under her command.

"I understand, Ms. Ross. Rita." Agent Galman pointed at the photos. "Let's use this one for both the APB and Amber Alert."

Rita nodded.

"Good. I'll scan it over right away."

Two uniformed county deputies, male and female, stood beneath the arch dividing the dining and front rooms. They stepped aside as the agent disappeared out the front door into the afternoon drizzle.

Slink's eyes were steady. "You and Ben already searched the woods?"

Rita numbly said, "I found her yellow ball in the stream rocks." She indicated the item sitting atop the table inside a plastic evidence bag.

Along with Agent Galman, Slink had drummed through the usual questions, already aware of the stalker in the woods. They'd asked Rita if the family was arguing over finances or if Feather was prone to bouts of isolation or wandering off on her own for extended periods. They'd asked about drugs, though it had seemed odd to Rita how a home-schooled ten-year-old would be into such things. But she conceded times were different these days.

Agent Galman returned, stomping her shoes, trying not to drip in rainwater. She produced a tri-county map and spread it atop the dining room table.

She gazed at Rita. "This is the creek over here, right?"

Rita nodded. Yes, it was called Tar Creek, she informed. It ran alongside the DeSaul property, then past a decrepit old hay barn. She looked up. "Ben and I checked there already."

"Lots of deserted barns and old hunting sheds around these parts," the agent said knowingly. "Meth heads, party kids. They visit them on weekends."

"Our woods are about forty yards across," Rita told them. "The stream flows down its middle."

They focused on the map.

"You mentioned the DeSaul place?" the female deputy said. "He's Fillmore Farms CEO, right?"

Rita agreed he was.

Galman shifted to Slink. "You said this other guy, this Mr. Kemp. He lives there also?"

"Corporate security head. Been lodging there the past few months."

If they found it odd, no one commented.

Rita explained the property also had a guest house a short distance behind the main manor. She pointed at the map and indicated a third structure: it was a massive, converted feed barn situated closer to Tar Creek. The barn house was even more extensive than the three-story main house.

As they calculated the geometry of the DeSaul property, Slink said, "I never knew farming paid so well."

"It doesn't." Rita's comment left no room for doubt.

Agent Galman asked if Feather could have wandered up through the woods? Crossed the stream? In effort, perhaps, at escaping the storm?

Rita shook her head. Not a chance.

"Something had to have happened," Slink put in. "Turned an ankle? Or her dog got hurt?"

Rita rose from her chair, unable to sit any longer. "Ben drove to check the DeSaul house over an hour ago," she informed. He phoned me, saying their housekeeper hasn't seen or heard anything."

A wind gust rattled the pane, and the room's air smelled metallic from the moisture.

Agent Galman explained the search plan. A dozen officers and local volunteers—over thirty searchers in total—would split into three sectors. One group would comb across the DeSaul grounds; another would search the woods going north, starting here from the Ross' house; a third group would work along the creek banks and roads, all the way back down to where they now sat.

Slink told Rita, "We're going to find her before dark."

The officers all appeared determined, and they headed out the door. At the front steps, Rita called after them, "Please find her, guys. She means, well…"

Her voice hitched as she watched them nod seriously and their vehicle doors slam closed.

Behind the layers of ornery clouds, the sun was commencing its downward arc in the western sky. The stiff wind whipped in erratic gusts, and the cooler bobbed through the undulating water. Somehow Cale held onto the handles and lay draped atop his raft, fading in and out of consciousness.

By now, the rain had let up, and the jungle drums in his head disappeared. He thanked the Almighty for reminding him how insignificant a lump of clay he was in the cosmos.

Remember, man, that you are dust…

He let the rest go, knowing he could barely string two thoughts together, let alone turn philosophical.

Still, during his brief spans of clarity, Cale focused on where his life stood at present. If he survived this ordeal, some things needed fixing. First, he had to put things right again with the Department's brass, who had suspended him. And for what? Promising families he'd search for their daughters who had been sold to human traffickers? Of course, that was only half of it. He could never have predicted the insane witch doctor following him home and attacking his family before getting shot dead on his living room floor. But that's what had transpired, so everyone had to accept the facts as they were.

The dead man's diplomatic immunity had resulted in Cale's thirty-day suspension. An unfair punishment, he'd argued, but it was how things worked in today's "woke" society.

He was not sorry Colonel Mabutu had met his untimely demise. He just wished he'd been the one who had pulled the trigger instead of Maggie.

Cale shrugged these images away, his thoughts turning, instead, to his upcoming marriage. Mostly with regards to

Maggie's pregnancy. Shouldn't he be more upset that the baby might not be his? That her rapist, Tobias Crenshaw, could turn out to be the child's actual father? Of course, Cale had already made peace with the bizarre situation. His love for Maggie had trumped all else, and they'd decided to raise the child together as their own.

They agreed it was the right thing to do.

Cale now forced his mind back to the more urgent situation at hand. Miguel—along with the gangster Frank Kemp—had tried to murder him. By now, they would assume that they'd succeeded. Cale's task, therefore, was to will himself to survive. Not merely for justice's sake but for everyone else involved as well.

He had confessed to Dr. Pam how he usually sided with the underdogs of the world. Yet here he was, adrift in deep water, battling rain, wind, and rolling waves. If you fight for the little guys—his brain now nagged—then how about battling a little harder to save yourself?

Closing his eyes, Cale felt himself drift off again. Moments later, he lurched awake, coughing and spitting water. He scolded himself: You almost let go of the handles, moron!

He blinked twenty times, realizing he'd lost all concept of time. Cale recalled a strategy he had employed during past crisis modes. The "KISS" method he'd learned from his father. Keep It Simple, Stupid!

Thus, his new plan consisted of a mere three details: *A)* hold the cooler for dear life, *B)* stay awake, and *C)* like it or not, force down sips of water. His rules for survival.

And don't forget *D)* keep breathing. But only when your head is above the surface.

The air and water temperatures had fallen, and darkness captured the storm clouds, checkmating any final hint of sunlight. Cale recalled his shivering hours ago—or had it been minutes? The demented entity inside his head causing the jungle drums, along with his headaches and fever, had somehow warmed his body enough to keep him alive.

Could he summon the same warmth back again on his own? The way Hindu yogis could warm themselves by sheer force of will? He figured it wouldn't hurt to try, though maybe later after he'd rested a bit more and felt stronger.

Such were Cale's thoughts as he bobbed along with the rolling waves. At times, he imagined a massive sea creature rising from the depths to swallow him whole. Would it not be a fitting end? Put him out of his misery?

Another wave slapped him in the face, but he didn't release his grip on either handle. He cackled at the absurdity, knowing he sounded like an asylum resident. Was this how being in a straitjacket felt? Unable to move your arms and floating at the whims of fate?

Sometime later, a far-off image caught his attention. It drifted at the horizon, reminiscent of a heap of wet firewood. Squinting through edematous eyes, Cale observed the snaking shadow as it dipped in and out of sight. This new mirage appeared to be posing as a strip of land.

Or at least how land might appear to the half-closed eyes of a dead man drowning.

CHAPTER 32

The troop of searchers had assembled in front of the DeSaul manor house. Cruisers and police SUVs with flickering lights stood parked at angles along the front driveway circle.

The officers were joined by hastily summoned volunteer students, church members, and neighbors dressed for the outdoors. All were issued yellow hazard vests. The Amber Alert for Feather Ross was running statewide. It extended downstate to Milwaukee, Racine, and Madison, north to Michigan's Upper Peninsula, before expanding west to the Minnesota border.

Agent Gwen Galman held a federal warrant as she rang the doorbell of the moss-covered manor house. Slink Dooley stood a step behind. The housekeeper, Mrs. Flench, greeted them. No, she informed, neither Mr. DeSaul nor Mr. Kemp was at home. When presented with the federal search warrant, she widened the door and stepped aside.

Slink led a search group around the side of the house, where they'd comb the bushes and examine the garages, then search the guest house.

Agent Galman led the inside search team. She remained beside Mrs. Flench on the front room couch while her agents performed room-to-room inspections. As the officers searched the three-story premises, the housekeeper's calls to both masters of the house had gone unanswered. She left messages on their phones.

Footsteps thumped throughout the home.

"Your neighbor Ben Ross?" Galman questioned, her voice flat and professional. "The missing girl's uncle? He was here earlier, right?"

Mrs. Flench nodded. Yes, she'd allowed him to search inside the house, garages, and outer lawns, along with the pair of adjacent structures on the property—which were always locked, she confessed, and she possessed no keys. Having discovered

206

no signs of the missing young girl, the man had driven his truck away in frustration.

"Did he say where he was going?"

The housekeeper shook her head. "He was polite, though. Waved thanks as he drove off."

The pounding footsteps continued across the upper floors. Galman pressed Mrs. Flench with further questions, and her answers were firm and concise. The agent always felt she could spot a liar from an acre away, but her inner radar failed to rise with this lady. She seemed honest and sincere in her dismay.

Agnes Flench was a 47-year-old widow in Mr. DeSaul's employ for almost two years now. She informed the agent her daughter, Sherise, twenty years younger, frequently assisted her with cleaning. And no, neither Frank Kemp nor Mr. DeSaul had shown any romantic interest in her daughter.

Or herself, for that matter.

The half-dozen deputies returned outside. Their leader reported no traces of the missing young girl. Before Agent Galman departed, she asked the housekeeper when Mr. DeSaul might return. As was protocol, she'd prefer questioning him herself, in person.

The lady's hand rose to her mouth. "You mean you haven't heard?" She appeared surprised.

"Heard what?"

"The boating accident? Earlier?" The housekeeper's cheeks flushed. "I thought it was the *real* reason you were here."

Agent Galman's confusion prompted Mrs. Flench to add, "Mr. Miguel's in the hospital. He almost drowned in the bay this afternoon."

The afternoon drizzle had at last ceased. Tree leaves remained soggy, and occasional droplets fell on the heads and shoulders of the search party's members.

The search party had spent the past hour examining the property's garages and outbuildings, the guest house, and the massive barn house. They'd jimmied the locks, per their warrant, for a thorough look-see, securing them after leaving. No signs of young Feather had turned up. A pair of sniffer dogs who'd been given the missing girl's scent had also come up empty. The canine officers informed Agent Galman there was "zero chance" the girl had been on the property today.

Galman also informed Slink of Miguel DeSaul's unfortunate boating accident. And how Mrs. Flench had confirmed Cale's lunch meeting with Miguel had been canceled ahead of time.

The agent next led her small troop down along both sides of Tar Creek. They would provide a fresh set of eyes to the first unit team, who had already combed the woods thirty minutes before. Galman led her squad along the muddy banks of the rain-washed stream. They would all eventually rendezvous back at the Ross dairy farm.

As they stepped over the uneven terrain, Slink Dooley continued checking his phone for updates. He dialed Cale's number and received another pair of "No Service" messages.

"Anything from Cale so far?" Agent Galman asked. She was walking behind Slink, both spraying the damp forest floor with their flash beams.

"Phone issues, it looks like."

She thought about it. "Any chance he'd have gone out on the water with Miguel DeSaul?"

Slink shook his head. "The guy's a sleazeball. Cale would never get into even a rowboat with the guy."

The woods smelled mossy as they progressed forward, a graveyard feel. The stream gurgled nearby, water flowing over the mud-crusted rocks. They paused after fifteen minutes. The weatherworn "haunted" barn stood a short distance off. It was perched between the gloomy tree branches ahead, appearing as if some shipwrecked Spanish galleon had been dropped there by God's hand.

The dusky twilight had crept in around them, and Slink couldn't say how he'd spotted the object. Plain dumb luck, he would later confess. But whatever the case, he spied a brassy glimmer at the penumbra of his flash beam.

Stooping, he held the item up and studied it in the light. The band had been sliced, leaving no evidence of blood spatter. The animal might have been either unconscious or even deceased when the slice had been accomplished. The bronze ID tag read: "Trey." Below it was engraved Ben Ross' phone number.

Slink bagged the collar. They'd run it through the lab for fingerprints and possible DNA. Maybe even more dumb luck might help them ID a potential suspect from some database.

Stepping to a dry spot above the bank, Agent Galman spoke into her walkie. "All units. Positive on the dog's collar. No signs of the animal or girl."

The troop continued forward, beams sweeping the sodden woods. They moved southward along both sides of the stream. Trailing behind the agent, Slink asked, "Think they killed the dog, Gwen?"

"They'd want it alive. Threaten it with harm to control the girl."

"Killing him would frighten her into compliance as well, wouldn't it?"

Galman said nothing, and they continued their march toward the Ross farm.

Frank Kemp's scheme dictated his next moves.

He had anointed himself a puppet master years ago. He enjoyed pulling strings, dictating how lesser players responded to his orchestrations. With Miguel now confined to his hospital bed, cast as a "survivor," Kemp still had a few scenes left to round out their performance.

He moved now into an empty hospital room and closed the door. Sitting on the edge of a crisp-sheeted bed, he dialed his phone and demanded the switchboard operator put him through to Detective Sgt. Slink Dooley. He learned the man had just returned to the station. Yes, it was urgent. Dammit, it *was* an emergency. It had to do with the recent double-murder case.

Kemp's mobile flashed a minute later.

"Mr. Kemp," came Slink's uncertain voice. "I hear you have information regarding the Cho Lin murders?"

"More than that, Detective." Kemp's tone conveyed the proper gravitas. "My boss, Miguel, had lunch earlier today with your partner."

"They canceled it. According to your Mrs. Flench."

Kemp softened his voice like a funeral director. "Not so. They moved it to the yacht club in Oconto. Then afterward, they took Miguel's new power boat out for a test on the bay." He allowed his words to sink in. "Right before that killer storm hit."

Silence. Kemp gave the detective time to process the information before adding, "The storm was savage, Detective. They think a giant swell might have capsized their boat."

"I'm not sure I—"

"Let me finish." Kemp swallowed hard. "I thought you should know before the news hits the airwaves."

"Know what?

"Miguel's in the hospital, barely alive."

Slink was stunned into silence.

"Your partner is, well, it sounds as if…" A dramatic pause. "I hear the Coast Guard's putting a rescue chopper in the air."

Kemp imagined the detective was calculating the odds of the story being true. Also, he might be estimating how much time his partner had spent in the chilly waters of the bay."

"I figured you should know. In case you need to…with his fiancée and all?"

Silence again, until Slink blurted: "I'll call the Coast Guard, myself." He ended the call.

Kemp pocketed his mobile, mentally checking another mark from his list—the dutiful, heartfelt notification. He departed from the room, striding down the corridor toward the hospital's front reception area.

CHAPTER 33

The afternoon rains had washed the Van Waring house. The gloomy dampness made the lawn appear greener. The tires of Maggie's Mazda whooshed as she navigated up the driveway.

She opened the backdoor while carrying a grocery bag. She'd been at her doctor's appointment, and things were progressing well at the ten-week mark. The house was silent as she entered. Cale was at his lunch meeting or whatever, and he'd have called if anything important had come up. Having heard her car pull up, Hank stretched and entered the kitchen, purring as she reached down to fluff his head.

Maggie had spent most of the day thinking about the job opportunity Cale had been offered. Her initial reaction was skepticism. Head of security for an industrial farm? A six-figure salary? It sounded ludicrous. After all, what was there to do all day? Guard the tractors? Ward off cattle rustlers? Admonish the workers for smoking pot while milking cows?

Giving it more thought, she understood every decent-sized business required a security head these days. And Fillmore Farms employed over fifty people already and planned on expanding. As an attorney, she knew how corporations functioned in this age of litigation—employee benefits, safe work environment, workforce stability, along with a full-time security team. The security unit not only protected the workers but also had to contend with outside forces.

Maggie had read reports about groups picketing farms against pollution run-off, air toxicity, and other concerns. Also, anger was mounting involving government-subsidized corporate farms destroying smaller independent farmers' lives, hurting their businesses, taking away their ability to feed their families and earn an honest living off the land.

Tempers flared when livelihoods were at stake.

Thus, upon further review, Cale's job offer didn't sound as outlandish as she'd initially imagined.

And with a baby in their future, his leaving police work might not be the craziest idea in the world. A corporate security position would carry less stress than police work, and he'd gain a substantial salary increase. Not to mention regular hours with no late-night murder scenes to attend. It meant he'd be home more for both her and the munchkin. After her maternity leave, Maggie might even decide to give up her Public Defender's job. A stay-at-home mom? It was an idea she'd never have considered back in law school.

On some maternal level, it sounded appealing. Right now, however, it made her think of her own mom, and her eyes welled up.

As Maggie placed a head of lettuce in the refrigerator drawer, her phone buzzed. Slink's cell number, with the text demanding she call him ASAP. She hit redial and said, "Hey," after he picked up.

No clever wisecracks from Slink, and she sensed a wave of unusual sobriety. "Mags," he said, "I was out on the missing girl search all afternoon."

"I heard the Amber Alert on my car radio."

"Listen," he shifted topics, "there've also been reports of a boating accident out on the bay."

"Not the little girl—"

"No. It's Cale." Slink's voice flattened the way cops convey disturbing news. "Something might've happened…and right now, he's missing."

Kemp hurried down the corridor and through the swinging doors, which led to the hospital's front reception area. He carried a folder in one hand, notes stuffed in his front shirt pocket.

Pausing in the hallway, he mentally rehearsed his lines like a stage actor.

Kemp wanted to sprint to his Regal in the parking lot and speed for home. Thanks to Miguel's nurse, he now possessed the login passwords from his partner's phone and was anxious to get to his keyboard, surf the dark web, access Cho Lin's hidden account. Retrieve the missing half of the fentanyl formula.

The numbers compounded in his head the way computer programs add automatic zeros. Once word got out that a non-lethal opioid was hitting the market, users and dealers would clamor for the product. Cookers would be unable to produce the stuff fast enough. Demand would sweep the U.S., Mexico, Canada, and everywhere else. The latest and greatest! Street pushers would hype the stuff. Rural dealers would plead for "Turquoise Ice," or whatever the name would be, by the truckload.

Kemp grinned. As things stood, he and Miguel didn't have to move to Belize. Hell, they could frigging *buy* Belize! The entire country. Maybe throw in Puerto Rico for good measure.

But first things first. Stay focused, he reminded himself, breezing through the doors and into the front lobby. He nodded respectfully to the administrative director.

Minutes later, Kemp stood at a small podium in the corner of the extended reception area. A gaggle of local reporters was gathered—phones, notepads, wireless video cameras. RNs and other medical staff were present, blended with a dozen waiting room patients, all listening with rapt attention.

Kemp tested the mic, withdrew his notes, spoke soberly.

"On behalf of Fillmore Farms," he said, "I want to express my gratitude to the professionals here at Oconto Memorial. They have worked tirelessly to save the life of our company president, Miguel DeSaul."

There were smiles and nods and scattered handclaps.

Kemp continued: "Mr. DeSaul, as some of you have heard, washed ashore this afternoon during the violent typhoon. He suffered dehydration, hypothermia and was in severe shock. The doctors say he's not out of the woods yet." Kemp paused, swallowing hard. "But one thing we know about Miguel is he's a fighter."

Recorders and devices were extended even closer to the small podium where Kemp stood. Furious notes scribbled.

Kemp pressed on. "The Coast Guard and County Rescue Services will continue searching for other survivors. We pray that God will protect them, along with the brave rescuers who have put their own lives in danger. They and their families are in our prayers."

Searching the room with sober eyes, he added, "Due to the gut-wrenching nature of today's tragedy, which has stricken all of our Fillmore Farms family, no further questions will be taken at this time."

Chewing on his quivering lower lip, Kemp spun on his heel and strode from the reception area. He exited out through the hospital's automated front doors.

4:35 p.m. The old Dutch grandfather clock in the dining room gave a single, mournful chime. Fifteen feet away, Rita and Ben sat on the sagging couch in the front living room. The last two deputies had departed, and shadows formed in the corners of the room. Their thoughts galloped through the silence. After a minute, Rita covered her face and began to weep again.

Ben placed his arm around her shoulders, and they cried together. Rita tried speaking but couldn't form words through her tears. Her brother whispered, "They'll find her. I know they will. We won't give up hope—"

"But if the police can't—"

"Think positive. C'mon."

She knuckled her eyes and lifted them. "But Trey's collar. And the ball. He would never have left her."

"We know he wouldn't."

"So it means…"

Ben rose. "He's with her right now. Somewhere."

"We should go back out. We must've missed something."

Ben was silent, and he focused through the rain-streaked window at the gloom. He turned and faced her.

"Fifty people have already searched the woods and the whole DeSaul property. Even that haunted old barn again." He strode to the nearby dining table and used the light to search his phone for the fiftieth time this hour. Without looking up, he said, "Besides, it'll be dark soon."

Rita began sobbing again.

"She knows our numbers," Ben insisted. "She'll call when she gets to a phone."

It was just after 5:00 p.m., and the streets remained damp, the storm sewers working overtime.

Slink swung the pewter-colored Taurus left at the stoplights, grill flashers on. He listened for updates on the scanner, reports trickling in from the wind-whipped waters of the bay. Minutes later, he accelerated up Cale's driveway and parked on the apron alongside Maggie's Mazda.

With the barest of knocks, he let himself in.

Slink located Maggie on the family room couch, holding her phone, eyes staring at a TV reporter in a windbreaker and rain hat. She stood on the bay shore with a microphone in hand, her hat brim flapping in the wind.

"...Reporting the thirty-foot fishing cruiser was about a mile from the Oconto shoreline when gale-force winds and waves swamped the vessel. The two men aboard were flung into the fifty-degree water...."

"Life vests!" Slink barked, causing Maggie to glance at him. "They would've had on life vests!"

They focused on the screen, the reporter continuing:

"Miguel DeSaul, age 35, CEO of a large industrial dairy farm, along with a second Green Bay man, Cale Van Waring, age 37. They remain the only reported victims. Van Waring is a senior detective currently on leave from the city's police department."

215

"For Christ sakes," muttered Slink. He rose and stomped in a circle, listening to the TV voice:

"Lt. Commander Niles Ray Moorhouse of the Sturgeon Bay Coast Guard Unit informs us that a full search and rescue operation is underway. A Jayhawk helicopter from Traverse City Air Center has been deployed, along with a 25-foot Response-Boat and rescue crew, which launched from Washington Island an hour ago."

Slink resignedly positioned himself on the couch arm.

"According to Moorhouse, the Coast Guard will continue searching through the night if need be."

Maggie flicked off the TV. Neither of them spoke. After a minute, she turned his way. "If you know anything about all this, please tell me."

Slink rubbed his face. "He was meeting DeSaul for lunch. They switched locations. God knows why."

"It's not some crazy drug story you guy's hatched, is it? To bait those opioid dealers?"

"Don't I wish?"

Maggie's eyes welled. She buried her face in her hands and waved him away as he moved to comfort her.

Connie stood in the front room of the B&B and stared out the window at nothing. She answered her phone marked PRIVATE when it buzzed and found herself speaking to a Sgt. Mileski of the Wisconsin State Patrol. He'd gotten her contact information through the Minnesota DMV. No, he couldn't discuss the matter over the phone.

He'd be over in ten minutes.

Watching the state patrol SUV pull into her driveway, Connie sighed. She was relieved the flashers were quiet. Nevertheless, a tightness gripped her stomach. She opened the front door before the officer could knock.

Trooper Mileski declined her refreshment offer. Not a social visit, he informed. When Connie directed him to the front room, he requested she take a seat. The man sat across from her on a chair's edge. Connie ID'd Syan's DL photo and confessed her secretary had left three hours ago to run errands. When she hadn't returned after ninety minutes, she'd left several messages on her mobile.

The man gave a solemn nod, and Connie cried, "What is all this about? Is Syan okay?"

"I'm afraid it's serious, Ms. DeSaul." Trooper Mileski removed his hat, held it by the brim. "We discovered Ms. Hng inside her vehicle. Parked on a side street near a strip mall."

"Syan doesn't drink if you're thinking—"

"She OD'd."

His blunt words hung in the air. He added, "Needle. Empty vials on the vehicle floor." He paused. "She's been deceased for at least a few hours now."

Connie's forehead flushed, and her world turned pale. She waited for the man to smile, but no smile came.

A moment later, she found herself looking down at her own body from up near the ceiling. She viewed her arms flailing as the officer reached for her, watched herself fight him off like an attacker. It was a pantomime, she understood, the way actors rehearse a scene.

Then the actress playing her was lying upon the front room's rug sobbing, curled fetal, as the kneeling trooper placed an arm around her shoulders in a comforting gesture.

CHAPTER 34

5:55 p.m. Frank Kemp had raced along the country backroads, at last arriving at the English manor house. As he'd cruised up the lane to the circular front drive, his eyes scanned the place. Mrs. Flench had left a frantic message. The police and DEA investigators had invaded the property, searching everywhere for the missing young Ross girl.

They'd had search dogs with them. And there remained an active Amber Alert out.

The "dog part" had caused Kemp's stomach to clench, especially if they'd explored the converted barn house on the property. After taking a deep breath, though, he recalled how sniffer canines were trained to lock onto a victim's scent and would never be distracted—not by hot dogs or candy or even packages of narcotics wrapped and hidden behind walls.

The searchers were gone now. Kemp sighed with relief as he parked the Regal in front. Nothing appeared amiss. The housekeeper had departed at five o'clock, so he didn't have to deal with her hovering about and gnashing her teeth.

Kemp swept through the house and up the stairs, where he barged into his private bedroom on the third floor. It was a magnificent suite, three times larger than any standard apartment. A matching trio of quarter-paned, floor-to-ceiling windows looked over the property's back, across the treetops, farm acreage, and distant roadways. The two-story guest house was positioned straight back. Beyond it ran a county road that separated miles of open fields. If he opened the French doors and stepped out onto the spacious balcony, Kemp could observe the massive, three-floored, remodeled barn house perched further east, shielded by a copse of towering elm and ash trees.

No time for sightseeing. His laptop remained on the writing desk where he'd left it, appearing unmolested. The closet doors were half-open. At least they hadn't disturbed his shoe rack, where over thirty exact pairs of wine-colored loafers awaited their turn in the rotation. He could feel how the searchers had stirred the interior dust. They'd left trace odors of dampness tinged with cheap aftershave.

Kemp powered on the laptop. The cops wouldn't have wasted time trying to solve his passwords. If they had been examining for kiddie porn, they'd have confiscated his computer. No. It was just as Mrs. Flench had reported. They were searching for a missing young girl. But for his peace of mind, he examined his search history. All clear. Just as he'd left it.

He now relaxed, reminding himself it didn't take a genius to navigate the dark web. Not if you possessed half a brain.

Frank Kemp had previously allocated secure, private server systems for the half-dozen Fillmore Farms side-businesses. These servers were stand-alone, dedicated to documenting only narcotics sales and revenues. They were connected to a core server via a series of VPN-encrypted routers, which changed at random and were untraceable. The system further allowed Kemp to move crypto funds in-and-out of offshore accounts. It was a necessary component in the fluid global chess game that every player in the Narco Sector inhabited these days.

Kemp sat forward and cracked his knuckles. Cho Lin's dark web account was mere minutes away. He located the site he had accessed before. He stared at the empty login boxes, perhaps with the same anticipation archaeologists experienced before crowbarring their way into some ancient tomb.

He had copied and recopied the logins from Miguel's phone three times, ensuring no errors.

Kemp typed the unique letters and symbols into the boxes. He double-checked each keystroke. Every case and spacing had to be precise. A typo was as devastating as a hand grenade. Tapping in the sequences, at last, he clicked the Enter button and waited.

Two seconds later, Kemp scowled at the return message. "Password Incorrect."

He tried again, making extra certain.

"Password Incorrect."

His instinct was to blast his right fist through the screen. Instead, Kemp decided to accept the results as a glass-half-full. The message meant the login was correct, but the password remained the culprit.

He blinked and stared at the numbers and symbols again, studying every inversion and variation of the password Miguel had procured. Kemp was aware there were limits on his allowed attempts, so he disciplined himself from typing in symbols willy-nilly.

Ten minutes had turned to thirty. He pushed his chair back, mulling over the puzzle until the answer finally registered—it was apparent the drowning detective had concluded Miguel would sail away without him, regardless. And thus, it was now evident he had dummied the passwords at the last second.

Without knowing why Kemp laughed out loud like a lunatic. In this darkest of moments, insight struck him with force. There remained a solitary correct answer amid thousands of wrong ones.

And best of all, he knew now where this answer was hidden.

Kemp lifted from his chair and stepped across the room. His phone buzzed atop his bed, and he stared down at the readout: Ferlando.

He wondered now what?

At the Mood Indigo Beauty Emporium, Chloe listened to the 6:30 radio news in the background. A pair of boaters had suffered a tragedy out on the bay's stormy waters. When the men's identities were revealed, her open scissors froze in her fingers. Jenna would take over her client's color job. Everyone seeing Chloe's face understood it was best that she depart at once.

"I just heard," Chloe said into her phone, opening her car door. "I'm on the way over." She hung up before her sister could reply.

Minutes later, she pulled onto Maggie's driveway apron. The evening was damp and wind-swept, and it gave off an ominous vibe. Chloe's mind flashed back to the night of the crazy intruder's attack six weeks ago. She could picture it like yesterday. Chants, shakers, pounding jungle drums...the evil Buddha statue...the demonic sulfurous cloud floating through the house.

The crazed zombie attacking them.

The invasion had been orchestrated by the insane voodoo priest—the lunatic who'd come close to destroying their lives. Chloe had been assaulted, tossed about the way a dog flings a rag doll. She had still not recovered her mojo and wondered if she ever would.

Two quick knocks and she let herself in through the kitchen door. Spotting Maggie sitting in the dining room, she rushed over and hugged her sister, tears filling their eyes. Chloe whispered they'd find Cale in short order, how it must all be some mistake. He was invincible. He'd proven it to them before.

When she pulled back, Maggie's eyes were glazed. "I blame myself."

Chloe stooped down to eye-level, shaking her head.

"A job interview Cale was looking into," Maggie added. "Private security. Trying at a safer life for us—"

"Leave police work? Cale? No way."

"There was also some shady business guy." Maggie spoke without looking at her. "Two birds, one stone sort of thing."

"It was an accident, Mags. But it's going to be—"

"I was too negative." Tears seeped down Maggie's cheeks. "I shouldn't have been so stubborn!"

Chloe hugged her sister again. It was going to be a long night. It didn't take a psychic to figure that out.

221

The trooper had departed, and Connie climbed the stairs to Syan's room, where she sat on the edge of the bed. Her best friend was gone because of their stupid gun argument. Syan had slammed the front door and driven off to town, angry and frustrated.

They'd never even said goodbye.

Downstairs now, Connie poured herself a half-tumbler of bourbon. She felt lost in her head, halfway between denial and contemplating the benefits of the pill bottle up in her dresser drawer. Instead, she decided on a plan she'd learned years ago.

"There's only one way to deal with heart pain, sweetie," her mother had shared once upon a time. "Crack open a bottle of Numb and keep swallowing till it fades away."

Connie decided she would honor Syan by toasting her out on the backyard deck. The cold dampness suited her mood, and she could commiserate with the weeping willow Syan had loved so much. Gazing up at the moody purple sky, she knew her friend was smiling awkwardly down at her.

Connie slugged down the amber fluid in two gulps. She refreshed her glass from the bottle—*one for my baby and one for the road.*

She had on a knit wrap-around sweater, sitting at the round table spotted with damp leaf bits. The breeze carried a coppery scent. The full bottle soon turned half that, fifteen minutes stretching into well over an hour. Connie wondered if the dark shroud covering her heart might be inherited, something embedded in her DNA. The daughter of Sevvie DeSaul and all that. The idea caused her teeth to clench.

Connie raised her glass aloft, the same as they do at Irish funerals. She slurred her words toward the purple heavens, proclaiming to Syan and Jesus and Edgar Allan Poe, and anyone else who might be listening:

"As God is my witness, that prick will pay for this."

Connie belted down her final swallow. "So it be," she whispered to the dreariness, allowing her words to swoop away like ravens into the colorless gloom. She flung the glass against the low deck wall, where it shattered.

The bargain was complete.

Back inside the house, Connie reached for her phone. She dialed the private number she'd discovered inside Syan's bedstand and let it ring until a hesitant voice answered.

"Connie? What a surprise."

Connie was speaking to a dangerous woman. One who lived in a world with people who enjoyed looking through laser sights and pulling triggers. Nevertheless, she wasn't going to play cutesy. Not with two pints of Kentucky's finest sloshing around in her gut.

"I blame you, Jackie." Slurring her words. "Just so that you know it."

The accusation caught Jackie by surprise. "I thought we were past the schoolgirl BS—"

"Not why I'm calling," Connie interrupted, exhaling. "You distracted her. Made her careless. And now…" Her voice trailed off.

"Now what? What are you talking about?"

"Syan's dead, you stupid bitch." A long second passed. "They murdered her."

Quiet built between them, and at last, Jackie asked, "Who did? Who's *they*?"

"My *bastard* half-brother—who the hell else?"

CHAPTER 35

Frank Kemp's phone buzzed a second time, and he grabbed it from atop his quilt. Ferlando. Calling from the Farm's headquarters. "Yeah?" His voice was tight. He had a dozen more important things on his mind right now.

"Two problems, Mr. Kemp," the man nervously reported. "First, the press keeps calling for updates on Mr. DeSaul."

"I gave our statement at the hospital," snapped Kemp. He turned and stared out the high windows. Twilight was settling in.

"They want some video of the farm facilities. For their news reports. I told 'em you handle the PR stuff."

Kemp felt his forehead warm and turned back to the room. "Mr. DeSaul is fighting for his life! Tell the media parasites to show some courtesy for a change." His jaw was tight. "Is that all?"

Ferlando hesitated. "*Problemo dos, senor.* I figured you should know."

"I've got a half—"

"It's with Clive Bawdy, sir."

Kemp glanced over at the laptop screen.

"Bawdy? What the hell's he got—"

"Remember Cheezer?" Ferlando interrupted. "One who helped us with deliveries two months back?'

"Somewhat. Bald guy, right?"

"Claims he always knew Bawdy had some screws loose," Ferlando's voice rose a notch. "But he never guessed he was a *pervert*, besides."

Resigned now, Kemp sat down on the edge of his mattress. "Okay. Tell me what I need to know."

Cale felt the delirium take hold again, shivering while he floated in the pitch-black water. Despite this, the waves around him felt less choppy, though they continued to roll and undulate the way Brazilian hips sway to Samba.

The floating cooler beneath him seemed guided by some sentience. Yet for him, both time and reality had remained uncertain for the past few hours, as he'd watched the mirage-like trees and shoreline continue to expand in size.

When at last convinced they were solid, Cale considered releasing the plastic handles—attempt a valiant swim for land. However, his inner voice cautioned that since he'd floated this far, wouldn't it be wiser to ride it to the end?

The moon remained hidden behind a leaden sky, and the wind at his back propelled him through the churlish, gunmetal water. Draped across the small raft with his teeth chattering again, sometime later, when his shoes touched the weedy bottom, then his knees moments later, he rallied his final bit of strength.

Easing his cramped fingers from the plastic handles, Cale released himself. He recalled how people had drowned in mere inches of water, so with his legs nearly having forgotten their function, he began slogging toward the dark, shadowy beach. Minutes later, after staggering exhaustedly over the uneven bottom, Cale collapsed onto the weed-strewn shore. He army-crawled to where the moist sand became a cluster of unkempt brush. There his head flopped to the ground, and his mind went black.

Sometime later, Cale's senses failed to register the snuffling sounds nearby. Nor could he make out the tinkling notes, huffs of breath, or the voice reaching him as if from some far-off land.

"Whatcha got there, Buster? Whatcha find there, boy?"

PART THREE

PLEASE DON'T HURT HIM, MISTER

"They (demons) will inflict people with a painful torment, so excruciating that people will plead for death but not die."
— Book of Revelation 9:6

CHAPTER 36

It was the most strenuous physical task Dr. Ernst Drissey had attempted in quite some time. Or at least since he'd retired from his medical practice eight years ago—that of dragging an unconscious body ninety feet up a windy, rain-soaked strip of muddy beach.

It sure as heck trumped his weekly racquetball game.

After checking the swimmer's vitals, he removed his light jacket, wrapped it tight around the man, and knotted the sleeves. The doctor knew there was no one to respond to his shouts for help. And by the time Rescue Services would arrive, the man might perish from hypothermia. His dog Buster was no Rin Tin Tin, so sending him off to rouse a rescue posse was pointless.

One solution was left: good old-fashioned elbow grease.

Gripping the man beneath his armpits, once Drissey had managed a step-by-step backward rhythm, he proved equal to the task. Buster, the dog, acted as both an accomplice and cheerleader. He dashed ahead then waited, staying ten yards in front the entire way. Occasionally, he'd offer a low bark.

After twenty minutes of steady progress, the well-seasoned doctor paused to rest. Darkness had descended, and the night shadows thickened. As he turned from the beach onto a stone walkway leading up a slope to his elevated house, he pictured himself in the final minutes of a football game, when wins or losses are decided.

Arriving at his garage, nearly exhausted, Drissey hoisted the doors and dragged the man along the cement floor of an open stall. Sweating worse than a Barcelona matador, he pulled the victim inside the house and down a long hallway. One limb at a time, he levered him up onto the front room couch. The journey's jostling seemed to have restored some pink to the unconscious man's sunken cheeks.

Dr. Drissey recaptured his ragged breath and withdrew a stethoscope from his worn leather medical bag. He cut away the soaked clothing with his surgical scissors. While doing this, a voice in his head reminded him that it was doubtful the man would have survived the night alone on the desolate beach in his current hypothermic condition.

Not far away, Buster lay upon his sleep mat. He watched the doctor's every move and whined as he observed things, mainly providing emotional support.

Drissey listened to the uneven heartbeat and checked the pulse and breathing. Pupils were responsive. The guy might survive if he managed to warm him enough. His ingestion of water—planned or not—had staved off dehydration. He wrapped his patient in blankets, then cranked the gas fireplace up into the 80s. It might take an hour or so, but the man would come around. He considered calling 911 but decided he could administer his own saline IV faster than waiting for Rescue. Right now, saving the stranger's life was his primary goal. The oath he'd taken years ago trumped all else.

As the room temperature warmed and with things under relative control, the physician rummaged through the man's sodden clothing. He discovered a drenched travel wallet and a cell phone in the pants pockets. The mobile was dead, so he examined the wallet's contents through his trifocals. Located an ID.

"A policeman, eh, Buster? Who'd a thunk it?"

Buster answered with a supportive whimper. It was long past time for his evening snack.

Kemp now sat perched on the edge of his California-king mattress, the phone at his ear, listening as his farm manager and narcotics right-hand man conveyed the seriousness of the situation.

"He's gone nuts, Mr. Kemp." Ferlando blurted this out.

"What do you mean nuts? The short version?"

"Cheezer told me Bawdy had some plan to kidnap her. The little Ross girl." The man's voice was jittery. "Sell her to traffickers in Minneapolis. Czechs or something."

"Sell her? What does…for how much?"

"Eighty-K's what Cheezer heard."

"She's ten years old, for God's sakes!"

"It gets worse. Bawdy says he can't help himself—she's so beautiful to him."

What the hell next? Kemp fumed.

"But he's canceled the deal now," Ferlando continued unabashedly. "Told Cheezer he's in love. Wants her himself."

Kemp cursed as he digested what he was hearing. His heartburn flared in his chest. How could he have been so blind? With all the morons, criminals and lowlifes he'd run across over the past decades, why hadn't he seen this one coming?

With Miguel tucked safely in a hospital bed, he now had yet another brush fire to extinguish. The missing passwords could wait until later. Right now, Kemp had to deal with the idiot Clive Bawdy. Deal with him fast and harshly.

Sex sicko. Pervert. Moron.

Kemp understood they couldn't risk any TV news clowns sniffing around the Farm's headquarters. And they sure as shit didn't need more county deputies and state patrolmen tromping around their property. Theirs was an under-the-radar operation. Due to the sick bastard, Bawdy's what—Indiscretion? Lunacy? Perversion? He didn't know what to call it, but the bonehead had put them all at risk.

And there was no time for playing games with Ferlando. "Where are they now?" he demanded. "And don't BS me."

"We stashed the new drug supply up at the barn house yesterday. Like you said to."

"Where are they *right now*?"

A pause. Then: "With all the excitement before, the cops searching the woods and your house, Cheezer says Bawdy's doubling back."

"What's that supposed to mean?"

229

"He's taking her to the old barn in the woods."

"That rat hole? Down a ways from Miguel's house?"

"Si. The cops checked it out already. Bawdy thinks no one will show up there again."

Kemp ended the call. The entire house was empty, so no one was around to hear him blister a string of curses vile enough to make a demon blush.

It was an hour now since he'd talked to Ferlando. Kemp walked outside around the garages, entering through the back entrance. It was pitch black out, no moon, but at least the rain had ceased. Sliding into his Regal, Kemp inventoried the glove box. On the bright side, if he managed to avoid any rutting deer jumping out from the trees, his destination was just twelve minutes away.

A funeral pall had fallen over the family room. The sisters sat in gloomy silence save for the ticking grandfather clock in the room's far corner. It tolled 9:30. The heirloom was one of Maggie's most cherished possessions, which she'd brought along when moving into Cale's house a year ago. It had belonged to her and Chloe's mother.

She had her stocking feet tucked under her on the couch, covered by a patterned afghan. Her face, flushed from hours of tears, made her look like a flu sufferer. Chloe had Hank on her lap in the nearby rocker, brushing him absentmindedly as the chair moved up and back. The TV across the room stood dark. The sisters spoke in intermittent fragments, cautious of uttering anything negative. Yet the worst-case scenario hung silently between them, unstated.

Maggie's phone buzzed. She grabbed it from the coffee table, thinking it might be Slink with a Coast Guard update. Yet, the number on the screen was unfamiliar.

The voice sounded unintelligible and raspy like sandpaper pieces rubbed together. "Hey, babe. Miss me?"

The familiar tone was gravelly and far off. It couldn't be Cale's voice, and she imagined some sadistic prank being pulled. "What?" she said in a low tone. "Who is this?"

Chloe froze in the nearby rocking chair.

"Had a long swim," the voice grated. "Then, thankfully, I met the best Doc in fifty states. Should have his picture hanging at Mayo Clinic."

If the call weren't a sick joke, she'd envision Cale winking at some stranger across the room. Was it some physician who perhaps had saved his life?

"Cale?" Maggie's voice was tentative. "But the news—"

"Exaggerated." He coughed. "No worries, Doc promised he'll stay mum, play it my way." He coughed again for ten seconds. "He's retired. So, I agreed to rest here tonight."

Maggie was sitting upright on the couch for real now and remained in disbelief. She wondered if, by some miracle, he could have survived. Her eyes widened at Chloe across the room, whose own face frowned with suspicion.

"I'll drive wherever you are, Cale. Pick you up."

"Unh-uh. Got to sleep." She could feel his energy fading. "Call Slink. Call off the search, save taxpayers some dough."

Maggie pictured him withered, dehydrated. Especially if he'd been in the water half the day struggling for survival.

"I'll call...in the morning, Mags." Cale croaked out the words. "Say hi to Chloe and Hank. Love you."

He hung up.

Maggie stared at her phone as if she'd dreamt the bizarre call, had maybe dozed off into fantasy land.

Across the room, Chloe was stunned. "Was that for real?" she asked, her suspicion not dissipating.

Maggie grinned for the first time in hours. Yes, it was real. Only Cale would know they'd all be sitting mournfully together here, feeling sorry for themselves. To Chloe, she said, "He says Hi to both of you."

Chloe lifted from the chair, dumping Hank in the process. She rushed to her sister, and they hugged one another tight. The old clock's ticking grew louder as tears filled their eyes until, at last, they separated. Maggie waved her phone in the air, saying, "I've got to call Slink. Call off the rescue search."

Chloe grabbed her empty wine glass from the end table. She moved off toward the stairs, raising the goblet, calling over her shoulder:

"When a drowned ghost calls, it's time to celebrate."

Kemp cut the Regal's headlights and swung to the road's soft shoulder. He nosed the sedan into the thick bushes, silenced the engine, pulled his 9mm from under the passenger seat. He then screwed a four-inch suppressor to the barrel, muted his phone, grabbed a crowbar from the backseat, and exited the vehicle.

Kemp didn't know what kind of monster Bawdy had become. If the jerkoff had gone nuts over a prepubescent girl, he might be dealing here with mental issues beyond your everyday sociopath. Whatever the case, with human traffickers in the mix, Bawdy no doubt armed.

Kemp wondered if he could talk sense into him. Get him to give up the girl without a struggle. As things stood, they had over fifty packs of meth ready for delivery. If Bawdy was incapable of reason, well, Kemp hadn't gained the moniker "Two tap" over the years for nothing.

He moved now through the damp, wet underbrush, his footsteps hushed and spongy from the rains. Bawdy was expendable, of course. The other guy, Cheezer, could help Ferlando with moving the drugs. Pay him double for short notice.

So, tap-tap it would be unless he found a better choice. But first, Kemp needed to separate the girl for her safety.

The worm-eaten barn loomed ahead in the dark, perched among the trees like a giant tumor. A breeze swayed the high branches, and the moon stayed hidden. The dampness brought forth a pungent odor that wafted in the humid air.

Kemp approached upwind, coming at the decrepit structure from behind, not risking Bawdy taking a pot shot at him. The guy was local and had grown-up shooting bottle caps off fence posts at fifty yards. Kemp wouldn't be a sitting duck for some jackass with lover's nuts—especially one who'd gone apeshit over some underage Lolita.

He worked his way around the place until he'd slipped close to the weathered main doors, which remained cracked open two feet. High weeds were splayed all around, stooped from the recent rains.

Bawdy had gone looney-tunes. A thousand different songs claimed love could do it to a young guy: or an older dope as well, for that matter. Kemp would use it to his advantage. Right now, Bawdy might be stoned, hop-headed, or even drunk on his ass. *Or drunk on love*, his inner voice needled. The problem wasn't putting two rounds through the cretin's skull—the way a farmer would put down a rabid skunk. The problem was doing it without the girl ID-ing him in the process.

Kemp had been to the decaying old barn twice in the past. The place was a boneyard. It ought to be burned down, put out of its misery. But Miguel had argued against it, claiming a deliberate fire might turn on them, sweep up through the woods and engulf their property the way those California wildfires often did.

He supposed Miguel had a point, albeit a somewhat paranoid one.

An owl hooted. Rainwater dripped from the upper leaves, and the nearby lavender bushes emitted a pungent smell. Kemp set his crowbar down in the weeds. Voices were coming from inside, the hayloft if he had to guess. He listened closer. A one-sided talk. Bawdy, he recognized, was trying to convince the girl he was a brilliant "entrepreneur."

A ten-year-old, for chrissakes!

Slipping noiselessly inside the cracked barn door, Kemp tiptoed to a dark corner along the inside wall. There he lowered to one knee, listening as Bawdy flapped his jaws in the upper loft like some tavern drunk.

Kemp swept together a small pile of straw and hay and whatnot from the floor. He fished a silver Zippo from his jacket pocket. Soft as a sigh, he cupped his hands and held the lighter to the pile.

CHAPTER 37

The guy just kept talking and talking. Feather had stopped listening about two hours ago. She had no clue what he was blabbering about.

In the barn's upper loft, she sat coated with filthy dust and grime. Beside her, his neck tied with a long cord to an old broken beam, Trey began to whine. Something wasn't right. Feather lifted herself, coughing, and her eyes starting to water. She spotted a campfire of flames below them. Her sudden shouts jarred the blonde-haired man to his senses. Bawdy's eyes focused at where she pointed, widening as he witnessed streams of rising smoke. Flames had ignited in scattered clumps of straw across the lower floor and threatened now to leap and lick at the moldy wood of the sidewalls.

"Holy Jesus—!" Bawdy called out.

Trey's barking caused Feather to rush back to his side. The skinny man remained at the loft's edge, hypnotized by panic. "The ladder!" he shouted over his shoulder. He side-stepped his way along the high edge of the loft. "C'mon. Let's go!"

"Not without Trey!" her voice matched his demand. "I'm not leaving him up here to die!"

Clive Bawdy froze with indecision. He didn't give a donkey's schlong about the dog, but he *needed* the girl. Needed her alive. He glanced down, then looked over at her. Her thin arms were wrapped around the animal's neck, its eyes white with fear.

Flames danced across the barn floor and climbed higher up the warped and rotted walls. Smoke rose in swirls, forcing Bawdy to spring into action. He moved back and knelt beside the whimpering animal, then sliced the electrical cord from around its neck with his knife. Then he pulled Feather toward the top of the hayloft ladder. Behind them, Trey refused to budge, wary of the smoke and flames below.

"You have to carry him!" the girl cried. "It's too high to jump."

Bawdy studied the ladder, then sized up the dog. The seventy-pound animal had an injured flank. It might snap at him if he tried lifting it. Yet, he also understood the girl would be useless to anyone if he allowed her dog to perish.

"Down! Now!" he ordered. "I'll carry him right behind you."

"You better not be—"

"I promise."

With those words, he sprang into action, easing his way back to the canine. The animal bared his teeth and snarled at the man's approach.

Feather shouted, "Let him carry you, Trey! It's all right— good boy!"

Bawdy hoisted the animal from beneath, using both his arms. It would be an effort to cart the dog down the ladder, but he was out of options.

"Get going!" he commanded the young girl. He watched as she began descending the shaking ladder. She single-stepped down as fast as she dared.

When she neared the bottom, he began his own descent. The whimpering animal's weight, which he leveraged against the inside ladder rungs, proved helpful for balance. In less than a minute, his feet landed on the flame-spotted floor.

Her elbow over her face, Feather hopscotched toward the half-open barn door. The dog wormed itself free from Bawdy's arms and limped after her, ignoring the spreading flames around them.

Bawdy crocked his arm over his nose and wove his way after them. He watched them disappear through the smoky opening, escaping into the night's fresh air. He shouldered the door wider seconds later, bursting free of the death trap. His eyes watering, Bawdy discerned the high bushes and trees that formed a dark curtain around the entire barnyard, all reflected orange by the flames they'd just escaped.

He failed to spot the presence lurking to his left as he stepped clear of the doors. Nor did Bawdy hear the whistle of iron arcing through the night air. He did sense a pressure against the back of his skull, then a starburst of pain. Still, he uttered nothing as his thoughts went dark, and he was unconscious before his face planted into the weed-covered turf.

While the girl and her dog knelt on the ground in shock, Kemp tossed aside his crowbar. He grabbed the unmoving body by the ankles and dragged Bawdy back inside the barn. Seconds later, he reemerged, backlit by orange flames and smoke. Kemp picked up the long iron weapon and walked straight at the pair like some movie screen psycho. Feather shrank at his approach. She was too paralyzed to either run or scream. After witnessing him drag the other man to certain death, her eyes were frozen with terror.

She cowered against the chest of her dog.

"Get up!" Kemp ordered. "You're coming with me."

"I only live over there, mister. Just down through those woods."

Kemp motioned with the metal bar, pointing opposite. "Now. I'll drive you."

She shook her head. "I'm not leaving Trey."

"Bring the mutt. Let's go."

Feather's tears had no effect on him, and he reached for her elbow and yanked her to her feet. The dog was up in a flash, baring his teeth.

"Back him off!" Kemp ordered, raising the crowbar. "Or Fido here winds up same as the other guy."

The young girl put her hand on her pet's head, calming him. Kemp guessed she knew no one would be out looking for her this late, and any screams she made would go unheard. She had no choice but to obey.

237

With the flames growing higher behind them, they heard the hayloft's loud collapse. The girl jerked back at the sound, but he nudged her forward. She stepped alongside him through the bushes and soggy underbrush, headed toward where Kemp's vehicle was parked.

The dog limped gamely along behind them.

By eleven p.m., Kemp had things back under control. The girl and her pet were secured in a storage room on the third floor of the vast barn house, which stood at the back corner of the DeSaul property. It was secluded, separated from the main residence by high trees and a dense thicket of bushes. Its opposite side-lawn extended across to the banks of Tar Creek.

The barn house was always locked via security keypads front and back, and sensors guarded the windows. These measures were not for luxury but necessity. It was where they stored their product until the time for the next delivery.

Kemp had decided to keep the girl confined. At least until he figured out how to handle this latest mess. He'd weighed dropping her and the dog off at her house, safe and sound, but her parents would notify the authorities. They'd quickly discover the fire in the nearby woods and, with it, Bawdy's charred body inside the burned-out barn.

Having seen his face, the girl could finger him from a mugshot file. By tomorrow morning, he'd be facing a team of arson, abduction, and homicide investigators. Not to mention those ass clowns from the DEA.

Kemp decided the girl was safe now, and he needed to devote his time to crisis management. If he made the right moves and could win her trust as the man who had saved her from a psycho pervert, hell, he might even be hailed a "hero" in the deal.

In the meantime, he had more urgent matters to deal with. Kemp had to get his hands on Cho Lin's passwords. With the fentanyl formula in hand, he could dictate the chess moves on his own terms. Over the years, he had learned there was one surefire strategy to wrangle yourself out of any situation: cold hard cash.

The more of it, the better.

He glanced at his watch. Kemp still had an hour to prepare for his next mission. A hot shower would wash away the lingering smoke odor. Thank God for Mrs. Flench's Midwest work ethic. She kept the kitchen stocked with food and leftovers.

Besides, with everything he had been through today, a little regrouping would help recharge his batteries.

Maggie settled between her blankets, commanding herself to relax and fall asleep. No simple task after her phone conversation with Cale. By some miracle, he was alive. She asked herself: How many times do you lose and regain your beloved in a single day?

She sighed, releasing the tension, knowing she had to put it out of her head. Tomorrow wouldn't be much of a reunion if she couldn't keep her eyes half-open.

She took deep yoga breaths to clear her mind. Maggie recited a mantra she sometimes used. Yes. She felt herself relaxing, tricking her brain the way a hypnotist does.

Yet the truth was she hadn't slept very well since the crazy break-in weeks ago. It was worse when she was alone at night, which wasn't often, with Cale's suspension keeping him home most evenings. Regardless, she'd be the first to admit she still slept with the proverbial "one ear open." Though not by any choice of her own.

Maggie was just dozing off when Hank pricked his ears up. It was a signal between them, and she was on instant alert, the hairs on the back of her neck tingling.

She listened as a tree branch caressed the high gutter along the roof's corner. It had been a rainy, wind-swept day, and she decided the sound was insignificant. She shifted on her pillow, ordering her brain to close itself down.

Her brain refused.

A glance at the bedstand radio. 1:08 a.m. A glass of water from downstairs might calm her, she decided, erase away any concerns. With the lights off, she drifted specter-like down the steps and through the house's inner shadows. She had on PJ bottoms and a tank top. She'd skipped her robe, knowing she would be back in bed in minutes. The lower house displayed light streaks around the closed window blinds. The locks and outside security lights had been upgraded since the intruder attack. Glancing out the kitchen window, she noticed the sway of high branches. It was a cloudy night, the moon concealed.

A different noise came now. It was a faint scratch, but it set Maggie's heart pounding. She put down the glass and slipped across the kitchen floor. In the hallway, she eased open the door of the walk-in closet and waited there, hand on the handle, listening to the house breathe.

The scratch sounded again.

Instinct told her to slip inside the closet. Maggie did so and eased the door closed behind her. She froze within the black cocoon, praying Hank was still asleep upstairs.

The deep closet had a high shelf above the hanger bar. Upon it sat the leather box holding her Kahr PM9 and a full ammo clip. Another distant scratching sounded. She became an ice sculpture, listening. With the closet door closed, the sound had been very frail, the way a leaf skitters along cold asphalt. A flat voice whispered in her head: *Someone's inside the garage.*

Maggie raised on her tiptoes and withdrew the leather box, easing it to the floor at her feet. She removed the handgun and pre-loaded clip, then wrapped the weapon inside her wool autumn coat, which hung inches away. It muted the sound of the clip sliding into the handle, and she eased a round into the chamber and thumbed the safety off.

Maggie turned to face the door again, listening hard.

A minute later, she sensed a breeze, reminding herself that old houses sighed at night. Was she paranoid? Then came the sound of creeping footsteps, the soft-soled movements of a ballerina.

Someone was advancing through the house.

Maggie's phone was on the bedside table upstairs. No calling for help. Her palm sweated on the gun handle. She held the weapon low but raised it now. If the knob turned and the door swung open, she would fire at chest level.

But what if it's Cale? Deciding to return home? Sneaking in, so he didn't wake her?

Silence, as if someone were listening. Then the entity—or whomever—slid past and moved farther up the hallway. It paused outside the open den door. The windowless room would reveal the desktop computer's shadowy outline, the half-couch to one side, bookshelves on the wall opposite.

What was he looking for?

One answer: *Me.*

She'd find out in a moment. Either he would ease up the stairway to the bedrooms or navigate further down the hall, climbing the six steps to the family room. A jewel thief? An opportunist? If he'd heard reports of Lt. Cale Van Waring's drowning earlier that day, he might be one of those "death thieves," known to ransack homes while family members were often heavily sedated in their grief.

What is he after?

A shift in the atmosphere changed things. While the intruder was contemplating his next move, Hank had soundlessly slipped down the stairs to investigate. From behind the invader now, he offered a loud *Meow!*

The startled man leaped back in surprise. Maggie had desired to remain hidden, but Hank was now in danger. She flung open the closet door. The burglar was further shocked by someone leaping out from a dark, shadowy closet.

"Freeze!" she shouted. The man stumbled backward toward the hallway steps. She could discern it wasn't Cale. "On the ground—*NOW!* Or I shoot!"

The stranger spun around instead and began scrambling up the steps toward the split-level room. He was near the top when she fired. She'd meant it as a warning, but the bullet caught him in the heel of his left foot.

He landed chest down on the upper landing, gasping in pain. The intruder scrambled to his feet, cursing, and as if familiar with the layout, he ripped open the family room's sliding door and hobbled onto the outside deck. There the man gimped down the outer steps, hoofing his way across the lawn like a runner toughing through a charley horse.

Maggie emerged onto the deck moments later. She could have emptied the clip after him but held her fire. She watched the man disappear through the dense bushes at the lawn's corner and at last lowered her weapon.

Inside the house, she grabbed the landline phone from the nearby table. With her brow sweating, hands shaking worse than a morning alcoholic, she punched 911.

CHAPTER 38

Frank Kemp awoke Thursday morning from a graveyard slumber. Before remembering the previous night, he rose from his wide bed and shrieked when his injured foot hit the floor. It was stunning how such a high-pitched, girly sound could emit from his vocal cords. His inner voice chided: Some ruthless assassin, aren't you, Frank?

Kemp gulped down four elliptical white pills to temper the pain. Then he hobbled to the shower, where he cringed as he soothed the heel of his left foot with warm water. While under the spray, he recalled what had happened after the late-night gunshot had surprised him, sent him...

Running for my life and driving from the city in shock. Keep the car straight, no speeding. Bottle of Hydrocodone in the glove box, swallow three...bottle of Jameson wrapped in trunk...pull to side street...glug down Jameson, then glug more again...driving, driving, keep it chill and steady...narrow and straight...stay between lines...

Glug more Jameson.

Dressed now post-shower, post-coffee and scrambled eggs, Kemp had driven to the Fillmore Farms main building parking lot. There he limped to the veterinary infirmary and didn't require permission to slip down a hallway beyond the front desk. He ran the freaking place for chrissakes. Moving to the back, Kemp observed the shelves loaded with bovine antibiotics, anti-inflammatories, hormone pills, and other various boxes and bottles of medications. He knew most of them worked for cattle as well as humans.

On-site care was part of their employment contract. Yet, it was common knowledge that qualified veterinarians could administer this type of care as ably as RNs or PAs. All on the down-low, of course. Veterinary assistants, with far less oversight, were an even better option.

Kemp had once informed Miguel: "They all nurse from the same teat, don't they? White coats fix what ails you. So, in the long run, who cares about their titles?"

The VA named Elliot was on duty. No appointment needed. Who was going to complain? Some waiting room full of dairy cows? Kemp requested the "Doc" take a peek at the torn and puckered flesh of his left heel. Upon the padded table, after undoing his amateur wrap job, Elliot gave a soft whistle.

"Stepped on some sharp wrapping wire last night," Kemp said dryly. "Lifting a couple of heavy milk crates."

The tech didn't flinch. Eighteen stitches, a Vicodin reload, and a bottle of antibiotics later, Kemp was back out the door. His previous handful of Hydrocodone was already playing a rumba inside his skull. He'd been floating, despite his limp, as he'd entered the infirmary.

Now he'd float even higher driving home with a fresh new bottle of the stuff.

Kemp navigated the Regal back to the manor house. Sunlight graced the front room like a morning church, and he built himself a screwdriver. Made it a double. After the first swallow, he heard Ferlando's Dodge Ram rumble up the front drive. Close behind was Miguel's midnight-blue Range Rover. He had checked himself out of the hospital, Kemp knew at once. Ferlando would have driven him back to the yacht club to pick up Miguel's SUV.

Kemp perched on the arm of the couch. He was aware that if he sank too low on the cushion, he'd be unable to pull himself back up. Miguel came strolling through the front door, happy as a dog with a raw steak.

"We all clear then, Frank?" Miguel asked, hopeful. He strode to the wet bar to pour himself a morning bracer.

Kemp knew he meant regarding the login and password codes, which his partner had risked his life to retrieve. "Minor snag. But I'm working out some kinks."

They heard Ferlando's truck roar off. Kemp imagined the man was steering clear of him due to the Bawdy screwup.

244

Miguel arched his eyebrows. "I'm starting to wonder if…"

"I said we're good!" Kemp snapped. Take it easy, pal, his mind warned. You're close to the finish line here.

Miguel returned to his task. "They find that detective's body?"

"Coast Guard searched all night, I guess."

"It'll float up in a week. Or in the fishing lines."

Kemp's forehead creased. "You couldn't have stayed in the hospital a few more days? Until all this blows over?"

Drink in hand now, Miguel took a seat in the leather armchair opposite him. He had on pressed tan slacks and a chestnut button-down, clothes Ferlando had supplied for his hospital departure. "We slipped out the back-laundry delivery. Nobody around. Doubt they know I'm even gone yet."

Kemp had swallowed two of the new Vicodins on his return drive back from the vet. He wasn't feeling half bad but imagined he'd need a couple more in an hour or two. He eyed Miguel, who kept licking his lips as if he'd sucked on a lime.

Miguel asked him what was with the holdup? And Kemp explained he was battling an annoying computer glitch. And, besides, chemistry equations were frequently complicated, weren't they? It wasn't some two-bit E-equals-MC crap.

It was Miguel's turn to frown.

"Not to mention," Kemp sipped his drink. "We've got a new batch of meth prepped for tonight's delivery. And there's a lineup change—that Cheezer guy's replacing Bawdy."

"I thought we were through with the penny-ante stuff?"

"We are. Soon as we're flush."

Kemp lifted from the couch arm. He limped to the wet bar on the toes of his left foot. He had razor-ed out his loafer's heel and clear-taped the shoe to the sock of his bandaged foot.

"What's with the hoof?" Miguel asked.

"Those crazy barn house stairs. Christ!" Kemp splashed orange juice onto four fingers of Grey Goose. A new scoop of ice. "Got forty-nine right out of fifty." He laughed at his joke.

"You better wrap it. Swelling, you know?"

"Plenty of ice right here." Kemp hoisted his cocktail glass without turning, then took a long slug.

Miguel rose. He appeared antsy from lying too long in the hospital bed. "So, Bawdy's out? Flu or something?"

Back at mid-room, Kemp chose not to sit this time. The opioid reloads, bolstered by the vodka, were giving him jitters. He could tango around the room right now if he had to. Maybe win an award for it.

"Ferlando's got the thing covered," he said. "I texted him already." Kemp bottomed his drink and set the glass down. Then he turned and made for the room's hallway arch.

"Time, Frank?" Miguel said, tapping a finger on his watch dial. "We're running out of it."

"So's every other jackass on the planet."

Kemp departed with a headshake, heel-toeing-it down the hallway.

CHAPTER 39

"You've slept for over a month!" Cale's inner voice shouted with alarm.

He awoke in the guest bedroom of Dr. Ernst Drissey. His heart was racing, and his brow and chest were damp with sweat.

The two-story domicile was nestled among the coastline trees, a hidden gemstone perched along the east bay shore. It was a half-mile up from Edgewater Beach. Cale stumbled into the kitchen at half-past noon, where the doctor cracked wise about Rip Van Winkle's descendants. It had taken him close to fifteen minutes to empty his bladder. He'd swallowed a few gallons—how it felt—of water the day before.

The rest of it seemed to be someone else's dream. Images of floating in deep water flashed through his head. Of his rescue, Cale remembered nothing. His late-hour phone call to Maggie also seemed hallucinatory. On the plus side, while he'd slept, the good doctor had washed and dried his clothes—even his shoes somehow.

The shower felt wondrous. One-hundred-five-degree water trumped fifty degrees any day of the week. After turkey sandwiches and fifty pats on Buster's soft head, Cale was ready to depart. The doctor asked if he'd be required to report having discovered him, but with his recovering without ill effects and the rescue search called off, they both agreed it was akin to Drissey having stopped and rendered him roadside medical aid.

"No harm, no foul," Cale had shrugged while promising to keep the good doctor updated.

He waved goodbye to his rescuers at half-past one. Dr. Drissey had asked few questions, and Cale thanked both him and Buster. He promised they'd keep in touch, then boarded an Uber ride back to the city.

The driver's name was Amy. She was pleased to lend him her mobile phone during the thirty-minute drive. With the blue sky feathered with perky clouds, Cale's first call of his new life was again to his fiancée.

Instead of squeals of joy, however, Maggie reported straight up: "I shot him." Her words sounded as emotionless as three slugs from a .45.

"Shot who?" He watched Amy's eyebrows arch.

"Solid guy. Not quite your height," Maggie reported. "Steel wool hair, hawk nose. Beady eyes."

It was a spot-on description of Frank Kemp. Cale reset his brain. "Can I ask what you're talking about?"

She explained how the post-midnight home invasion had gone down. She condensed it to chapter headings, skipping the dramatic verse—the noises, closet, her handgun, the cat screech; then the fleeing intruder, followed by her gunshot.

"I was trying to scare him," Maggie confessed. "A warning shot."

Cale was unsurprised at her hesitation. Only six weeks ago, she'd shot the nutjob home invader in their living room. Another dead body so soon would look suspicious on her legal resume.

"How bad?" he asked.

"His foot. Limped away. I could have shot more but—"

"You called it in, right? The cops?"

Cale now heard their house doorbell sounding in the background. Maggie said, distractedly, "Yes. Slink knows. They were here half the night."

He thought about it. "Do you need an attorney?"

"I am an attorney."

"You know what I mean."

"Got to run. The sketch artist is here." She added, "Hurry home, Cale. I need you back here."

He handed the phone back to Amy. She accepted the mobile without comment as if midnight shootings and home invasions happened on her watch all the time.

248

Ten minutes of silence passed as Cale worked the puzzle. The crazy case had begun as a simple favor—helping an ex-con get handed a notebook—and turned into a battle for survival. Cho Lin's innocent phone call had proved anything but. As the facts stood, the mysterious fentanyl formula seemed to be a magnet for death and destruction.

Most of what he knew remained murky. Frank Kemp, no doubt, was involved up to his eyeballs. And what about Syan? Was she a mere victim of circumstance the way she claimed? Or more deeply involved? As for Miguel, he had offered Cale his life in exchange for Cho Lin's passwords. Yet despite handing them over—albeit phony ones—the man had left him to drown. It had been attempted murder, only defined as "attempted" thanks to his miraculous survival.

He'd get to that part later. But first things first.

Adding Cale to the body count hadn't seemed to trouble Miguel in the least. Nor did the fact he was a cop. One proven sociopathic trademark is no fear of the police. And thus, both Miguel and Kemp appeared to be killers willing to stop at nothing to achieve their goals.

Cale couldn't decide how Connie DeSaul or her secretary fit into the mix yet, but their vibe had been anti-Miguel and Kemp. Thus, it put them on the side of the good guys, didn't it? The enemy of my enemy?

Cale surmised Kemp had murdered the courier for his notebook, then executed Cho Lin in his hotel room. He'd then grabbed Cho Lin's phone and computer, figuring one of them contained his half of the drug formula. Kemp may have learned all this from his son Kilo, who was Cho Lin's former cellmate. And yet, despite possessing both pieces of the equation, they hadn't been able to put it together. They still, apparently, needed Cho Lin's passwords. Miguel's demand for them out on the water proved as much.

Drowning a cop was a desperate move—even with an approaching storm providing cover. It had almost worked. The odds predicted Cale's waterlogged body should be floating in deep water right now. The fact it wasn't remained nothing short of a miracle.

Staring out the Uber window as they neared the sprawling city below, Cale analyzed the puzzle parts he had assembled. Miguel DeSaul's phony job offer, the lunch meeting, the boat ride—they were all an elaborate ruse, one he'd been too careless to spot at the time.

Some detective, he chided himself. More proof that he deserved his current thirty-day suspension. Cale shook these negative thoughts off and focused, instead, on Frank Kemp.

After realizing the login passwords he'd provided them were phony, Kemp had guessed the actual ones were hidden at Cale's home. His midnight break-in was a logical next move.

Except he hadn't counted on Maggie going Annie Oakley on him in the middle of the night, first wounding him, then chasing him from their house like a backdoor creeper.

Lining up the pieces now, Cale accepted that a significant challenge lay ahead: How to prove the pair had tried to murder him. He, no doubt, required more solid evidence than simply accusing Miguel of pushing him off the boat in a torrential downpour.

And yet, the odds were not entirely stacked against him. He now possessed a hidden ace up his sleeve.

His killers assumed he was dead.

Cale borrowed Amy's phone again as they approached the outer rim of the city. He tapped in Slink's mobile number.

"If it isn't Michael Phelps," his partner joked. "Wondered when you'd call."

"Heard you were hassling my fiancée again."

"Tell her to stop shooting people in the middle of the night."

Slink had a point. "You know it was Kemp, right?" Cale said. "The guy we met the other day with DeSaul?"

"Got proof? I'll meet you at the DA's in ten minutes."

"I'm dead, remember? Think they'll take a statement from a ghost?"

Cale gave his partner the condensed version of his water adventure. Slink was dumbfounded at first, then amazed. He informed Cale that DeSaul's boat had reportedly sunk in deep water. Miguel barely made it ashore and was rushed to a trauma center.

"The sonofabitch tried to drown me."

"He claims a swale swept you both overboard. EMTs found him close to his final breath."

"You're doubting me?"

"I'm saying we can't yank him from a hospital bed." Slink painted the picture. "Wheelchair and blanket, a feeble wave to the news cameras?" He added, "His lawyers will be buying drink rounds while viewing the coverage."

Cale understood Slink was right. The media would play the sympathy card for higher ratings. *Police Arrest Near-Drowned Farmer*. Something along those lines.

"Maggie's sketch will finger Kemp for the break-in."

"Wonderful," Slink said. "I'll bring him in for questioning, soon as the DA signs off."

"She shot him in the foot." Cale smirked. "Even you might be able to run him down."

"Touche."

Cale used the silence to study the scenery through Amy's windshield. The city's landmarks focused in as they neared. The arching Tower Drive Bridge spanned the river's mouth, set against the backdrop of tall buildings and factory smokestacks. Opposite the bridge, the bay was a gorgeous aquamarine quilt stretching to the northern horizon.

Looks can be deceiving, his brain reminded.

"One more thing," Slink said reluctantly. "As if yesterday weren't crazy enough, the young Ross girl went missing."

"Missing how?"

"Suspected abduction. Agent Galman put out an Amber Alert."

The news slapped Cale harder than any wave. Feather had warned them about the stalker lurking in the woods. Cale considered the timing, unable to see how the young girl's disappearance related to his being pushed off Miguel's boat. Yet alone the fentanyl case.

"Galman led the search," Slink reported. "We combed the entire DeSaul property. Searchers, dogs, the works. Then we walked the stream down through the woods." Frustration darkened his tone.

"Nothing, right?"

"Just the dog's collar. Sliced clean through with a knife."

CHAPTER 40

The Uber pulled into Cale's driveway. Maggie's gray Mazda stood parked alone on the apron. He tipped Amy extra using his dried-off credit card, and she drove away with a good-luck salute.

Maggie met him at the top of the driveway. They hugged thankfully, with Cale swiping the wayward bangs from her forehead.

She sized him up and said, "You lost weight."

"Eight-hour swims. My new workout program."

They entered the kitchen with his arm tight around her shoulder. She turned to him with sorrowful eyes. "I can't believe this all happened."

He agreed.

"It's some Stephen King nightmare," she said, shuddering.

They sat at the dining room table, both sipping iced teas. Just yesterday, Maggie had been typing her legal brief while Cale mowed the lawn—bland suburbia. Now, thirty hours later, they were fortunate to be alive.

"How'd it go with the sketch artist?" he asked.

"The break-in happened so fast—plus it was pitch black."

She recited the full re-cap, up to when the officers had departed after two-thirty a.m. Cale smiled at the part where Slink had stepped in and got the break-in recorded as a "failed burglary attempt." How Maggie had fired a "warning shot" to frighten off an intruder.

He'd thank Slink later for keeping the home invader's "possible" gunshot wound off the record.

"Hank's the real hero in this," Maggie confessed. "The guy almost jumped out of his skin."

And speaking of heroes, her comment made him wonder how much he should reveal about the hallucinations he'd experienced in the water. About his crazy conversation with

253

Colonel Mabutu—real or imagined—the witch doctor whose life Maggie had ended weeks ago with a gunshot through the eye of his voodoo mask.

"I may have been saved by a ghost," he admitted. "I'll tell you about it sometime."

Her eyebrow arched. "At least tell me how it happened in the first place? Falling off a boat?"

"Blindsided by DeSaul." He appeared sheepish. "Geez, was I stupid for not seeing it coming."

"Still, eight hours in chilly water?" She studied him. "Who survives that?"

"Help from above. Like I said."

Maggie didn't press. She had been through the wringer enough herself thinking he had died, then being attacked in the middle of the night. Cale shifted topics, informing her about young Feather Ross going missing. Yes, she'd seen the Amber Alert. He shared how he'd met the girl when he and Slink had spoken with the farmers' group days ago.

"The group being bullied by Fillmore?"

He nodded.

"The same CEO who faked a job offer and tried drowning you?"

"I'd guess his offer is off the table."

Before she could comment, he rose and stepped down the hallway. Maggie followed. Inside the den, Cale pulled the novel *Shoot For the Stars* from a bookshelf. He withdrew the envelope Cho Lin had bequeathed him and studied the folded note, ensuring it was the original.

Behind him, she said, "Hon, you're scaring me."

"This is what he was after." Cale waved the note between them. "Cho Lin's passwords. It's what almost got us both killed."

She appeared puzzled. Cale refolded the note and stuffed it in his upper shirt pocket. "I'm keeping it on me from now on."

By mid-afternoon, Cale recognized how caged tigers felt. After hours of floating, followed by lying near comatose in the doctor's house, his body craved motion. He felt lost without the Bronco. Maggie offered to drive him back to the yacht club, where he'd parked it before having lunch with the man who had tried to murder him.

When she dangled her Mazda keys in the air, Cale grabbed them, anxious to drive. After all he'd been through, he longed for control over his forward motion.

During the drive, Maggie suggested a relaxing evening at home would benefit them both. Reconnect their bodies and souls. She also informed him Chloe might stop by later. Her sister demanded to see Cale in the flesh to ensure he wasn't some pod person. Cale asked if her sister was still seeing Father Larchezzi about her "soul-cleansing."

"They dropped the idea," Maggie said. "She's going to write a book, instead. For 'catharsis,' she says."

"On what? Demon attacks?"

"Guess you'll find out when you ask her."

They crossed the lengthy Tower Drive Bridge and were headed north. The same road Cale had driven to his death-defying "swim" yesterday. He'd already phoned the county deputies to ensure the Bronco hadn't been towed.

The warm June air smelled clean, and the wide bay stretched before them, a flat blue scroll. An excellent day for sailing, but the thought of deep water caused Cale's guts to clench.

Maggie's phone buzzed in her lap. It was Slink, and she handed it over to Cale.

In his ear, Slink said, "This crazy shite keeps getting more crazy."

How can it? Cale wondered.

"Just received a report on my desk." Slink paused. "The Asian secretary you interviewed the other day? Connie's assistant?"

"Syan Hng."

"Deputies discovered her body. OD'd in her SUV."

Cale pictured her Toyota driving past the warehouse the night the courier was murdered. Also recalled her on the breezy backyard deck, her arms wrapped around small shoulders, quivering with fear as she spoke about Frank Kemp."

"County recorded it as an accidental suicide," Slink said. "Vials and needle discovered on the floor of her SUV."

"It's BS. Got to be planted."

Cale sensed his partner's nod.

"Doc's scheduled her slab appearance for tomorrow. Should get the tox prelim in a day or so."

For Cale, the news only added to the surrealness of the past three days. As if it were all some college prank or sick game show, where hidden cameras would jump out at any moment.

"One more thing," Slink added. "Does the name Clive Bawdy ring any bells?"

Cale said it didn't.

"Fire and Rescue responded to a barn blaze late last night. Some abandoned junk heap in the woods, not from the Ross farm."

Cale waited for the next shoe to drop.

"Trees were too soggy for the flames to spread. Arson's a safe bet"—Slink let it hang—"but want to guess whose body they found inside?"

"Someone named Clive Bawdy." Cale paused. "And don't tell me it was suicide."

"Burned extra-crisp. But they described him as best they could: a young skinny guy with stringy blond hair."

CHAPTER 41

Eight-thirty-six p.m. The hazy purple gloaming blanketed the surrounding forest like a diaphanous fog.

Kemp eyed Miguel as they stood in the high-ceilinged front room of the manor house. His partner peered out the tall, quarter-paned windows, staring at nothing in the twilight. At his own reflection, Kemp snickered to himself. Sometimes he wondered if the guy had the nads enough for their scheme. Maybe the stage was too big for him.

"I'm pissed-off, Frank." Miguel turned back. "None of this is going the way we planned."

At the wet bar, Kemp poured two-fingers of brandy. He used it to slug down another pair of oxys. The sun had set, so he'd switched to colored booze.

"With Bawdy, you mean? That barn fire?"

"What kind of *accident* could have happened?" Miguel strode back toward the chairs. "That putrid old barn, for Christ's sake." He swirled the ice in his glass.

Ferlando had informed them the county deputies had also been at the Farm's headquarters, sniffing around. A few locals were suggesting Bawdy had connections to Fillmore. Ferlando, of course, denied knowing anything. Said he'd check with Personnel, give them a holler back.

Kemp had already deleted Bawdy from his memory file. The drug cooker was a pervert and got what he deserved. He said, "Nothing to do with us, thank God."

Miguel studied him. "You're supposed to be on top of all this crapola—or so you said."

Kemp gimped a few steps to the couch. He didn't sit. "In case you forgot, I was busy saving your ass yesterday."

"Driving around in circles? Blabbing off useless press statements?"

When Kemp smirked, Miguel added, "You forget who dumped the cop in the bay, Frank? Who got us the passwords? Who swam a frigging mile underwater and washed-up half-dead?"

Kemp kept his cool. Best to let his partner air it out.

"The *real* question is, what else aren't you telling me?"

Kemp assumed he meant the passwords. Why hadn't he hacked Cho Lin's account by now? Didn't have the drug formula in hand? Why weren't they halfway to Belize?

The investigators, Kemp understood, would be piecing things together as they spoke. They might already be closing in. Still, there was no point pushing Miguel any closer to the edge.

"Listen to yourself, would you?" Kemp kept his tone neutral. "You're a panicky schoolgirl."

"Screw you."

"What, then? Should I have called you in the middle of the night? Told you Bawdy's a pedophile?" He limped back to the wet bar for another refill, saying over his shoulder, "I'd have filled you in at the hospital, only you recovered from drowning faster than Lazarus."

The room was quiet.

"And the password thing?" Miguel sipped his drink. "Do we have the formula or not?"

"Nearly there." Kemp remained unconcerned. "Your daddy always told us. 'No patience—it'll fry your ass faster than a Dutch oven!'"

"I don't remember that one."

"You were probably too young."

They brooded in silence. "I got a call from the Euro drug rep," Miguel said, shifting topics. "While you were out dicking around."

"And?"

"And we're both King Midas-es if we rig it so they get the final bid."

Kemp knew about the proposition. The soft-voiced shot-caller from the European pharmaceutical giant had phoned him as well. They were, in essence, a drug cartel called "EU DrugXotica." Each of their five international companies was larger than any of the top three narco cartels combined. Whatever the highest bid in the fentanyl auction was, the EU drug conglomerate had promised to double it.

Payment, of course, would be of their choice. Crypto or cash deposited into their Cayman or Bermuda accounts. Even Switzerland, if they chose. Once the formula was in EU DrugXotica's hands—and reproduction verified—it would revolutionize the worldwide pain relief industry. Further, it would also cut into the profits of heroin, cocaine, crystal meth, and other synthetic opioids across the world market.

"A non-lethal form of fentanyl," the soft-voiced rep had informed Kemp. "A hundred times stronger than morphine. I promise you—it will be the most exciting drug to hit the planet since bottled water."

On this point, both Kemp and Miguel agreed: they were far better off dealing with international businesspeople than the cartels. Kemp conceded they were no less criminal, but at least they weren't narco-sadists who'd machete your head from your neck without warning. Besides, the offer to pay double the highest auction bid was by far their most lucrative play.

It was where things stood at present.

All Kemp had to do was get his mitts on the passwords, the *real* ones this time. He'd do it later tonight after Ferlando and Cheezer picked up the drug stash for their final delivery. He would return once more to the house of the drowned detective, where his stupid bitch had pot-shotted him last night in the dark.

Kemp promised himself one thing: his revenge would be sweeter for him than for her and her loudmouth cat. The "Rule of the Streets" was in play, where payback was triple the original insult.

Just ask Biggie and Tupac. Or Scarface Al Capone.

Or ask the other slut, Syan, whom Kemp had known he couldn't trust with a secret. He had blackmailed her into helping him at the warehouse that night, paid her to pose as an Uber

259

driver, and intercept the courier at his hotel. The guy was a sitting duck before he'd entered the dark building. With Kemp's 9mm barrel aimed at his face, the courier had handed over his part of the formula without protest.

The neck slice had been his departure gift. "No loose ends" was Kemp's motto. The same went for the two-timing Syan. Her "accidental" OD was best for everyone concerned. He'd learned long ago how every snake comes back to bite you sooner or later.

Kemp now crossed his tender leg while leaning back against the wet bar. At least the conversation with Miguel had returned to civil. Talking about becoming wealthy beyond their dreams had dropped the drama level down a few notches.

"While you were napping before, Connie called," Miguel said. "A cussing lunatic. Saying I wouldn't know 'true love'— he made finger quotes—'from a cow's ass.'"

Kemp replenished his glass with another two fingers of St. Mark's. He swallowed the amber liquid down, then set the tumbler on the chrome serving tray. He said, "Connie was nuts before her baby doc slapped her."

"Still, if she goes whining to our dad, and he puts her in charge?" Miguel said this with a head shake. "And there'll be even more heat if this Bawdy thing flares up."

Kemp was tired of empty speculations. He was also tired of penny-ante drug sale payoffs, so he limped from the room toward the hallway stairs. "Leave old Sevvie to me," he grumbled.

"Get some ice on that foot, Frank," Miguel raised his glass supportively. "And get moving on those passwords—*por favor.*"

"I'll be out at the barn house later," Kemp called back. "Helping load the delivery."

"Just to stay flush, right? Until we escape this hellhole?"

Kemp needed another pair of oxys. With his lips pressed tight, he climbed the steps like a geezer low on fuel.

Cale and Maggie sat together on the family room couch now, listening as the grandfather clock ticked in the room's far corner. The sun was down, and the outside security lights were ablaze. The Bronco sat napping in the garage.

Earlier, Maggie had reheated a tuna casserole. She hadn't felt in the mood for cooking. Cale devoured two-thirds of it. Giving him sidelong glances, she'd decided his consumption must be some survival mechanism. When you escape certain death, perhaps your appetite gets revved up? Some innate reptilian response?

Unable to sit in silence, she had flipped on the TV and searched through documentaries—something to reset their brains back to normal.

Maggie felt comfortable again, enjoying the time they were sharing. They both had experienced life-threatening traumas. Survival was its own reward, yet there was always a need for reconnection. The way plane crash survivors felt compelled to reunite. Nevertheless, an unspoken tension hung in the air between them. A heaviness she could sense but couldn't put her finger on.

Chloe had texted her earlier, informing them she was delayed. She'd message later regarding her stopping by or not.

After spending the past half-hour watching a YouTube video on famous art thefts, Cale sat with one stocking foot extended along the coffee table's edge. He sipped from his water glass as he massaged her shoulder. Hank was perched contentedly between them. When Maggie glanced Cale's way, she noticed his opposite foot twitching faster than a Flamenco dancer's.

They had been through too much together for her not to recognize the syndrome. Especially with Slink reporting on some old barn burning down late last night, an Asian lady's death, and young Feather Ross' disappearance.

Maggie could read Cale's mind easier than she could the preview channel.

"Just go, then," she said, at last, heaving a dramatic sigh. "Before you give yourself an ulcer."

"That obvious, huh?"

She scooped Hank onto her lap. "Like a fourth-grader needing the bathroom."

Cale rose and pecked her cheek. "Mind if I borrow your phone? I'll call the landline with any updates."

"Just promise me you'll come back in one piece, Cale." He promised he would.

She aimed the remote the same way she'd shot her gun at last night's intruder, upping the TV volume. When she glanced back across the room seconds later, he was gone.

Perhaps he was a ghost after all.

CHAPTER 42

A strangeness had invaded their lives, something odd and unhealthy. Cale decided there was no other way to describe it. At the epicenter of it all, it seemed, was the home of Miguel DeSaul. Thus, before leaving, he had grabbed the pair of the weapons he'd purchased from Jackie No Name—the pirate-handle shotgun and the holstered Sig 9mm.

Forty minutes later, he caught the same county exit they had taken two days earlier. Soon afterward, he navigated the Bronco through the darkness, following his headlights along the county roads surrounding the expansive acreage of Fillmore Farms.

The moon was a hazy blur between the night clouds, and in the distance, Cale spotted the eerie spray of lights emitted from the milking carousel. No surprise. Ben Ross had informed him that three-thousand-head cow herds needed draining three times a day, so teams of milkers labored around the clock. It was eerie seeing the structure aglow after dark, looking like some lunar launching site. Tall electrical poles stood along the country roads as the Bronco swept past, stiff as guardians at their posts. All was otherwise peaceful across the flat farm fields and inside the intermittent clusters of thick, dark forests.

While he drove, Cale's thoughts flashed back to his time in the water. He'd been rendered as insignificant as a piece of drifting cardboard. His plan tonight was to flip the script. He needed evidence to unravel the case while also exposing those responsible for his attempted murder.

As things stood, it was his word against Miguel's—with no other witnesses upon which to rely. "He said, he said," as Slink had warned. Mere accusations were useless without concrete evidence, no different than any other case. Cale's experience

263

told him it always boiled down to the bad guys' motivation. Why had Kemp and Miguel conspired to murder him?

Why indeed? The million-dollar question.

To him, at least, the answer seemed obvious. He had become a barrier to them getting their hands on the fentanyl formula. And yet, lacking solid proof, wasn't he merely the breathing ghost of his own miraculous survival?

Cale supposed so. The fact he remained alive seemed in defiance of all odds and should never have turned out the way it had.

Casting these thoughts aside, he concentrated on the road ahead. The Bronco's beams kept the wildlife at bay, and the woods appeared denser as the two-lane ribbon of asphalt narrowed. He reduced his speed while cruising along the DeSaul property's northern border.

Nearing his destination, Cale cut the Bronco's headlights and crawled along the road's dirt shoulder. Twenty yards further, he edged off the asphalt and angled the front tires into a massive cluster of bushes. He hoped they would somewhat conceal the SUV from passing headlights.

Thus far, his was the lone vehicle on this desolate road tonight.

Cale distinguished the guest house's dark form standing thirty yards away, peering through the bushes and trees to his right. It stood shadowed beyond the gently swaying branches. Shimmers of the dusky sky darkened the back windows, showing no inner lights. A few lingering ghosts inside, perhaps, if he allowed his imagination free rein.

Cale turned off the ignition, and his heart jumped when Maggie's phone buzzed in the pocket of his windbreaker. He had texted Slink upon leaving his house, informing him he had borrowed her mobile.

"We're just finishing up with the warrant," his partner reported. "Judge Cowles is signing off on it."

"Which Cowles?" Cale knew there were two.

"David. The one we trust with this kind of stuff."

"How about DEA? They in as well?"

"Agent Galman has her team ready."

"Way ahead of you," Cale said. "I'm at DeSaul's right now. Figured I'd look around those back buildings. Pricey homes where nobody lives? Seems hinky to me."

"Watch yourself, hombre. Two more bodies yesterday ups the stakes."

"You called them 'crazy farmers' the other day."

"And crazy farmers own sharp pitchforks, don't they?"

Ending the call, Cale muted Maggie's phone and pocketed it. He grabbed the holstered Sig, made sure the mag was full and clipped it inside the inner pocket of his windbreaker. He zipped it halfway up, so the weapon wouldn't bounce, then grabbed a small TAC flashlight from the glove box, exited, and gentled the door closed.

Slipping between the trees, he felt more commando than a cop. The guest house remained angled to his right. With its solitary spire, it appeared the way haunted houses often do in moonlit photos. Cale veered left across the back lawn to another stand of tall elms. This group separated the guest house lawns from the neighboring barn house, which featured an extended backyard.

He listened to the night as his eyes searched the stillness. A lone airplane blinked between tufts of high clouds, and the surrounding woods felt suffocating. He approached the large structure from the back, edging between the thick tree trunks. A soft gurgling sound came from Tar Creek, which flowed thirty yards off, on the opposite side of the shadowy building.

The converted barn was massive, at least twice the size of the guest house, and even more extensive than the three-story main house. Once a giant equipment storage barn, Miguel had informed, it had been refurbished back when Fillmore bought up much of the surrounding farmlands. They redesigned the lower floor for entertaining groups of visitors and guests. The second level comprised private bedrooms and boardrooms, with the top floor reserved for storage and whatnot.

265

Cale studied the layout in the shadows. The back of the place appeared as sheer as a dark granite cliff face. A low fence surrounding the brick patio at ground level led to the backdoors, and a sizeable service lift ran outside the building from the ground to the uppermost floor. It appeared double the size of a regular model. An old freight elevator if he had to venture a bet. It would assist in moving furniture and large appliances in and out. Whatever else, he could only imagine.

The exterior security lights were off, and a pathway around the house's side disappeared between clusters of thick, unkempt bushes. Off the edge of the patio stood a delivery station designed for caterers and food transport. Cale stepped over the low patio wall and crept toward the back doors. All locked, of course. He imagined vagrants and vandals could be an issue out here, as isolated as the large empty houses were.

He searched around for security cameras and spotted none. He considered jimmying the lock but breaking a small window appeared more straightforward. They'd write it off as wind damage.

Cale aimed his TAC light along the door and window edges, searching for hidden alarm triggers. He focused the beam no longer than a four-second count. Satisfied, he flicked it off. His next move, though, came unplanned. He felt the sudden bite of cold metal against the back of his neck, followed by an unexpected whisper in his left ear:

"One false move, jackass, and your ghost act ends right here."

Cale stayed frozen. He hadn't heard the man's approach due to the sway of the high leaf cover. He'd been careless, off his game. Nonetheless, it didn't take a genius to guess who held the weapon.

"Easy, Kemp," he said. "Out for a moonlight stroll?"

The heavier man elbowed him roughly against the house before stepping back. He stayed out of range, wary of the flashlight swinging backward.

"Sound carries out here," Kemp said. "Something you city dopes wouldn't know."

"Your breath smells a little Scotchy. Didn't get you out of bed, I hope."

The man ignored the jab. "Stretch your arms wide, funny guy. Way out." Kemp watched him comply. "Now turn around slow." Cale performed the robotic tasks. "Two fingers now. Toss the gun under your jacket to the ground."

A training school voice in his head screamed, "Never give up your weapon!"

"Do it!" Kemp waved his weapon's extended barrel. "I'm lubed enough to empty this clip in your chest. And guess who's gonna hear it?"

The tone of a man used to issuing orders. Cale tossed the holstered weapon onto the patio, annoyed when the rough edges threatened the handle's finish.

"On your knees." Kemp motioned again. "Now, hand over your phone."

Cale knelt on the hard cobblestone and withdrew Maggie's mobile from his inner pocket. Kemp's 9mm remained steady as he grabbed the device. He powered the phone off, then flung it into the heavy bushes some distance away.

Withdrawing a key from his front pocket, Kemp stepped ten feet along the back of the house. He unlocked the outer freight elevator switch. An inner light blinked on, and the wide doors slid smoothly open.

Kemp motioned with the gun barrel.

"Lay face down against the sidewall, there."

The man kept his weapon steady. Cale laid inside with inches to spare beyond his head and shoes. Kemp stepped in and flipped a wall switch. The doors closed, and with a jerk, the car rose along the backside of the tall structure.

"You're supposed to sleeping with the mitten crabs." Kemp showed a flicker of surprise.

"Too salty for them, I guess."

In the business too long to be ruffled, the burly man kept his poker face. "No worries. They'll get another crack at you soon enough."

CHAPTER 43

Cale moved along the tight third-floor corridor. Kemp's weapon prodded his back every few steps. The cavernous open space over the railing to their left was fifty feet down to the first floor. There was a wide area displaying leather couches and cocktail tables, a mirrored mahogany bar, the settings grouped for business gatherings and financial discussions. Soft valence lighting illuminated the lower floorboards, providing a subtle glow throughout the place.

Cale could detect a second-level balcony area twenty feet below them. The entire three floors of the enormous space were painted in layers of murky gray-black shadows.

The expansive barn house was as silent as a mausoleum, and he now recognized the man behind him was limping. He hadn't noticed it outside, but Maggie had sworn she'd hit last night's home invader in the foot. The man who'd likely been searching for Cho Lin's hidden passwords—confirmed now as Frank Kemp.

As they moved up the hallway, Cale observed a stairway running along the far wall some distance ahead of them. It ran down to the second-floor landing. The landing was visible over the near railing, and he could discern a long central stairway descending from the second level down to the bottom floor. Cale considered his options. If he leaped over the balcony railing right here, he might luckily land on the second-floor landing. But just a few feet too far, and he'd continue falling to the polished hardwood of the first level.

Few humans could survive a fifty-foot drop. Besides, his luck was already running on empty.

"Stop. Right here," Kemp ordered.

They remained a good thirty feet from the hallway's end and had paused in front of a closed-door with an eye-level deadbolt. Kemp ordered him prone on the floor again as he slid aside the bolt and keyed the lock. The door's wood was pine, Cale noted, varnished to appear as higher-quality oak. Perhaps to save a few bucks.

Kemp kept his gun level. He ordered him to rise and enter the room. The light inside the extra-wide apartment was almost absent, with only a faint moonglow seeping in through a solitary, half-curtained window. As Cale's eyes adjusted, he detected a small card table and three chairs set off to one far left corner. The chairs were empty, as was the rest of the place. No beds or other furniture.

But wait. Hidden in the bleak shadows beyond the card table, he discerned two small forms huddled together in the room's farthest corner.

The animal's soft whine gave things away.

"You sick bastard," Cale muttered without turning his head. "Ever hear of insurance?"

Cale cautiously approached the figures sitting together upon a worn floor rug. The girl had a green army blanket curled over her jacket, and her narrow shoulders appeared gaunt in the dimness.

"Feather? Is that you?" He already knew the answer.

Her eyes widened at his voice. The slight bob of her head was difficult to distinguish in the room's pale light. He eased forward, with Kemp remaining a safe distance behind.

"I'm the policeman. I'm Cale," he offered, moving closer. "We talked at your house a few days ago."

She nodded and said, "They were all yelling. But you were nice."

Cale stooped down near them in a catcher's stance. He patted the dog's head, and the animal gazed up with wet brown eyes. "Is Trey okay?"

"His leg's hurt. The skinny man kicked him three times." She meant Clive Bawdy.

"Very touching," Kemp called from the room's center. "Straight out of *Old Yeller*."

Cale glared at him. "You're feeding them, I hope."

270

"A food bowl. Each." Kemp's steady voice. "I saved her from dying in that barn fire. She ought to be thanking me like a good little girl."

Rising again, Cale advanced on the man with his fists clenched. Kemp lifted his weapon's barrel, stopping him as he neared the room's center.

Cale said, "You mean the fire where the guy burned up?"

"The guy who planned on selling her to a lifetime of sick sex acts?"

Cale held his tongue, knowing Kemp might not be lying. His bulk alone indicated he wasn't the stalker the girl had described.

Kemp said, "Ask her yourself."

"And now she's your prisoner? A real hero, aren't you, Kemp?"

The man's eyes flashed. He stepped around Cale while holding his gun on him, angling closer to where the girl and dog were huddled. Trey gave a low growl, ready to defend them. Without turning, Kemp said. "You've got five minutes, Van Waring. Then I come back and put the mutt here out of its misery."

He kept the barrel trained on Cale's chest while he gimped gingerly back toward the open door.

"I should've mentioned it before, Kemp. The DEA's got a task force on the way."

"BS. They were just out here yesterday. Found nothing."

Cale thought about it. "So, you're giving me five minutes for what exactly?"

"The passwords, moron. The *real* ones this time."

Kemp exited the room, and they heard the lock click and bolt slide back in place.

The lightless area around them breathed again. Cale stepped back over and petted Trey's head. Feather cast her blanket aside and moved into his arms. He brushed her hair and held her as she trembled through sobbing tears. Her crying increased until, at last, she blurted out:

271

"I don't care if he shoots me dead—but not Trey!" She swallowed a sob. "He didn't do anything wrong!"

"Trey's going to be fine. And so are you." Cale reached inside his jacket to his upper shirt pocket. He pulled free a folded piece of paper and held it in front of her.

"This is what he wants."

The girl frowned at the note in the faint light.

"A recipe for making drugs," he said, knowing she wouldn't understand.

Feather's forehead creased. She rose and stepped across the room to a concealed closet door barely outlined in the low light, whispering over her shoulder as she moved, "Quick. There's a thing in here I'll show you."

The manor house was stone silent with no one around. No music playing or television laugh tracks. Miguel peered at his phone for the twentieth time. Ferlando should be up at the barn house by now, loading the delivery truck with the drug batch for tonight's transport. Kemp, he knew, would also be there, supervising things.

Perched on a leather front room chair, Miguel sipped a vodka tonic. Tonight's delivery should provide one final influx of cash before they flew this chicken coop. He was fatigued by the two-bit drug business and pictured himself lolling under a beach umbrella in sun-drenched Belize. Like the actor in those Corona commercials. *Se la vie.* Connie could, at last, become the "Farm Queen" she so desperately desired.

Miguel hadn't spoken to his half-sister since her phone rant. They were not what you'd call close. He would render her a courtesy call after she'd settled down, of course. *Sorry for your loss.* She'd be distraught over her best friend's death, so the sympathy play was to wait a day or two, allow all her emotional garbage to subside. He would attend Syan's funeral out of family respect. Whatever kind of funerals her people had. Maybe ashes into a volcano, for all he knew.

Miguel rose and moved to the wet bar. He had made a clever move escaping the hospital earlier. If not, he'd be going stir crazy by now. They ought to be thanking him for leaving, opening a bed. Performing his civic duty, wasn't it?

He tipped more vodka into his glass and worked the ice tongs, squeezed in a fresh lemon wedge.

There was also the bizarre ordeal with the detective, Miguel thought. His drowning had been unfortunate—but business was business, wasn't it? Getting the drug formula was the endgame here, and the detective's accident during the typhoon was considered collateral damage.

Yet, even for Miguel, too many strange occurrences were converging. He wished Kemp would fess up that he had the fentanyl formula figured out, how they'd be escaping this hayseed farm life pronto.

He gazed around at what had been his home for two years now. All was quiet on this summer night, almost eerily so. His phone buzzed. Kemp? Hopefully, with decent news for a change. Miguel set down the tongs and answered. His partner was shouting as if his shirt was on fire.

"Get out of there, Miguel! Right now! The DEA's coming back with a warrant!"

"Why would they—"

"Shut up and listen!" Kemp barked. "We need the gray leather satchel from up in my room. Closet shelf. Take the back stairs, and no dicking around. I'm serious."

"What about the shipment?"

"Listen to me, you dumbass!" Kemp barked, "I've got the *actual* formula now. If you still want to be a rich dick, then get out of there now. Wait for me on the other side of the creek—"

"The creek? Where?"

"—the stretch of woods. Where you shot that fawn last fall."

Miguel's eyes searched around the room. Every shadow was listening. Kemp was still yapping in his ear, saying something about "The U.P. or Canada," before he shouted once again:

"Get out now!"

273

Feather had slid open the hidden double-closet doors. She'd flicked a toggle switch before sliding a false back wall panel aside. When she tugged on a string light, a spacious hidden storage area was revealed.

Cale was at her left shoulder, peering inside. More than fifty plastic-wrapped packs of illegal narcotics—methamphetamine, from the looks of it. He exhaled and glanced at his watch.

Time was not their ally.

"The man with the gun came here this morning," Feather reported. "After he left, I tried finding some way out." She pointed to the closet. "When I flipped the switch here...." She shrugged as if they were eyeing store produce.

Cale had witnessed similar stashes numerous times during his days with the Narcotics unit. The amount here flashed the math in his head: an easy $3 million street value. He reached in and killed the light, closed the panel, shut the closet doors.

Just in time. They could hear a fumbling in the hallway outside the door.

Feather sped back across the room to Trey. She knelt beside him, and he whined as if knowing their lives together might be over in the next few minutes. Cale remained apart from them, lingering steps away from the hidden closet.

The room door eased open. Kemp edged warily into the place, the faint hallway light spilling in behind him. The 9mm in his hand added menace to his sneer. He kept his left heel raised, and his burgundy loafers appeared scuffed. He pointed the weapon at Cale.

"Time's up." He tossed a small notebook with an attached pen over. Cale caught it midflight, the pen dangling. "Write 'em down now—the passwords," Kemp ordered. "You play cutesy this time, well...a bullet costs a buck."

Kemp edged two sidesteps toward the dog. Trey lay on the worn circular rug with his head on his paws, eyes moist and wary. Feather had an arm around his neck and tears in her eyes.

She said, "Don't do it, Mister. Please don't hurt him."

Kemp swung back to Cale, who finished scribbling and tossed the notebook on the floor at his feet. In the faint pool of light, Kemp read the bold letters on a notebook page. **F.U.**

"Shit for brains, Detective." Kemp exhaled, disappointed.

Cale reached into his shirt pocket and withdrew the folded piece of notepaper. He held it out at arm's length with a steady hand.

Kemp kept his gun level. "The hell's this?"

"Courtesy of James Cho Lin." Cale tasted bile but kept his expression blank. No time for heroics.

Kemp leaned forward and snatched up the item with his free hand. The stationary top was stamped *Union Hotel*. Angling it toward the hallway light, he studied the numbers and symbols for a moment. When he lifted his head again, he smirked.

He now had what he needed.

CHAPTER 44

The five-stall garage was attached to the east side of the main house. Miguel spotted Kemp's parked Regal and knew his partner was still helping with the drug stash. He backed the Range Rover out and eased around the rear of the garages, headlights off. He cruised the narrow pathway along the house's back, past the guest house drive-up, until he entered the woods along the property's edge. An exit lane curled through the heavy tree thicket, used chiefly for delivery people and maintenance workers.

After two years of residence, Miguel could navigate every cranny and tree cluster with his eyes closed. His gangster father had drilled him at a tender age: "Always know your bolt holes, kid."

The path through the backwoods had once been an old fire lane, kept free of branches. No one converging on the front of the house—a DEA task force, for instance—would spot a lightless vehicle escaping along the outer back edge of the property.

Miguel snickered. Kemp was the panicky schoolgirl now, blowing things out of proportion. Still, he couldn't take the risk. If another raid were on the way, then fleeing was the shrewdest move in their playbook.

Especially now that Kemp had the formula figured out.

The Range Rover emerged onto the dark county road and swung right, continuing to navigate without beams. Miguel's eyes were alert. Broadsiding an animal in the moonlight, he admitted, would be a small price for escaping unseen.

Covered by darkness, the DEA task force—comprised of a half-dozen Sheriff's deputies, three Green Bay officers, and a trio of federal agents—parked their vehicles in the deep shadows along the tree line. They were armed and vested, wearing night goggles, communicating via com-units and hand signals.

Twenty feet away, Agent Galman motioned Slink Dooley forward. He hunched his way up behind a box elder and studied the manor house from a new vantage point—three stories of brick, broad windows, creeper vines halfway up the sides. Mrs. Flench had greeted them just days ago.

He doubted she was inside now.

The glow of exterior lights created pockets of shadow outside the home. The inside was gaudily lit, and it gave the team pause. A dozen armed DeSaul gang thugs might be gathered in there for a pow-wow, for all they knew.

Slink was aware of how tricky nighttime raids could be. He had almost been blown to his grave confronting a wired shoreline boathouse not long ago. He could feel sweat spreading along his lower back.

A nightbird chirped, and Agent Galman motioned them forward again. Slink stepped with the others, his sidearm low. They advanced toward a clump of tangled bushes and spread out, holding their ground while awaiting the next signal.

Jackie sat at the wheel of her F-150, parked a quarter mile down from the Ross farm. Navigating the backroads for the past five hours, she'd searched waysides and truck stops and the restrooms of county parks. And every two-bit motel she could think of where some pervert might try hiding a ten-year-old girl.

With her lights off, she stared out the pickup's dark windows. Her phone was on her lap, and she'd never felt more useless in her life.

Jackie longed to call Rita, understanding how her friend needed emotional support. However, Rita was playing by the rules, accepting no visitors or calls, keeping her phone line clear. Feather had been gone for thirty hours now, and whoever had taken her could be just about anywhere by this time.

Tears burned Jackie's eyes. Her inner voice prayed: Jesus, but I love that little squirrel. Please, God! Please let Feather be okay.

The events of the past two days had imploded Jackie's world. First, Syan was murdered—made worse by Connie's claiming that she (Jackie) was responsible. Shortly afterward, news broke of Cale Van Waring's drowning in a violent storm on the bay. Though unconfirmed, anytime the Coast Guard officially called off a search, things seldom turned out positive.

Topping things off, Feather's abduction stabbed her in the heart. Jackie blamed herself. Rita had warned her a month ago about some mysterious stalker in the woods. Yet, along with everyone else, she had been too slow to react.

Jackie's gut told her these events all somehow connected back to Fillmore Farms. With their narcotics side-business, they were beyond corporate boogeyman. The proof was in the body count. And facts being what they were, she held one individual accountable—the CEO behind the curtain, the ringleader manipulating the puppet strings:

Miguel DeSaul.

In Jackie's business, it was necessary to maintain a fair degree of balance. At the same time, there wasn't a client she knew who'd have the slightest trouble spelling the word "Revenge."

Frank Kemp hobbled to the end of the third-floor hallway and worked his way down the stairway along the far wall. He needed three more oxys and a slug of bourbon but knew he could tough things out. The craziness was behind them.

He held the password note in his hand now, and Kemp was already thinking four moves ahead. The best image was of him flying south through lavender, cloud-puffed skies.

He gimped along the second-floor landing and stopped at the top of the steep central staircase. There he withdrew his phone while debating if he should go back and eliminate the three witnesses—the girl, the dog, and the ass-pain Van Waring. On the other hand, if the detective hadn't been BS-ing about another DEA raid in the works, then the most sensible move was to leave well enough alone.

He had the passwords in his possession. Lady Fortune was again back on his side.

He pressed the phone button, and Miguel answered. "Where are you right now?" Kemp asked, staring down the stairs at the pool of darkness. Around the edges of the place, the recessed floor lights faintly glowed. It reminded Kemp of an art gallery he and Sevvie had looted thirty years ago.

"Other side of the stream," Miguel reported. "The woods where you said. I've got eyes on you. Where's Ferlando with the truck?"

"No matter. You grab my satchel?"

"Yeah. Gray leather with the laptop and stuff inside."

Kemp grinned. "Congrats, *amigo*. We're now the world's newest pair of millionaires."

"For real this time, Frank?"

"Got it in my hands right here." He fingered the folded note. "I'll be there in ten minutes, even if I have to swim across. Then we blow this joint for good."

Ending the call, Kemp sensed a dark form moving in the frozen space behind him. He turned instinctively, but the rushing shadow was upon him before he could react, and a sharp blade entered just beneath his rib cage.

The assault left him unbalanced on the uppermost step. His arms windmilled, and his unsteady feet rocked until gravity won out, and he was airborne. The room spun as he bounced down the steep staircase, and he heard hollow echoes and felt one thump-thud after the next as his body somersaulted down to the bottom.

He landed on the floor at the base of the steps.

Only then did the caterwauling wails—echoing off the fifty-foot walls—register in Kemp's mind that they had been his own. Then a dark wave of silence washed over him.

279

Inside the sparse third-floor room, their captor had locked the door after departing. Before his footsteps faded, Cale moved to where Feather knelt beside her dog.

"What's going to happen now?" she asked. Her cheeks were streaked, and she swiped them with the back of her hand.

"We find a way out. They'll be coming for the drugs soon."

"But the man said—"

Her comment was interrupted by the sounds of distant clamor. Shouts rose from somewhere inside the spacious barn house. A screeching-echo voice cried out, and it was followed by pounding and thumping as if a bar brawl had broken out.

An eerie silence followed.

Cale moved to the door, his ear pressed, listening. It was quiet now but remaining in the room was dangerous. He felt the door and frame to assess their strength. Feather stood a yard behind him in her jacket, watching nervously.

Cale stepped and kicked the door, his right foot landing inches below the knob. No luck. He kicked next at the lower door panel, firing a series of sidekicks until the old wood splintered and shattered outward. He stooped and cleared away the wood, widening the opening. Feather was more agile, so she went through first. Trey followed them both, half-hopping through the hole and into the low-lit hallway.

Grabbing a foot-long dagger of wood, Cale considered the rear elevator. No operation key. Instead, he led them down the carpeted corridor, the atmosphere dense with shadows. They descended the stairway at the far wall, and he wished he had his TAC light now. Even better, his Sig.

They paraded along the second-level balcony rail, and Cale sensed dark energy lingering near the top of the stairs. He could barely see into the blackness but detected a faint metallic odor.

Trey also sniffed the air.

Gazing down the central stairway, he spied a sack-like clump at the very bottom. The outline failed to move. Feather remained behind him as they descended. They noticed inky wet splashes along the steps and side-rails and the same substance pooling around the unmoving figure at the base.

Feather whispered, "Is that—"

"Yes."

At the bottom, Cale avoided the blood pool while turning the body's shoulders over. Frank Kemp's eyes stared somewhere far beyond them. He pictured the deadly event sequence: the victim was likely stabbed first, then shoved down the stairs. The attacker had trailed Kemp to the bottom and slashed his throat, slicing his body again and again—rage taken to an alpha level.

Feather held her hands over her mouth. Cale guided the young girl a half-dozen steps away. "It's okay," he said soothingly, rubbing her shoulder. "He can't hurt us anymore."

Spotting the item in the nearby shadows, Cale plucked Kemp's mobile phone from the floor. Who knew where his gun had bounced? He scanned the last call—to Miguel, just before the attack. He turned and studied where the body lay, searching the area for Cho Lin's note. No luck. In Kemp's pocket if he had to guess. The crime scene techs would discover it and log it into evidence. Unless, of course, the crime's perpetrator had found it before fleeing. He considered Miguel, the man who'd pushed him off the powerboat. Had they had a falling out? Were both men capable of murdering one another?

All speculation at this point.

Cale wiped his prints from Kemp's phone and slid it back along the floor. They started toward the high front foyer with Feather alongside him, the glow of the floorboard lights guiding their path. Trey ambled behind, leaving auburn paw prints on the polished wooden surface.

Their sober exit, though, was interrupted when the tall front doors were suddenly battered open. Sweeping light beams crisscrossed the interior darkness, and shadowy figures in black swarmed in shouting: "Police! Freeze!" With others chorusing: "Get back! Away from the door!" And adding: "Everyone on the floor *Now-Now-Now!*"

The halogen brightness forced them to cover their eyes, and Trey barked wildly at the chaos. The beams continued sweeping over them with continued shouts of: "On your knees! Get down! Stay down!"

And a single angry voice shouting: "Somebody shut that dog up!"

Their arms extended, Cale and Feather had both fallen to the floor. She was crying desperately, sobbing: "Be quiet, Trey! Please be quiet!"

"Police officer! Police officer!" Cale repeatedly called out a third, fourth, and fifth time…until a voice, at last, echoed over the others.

"Hold up! Hold up—we got a cop here!"

And a saving voice above the rest. "Stand down, damn it! He's my partner!"

CHAPTER 45

The raid of the drug house went off without a hitch. The officers and crime techs professionally executed their roles.

However, there was one significant difference for Lt. Cale Van Waring this time—he was on the other side of the thin blue line. No weapon. No badge clipped to his belt. He hovered somewhere between suspect, victim, and witness, with all three roles vaguely overlapping.

Some officers and techs performed double-takes, either surprised by his presence or wondering if they might be viewing his ghost hovering about the crime scene. One photographer even snapped Cale's picture, half-convinced the image would show up as a spectral orb.

And yet, one fact was indisputable. The cooling carcass of Frank Kemp remained at the base of the stairs. It was the focus of their presence here, awaiting the arrival of the coroner and body transport van.

Cale had provided his statement to both Agent Galman and the county sheriff's investigators. He'd done so while keeping an eye on Feather and Trey, making sure they were comfortable. He also observed a tech storing Kemp's phone inside an evidence bag, understanding they'd do the same with the drug formula note after locating it.

The beehive of chaos continued. More crime techs arrived in Tyvek suits and began combing through the house and the outer grounds. They put up glow lights and stretched yellow scene tape halfway around the massive barn house. Cale guessed that with the structure's size, they'd be here until daybreak.

He had borrowed Slink's phone and contacted Rita. After informing her Feather was safe and secure, he smiled at her cries of happiness. At her ear, Ben was no less enthused.

Rita wanted to drive right over. Cale informed that an officer would transport her daughter and Trey home, leaving in the next minute. The message conveyed, he bid farewell to Feather with a heartfelt hug, telling her he'd visit her soon. The young girl waved shily, and she and Trey followed Sgt. Emily Tan out the front door.

Cale overheard the officer telling Feather that, yes, she could ride upfront; and of course, she could work the flickering lights during the mile ride back to her home.

After they'd vanished, Cale used Slink's mobile to contact Maggie on their house phone. He relayed the condensed version of what had transpired. Maggie's pithy commentary ran the emotional scale range.

After a pause, she'd added, "I swear you've got nine lives, Van Waring."

"After this week, I'm under a half-dozen."

She advised him to avoid speeding. And like the famous radio ad, she promised to leave the lights on for him.

Cale returned Slink's phone just as a boisterous commotion erupted at the back entrance. Two sheriff deputies advanced along the polished wooden bar, which ran the length of one sidewall. Its long mirror reflected the rows of glistening liquor bottles. Behind the deputies trailed a muscular state trooper who frog-marched a handcuffed Connie DeSaul by the elbow.

Along with the others, Cale stared at the scene in disbelief.

Connie appeared disheveled and combative—wild hair, eyes sunken, dark jeans, running shoes, a hooded sweatshirt. The hoodie was blotched with stains that Cale guessed would match the substance pooled around Frank Kemp's lifeless body.

Agent Galman stepped forward, and they halted. The trooper informed: "Caught her in the woods, ma'am. Attempting to reach her vehicle."

Connie's eyes were glassy. Cale imagined she'd ingested the old standby combination of pills and alcohol.

She barked out, "I own this place, you morons! I'm Connie DeSaul!"

"We also found this," the straight-faced trooper reported. "In the bushes near her vehicle."

He held up a plastic evidence bag. Inside was a curve-bladed knife with finger-grips and a metal loop at its base. The blade was aggressively serrated.

"For protection." Connie slurred in protest. "Wolves and animals…all over this damn place!"

"A karambit knife," Agent Galman said. "Lethal as hell."

They studied Connie together.

"Might be stains on the blade?" suggested the trooper.

Cale decided they didn't need Hercule Poirot to figure this one out but kept his thoughts to himself.

"Place her on a mental hold," Galman ordered. "If she's part-owner of this circle jerk, we can book her under the federal warrant."

They watched as Connie was escorted out the front door, cursing and struggling with every step. After she'd disappeared, Cale turned to Galman. "Did you arrest Miguel DeSaul? During the raid?"

"Houdinied it. Maybe received a heads-up." She sighed, frustrated. "His SUV wasn't in the garages. We've got a four-state APB out."

Cale guessed she was correct. With a sufficient head start, Miguel DeSaul could be across any of four state lines by now. The fact Kemp had phoned him meant the man was on the run somewhere.

"One thing before I leave." He offered this almost as an afterthought. "While a prisoner, young Feather Ross uncovered a drug stash upstairs. I think a large reward is in order, with her picture on every news outlet in the state."

At their puzzled looks, he pointed upstairs. "Top floor. Room with the kicked-out door."

A deputy and two techs began climbing the stairs.

"It makes sense," Galman nodded. "We busted a Fillmore hombre named Ferlando on the drive here. He was en route with another guy for a supply pick up."

"How'd you know to stop them?"

"Anonymous tip," Slink interjected. "They were driving a *love* truck."

Galman rolled her eyes.

"Animal husbandry," Slink added for Cale's benefit. "It's how they've been disguising their narcotics deliveries across the neighboring counties."

Slink strode off toward a pair of uniforms stationed at the front door. Cale was thankful he didn't have to look his partner in the eye now due to his description of the vehicle. They'd laugh about it while sipping beers this weekend.

Cale thanked Agent Galman for not giving up on the case. He exited from the barn house with a nod to Slink, knowing he'd need to explain the details of how he'd managed to survive drowning yesterday.

Flickering lights reflected off the grass and bushes, rising above the trees in a fireworks display. Cale stepped along the house's side lawn, careful to avoid evidence markers. Things were less intense on the back patio this time around. He searched for his Sig and TAC light, guessing they'd already been bagged. He'd retrieve them in a day or two from Evidence. Along with Maggie's phone, assuming they had discovered it already.

Walking back to the Bronco, Cale marveled at how things had turned out. He'd survived drowning, rescued a young girl and her dog, helped break up a drug ring, and escaped with his hide intact.

Nonetheless, he pictured a chilly reception awaiting him at home. No matter how heroic his endeavors might have been, Maggie's annoyance over losing her phone would place him squarely in the doghouse.

CHAPTER 46

The Bronco remained tucked in the bushes where he'd left it. Cale relaxed in the dark inner silence, reflecting on how his latest excursion had almost cost him his life.

He recalled an old cliche about things ending well and decided it applied with Frank Kemp's demise. He had avenged Cho Lin's execution and assisted in pulling the plug on a decent-sized drug operation. A win-win by his book.

No longer in a hurry, he decided to take the rural route home. The backroads this late would be almost deserted.

Cale navigated over the old tractor bridge spanning Tar Creek. He turned right at the four-way stop and headed south between the alfalfa fields and the forest, whose thick trees stood opposite the stream from where he'd just been.

The road ran straight along past the Ross farmstead. By now, Feather's exhaustion would have kicked in. She'd be showered and tucked beneath a cozy quilt, dreaming of sugar plums or whatever kids her age dreamed about these days.

He hoped not techno music.

The Bronco's twin beams swept the country road. Wary of leaping deer, Cale almost missed the flash of metal in the deep tree shadows. Still, he'd caught enough glimpse to slow and more intently search the forest on his right. There it was once more—no mistake—the shadows concealing an SUV hidden just inside the tree line's high bushes.

On closer inspection, Cale found himself looking at the familiar midnight-blue Range Rover. The identical vehicle he'd seen yesterday in the yacht club's parking lot.

Agent Galman had informed him earlier that Miguel escaped the task force raid on his house. Might he have discarded his SUV here, in the dark woods, then caught an Uber ride off to heaven knows where?

At this point, anything seemed possible.

On the other hand, what if he had chosen not to flee? Instead, decided to hide his SUV here in the brush while waiting for Kemp to arrive with the drug formula? Then they'd escape together into the sunset, both men soon to be wealthy and free.

A huge What If.

In his head, Maggie's stern voice asked, "What is it about suspended you don't get, Cale?"

Regardless, he was still wound-up from the evening's events. A five-minute look-see would at least help him sleep better.

Cale reversed the Bronco back twenty yards along the road's shoulder and was now a decent distance from where the Rover was hidden. With his Sig long gone, he pulled the Mossberg shorty shotgun from under the driver's seat. He loaded six shell rounds from the carton in the glove box, then tucked it into the pocket of his windbreaker.

Cale stepped from the vehicle, easing the door closed, noting the pine scent on the breeze. He could hear the stream gurgling thirty yards into the woods.

An invisible path cut through the forest just behind the parked Range Rover, where the sawgrass had been tamped down. Following the makeshift trail for fifteen yards, Cale paused and listened like a tracker. Sighs rustled from the breezy high grass, and darkness shrouded in around him. Crickets chirped from the banks of the stream up ahead.

He eased his way forward beneath the tree cover, staying invisible, peering out through open spots between bushes and moss-covered trunks.

The far-off distance revealed flickering police lights at least sixty yards away. Cale now stood opposite the stream from where he'd been fifteen minutes ago. Lights spilled from the giant, oversized barn house, and officers and crime techs moved about with purpose. The DEA agents would be photographing the drug stash, preparing to haul it away by this time.

Capturing Cale had allowed Frank Kemp a final shot at the fentanyl formula. He had almost succeeded. Kemp, however, hadn't planned on the retribution of Connie DeSaul—a woman hell-bent on revenge. Whether blind or not, frontier justice had prevailed.

Yet Miguel remained at large. If the man had hidden the Rover here hours ago, he could be sitting in an airport lounge right now, awaiting his partner's arrival. Or perhaps Miguel had swapped vehicles here, then escaped to some hunting cabin deep in the forest? Or flew off to some exotic locale the way they did in movies?

Cale's logical mind simplified the bottom line: the guy could be just about anywhere.

He now stood at the base of a tall chestnut tree. A cold shiver ascended his spine. He wondered if Miguel had stood in this very spot hours ago, watched the events unfold in the barn house across the creek.

The question nagged him: Where is the man right now?

A shell husk behind him cracked. Cale didn't hesitate. He dropped to one knee and spun around, raising the shotgun. His eyes scanned the blackness—no target, no shot—until the *whoosh* of liquid spray blasted him in the face. He roared in pain, dropping the weapon as both his hands flew up. The acid spray had caught him flush, blinding, choking him. He rolled into a ball on the uneven ground, cursing and spitting, unable to breathe.

Cale understood how pain felt, and this was worse. His brain registered now that he hadn't been sprayed with acid but with an even more painful substance—high-powered capsaicin. Bear mace. The stuff they used when 700-hundred-pound grizzlies attacked. Tucked on his side with his knees curled fetally, Cale wailed in agony. He wanted to sprint to the water, plunge his face in deep, claw his flesh off if he had to—anything to stop the burning.

Miguel had emerged from around the tree trunk with his propellant. He'd stepped aside as his victim went down, and he circled behind him. Cale struggled to one unsteady foot now, attempting to rise. A kick at the back of his knee put him down again. A follow-up stomp between his shoulder blades forced his face to the loamy soil.

Miguel plucked the shotgun from the ground and flung it, spinning toward the stream. It landed in the muck along the nearby bank.

Cale's burning eyes saw dancing lights far off, blurry sparkles of color. He wondered if screaming might help, but a glimpse over his shoulder showed Miguel now training a handgun on him, its long barrel suppressed. Even if the cops heard the *spuutt spuutt spuutt,* it was doubtful they would detect anything amiss from this distance away.

"Remove your jacket, dipshit," his assailant ordered, emotionless.

Cale struggled to his knees. His face contorted as he wormed his arms free of the nylon windbreaker. The ammo box rattled to the ground, spilling shells. His captor grabbed the jacket from behind him, ordering: "Make your arms stiff at your sides."

"Kemp is dead," Cale rasped. "It's over."

"Shut up. Or I spray you again."

Cale had no saliva left. His lungs felt seared by kerosene.

Standing behind him, Miguel spun the jacket like a damp swimming towel. He continued holding his weapon. "Freeze now. Move a muscle, and your brains splatter."

Cale stayed rigid as the man wrapped the rolled jacket around his torso, crossing it behind him, knotting it tightly. The sleeves pinned his arms to his sides. Miguel then yanked him to his feet, keeping the gun steady with his opposite hand.

"I should've plugged you in the water yesterday."

"You're not a killer, DeSaul. Kemp's the psycho."

"Who pushed you off the boat, jackass?"

DeSaul's voice held an edge as if knowing his world was unraveling around him. At the same time, Cale asked himself, Who am I to talk?

Miguel poked his shoulder with the gun barrel, prodding him back the way they had come. Cale trudged through the forest, armless and stumbling, guessing at the direction in the gloom.

They stepped through weeds and bushes. Miguel jabbed him with the barrel every few strides, steering him this way or that.

"I can get you the drug formula." Cale's voice came out hacking, desperate, and he imagined the enamel had melted from his teeth.

"Shut up. Or the next spray goes down your gullet."

The thought caused his gorge to rise, and he swallowed bile and felt the flesh dripping from his face. Cale's eyes were seeping tears. The woods ahead thinned, and the shades of charcoal shadow formed outlines. They were nearing the road. He remembered the closest light pole was back at the four-way stop a quarter mile behind them.

Cale doubted Miguel had any plan. He had spotted the Range Rover in the bushes by pure blind luck, one-in-a-hundred. He figured the guy must be calculating his next moves, what to do with him, then how to escape.

He might drive to some warehouse, spray Cale again and again, listen to his final simpering attempts at trading his life for Cho Lin's login data. He imagined by now the techs had discovered the passwords note hidden on Kemp's bloody corpse.

On the other hand, perhaps Miguel was tired of the headaches. His father was wealthy, his inheritance secure. So why bother with all the BS? Why not just fire three quick bullets into the detective's body and dump the carcass in a ditch? Miguel disappears into the wind, leaving no trace.

Cale's snarky brain goaded him, concluding that shooting him would be Miguel's most logical solution. Besides, he had almost murdered him once already, hadn't he?

A cluster of heavy bramble-bush formed ahead of them. Bracketed by a pair of tall trees, within the bush's scrubby branches, stood the shadowy outline of Miguel's SUV. The man fobbed the locks and angled himself in closer, forcing the passenger door open wide. He stiff-armed his prisoner into the Rover. Cale continued attempting to loosen his arms but accepted the futility; it was why straitjackets had been invented.

He landed halfway in, tumbling onto the seat, before curling his legs inside.

The door thumped closed behind him.

Miguel reappeared at the driver's door. The dome light blazed again as he slipped inside, and the brightness forced Cale to clamp his dripping eyes shut. His captor closed the door, and all turned dark again.

Silence. Black, intense, engulfing. Cale noted the interior smelled of bleach, the way killers scrub a murder scene. Same as how Cho Lin's room had smelled the night he was two-tapped. With his weapon level again, Miguel reached over Cale with his left hand for the passenger seatbelt. He pulled and snapped the clasp closed.

Even less wiggle room.

Miguel shifted the gun to his left hand and keyed the ignition. Moving in reverse, he backed the vehicle while keeping the weapon steady, using just the parking lights to guide them. With his head half-turned, his eyes fought the darkness as the SUV bounced over uneven terrain. It dipped and rocked, reversing across the shallow culvert, before powering back onto the asphalt road in the shadows.

Slamming the shifter into park, Cale sensed Miguel studying him in the dimness. He'd been jostled during the backup, but the seatbelt had prevented his slamming into the front dash or side door. With his head hung low, he accepted there was no point in squirming against his bindings. He knew his face looked half-melted. He'd witnessed explosion victims before.

Miguel was a lurking presence beside him, a specter with a canned 9mm. The road ahead and behind showed nothing but twin dark tunnels stretching to infinity. The loud rumble of a vehicle sounded somewhere in the night.

"We're switching seats," Miguel announced. "My aim's steadier if you drive."

"You try driving without arms, genius."

"You only need one." Miguel sneered.

He pressed Cale's seat belt release. Keeping the weapon fixed, he opened the driver's door and stepped out onto the center of the dark, two-lane road. The dome light was on again, and both men glared at one another in the glow.

"I'm coming around," Miguel stated. He felt his pockets for his spare ammo clip and looked down, distracted.

Cale decided against trolling the man with the gun any further, so he kept his trap shut.

The low growl of an engine echoed again. Cale pictured a diesel semi-truck downshifting as the distant rumbling noise grew louder. And seconds later, the sound increased by decibels until there was no mistaking it—something powerful was coming their way, coming fast. The low-blatted throbbing caused Cale to cut his eyes back down the shadowed road behind them, and as he did, the volume quickly turned into a charging, guttural noise.

Standing outside the open driver's door, Miguel suddenly peered behind them as well. As he did, his eyes were blinded by a dual pair of igniting halogen headlights—accompanied by the oncoming engine roar.

Raising his gun hand to shield his eyes, Miguel realized he was trapped between the Range Rover's open driver's door and the accelerating vehicle. He barely had time to bleat a cry out before the front grill bore down on him, an angry charging locomotive. With nowhere to escape, both man and SUV door were blasted high into the night air, the metal ripped clean from its hinges.

The massive object sailed toward the road's opposite ditch, wedging into the ground like a crashed cockpit hatch. Miguel hit the pavement yards ahead of the onrushing pickup. As the aggressive truck accelerated—thick tires and undercarriage slamming over him—Miguel's body was a ragdoll, flipped three times before coming to final rest.

The Rover itself had been spun around by the impact, shoved ten yards aside to the road's dirt shoulder. Cale was pressed against the passenger door but remained upright, unscathed by the violent jolt.

It had happened so fast that Miguel's death shriek still echoed in the night air. It dissolved then, swallowed by the fading sounds of the muscular F-150 as it sped off into the night. Cale watched the crimson taillights vanish like a pair of demon eyes.

A dish best served cold, he thought.

He'd have to struggle to free himself, then locate Miguel's phone if it hadn't been crushed. The safest play was calling the county 911 dispatch, reporting the fatality. Cale's scorched appearance would confirm his kidnapping and the mace assault by a lunatic. His eyes—the deputies would admit—were swollen and damaged, incapable of identifying the hit-and-run vehicle's color or make.

Yet alone the driver.

The officers would eye Cale carefully. The incident had happened on a barren stretch of country road, darkened by clouds and the faint hint of moonlight. Made more suspicious, perhaps, because wasn't he the same policeman who had been reported drowned in a storm the day before? A violent squall? His bloated body still unrecovered from the murky waters of the bay?

After months had passed, these same deputies would exchange stories at their local Tuesday night watering hole. There they might wonder if the statements they'd taken that night were from an actual flesh-and-blood person. Or might they have been conveyed, instead, by the wandering spirit of a drowned cop? One whose ghost still patrolled a lonely stretch of country road on moonless nights, searching for final justice.

That is, if one believed those sorts of things.

CHAPTER 47

It had taken over a week for the press to die down. The silver Bronco now sat parked in a half-filled, downtown lot. The familiar five-story office building overlooking the river, which housed clinical psychologist Dr. Pamela Ranula, Ph.D.

Dr. Pam stepped from behind her mahogany desk with her phone in one hand, notepad in the other. She seated herself in a comfortable chair opposite the ox-blood leather couch. Today she wore a teal blue pantsuit, white blouse, and a thin burgundy necklace. Her dark hair was pinned up professionally.

On the couch, Cale sat with one leg crossed guy-style. To his left, Maggie wore a demure skirt and blouse ensemble. She studied the therapist with hopeful eyes.

Dr. Pam set her mobile on the coffee table between them. The recording app was turned off. She crossed her legs be at the ankles, the notepad on one thigh. She softened her features to convey empathy, letting them know she was the most soulful listener with whom they would ever share their deepest secrets.

"Thanks for coming in, guys," Dr. Pam said. She assessed their demeanors without appearing to do so. "I've been hoping for a chance to talk to you together."

Cale's face showed signs of returning to normal. Less flushed and blistered. Though evidence of his recent burns and lacerations remained, he might pass as a sunburn sufferer beginning to heal.

He said, "Does this count as my third official visit?"

"Afraid not, Lieutenant." Dr. Pam's eyebrows narrowed. "This is considered a couple's visit, arranged by Maggie. Strictly voluntary."

"Figures."

After jotting on her notepad, the therapist's brown eyes widened at them. "Okay, who wants to jump into the deep end first?"

He shifted his eyes to Maggie, gestured with his left hand, palm open. "All right," Maggie said agreeably. "What's the topic?"

Cale hoped it was more profound than the tragic loss of her cell phone.

Dr. Pam blessed them with an earnest look. "How about, let's see... Why don't we start by talking about the new baby on the way?"

EPILOGUE

The vast barn house stood in moody silence. Sparse moonlight seeped in through the skylights and upper windows. The house felt tired from the recent commotion, and even her old ghosts were exhausted.

Around this time a week ago, Frank Kemp had held a folded note as he limped along the second-floor landing. He'd paused at the top of the main staircase and made a phone call while glancing at the message. Doing so, he failed to sense the lurking attacker who'd rushed out from the recessed shadows behind him.

The thrust of the serrated blade had slashed beneath his rib cage, nicking bone and lacerating his liver. Kemp had gripped the folded note tight as he rum-tummed down the long stairway, performing an A-plus impression of a frat house drunk.

The attacker trailed after him, stabbing, slicing, concluding her business at the base of the stairway. She then moved past the long mahogany bar and out the backdoor, escaping into the somnolent night. Kemp's final act had been his gnarled fingers uncoiling with a lifeless twitch. Flecked with blood, the note remained folded where it lay upon the hardwood floor.

Minutes later, the detective and young girl—followed by her limping dog—had trailed cautiously down the bloodstained stairway. After assessing the body at the bottom, they'd moved to the front foyer, intent on exiting the crime scene.

However, neither had noticed the folded note, which had flypapered itself to the animal's left rear paw.

By the time the police and DEA agents stormed through the front doors, the note had fallen away due to the dog's wild and incessant barking. Unbeknownst to one female deputy, though, the item had adhered to the sole of her work boot as she'd charged through the foyer, headed toward the back kitchens.

297

With little to see in the faint light of the rear outer patio, she'd spun around and made her way back inside the house.

It was on a single square of patio flagstone that the note, once again, had become dislodged during the officer's hasty reversal. In the breeze above the back lawns, floating like a beige-colored moth, the notepaper capered and pirouetted. It flitted across the grass, over bushes, and between the trees, where at last it lodged against a mud-rock half-buried along the bank of the gurgling creek.

There it remains, soiled and discolored, yet ready to reveal the login passwords to a dark website where a fentanyl formula, worth millions, awaits whoever might happen upon it.

Printed in Great Britain
by Amazon

42233737R00173